A Vintage FROM Atlantis

THE COLLECTED FANTASIES OF
CLARK ASHTON SMITH

VOLUME THREE

A Vintage from Atlantis

THE COLLECTED FANTASIES OF
CLARK ASHTON SMITH

VOLUME THREE

EDITED BY SCOTT CONNORS AND RON HILGER

WITH AN INTRODUCTION BY MICHAEL DIRDA

NIGHT SHADE BOOKS
NEW YORK

A Vintage from Atlantis © 2007 by The Estate of Clark Ashton Smith
This edition of *A Vintage from Atlantis* © 2016 by Night Shade Books

Introduction © 2007 by Michael Dirda
A Note on the Texts © 2007 by Scott Connors and Ron Hilger
Story Notes © 2007 by Scott Connors and Ron Hilger
Bibliography © 2007 by Scott Connors and Ron Hilger

Night Shade books may be purchased in bulk at special discounts for sales promotion, corporate gifts, fund-raising, or educational purposes. Special editions can also be created to specifications. For details, contact the Special Sales Department, Night Shade Books, 307 West 36th Street, 11th Floor, New York, NY 10018 or info@skyhorsepublishing.com.

Night Shade Books® is a registered trademark of Skyhorse Publishing, Inc.®, a Delaware corporation.

Visit our website at www.nightshadebooks.com.

10 9 8 7 6 5

Library of Congress Cataloging-in-Publication Data

Names: Smith, Clark Ashton, 1893-1961 author. | Connors, Scott, editor. | Hilger, Ronald, editor.
Title: A vintage from Atlantis / Clark Ashton Smith ; edited by Scott Connors and Ron Hilger ; with an Introduction by Michael Dirda.
Description: New York : Night Shade Books, 2016. | Series: The collected fantasies of Clark Ashton Smith ; volume 3
Identifiers: LCCN 2015050035 | ISBN 9781597808514 (paperback)
Subjects: | BISAC: FICTION / Fantasy / Short Stories. | FICTION / Science Fiction / Short Stories. | FICTION / Short Stories (single author). | FICTION / Horror. | GSAFD: Fantasy fiction | Science fiction | Horror fiction
Classification: LCC PS3537.M335 A6 2016 | DDC 813/.54--dc23
LC record available at http://lccn.loc.gov/2015050035

Cover artwork © 2007 by Jason Van Hollander
Cover design by Claudia Noble
Interior layout and design by Jeremy Lassen

ISBN: 978-1-59780-851-4

Printed in the United States of America

CONTENTS

Contents

INTRODUCTION

By Michael Dirda

Clark Ashton Smith (1893–1961) was one of the three great contributors to *Weird Tales* (along with H. P. Lovecraft and Robert E. Howard, creator of Conan)—and, just possibly, the greatest of all.

Consider the testimonials: Lovecraft himself maintained that "in sheer daemonic strangeness and fertility of conception, Clark Ashton Smith is perhaps unexcelled by any other writer dead or living." Two of our contemporary grandmasters of fantasy and science fiction, Jack Vance and Ray Bradbury, clearly modeled their own early "poetic" styles after his. According to Bradbury, Smith "filled my mind with incredible worlds, impossibly beautiful cities, and still more fantastic creatures on those worlds and in those cities." And he did this largely through his gorgeous style and the courtly pacing of his sentences. "Take one step across the threshold of his stories," declares Bradbury, "and you plunge into color, sound, taste, smell, and texture—into language."

Smith's formal diction and syntax have often been likened to prose-poetry, or even incantation. Some people can't bear this "grand manner," as Smith once described his taste for the ornate, and simply resent "all that savors of loftiness, exaltation, nobility, sublimity, and aristocracy." Yet as he explained in a letter, his reason for resorting to a luxuriant vocabulary was solely "to achieve precision, variety and richness. The words are never plugged in for their own sake, but simply because they expressed a finer shade of meaning or gave the tone-color that I wanted." You can hear Smith's "painted speech" at its best, in the opening sentences of his very first fantasy story, "The Abominations of Yondo" (1926):

"The sand of the desert of Yondo is not as the sand of other deserts; for Yondo lies nearest of all to the world's rim; and strange winds, blowing from a gulf no astronomer may hope to fathom, have sown its ruinous fields with the grey dust of corroding planets, the black ashes of extinguished suns. The dark, orb-like mountains which rise from its pitted and wrinkled plain are not all its own, for some are fallen asteroids half-buried in that abysmal sand. Things have crept in from nether space, whose incursion is forbid by the watchful gods of all proper and well-ordered lands; but there are no such gods in Yondo, where live the hoary genii of stars abolished, and decrepit demons left homeless by the destruction of antiquated hells."

Frankly, I think this excellent prose of its kind—elegant, rhythmic, original in diction, sonorous in tone, at once evocative and precise.

In Smith's best stories, this style serves the operatic, death-obsessed grandeur of his vision. For example, "The Dark Eidolon"—arguably Smith's finest story (yet to come in the Night Shade Collected Fantasies)—requires a language full of majesty just to match a sorcerer's grisly, poetic vengeance on the king who wronged him. It begins this way:

"On Zothique, the last continent of earth, the sun no longer shone with the whiteness of its prime, but was dim and tarnished as if with a vapor of blood. New stars without number had declared themselves in the heavens, and the shadows of the infinite had fallen closer. And out of the shadows, the older gods had returned to man: the gods forgotten since Hyperborea, since Mu and Poseidonis, bearing other names but the same attributes. And the elder demons had also returned, battening on the fumes of evil sacrifice, and fostering again the primordial sorceries.

"Many were the necromancers and magicians of Zothique, and the infamy and marvel of their doings were legended everywhere in the latter days. But among them all there was none greater than Namirrha..."

After reading sentences like that you know you're embarking on a real Story by a real Storyteller, one working in the tradition of the fairy tale, the Arabian Nights, and the fin-de-siècle decadents. This is vision, opium-dream, imagination at work, not some disguised memoir or slice of life about adultery in Connecticut. That paragraph also conveniently mentions three of Smith's favorite fantasy realms: the ancient lands of Hyperborea and Poseidonis and the over-ripe, far-future Zothique. A fourth is Averoigne, a part of an imagined medieval France, a darker version of James Branch Cabell's Poictesme. In all of them magic and sorcery are the tools of ambition, avarice and lust. By contrast, Smith's Golden Age-style science fiction stresses sheer wonder and the utterly alien, while his occasional straight horror tales call to mind a gruesomeness we associate with old comics like *Tales from the Crypt*.

Fantasy realms of magic, the fates of empires, Grand Guignol horror, the completely "other," the last days of Earth—such colossal themes encourage a grave or formal diction, full of descriptions of the undescribable, and always balancing the ineffable and sublime against the histrionic and sententious. When Smith takes a misstep or simply goes overboard, his baroque vocabulary and elaborate harmonies may actually cloud our minds and dull rather than illuminate his transcendental visions. To my mind, his most effective work nearly always focuses on the fate of individuals. But Smith shared with Lovecraft the belief that in a tale of wonder "the real actors are the terrible, arcanic forces, the esoteric cosmic malignities," and so often downplayed his human characters.

That said, Clark Ashton Smith doesn't, in fact, always sound like the young M. P. Shiel on steroids. He can vary his approach considerably, as the stories in this volume testify. A science fictional adventure, like "Seedling of Mars" or "The God of the Asteroid," can relate an alien encounter with clipped, Asimovian efficiency. "The Eternal World"—despite its longueurs—offers a cosmic vision of the universe in the grand manner of Olaf Stapledon, with a touch of H. G. Wells' *The Time Machine.* "A Vintage from Atlantis" might almost be one of the leisurely club tales of Lord Dunsany's Joseph Jorkens, just as "The Weird of Avoosl Wuthoqquan" and "The Holiness of Azéda-rac"—two of my own favorites— possess something of the refreshing black humor of Jack Vance's Dying Earth stories. One could readily imagine "The Vaults of Yoh-Vombis" emerging from the pen of H. P. Lovecraft, while "The Seed from the Sepulcher," which takes up a similar theme, neatly complements well-known horror classics by William Hope Hodgson and John Collier. The plot of "Ubbo-Sathla" approaches a Borgesian fable of identity, almost a mixture of "The Aleph" and "The Circular Ruins." "The Double Shadow" even opens in a voice that recalls any number of Borges' stories:

"My name is Pharpeton, among those who have known me in Poseidonis; but even I, the last and most forward pupil of the wise Avyctes, know not the name of that which I am fated to become ere tomorrow. Therefore, by the ebbing silver lamps, in my master's marble house above the loud, ever-ravening sea, I write this tale with a hasty hand, scrawling in an ink of wizard virtue on the grey, priceless, antique parchment of dragons."

Much of Smith's finest work leavens his histrionic impulses with humor, generally sardonic or macabre. In these tales, the finale usually takes the form of the biter bit, the tables turned, the greedy or proud receiving their just, if unexpected, comeuppance. (See "The Weird of Avoosl Wuthoqquan" for a good example.) Smith's many decadent themes—black magic, doubles, Faustian pacts, metamorphosis, love potions, vampires and femmes fatales—readily invite such conte cruel treatment. But whatever the theme or plot, Smith's stories nearly always maintain their dreamlike and incantatory character, sometimes as the hypnotic testimonies of the doomed, at other times as folkloric legends of death and transfiguration recited by ancient bards. Smith's protagonists seldom come to happy ends—and those who don't would often prefer a clean death to the noxious destiny in store for them. For example, several characters in "A Vintage from Atlantis" become the host bodies, then the nourishment, for a parasitic alien entity.

Smith insisted throughout his life that his brilliantined style aimed to evoke "an atmosphere of remoteness, vastness, mystery and exoticism" and, unlike ordinary magazine prose, allowed him "more varied and sonorous rhythms, as well as subtler shades, tints and nuances of meaning." Certainly, "A Vintage from Atlantis" shows how well he could create his particular verbal magic, whether in visions of the sublime, spells of enchantment, or conjurations of sheer horror. Not every story in these pages is a masterpiece—after all, the great benefit of any author's collected works is that it allows us to see a master trying out ideas that don't quite succeed. Nonetheless, those drawn to Smith's work will be glad to have virtually everything readily available, not just the classics like "The Vaults of Yoh-Vombis," "The Seed from the Sepulcher," and "The Double Shadow." Because of the scrupulous research, textual scholarship, and expert annotation of Scott Connors and Ron Hilger, coupled with Night Shade's fine book-making, we can now read a major American author in an authoritative and handsome edition. This alone is cause for celebration.

Michael Dirda, a Pulitzer Prize-winning columnist for *The Washington Post Book World*, is the author of the memoir *An Open Book* and of four volumes of essays: *Readings, Bound to Please, Book by Book,* and *Classics for Pleasure.*

A Note on the Texts

C lark Ashton Smith considered himself primarily as a poet and artist, but he began his publishing career with a series of Oriental *contes cruels* that were published in such magazines as the *Overland Monthly* and the *Black Cat*. He ceased the writing of short stories for many years, but, under the influence of his correspondent H. P. Lovecraft, he began experimenting with the weird tale when he wrote "The Abominations of Yondo" in 1925. His friend Genevieve K. Sully suggested that writing for the pulps would be a reasonably congenial way for him to earn enough money to support himself and his parents.

Between the years 1930 and 1935, the name of Clark Ashton Smith appeared on the contents page of *Weird Tales* no fewer than fifty-three times, leaving his closest competitors, Robert E. Howard, Seabury Quinn, and August W. Derleth, in the dust, with forty-six, thirty-three and thirty stories, respectively. This prodigious output did not come at the price of sloppy composition, but was distinguished by its richness of imagination and expression. Smith put the same effort into one of his stories that he did into a bejeweled and gorgeous sonnet. Donald Sidney-Fryer has described Smith's method of composition in his 1978 bio-bibliography *Emperor of Dreams* (Donald M. Grant, West Kingston, R.I.) thus:

> First he would sketch the plot in longhand on some piece of note-paper, or in his notebook, *The Black Book*, which Smith used circa 1929-1961. He would then write the first draft, usually in longhand but occasionally directly on the typewriter. He would then rewrite the story 3 or 4 times (Smith's own estimate); this he usually did directly on the typewriter. Also, he would subject each draft to considerable

> alteration and correction in longhand, taking the ms. with him on a stroll and reading aloud to himself [...]. (19)

Unlike Lovecraft, who would refuse to allow publication of his stories without assurances that they would be printed without editorial alteration, Clark Ashton Smith would revise a tale if it would ensure acceptance. Smith was not any less devoted to his art than his friend, but unlike HPL he had to consider his responsibilities in caring for his elderly and infirm parents. He tolerated these changes to his carefully crafted short stories with varying degrees of resentment, and vowed that if he ever had the opportunity to collect them between hard covers he would restore the excised text. Unfortunately, he experienced severe eyestrain during the preparation of his first Arkham House collections, so he provided magazine tear sheets to August Derleth for his secretary to use in the preparation of a manuscript.

Lin Carter was the first of Smith's editors to attempt to provide the reader with pure Smith, but the efforts of Steve Behrends and Mark Michaud have revealed the extent to which Smith's prose was compromised. Through their series of pamphlets, the *Unexpurgated Clark Ashton Smith*, the reader and critic could see precisely the severity of these compromises; while in the collections *Tales of Zothique* and *The Book of Hyperborea* Behrends and Will Murray presented for the first time the stories just as Smith wrote them.

In establishing what the editors believe to be what Smith would have preferred, we were fortunate in having access to several repositories of Smith's manuscripts, most notably the Clark Ashton Smith Papers deposited at the John Hay Library of Brown University, but also including the Bancroft Library of the University of California at Berkeley, Special Collections of Brigham Young University, the California State Library, and several private collections. Priority was given to the latest known typescript prepared by Smith, except where he had indicated that the changes were made solely to satisfy editorial requirements. In these instances we compared the last version that satisfied Smith with the version sold. Changes made include the restoration of deleted material, except only in those instances where the change of a word or phrase seems consistent with an attempt by Smith to improve the story, as opposed to the change of a word or phrase to a less Latinate, and less graceful, near-equivalent. This represents a hybrid or fusion of two competing versions, but it is the only way that we see that Smith's intentions as author may be honored. In a few instances a word might be changed in the Arkham House collections that isn't indicated on the typescript.

We have also attempted to rationalize Smith's spellings and hyphenation practices. Smith used British spellings early in his career but gradually switched to American usage. He could also vary spelling of certain words from story to story, e.g., "eerie" and "eery." We have generally standardized on his later usage, except for certain distinct word choices such as "grey."

In doing so we have deviated from the "style sheet" prepared by the late Jim Turner for his 1988 omnibus collection for Arkham House, *A Rendezvous in Averoigne*. Turner did not have access to such a wonderful scholarly tool as Boyd Pearson's website, www.eldritchdark.com. By combining its extremely useful search engine with consultation of Smith's actual manuscripts and typescripts, as well as seeing how he spelled a particular word in a poem or letter, the editors believe that they have reflected accurately Smith's idiosyncrasies of expression.

However, as Emerson reminds us, "a foolish consistency is the hobgoblin of little minds." Smith may have deliberately varied his spelling and usages depending upon the particular mood or atmosphere that he was trying to achieve in a particular story. As he explained in a letter to H. P. Lovecraft sometime in November 1930,

> The problem of "style" in writing is certainly fascinating and profound. I find it highly important, when I begin a tale, to establish at once what might be called the appropriate "tone." If this is clearly determined at the start I seldom have much difficulty in maintaining it; but if it isn't, there is likely to be trouble. Obviously, the style of "Mohammed's Tomb" wouldn't do for "The Ghoul"; and one of my chief preoccupations in writing this last story was to *exclude* images, ideas and locutions which I would have used freely in a modern story. The same, of course, applies to "Sir John Maundeville," which is a deliberate study in the archaic. (*SL* 137)

Therefore we have allowed certain variations in spelling and usage that seem to us to be consistent with Smith's stated principles as indicated above.

We are fortunate in that typescripts exist for all of the stories in this book except for "The Immortals of Mercury." Rah Hoffman, a friend of Smith and one-time co-editor of the amateur journal *The Acolyte*, was particularly helpful in deciphering the textual mysteries of this story, and we gratefully acknowledge his assistance.

Smith is known to have revised two stories extensively to meet editorial requirements, but we have been unable to locate copies of these earlier versions. Smith was in the habit of writing the dates of completion on the last page of his typescripts, along with the dates of any revisions, if any. In the case of "The Eternal World" the surviving typescript is dated the same day he indicated he had first completed the story, and the differences between it and the published version are not as substantial as his correspondence would indicate. Steve Behrends has stated that Smith's original version of "The Invisible City" was modified to add "more science," although we have been unable to verify his citation.

"The Seed from the Sepulcher" was originally accepted by Harry Bates for

Strange Tales, but later had five hundred words cut from it in order to sell it to *Weird Tales* after the former magazine ceased publication. We compared the two versions of this story, restoring some descriptive passages trimmed from the *WT* version while maintaining Smith's elimination of much repetitious narrative present in the version accepted by Bates. We also have restored several lines that were inadvertently eliminated from the version published in *Tales of Science and Sorcery* and carried over to all versions reprinted after that.

Smith published six stories himself in a 1933 pamphlet, *The Double Shadow and Other Fantasies*, but later revised some of these for sale to *Esquire* (unsuccessfully) and *Weird Tales* (successfully) in the late 1930s. In these instances we use the version published by Smith himself.

We regret that we cannot present a totally authoritative text for Smith's stories. Such typescripts do not exist. All that we can do is to apply our knowledge of Smith to the existing manuscripts and attempt to combine them to present what Smith would have preferred to publish were he not beset by editorial malfeasance in varying degrees. In doing so we hope to present Smith's words in their purest form to date so that the reader might experience what Ray Bradbury described in his foreword to *A Rendezvous in Averoigne*: "Take one step across the threshold of his stories, and you plunge into color, sound, taste, smell, and texture—into language."

The editors wish to thank Douglas A. Anderson, Martin Andersson, Steve Behrends, Geoffrey Best, Joshua Bilmes, April Derleth, William A. Dorman, Don Herron, Margery Hill, Rah Hoffman, S. T. Joshi, Terence McVicker, Neil Mechem, Marc Michaud, Will Murray, Boyd Pearson, John Pelan, Alan H. Pesetsky, Rob Preston, Robert M. Price, Dennis Rickard, David E. Schultz, Donald Sidney-Fryer, and Jason Williams for their help, support, and encouragement of this project, as well as Holly Snyder and the staff of the John Hay Library of Brown University, and D. S. Black of the Bancroft Library, University of California at Berkeley, for their assistance in the preparation of this collection. Needless to say, any errors are the sole responsibility of the editors.

THE HOLINESS OF AZÉDARAC

I

"**B**y the Ram with a Thousand Ewes! By the Tail of Dagon and the Horns of Derceto!" said Azédarac, as he fingered the tiny, pot-bellied vial of vermilion liquid on the table before him. "Something will have to be done with this pestilential Brother Ambrose. I have now learned that he was sent to Ximes by the Archbishop of Averoigne for no other purpose than to gather proof of my subterraneous connection with Azazel and the Old Ones. He has spied upon my evocations in the vaults, he has heard the hidden formulae, and beheld the veritable manifestation of Lilit, and even of Iog-Sotôt and Sodagui, those demons who are more ancient than the world; and this very morning, an hour agone, he has mounted his white ass for the return journey to Vyônes. There are two ways—or, in a sense, there is one way—in which I can avoid the pother and inconvenience of a trial for sorcery: the contents of this vial must be administered to Ambrose before he has reached his journey's end—or, failing this, I myself shall be compelled to make use of a similar medicament."

Jehan Mauvaissoir looked at the vial and then at Azédarac. He was not at all horrified, nor even surprised, by the non-episcopal oaths and the somewhat uncanonical statements which he had just heard from the Bishop of Ximes. He had known the Bishop too long and too intimately, and had rendered him too many services of an unconventional nature, to be surprised at anything. In fact, he had known Azédarac long before the sorcerer had ever dreamt of becoming a prelate, in a phase of his existence that was wholly unsuspected by the people of Ximes; and Azédarac had not troubled to keep many secrets from Jehan at any time.

"I understand," said Jehan. "You can depend upon it that the contents of the vial will be administered. Brother Ambrose will hardly travel post-haste on that ambling white ass; and he will not reach Vyônes before tomorrow

1

noon. There is abundant time to overtake him. Of course, he knows me—at least, he knows Jehan Mauvaissoir.... But that can easily be remedied."

Azédarac smiled confidently. "I leave the affair—and the vial—in your hands, Jehan. Of course, no matter what the eventuation, with all the Satanic and pre-Satanic facilities at my disposal, I should be in no great danger from these addle-pated bigots. However, I am very comfortably situated here in Ximes; and the lot of a Christian Bishop who lives in the odor of incense and piety, and maintains in the meanwhile a private understanding with the Adversary, is certainly preferable to the mischancy life of a hedge-sorcerer. I do not care to be annoyed or disturbed, or ousted from my sinecure, if such can be avoided.

"May Moloch devour that sanctimonious little milksop of an Ambrose," he went on. "I must be growing old and dull, not to have suspected him before this. It was the horror-stricken and averted look he has been wearing lately, that made me think he had peered through the key-hole on the subterranean rites. Then, when I heard he was leaving, I wisely thought to review my library; and I have found that the *Book of Eibon,* which contains the oldest incantations, and the secret, man-forgotten lore of Iog-Sotôt and Sodagui, is now missing. As you know, I had replaced the former binding of aboriginal, sub-human skin with the sheep-leather of a Christian missal, and had surrounded the volume with rows of legitimate prayer-books. Ambrose is carrying it away under his robe as proof conclusive that I am addicted to the Black Arts. No one in Averoigne will be able to read the immemorial Hyperborean script; but the dragons'-blood illuminations and drawings will be enough to damn me."

Master and servant regarded each other for an interval of significant silence. Jehan eyed with profound respect the haughty stature, the grimly lined lineaments, the grizzled tonsure, the odd, ruddy, crescent scar on the pallid brow of Azédarac, and the sultry points of orange-yellow fire that seemed to burn deep down in the chill and liquid ebon of his eyes. Azédarac, in his turn, considered with confidence the vulpine features and discreet, inexpressive air of Jehan, who might have been—and could be, if necessary—anything from a mercer to a cleric.

"It is regrettable," resumed Azédarac, "that any question of my holiness and devotional probity should have been raised among the clergy of Averoigne. But I suppose it was inevitable sooner or later—even though the chief difference between myself and many other ecclesiastics is, that I serve the Devil wittingly and of my own free will, while they do the same in sanctimonious blindness.... However, we must do what we can to delay the evil hour of public scandal, and eviction from our neatly feathered nest. Ambrose alone could prove anything to my detriment at present; and you, Jehan, will remove Ambrose to a realm wherein his monkish tattlings will be of small consequence. After that, I shall be doubly vigilant. The next emissary from Vyônes, I assure you, will find nothing to report but saintliness and bead-telling."

II

The thoughts of Brother Ambrose were sorely troubled, and at variance with the tranquil beauty of the sylvan scene, as he rode onward through the forest of Averoigne between Ximes and Vyônes. Horror was nesting in his heart like a knot of malignant vipers; and the evil *Book of Eibon,* that primordial manual of sorcery, seemed to burn beneath his robe like a huge, hot, Satanic sigil pressed against his bosom. Not for the first time, there occurred to him the wish that Clément, the Archbishop, had delegated someone else to investigate the Erebean turpitude of Azédarac. Sojourning for a month in the Bishop's household, Ambrose had learned too much for the peace of mind of any pious cleric, and had seen things that were like a secret blot of shame and terror on the white page of his memory. To find that a Christian prelate could serve the powers of nethermost perdition, could entertain in privity the foulnesses that are older than Asmodai, was abysmally disturbing to his devout soul; and ever since then he had seemed to smell corruption everywhere, and had felt on every side the serpentine encroachment of the dark Adversary.

As he rode on among the somber pines and verdant beeches, he wished also that he were mounted on something swifter than the gentle, milk-white ass appointed for his use by the Archbishop. He was dogged by the shadowy intimation of leering gargoyle faces, of invisible cloven feet, that followed him behind the thronging trees and along the umbrageous meanderings of the road. In the oblique rays, the elongated webs of shadow wrought by the dying afternoon, the forest seemed to attend with bated breath the noisome and furtive passing of innominable things. Nevertheless, Ambrose had met no one for miles; and he had seen neither bird nor beast nor viper in the summer woods.

His thoughts returned with fearful insistence to Azédarac, who appeared to him as a tall, prodigious Antichrist, uprearing his sable vans and giant figure from out the flaming mire of Abaddon. Again he saw the vaults beneath the Bishop's mansion, wherein he had peered one night on a scene of infernal terror and loathliness, had beheld the Bishop swathed in the gorgeous, coiling fumes of unholy censers, that mingled in mid-air with the sulphurous and bituminous vapors of the Pit; and through the vapors had seen the lasciviously swaying limbs, the bellying and dissolving features of foul, enormous entities.... Recalling them, again he trembled at the pre-Adamite lubriciousness of Lilit, again he shuddered at the trans-galactic horror of the demon Sodagui, and the ultra-dimensional hideousness of that being known as Iog-Sotôt to the sorcerers of Averoigne.

How balefully potent and subversive, he thought, were these immemorial devils, who had placed their servant Azédarac in the very bosom of the

Church, in a position of high and holy trust. For nine years the evil prelate had held an unchallenged and unsuspected tenure, had befouled the bishopric of Ximes with infidelities that were worse than those of the Paynims. Then, somehow, through anonymous channels, a rumor had reached Clément—a warning whisper that not even the Archbishop had dared to voice aloud; and Ambrose, a young Benedictine monk, the nephew of Clément, had been dispatched to examine privily the festering foulness that threatened the integrity of the Church. Only at that time did anyone recall how little was actually known regarding the antecedents of Azédarac; how tenuous were his claims to ecclesiastical preferment, or even to mere priestship; how veiled and doubtful were the steps by which he had attained his office. It was then realized that a formidable wizardry had been at work.

Uneasily, Ambrose wondered if Azédarac had already discovered the removal of the *Book of Eibon* from among the missals contaminated by its blasphemous presence. Even more uneasily, he wondered what Azédarac would do in that event, and how long it would take him to connect the absence of the volume with his visitor's departure.

At this point, the meditations of Ambrose were interrupted by the hard clatter of galloping hoofs that approached from behind. The emergence of a centaur from the oldest wood of paganism could scarcely have startled him to a keener panic; and he peered apprehensively over his shoulder at the nearing horseman. This person, mounted on a fine black steed with opulent trappings, was a bushy-bearded man of obvious consequence; for his gay garments were those of a noble or a courtier. He overtook Ambrose and passed on with a polite nod, seeming to be wholly intent on his own affairs. The monk was immensely reassured, though vaguely troubled for some moments by a feeling that he had seen elsewhere, under circumstances which he was now unable to recall, the narrow eyes and sharp profile that contrasted so oddly with the bluff beard of the horseman. However, he was comfortably sure that he had never seen the man in Ximes.

The rider soon vanished beyond a leafy turn of the arboreal highway. Ambrose returned to the pious horror and apprehensiveness of his former soliloquy.

As he went on, it seemed to him that the sun had gone down with untimely and appalling swiftness. Though the heavens above were innocent of cloud, and the low-lying air was free from vapors, the woods were embrowned by an inexplicable gloom that gathered visibly on all sides. In this gloom, the trunks of the trees were strangely distorted, and the low masses of foliage assumed unnatural and disquieting forms. It appeared to Ambrose that the silence around him was a fragile film through which the raucous rumble and mutter of diabolic voices might break at any moment, even as the foul and sunken driftage that rises anon above the surface of a smoothly flowing river.

With much relief, he remembered that he was not far from a way-side tavern, known as the Inn of Bonne Jouissance. Here, since his journey to Vyônes was little more than half-completed, he resolved to tarry for the night.

A minute more, and he saw the lights of the inn. Before their benign and golden radiance, the equivocal forest shadows that attended him seemed to halt and retire and he gained the haven of the tavern courtyard with the feeling of one who has barely escaped from an army of goblin perils.

Committing his mount to the care of a stable-servant, Ambrose entered the main room of the inn. Here he was greeted with the deference due to his cloth by the stout and unctuous taverner, and, being assured that the best accommodations of the place were at his disposal, he seated himself at one of several tables where other guests had already gathered to await the evening meal.

Among them, Ambrose recognized the bluff-bearded horseman who had overtaken him in the woods an hour agone. This person was sitting alone, and a little apart. The other guests, a couple of travelling mercers, a notary, and two soldiers, acknowledged the presence of the monk with all due civility; but the horseman arose from his table, and coming over to Ambrose, began immediately to make overtures that were more than those of common courtesy.

"Will you not dine with me, sir monk?" he invited, in a gruff but ingratiating voice that was perplexingly familiar to Ambrose, and yet, like the wolfish profile, was irrecognizable at the time.

"I am the Sieur des Émaux, from Touraine, at your service," the man went on. "It would seem that we are travelling the same road—possibly to the same destination. Mine is the cathedral city of Vyônes. And yours?"

Though he was vaguely perturbed, and even a little suspicious, Ambrose found himself unable to decline the invitation. In reply to the last question, he admitted that he also was on his way to Vyônes. He did not altogether like the Sieur des Émaux, whose slitted eyes gave back the candle-light of the inn with a covert glitter, and whose manner was somewhat effusive, not to say fulsome. But there seemed to be no ostensible reason for refusing a courtesy that was doubtless well-meant and genuine. He accompanied his host to their separate table.

"You belong to the Benedictine order, I observe," said the Sieur des Émaux, eyeing the monk with an odd smile that was tinged with furtive irony. "It is an order that I have always admired greatly—a most noble and worthy brotherhood. May I not inquire your name?"

Ambrose gave the requested information with a curious reluctance.

"Well, then, Brother Ambrose," said the Sieur des Émaux, "I suggest that we drink to your health and the prosperity of your order in the red wine of Averoigne while we are waiting for supper to be served. Wine is always welcome, following a long journey, and is no less beneficial before a good meal than after."

Ambrose mumbled an unwilling assent. He could not have told why, but the personality of the man was more and more distasteful to him. He seemed to detect a sinister undertone in the purring voice, to surprise an evil meaning in the low-lidded glance. And all the while his brain was tantalized by intimations of a forgotten memory. Had he seen his interlocutor in Ximes? Was the self-styled Sieur des Émaux a henchman of Azédarac in disguise?

Wine was now ordered by his host, who left the table to confer with the inn-keeper for this purpose, and even insisted on paying a visit to the cellar, that he might select a suitable vintage in person. Noting the obeisance paid to the man by the people of the tavern, who addressed him by name, Ambrose felt a certain measure of reassurance. When the taverner, followed by the Sieur des Émaux, returned with two earthen pitchers of wine, he had well-nigh succeeded in dismissing his vague doubts and vaguer fears.

Two large goblets were now placed on the table, and the Sieur des Émaux filled them immediately from one of the pitchers. It seemed to Ambrose that the first of the goblets already contained a small amount of some sanguine fluid, before the wine was poured into it; but he could not have sworn to this in the dim light, and thought that he must have been mistaken.

"Here are two matchless vintages," said the Sieur des Émaux, indicating the pitchers. "Both are so excellent that I was unable to choose between them; but you, Brother Ambrose, are perhaps capable of deciding their merits with a finer palate than mine."

He pushed one of the filled goblets toward Ambrose. "This is the wine of La Frênaie," he said. "Drink, it will verily transport you from the world by virtue of the mighty fire that slumbers in its heart."

Ambrose took the proffered goblet, and raised it to his lips. The Sieur des Émaux was bending forward above his own wine to inhale its bouquet; and something in his posture was terrifyingly familiar to Ambrose. In a chill flash of horror, his memory told him that the thin, pointed features behind the square beard were dubiously similar to those of Jehan Mauvaissoir, whom he had often seen in the household of Azédarac, and who, as he had reason to believe, was implicated in the Bishop's sorceries. He wondered why he had not placed the resemblance before, and what wizardry had drugged his powers of recollection. Even now he was not sure; but the mere suspicion terrified him as if some deadly serpent had reared its head across the table.

"Drink, Brother Ambrose," urged the Sieur des Émaux, draining his own goblet. "To your welfare and that of all good Benedictines."

Ambrose hesitated. The cold, hypnotic eyes of his interlocutor were upon him, and he was powerless to refuse, in spite of all his apprehensions. Shuddering slightly, with the sense of some irresistible compulsion, and feeling that he might drop dead from the virulent working of a sudden poison, he emptied his goblet.

An instant more, and he felt that his worst fears had been justified. The wine burned like the liquid flames of Phlegethon in his throat and on his lips, it seemed to fill his veins with a hot, infernal quicksilver. Then, all at once, an unbearable cold had inundated his being; an icy whirlwind wrapped him round with coils of roaring air, the chair melted beneath him, and he was falling through endless glacial gulfs. The walls of the inn had flown like receding vapors; the lights went out like stars in the black mist of a marish; and the face of the Sieur des Émaux faded with them on the swirling shadows, even as a bubble that breaks on the milling of midnight waters.

III

It was with some difficulty that Ambrose assured himself that he was not dead. He had seemed to fall eternally, through a grey night that was peopled with ever-changing forms, with blurred unstable masses that dissolved to other masses before they could assume definitude. For a moment, he thought there were walls about him once more, and then he was plunging from terrace to terrace of a world of phantom trees. At whiles, he thought also that there were human faces; but all was doubtful and evanescent, all was drifting smoke and surging shadow.

Abruptly, with no sense of transition or impact, he found that he was no longer falling. The vague phantasmagoria around him had returned to an actual scene—but a scene in which there was no trace of the Inn of Bonne Jouissance, or the Sieur des Émaux.

Ambrose peered about with incredulous eyes on a situation that was truly unbelievable. He was sitting in broad daylight on a large square block of roughly hewn granite. Around him, at a little distance, beyond the open space of a grassy glade, were the lofty pines and spreading beeches of an elder forest, whose boughs were already touched by the gold of the declining sun. Immediately before him, several men were standing.

These men appeared to regard Ambrose with a profound and almost religious amazement. They were bearded and savage of aspect, with white robes of a fashion he had never before seen. Their hair was long and matted, like tangles of black snakes; and their eyes burned with a frenetic fire. Each of them bore in his right hand a rude knife of sharply chiselled stone.

Ambrose wondered if he had died after all, and if these beings were the strange devils of some unlisted hell. In the face of what had happened, and the light of Ambrose's own beliefs, it was a far from unreasonable conjecture. He peered with fearful trepidation at the supposed demons, and began to mumble a prayer to the God who had abandoned him so inexplicably to his spiritual foes. Then he remembered the necromantic powers of Azédarac, and conceived another surmise—that he had been spirited bodily away from the Inn of Bonne Jouissance, and delivered into the hands of those pre-Satanic entities that served the sorcerous Bishop. Becoming convinced of his own physical solidity and integrity, and reflecting that such was scarcely the appropriate condition of a disincarnate soul, and also that the sylvan scene about him was hardly characteristic of the infernal regions, he accepted this as the true explanation. He was still alive, and still on earth, though the circumstances of his situation were more than mysterious, and were fraught with dire, unknowable danger.

The strange beings had maintained an utter silence, as if they were too dumbfounded for speech. Hearing the prayerful murmurs of Ambrose, they seemed to recover from their surprise, and became not only articulate but vociferous. Ambrose could make nothing of their harsh vocables, in which sibilants and aspirates and gutturals were often combined in a manner difficult for the normal human tongue to imitate. However, he caught the word *taranit,* several times repeated, and wondered if it were the name of an especially malevolent demon.

The speech of the weird beings began to assume a sort of rude rhythm, like the intonations of some primordial chant. Two of them stepped forward and seized Ambrose, while the voices of their companions rose in a shrill, triumphant litany.

Scarcely knowing what had happened, and still less what was to follow, Ambrose was flung supine on the granite block, and was held down by one of his captors, while the other raised aloft the keen blade of chiselled flint which he carried. The blade was poised in air above Ambrose's heart, and the monk realized in sudden terror that it would fall with dire velocity and pierce him through before the lapse of another moment.

Then, above the demoniac chanting, which had risen to a mad, malignant frenzy, he heard the sweet and imperious cry of a woman's voice. In the wild confusion of his terror, the words were strange and meaningless to him; but plainly they were understood by his captors, and were taken as an undeniable command. The stone knife was lowered sullenly, and Ambrose was permitted to resume a sitting posture on the flat slab.

His rescuer was standing on the edge of the open glade, in the wide-flung umbrage of an ancient pine. She came forward now; and the white-garmented beings fell back with evident respect before her. She was very tall, with a fearless and regal demeanor, and was gowned in a dark, shimmering blue, like the star-laden blue of nocturnal summer skies. Her hair was knotted in a long golden-brown braid, heavy as the glistening coils of some eastern serpent. Her eyes were a strange amber, her lips a vermilion touched with the coolness of woodland shadow, and her skin was of alabastrine fairness. Ambrose saw that she was beautiful; but she inspired him with the same awe that he would have felt before a queen, together with something of the fear and consternation which a virtuous young monk would conceive in the perilous presence of an alluring succubus.

"Come with me," she said to Ambrose, in a tongue that his monastic studies enabled him to recognize as an obsolete variant of the French of Averoigne—a tongue that no man had supposedly spoken for many hundred years. Obediently and in great wonder, he arose and followed her, with no hindrance from his glowering and reluctant captors.

The woman led him to a narrow path that wound sinuously away through the deep forest. In a few moments, the glade, the granite block, and the cluster of white-robed men were lost to sight behind the heavy foliage.

"Who are you?" asked the lady, turning to Ambrose. "You look like one of those crazy missionaries who are beginning to enter Averoigne now-adays. I believe that people call them Christians. The Druids have sacrificed so many of them to Taranit, that I marvel at your temerity in coming here."

Ambrose found it difficult to comprehend the archaic phrasing; and the import of her words was so utterly strange and baffling that he felt sure he must have misunderstood her.

"I am Brother Ambrose," he replied, expressing himself slowly and awkwardly in the long-disused dialect. "Of course, I am a Christian; but I confess that I fail to understand you. I have heard of the pagan Druids; but surely they were all driven from Averoigne many centuries ago."

The woman stared at Ambrose, with open amazement and pity. Her brownish-yellow eyes were bright and clear as a mellowed wine.

"Poor little one," she said. "I fear that your dreadful experiences have served to unsettle you. It was fortunate that I came along when I did, and decided to intervene. I seldom interfere with the Druids and their sacrifices; but I saw you sitting on their altar a little while agone, and was struck by your youth and comeliness."

Ambrose felt more and more that he had been made the victim of a most peculiar sorcery; but, even yet, he was far from suspecting the true magnitude of this sorcery. Amid his bemusement and consternation, however, he realized that he owed his life to the singular and lovely woman beside him, and began to stammer out his gratitude.

"You need not thank me," said the lady, with a dulcet smile. "I am Moriamis, the enchantress, and the Druids fear my magic, which is more sovereign and more excellent than theirs, though I use it only for the welfare of men and not for their bale or bane."

The monk was dismayed to learn that his fair rescuer was a sorceress, even though her powers were professedly benignant. The knowledge added to his alarm; but he felt that it would be politic to conceal his emotions in this regard.

"Indeed, I am grateful to you," he protested. "And now, if you can tell me the way to the Inn of Bonne Jouissance, which I left not long ago, I shall owe you a further debt."

Moriamis knitted her light brows. "I have never heard of the Inn of Bonne Jouissance. There is no such place in this region."

"But this is the forest of Averoigne, is it not?" inquired the puzzled Ambrose. "And surely we are not far from the road that runs between the town of Ximes and the city of Vyônes?"

"I have never heard of Ximes, or Vyônes, either," said Moriamis. "Truly, the land is known as Averoigne, and this forest is the great wood of Averoigne, which men have called by that name from primeval years. But there are no towns such as the ones whereof you speak. Brother Ambrose, I fear that you still wander a little in your mind."

Ambrose was aware of a maddening perplexity. "I have been most damnably beguiled," he said, half to himself. "It is all the doing of that abominable sorcerer, Azédarac, I am sure."

The woman started as if she had been stung by a wild bee. There was something both eager and severe in the searching gaze that she turned upon Ambrose.

"Azédarac?" she queried. "What do you know of Azédarac? I was once acquainted with someone by that name; and I wonder if it could be the same person. Is he tall and a little grey, with hot, dark eyes, and a proud, half-angry air, and a crescent scar on the brow?"

Greatly mystified, and more troubled than ever, Ambrose admitted the veracity of her description. Realizing that in some unknown way he had stumbled upon the hidden antecedents of the sorcerer, he confided the story of his adventures to Moriamis, hoping that she would reciprocate with further information concerning Azédarac.

The woman listened with the air of one who is much interested but not at all surprised.

"I understand now," she observed, when he had finished. "Anon I shall explain everything that mystifies and troubles you. I think I know this Jehan Mauvaissoir, also; he has long been the man-servant of Azédarac, though his name was Melchire in other days. These two have always been the underlings of evil, and have served the Old Ones in ways forgotten or never known by the Druids."

"Indeed, I hope you can explain what has happened," said Ambrose. "It is a fearsome and strange and ungodly thing, to drink a draught of wine in a tavern at eventide, and then find one's self in the heart of the forest by afternoon daylight, among demons such as those from whom you succored me."

"Yea," countered Moriamis, "it is even stranger than you dream. Tell me, Brother Ambrose, what was the year in which you entered the Inn of Bonne Jouissance?"

"Why, it is the year of our Lord, 1175, of course. What other year could it be?"

"The Druids use a different chronology," replied Moriamis, "and their notation would mean nothing to you. But, according to that which the Christian missionaries would now introduce in Averoigne, the present year is 475 A.D. You have been sent back no less than seven hundred years into what the people of your era would regard as the past. The Druid altar on which I found you lying is probably located on the future site of the Inn of Bonne Jouissance."

Ambrose was more than dumbfounded. His mind was unable to grasp the entire import of Moriamis' words.

"But how can such things be?" he cried. "How can a man go backward in time, among years and people that have long turned to dust?"

"That, mayhap, is a mystery for Azédarac to unriddle. However, the past and the future co-exist with what we call the present, and are merely the two segments of the circle of time. We see them and name them according to our own position in the circle."

Ambrose felt that he had fallen among necromancies of a most unhallowed and unexampled sort, and had been made the victim of diableries unknown to the Christian catalogues.

Tongue-tied by a consciousness that all comment, all protest or even prayer would prove inadequate to the situation, he saw that a stone tower with small lozenge-shaped windows was now visible above the turrets of pine along the path which he and Moriamis were following.

"This is my home," said Moriamis, as they came forth from beneath the thinning trees at the foot of a little knoll on which the tower was situated. "Brother Ambrose, you must be my guest."

Ambrose was unable to decline the proffered hospitality, in spite of his feeling that Moriamis was hardly the most suitable of châtelaines for a chaste and god-fearing monk. However, the pious misgivings with which she inspired him were not unmingled with fascination. Also, like a lost child, he clung to the only available protection in a land of fearful perils and astounding mysteries.

The interior of the tower was neat and clean and home-like, though with furniture of a ruder sort than that to which Ambrose was accustomed, and rich but roughly woven arrases. A serving-woman, tall as Moriamis herself, but darker, brought to him a huge bowl of milk and wheaten bread, and the monk was now able to assuage the hunger that had gone unsatisfied in the Inn of Bonne Jouissance.

As he seated himself before the simple fare, he realized that the *Book of Eibon* was still heavy in the bosom of his gown. He removed the volume, and gave it gingerly to Moriamis. Her eyes widened, but she made no comment until he had finished his meal. Then she said:

"This volume is indeed the property of Azédarac, who was formerly a neighbor of mine. I knew the scoundrel quite well—in fact, I knew him all too well." Her bosom heaved with an obscure emotion as she paused for a moment. "He was the wisest and the mightiest of sorcerers, and the most secret withal; for no one knew the time and the manner of his coming into Averoigne, or the fashion in which he had procured the immemorial *Book of Eibon,* whose runic writings were beyond the lore of all other wizards. He was a master of all enchantments and all demons, and likewise a compounder of mighty potions. Among these were certain philters, blended with potent spells and possessed of unique virtue, that would send the drinker backward or forward in time. One of them, I believe, was administered to you by Melchire, or Jehan Mauvaissoir; and Azédarac himself, together with this man-servant, made use of another—perhaps not for the first time—when they went onward from the present age of the Druids into that age of Christian authority to which you belong. There was a crimson vial for the past, and a green for the future. Behold! I possess one of each—though Azédarac was unaware that I knew of their existence."

She opened a little cupboard, in which were the various charms and medicaments, the sun-dried herbs and moon-compounded essences that a sorceress would employ. From among them she brought out the two vials, one of which contained a sanguine-colored liquid, and the other a fluid of emerald brightness.

"I stole them one day, out of womanly curiosity, from his hidden store of philters and elixirs and magistrals," continued Moriamis. "I could have followed the rascal when he disappeared into the future, if I had chosen to do so. But I am well enough content with my own age; and moreover, I am not the sort of woman who pursues a wearied and reluctant lover...."

"Then," said Ambrose, more bewildered than ever, but hopeful, "if I were to drink the contents of the green vial, I should return to my own epoch."

"Precisely. And I am sure, from what you have told me, that your return would be a source of much annoyance to Azédarac. It is like the fellow, to have established himself in a fat prelacy. He was ever the master of circumstance, with an eye to his own accommodation and comfort. It would hardly please him, I am sure, if you were to reach the Archbishop.... I am not revengeful by nature... but on the other hand..."

"It is hard to understand how any one could have wearied of you," said Ambrose, gallantly, as he began to comprehend the situation.

Moriamis smiled. "That is prettily said. And you are really a charming youth, in spite of that dismal-looking robe. I am glad that I rescued you from the Druids, who would have torn your heart out and offered it to their demon, Taranit."

"And now you will send me back?"

Moriamis frowned a little, and then assumed her most seductive air.

"Are you in such a hurry to leave your hostess? Now that you are living in another century than your own, a day, a week, or a month will make no difference in the date of your return. I have also retained the formulas of Azédarac; and I know how to graduate the potion, if necessary. The usual period of transportation is exactly seven hundred years; but the philter can be strengthened or weakened a little."

The sun had fallen beyond the pines, and a soft twilight was beginning to invade the tower. The maidservant had left the room. Moriamis came over and seated herself beside Ambrose on the rough bench he was occupying. Still smiling, she fixed her amber eyes upon him, with a languid flame in their depths—a flame that seemed to brighten as the dusk grew stronger. Without speaking, she began slowly to unbraid her heavy hair, from which there emanated a perfume that was subtle and delicious as the perfume of grape-flowers.

Ambrose was embarrassed by this delightful proximity. "I am not sure that it would be right for me to remain, after all. What would the Archbishop think?"

"My dear child, the Archbishop will not even be born for at least six hundred and fifty years. And it will be still longer before you are born. And when you return, anything that you have done during your stay with me will have happened no less than seven centuries ago... which should be long enough to procure the remission of any sin, no matter how often repeated."

Like a man who has been taken in the toils of some fantastic dream, and finds that the dream is not altogether disagreeable, Ambrose yielded to this feminine and irrefutable reasoning. He hardly knew what was to happen; but, under the exceptional circumstances indicated by Moriamis, the rigors of monastic discipline might well be relaxed to almost any conceivable degree, without entailing spiritual perdition or even a serious breach of vows.

IV

A month later, Moriamis and Ambrose were standing beside the Druid altar. It was late in the evening; and a slightly gibbous moon had risen upon the deserted glade and was fringing the tree-tops with wefted silver. The warm breath of the summer night was gentle as the sighing of a woman in slumber.

"Must you go, after all?" said Moriamis, in a pleading and regretful voice.

"It is my duty. I must return to Clément with the *Book of Eibon* and the other evidence I have collected against Azédarac." The words sounded a little unreal to Ambrose as he uttered them; and he tried very hard, but vainly, to convince himself of the cogency and validity of his arguments. The idyl of his stay with Moriamis, to which he was oddly unable to attach any true conviction of sin, had given to all that had preceded it a certain dismal insubstantiality. Free from all responsibility or restraint, in the sheer obliviousness of dreams, he had lived like a happy pagan; and now he must go back to the drear existence of a medieval monk, beneath the prompting of an obscure sense of duty.

"I shall not try to hold you," Moriamis sighed. "But I shall miss you, and remember you as a worthy lover and a pleasant playmate. Here is the philter."

The green essence was cold and almost hueless in the moonlight, as Moriamis poured it into a little cup and gave it to Ambrose.

"Are you sure of its precise efficacy?" the monk inquired. "Are you sure that I shall return to the Inn of Bonne Jouissance, at a time not far subsequent to that of my departure therefrom?"

"Yea," said Moriamis, "for the potion is infallible. But stay, I have also brought along the other vial—the vial of the past. Take it with you—for who knows, you may sometime wish to return and visit me again."

Ambrose accepted the red vial and placed it in his robe beside the ancient manual of Hyperborean sorcery. Then, after an appropriate farewell to Moriamis, he drained with sudden resolution the contents of the cup.

The moonlit glade, the grey altar, and Moriamis, all vanished in a swirl of flame and shadow. It seemed to Ambrose that he was soaring endlessly through phantasmagoric gulfs, amid the ceaseless shifting and melting of unstable things, the transient forming and fading of irresoluble worlds.

At the end, he found himself sitting once more in the Inn of Bonne Jouissance, at what he assumed to be the very same table before which he had sat with the Sieur des Émaux. It was daylight, and the room was full of people, among whom he looked in vain for the rubicund face of the inn-keeper, or the servants and fellow-guests he had previously seen. All were unfamiliar to him; and the furniture was strangely worn, and was grimier than he remembered it.

Perceiving the presence of Ambrose, the people began to eye him with open curiosity and wonderment. A tall man with dolorous eyes and lantern jaws came hastily forward and bowed before him with an air that was half-servile but full of a prying impertinence.

"What do you wish?" he asked.

"Is this the Inn of Bonne Jouissance?"

The inn-keeper stared at Ambrose. "Nay, it is the Inn of Haute Espérance, of which I have been the taverner these thirty years. Could you not read the sign? It was called the Inn of Bonne Jouissance in my father's time, but the name was changed after his death."

Ambrose was filled with consternation. "But the inn was differently named, and was kept by another man when I visited it not long ago," he cried in bewilderment. "The owner was a stout, jovial man, not in the least like you."

"That would answer the description of my father," said the taverner, eyeing Ambrose more dubiously than ever. "He has been dead for the full thirty years of which I speak; and surely you were not even born at the time of his decease."

Ambrose began to realize what had happened. The emerald potion, by some error or excess of potency, had taken him many years beyond his own time into the future!

"I must resume my journey to Vyônes," he said in a bewildered voice, without fully comprehending the implications of his situation. "I have a message for the Archbishop Clément—and must not delay longer in delivering it."

"But Clément has been dead even longer than my father," exclaimed the inn-keeper. "From whence do you come, that you are ignorant of this?" It was plain from his manner that he had begun to doubt the sanity of Ambrose. Others, overhearing the strange discussion, had begun to crowd about, and were plying the monk with jocular and sometimes ribald questions.

"And what of Azédarac, the Bishop of Ximes? Is he dead, too?" inquired Ambrose, desperately.

"You mean St. Azédarac, no doubt. He outlived Clément, but nevertheless he has been dead and duly canonized for thirty-two years. Some say that he did not die, but was transported to heaven alive, and that his body was never buried in the great mausoleum reared for him at Ximes. But that is probably a mere legend."

Ambrose was overwhelmed with unspeakable desolation and confusion. In the meanwhile, the crowd about him had increased, and in spite of his monkish robe, he was being made the subject of rude remarks and jeers.

"The good Brother has lost his wits," cried some. "The wines of Averoigne are too strong for him," said others.

"What year is this?" demanded Ambrose, in his desperation.

"The year of our Lord, 1230," replied the taverner, breaking into a derisive laugh. "And what year did you think it was?"

"It was the year 1175 when I last visited the Inn of Bonne Jouissance," admitted Ambrose.

His declaration was greeted with fresh jeers and laughter. "Hola, young sir, you were not even conceived at that time," the taverner said. Then, seeming to remember something, he went on in a more thoughtful tone: "When I was a child, my father told me of a young monk, about your age, who came to the Inn of Bonne Jouissance one evening in the summer of 1175, and vanished inexplicably after drinking a draught of red wine. I believe his name was Ambrose. Perhaps you are Ambrose, and have only just returned from a visit to nowhere." He gave a derisory wink, and the new jest was taken up and bandied from mouth to mouth among the frequenters of the tavern.

Ambrose was trying to realize the full import of his predicament. His mission was now useless, through the death or disappearance of Azédarac; and no one would remain in all Averoigne to recognize him or believe his story. He felt the hopelessness of his alienation among unknown years and people.

Suddenly he remembered the red vial given him at parting by Moriamis. The potion, like the green philter, might prove uncertain in its effect; but he was seized by an all-consuming desire to escape from the weird embarrassment and wilderment of his present position. Also, he longed for Moriamis like a lost child for its mother; and the charm of his sojourn in the past was upon him with an irresistible spell. Ignoring the ribald faces and voices about him, he drew the vial from his bosom, uncorked it, and swallowed the contents....

V

He was back in the forest glade, by the gigantic altar. Moriamis was beside him again, lovely and warm and breathing; and the moon was still rising above the pine-tops. It seemed that no more than a few moments could have elapsed since he had said farewell to the beloved enchantress.

"I thought you might return," said Moriamis. "And I waited a little while."

Ambrose told her of the singular mishap that had attended his journey in time.

Moriamis nodded gravely. "The green philter was more potent than I had supposed," she remarked. "It is fortunate, though, that the red philter was equivalently strong, and could bring you back to me through all those added years. You will have to remain with me now, for I possessed only the two vials. I hope you are not sorry."

Ambrose proceeded to prove, in a somewhat unmonastic manner, that her hope was fully justified.

Neither then nor at any other time did Moriamis tell him that she herself had strengthened slightly and equally the two philters by means of the private formula which she had also stolen from Azédarac.

THE MAKER OF GARGOYLES

I

Among the many gargoyles that frowned or leered from the roof of the
new-built cathedral of Vyônes, two were pre-eminent above the rest
by virtue of their fine workmanship and their supreme grotesquery.
These two had been wrought by the stone-carver Blaise Reynard, a native of
Vyônes, who had lately returned from a long sojourn in the cities of Provence,
and had secured employment on the cathedral when the three years' task
of its construction and ornamentation was well-nigh completed. In view of
the wonderful artistry shown by Reynard, it was regretted by Ambrosius, the
Archbishop, that it had not been possible to commit the execution of all the
gargoyles to this delicate and accomplished workman; but other people, with
less liberal tastes than Ambrosius, were heard to express a different opinion.

This opinion, perhaps, was tinged by the personal dislike that had been
generally felt toward Reynard in Vyônes even from his boyhood; and which
had been revived with some virulence on his return. Whether rightly or unjustly, his very physiognomy had always marked him out for public disfavor:
he was inordinately dark, with hair and beard of a preternatural bluish-black,
and slanting, ill-matched eyes that gave him a sinister and cunning air. His
taciturn and saturnine ways were such as a superstitious people would identify with necromantic knowledge or complicity; and there were those who
covertly accused him of being in league with Satan; though the accusations
were little more than vague, anonymous rumors, even to the end, through
lack of veritable evidence.

However, the people who suspected Reynard of diabolic affiliations, were
wont for awhile to instance the two gargoyles as sufficient proof. No man,
they contended, who was not inspired by the Arch-Enemy, could have carven
anything so sheerly evil and malignant, could have embodied so consum-
mately in mere stone the living lineaments of the most demoniacal of all

17

the deadly Sins.

The two gargoyles were perched on opposite corners of a high tower of the cathedral. One was a snarling, murderous, cat-headed monster, with retracted lips revealing formidable fangs, and eyes that glared intolerable hatred from beneath ferine brows. This creature had the claws and wings of a griffin, and seemed as if it were poised in readiness to swoop down on the city of Vyônes, like a harpy on its prey. Its companion was a horned satyr, with the vans of some great bat such as might roam the nether caverns, with sharp, clenching talons, and a look of Satanically brooding lust, as if it were gloating above the helpless object of its unclean desire. Both figures were complete, even to the hindquarters, and were not mere conventional adjuncts of the roof. One would have expected them to start at any moment from the stone in which they were mortised.

Ambrosius, a lover of art, had been openly delighted with these creations, because of their high technical merit and their verisimilitude as works of sculpture. But others, including many humbler dignitaries of the Church, were more or less scandalized, and said that the workman had informed these figures with the visible likeness of his own vices, to the glory of Belial rather than of God, and had thus perpetrated a sort of blasphemy. Of course, they admitted, a certain amount of grotesquery was requisite in gargoyles; but in this case, the allowable bounds had been egregiously overpassed.

However, with the completion of the cathedral, and in spite of all this adverse criticism, the high-poised gargoyles of Blaise Reynard, like all other details of the building, were soon taken for granted through mere everyday familiarity; and eventually they were almost forgotten. The scandal of opposition died down, and the stone-carver himself, though the town-folk continued to eye him askance, was able to secure other work through the favor of discriminating patrons. He remained in Vyônes; and paid his addresses, albeit without visible success, to a taverner's daughter, one Nicolette Villom, of whom, it was said, he had long been enamored in his own surly and reticent fashion.

But Reynard himself had not forgotten the gargoyles. Often, in passing the superb pile of the cathedral, he would gaze up at them with a secret satisfaction whose cause he could hardly have assigned or delimited. They seemed to retain for him a rare and mystical meaning, to signalize an obscure but pleasurable triumph.

He would have said, if asked for the reason for his satisfaction, that he was proud of a skillful piece of handiwork. He would not have said, and perhaps would not even have known, that in one of the gargoyles he had imprisoned all his festering rancor, all his answering spleen and hatred toward the people of Vyônes, who had always hated him; and had set the image of this rancor to peer venomously down forever from a lofty place. And perhaps he would not even have dreamt that in the second gargoyle he had somehow expressed his own dour and satyr-like passion for the girl Nicolette—a passion that had brought him back to the detested city of his youth after years of wandering; a passion singularly tenacious of one object, and differing in this regard from the ordinary lusts of a nature so brutal as Reynard's.

Always to the stone-cutter, even more than to those who had criticized and abhorred his productions, the gargoyles were alive, they possessed a vitality and a sentiency of their own. And most of all did they seem to live when the summer drew to an end and the autumn rains had gathered upon Vyônes. Then, when the full cathedral gutters poured above the streets, one might have thought that the actual spittle of a foul malevolence, the very slaver of an impure lust, had somehow been mingled with the water that ran in rills from the mouths of the gargoyles.

II

At that time, in the year of our Lord, 1138, Vyônes was the principal town of the province of Averoigne. On two sides the great, shadow-haunted forest, a place of equivocal legends, of *loupsgarous* and phantoms, approached to the very walls and flung its umbrage upon them at early forenoon and evening. On the other sides there lay cultivated fields, and gentle streams that meandered among willows or poplars, and roads that ran through an open plain to the high châteaux of noble lords and to regions beyond Averoigne.

The town itself was prosperous, and had never shared in the ill-fame of the bordering forest. It had long been sanctified by the presence of two nunneries and a monastery; and now, with the completion of the long-planned cathedral, it was thought that Vyônes would have henceforward the additional protection of a more august holiness; that demon and *stryge* and incubus would keep their distance from its heaven-favored purlieus with a more meticulous caution than before.

Of course, as in all medieval towns, there had been occasional instances of alleged sorcery or demoniacal possession; and, once or twice, the perilous temptations of succubi had made their inroads on the pious virtue of Vyônes. But this was nothing more than might be expected, in a world where the Devil and his works were always more or less rampant. No one could possibly have anticipated the reign of infernal horrors that was to make hideous the latter months of autumn, following the cathedral's erection.

To make the matter even more inexplicable, and more blasphemously dreadful than it would otherwise have been, the first of these horrors occurred in the neighborhood of the cathedral itself and almost beneath its sheltering shadow.

Two men, a respectable clothier named Guillaume Maspier and an equally reputable cooper, one Gérôme Mazzal, were returning to their lodgings in the late hours of a November eve, after imbibing both the red and white wines of the countryside in more than one tavern. According to Maspier, who alone survived to tell the tale, they were passing along a street that skirted the cathedral square, and could see the bulk of the great building against the stars, when a flying monster, black as the soot of Abaddon, had descended upon them from the heavens and assailed Gérôme Mazzal, beating him down with its heavily flapping wings and seizing him with its inch-long teeth and talons.

Maspier was unable to describe the creature with minuteness, for he had seen it but dimly and partially in the unlit street; and moreover, the fate of his companion, who had fallen to the cobblestones with the black devil snarling and tearing at his throat, had not induced Maspier to linger in that vicinity. He had betaken himself from the scene with all the celerity of which he was capable, and had stopped only at the house of a priest, many streets away, where he had related his adventure between shudderings and hiccoughings.

Armed with holy water and aspergillus, and accompanied by many of the towns-people carrying torches and staves and halberds, the priest was led by Maspier to the place of the horror; and there they had found the body of Mazzal, with fearfully mangled face, and throat and bosom lined with bloody lacerations. The demoniac assailant had flown; and it was not seen or encountered again that night; but those who had beheld its work returned aghast to their homes, feeling that a creature of nethermost hell had come to visit the city, and perchance to abide therein.

Consternation was rife on the morrow, when the story became generally known; and rites of exorcism against the invading demon were performed by the clergy in all public places and before thresholds. But the sprinkling of holy water and the mumbling of stated forms were futile; for the evil spirit was still abroad, and its malignity was proven once more, on the night following the ghastly death of Gérôme Mazzal.

This time, it claimed two victims, burghers of high probity and some consequence, on whom it descended in a narrow alley, slaying one of them instantaneously, and dragging down the other from behind as he sought to flee. The shrill cries of the helpless men, and the guttural growling of the demon, were heard by people in the houses along the alley; and some, who were hardy enough to peer from their windows, had seen the departure of the infamous assailant, blotting out the autumn stars with the sable and misshapen foulness of its wings, and hovering in execrable menace above the house-tops.

After this, few people would venture abroad at night, unless in case of dire and exigent need; and those who did venture went in armed companies and were all furnished with flambeaux, thinking thus to frighten away the demon, which they adjudged a creature of darkness that would abhor the light and shrink therefrom, through the nature of its kind. But the boldness of this fiend was beyond measure, for it proceeded to attack more than one company of worthy citizens, disregarding the flaring torches that were thrust in its face, or putting them out with the stenchful wind of its wide vans.

Evidently it was a spirit of homicidal hate; for all the people on whom it seized were grievously mangled or torn to numberless shreds by its teeth and talons. Those who saw it, and survived, were wont to describe it variously and with much ambiguity; but all agreed in attributing to it the head of a ferocious animal and the wings of a monstrous bird. Some, the most learned in demonology, were fain to identify it with Modo, the spirit of murder; and others took it for one of the great lieutenants of Satan, perhaps Amaimon or Alastor, gone mad with exasperation at the impregnable supremacy of Christ in the holy city of Vyônes.

The terror that soon prevailed, beneath the widening scope of these Satanical incursions and depredations, was beyond all belief—a clotted, seething, devil-ridden gloom of superstitious obsession, not to be hinted in modern language. Even by daylight, the Gothic wings of nightmare seemed to brood in undeparting oppression above the city; and fear was everywhere, like the foul contagion of some epidemic plague. The inhabitants went their way in prayer and trembling; and the Archbishop himself, as well as the subordinate clergy, confessed an inability to cope with the ever-growing horror. An emissary was sent to Rome, to procure water that had been specially sanctified by the pope. This alone, it was thought, would be efficacious enough to drive away the dreadful visitant.

In the meanwhile, the horror waxed, and mounted to its culmination. One eve, toward the middle of November, the abbot of the local monastery of Cordeliers, who had gone forth to administer extreme unction to a dying friend, was seized by the black devil just as he approached the threshold of his destination, and was slain in the same atrocious manner as the other victims.

To this doubly infamous deed, a scarce-believable blasphemy was soon added. On the very next night, while the torn body of the abbot lay on a rich catafalque in the cathedral, and masses were being said and tapers burnt, the demon invaded the high nave through the open door, extinguished all the candles with one flap of its sooty wings, and dragged down no less than three of the officiating priests to an unholy death in the darkness.

Everyone now felt that a truly formidable assault was being made by the powers of Evil on the Christian probity of Vyônes. In the condition of abject terror, of extreme disorder and demoralization that followed upon this new atrocity, there was a deplorable outbreak of human crime, of murder and rapine and thievery, together with covert manifestations of Satanism, and celebrations of the Black Mass attended by many neophytes.

Then, in the midst of all this pandemoniacal fear and confusion, it was rumored that a second devil had been seen in Vyônes; that the murderous fiend was accompanied by a spirit of equal deformity and darkness, whose intentions were those of lechery, and which molested none but women. This creature had frightened several dames and demoiselles and maidservants into a veritable hysteria by peering through their bedroom windows; and had sidled lasciviously, with uncouth mows and grimaces, and grotesque flappings of its bat-shaped wings, toward others who had occasion to fare from house to house across the nocturnal streets.

However, strange to say, there were no authentic instances in which the chastity of any woman had suffered actual harm from this noisome incubus. Many were approached by it, and were terrified immoderately by the hideousness and lustfulness of its demeanor; but no one was ever touched. Even in that time of horror, both spiritual and corporeal, there were those who made a ribald jest of this singular abstention on the part of the demon, and said it was seeking throughout Vyônes for someone whom it had not yet found.

III

The lodgings of Blaise Reynard were separated only by the length of a dark and crooked alley from the tavern kept by Jean Villom, the father of Nicolette. In this tavern, Reynard had been wont to spend his evenings; though his suit was frowned upon by Jean Villom, and had received but scant encouragement from the girl herself. However, because of his well-filled purse and his almost illimitable capacity for wine, Reynard was tolerated. He came early each night, with the falling of darkness, and would sit in silence hour after hour, staring with hot and sullen eyes at Nicolette, and gulping joylessly the potent vintages of Averoigne. Apart from their desire to retain his custom, the people of the tavern were a little afraid of him, on account of his dubious and semi-sorcerous reputation, and also because of his surly temper. They did not wish to antagonize him more than was necessary.

Like everyone else in Vyônes, Reynard had felt the suffocating burden of superstitious terror during those nights when the fiendish marauder was hovering above the town and might descend on the luckless wayfarer at any moment, in any locality. Nothing less urgent and imperative than the obsession of his half-bestial longing for Nicolette could have induced him to traverse after dark the length of the winding alley to the tavern door.

The autumn nights had been moonless. Now, on the evening that followed the desecration of the cathedral itself by the murderous devil, a new-born crescent was lowering its fragile, sanguine-colored horn beyond the house-tops as Reynard went forth from his lodgings at the accustomed hour. He lost sight of its comforting beam in the high-walled and narrow alley, and shivered with dread as he hastened onward through shadows that were dissipated only by the rare and timid ray from some lofty window. It seemed to him, at each turn and angle, that the gloom was curded by the unclean umbrage of Satanic wings, and might reveal in another instant the gleaming of abhorrent eyes ignited by the everlasting coals of the Pit. When he came forth at the alley's end, he saw with a start of fresh panic that the crescent moon was blotted out by a cloud that had the semblance of uncouthly arched and pointed wings.

He reached the tavern with a sense of supreme relief, for he had begun to feel a distinct intuition that someone or something was following him, unheard and invisible—a presence that seemed to load the dusk with prodigious menace. He entered and closed the door behind him very quickly, as if he were shutting it in the face of a dread pursuer.

There were few people in the tavern that evening. The girl Nicolette was serving wine to a mercer's assistant, one Raoul Coupain, a personable youth and a newcomer in the neighborhood, and she was laughing with what Reynard considered unseemly gaiety at the broad jests and amorous sallies of this Raoul. Jean Villom was discussing in a low voice the latest enormities of the demons with two cronies at a table in the farthest corner, and was drinking fully as much liquor as his customers.

Glowering with jealousy at the presence of Raoul Coupain, whom he suspected of being a favored rival, Reynard seated himself in silence and stared malignly at the flirtatious couple. No one seemed to have noticed his entrance; for Villom went on talking to his cronies without pause or interruption, and Nicolette and her companion were equally oblivious. To his jealous rage, Reynard soon added the resentment of one who feels that he is being deliberately ignored. He began to pound on the table with his heavy fists, to attract attention.

Villom, who had been sitting all the while with his back turned, now called out to Nicolette without even troubling to face around on his stool, telling her to serve Reynard. Giving a backward smile at Coupain, she came slowly and with open reluctance to the stone-carver's table.

She was small and buxom, with reddish-gold hair that curled luxuriantly above the short, delicious oval of her face; and she was gowned in a tight-fitting dress of apple-green that revealed the firm, seductive outlines of her hips and bosom. Her air was disdainful and a little cold, for she did not like Reynard and had taken small pains at any time to conceal her aversion. But to Reynard she was lovelier and more desirable than ever, and he felt a savage impulse to seize her in his arms and carry her bodily away from the tavern before the eyes of Raoul Coupain and her father.

"Bring me a pitcher of La Frênaie," he ordered gruffly, in a voice that betrayed his mingled resentment and desire.

Tossing her head lightly and scornfully, with more glances at Coupain, the girl obeyed. She placed the fiery, blood-dark wine before Reynard without speaking, and then went back to resume her bantering with the mercer's assistant.

Reynard began to drink, and the potent vintage merely served to inflame his smouldering enmity and passion. His eyes became venomous, his curling lips malignant as those of the gargoyles he had carved on the new cathedral. A baleful, primordial anger, like the rage of some morose and thwarted faun, burned within him with its slow red fire; but he strove to repress it, and sat silent and motionless, except for the frequent filling and emptying of his wine-cup.

Raoul Coupain had also consumed a liberal quantity of wine. As a result, he soon became bolder in his love-making, and strove to kiss the hand of Nicolette, who had now seated herself on the bench beside him. The hand was playfully withheld; and then, after its owner had cuffed Raoul very lightly and briskly, was granted to the claimant in a fashion that struck Reynard as being no less than wanton.

Snarling inarticulately, with a mad impulse to rush forward and slay the successful rival with his bare hands, he started to his feet and stepped toward the playful pair. His movement was noted by one of the men in the far corner, who spoke warningly to Villom. The tavern-keeper arose, lurching a little from his potations, and came warily across the room with his eyes on Reynard, ready to interfere in case of violence.

Reynard paused with momentary irresolution, and then went on, half-insane with a mounting hatred for them all. He longed to kill Villom and Coupain, to kill the hateful cronies who sat staring from the corner; and then, above their throttled corpses, to ravage with fierce kisses and vehement caresses the shrinking lips and body of Nicolette.

Seeing the approach of the stone-carver, and knowing his evil temper and dark jealousy, Coupain also arose to his feet and plucked stealthily beneath his cloak at the hilt of a little dagger which he carried. In the meanwhile, Jean Villom had interposed his burly bulk between the rivals. For the sake of the tavern's good repute, he wished to prevent the possible brawl.

"Back to your table, stone-cutter," he roared belligerently at Reynard.

Being unarmed, and seeing himself outnumbered, Reynard paused again, though his anger still simmered within him like the contents of a sorcerer's cauldron. With ruddy points of murderous flame in his hollow, slitted eyes, he glared at the three people before him, and saw beyond them, with instinctive rather than conscious awareness, the leaded panes of the tavern window, in whose glass the room was dimly reflected with its glowing tapers, its glimmering table-ware, the heads of Coupain and Villom and the girl Nicolette, and his own shadowy face among them.

Strangely, and, it would seem, inconsequently, he remembered at that moment the dark, ambiguous cloud he had seen across the moon, and the insistent feeling of obscure pursuit while he had traversed the alley.

Then, as he gazed irresolutely at the group before him, and its vague reflection in the glass beyond, there came a thunderous crash, and the panes of the window with their pictured scene were shattered inward in a score of fragments. Ere the litter of falling glass had reached the tavern floor, a swart and monstrous form flew into the room, with a beating of heavy vans that caused the tapers to flare troublously, and the shadows to dance like a sabbat of misshapen devils. The thing hovered for a moment, and seemed to tower in a great darkness higher than the ceiling above the heads of Reynard and the others as they turned toward it. They saw the malignant burning of its eyes, like coals in the depth of Tartarean pits, and the curling of its hateful lips on the bared teeth that were longer and sharper than serpent-fangs.

Behind it now, another shadowy flying monster came in through the broken window with a loud flapping of its ribbed and pointed wings. There was something lascivious in the very motion of its flight, even as homicidal hatred and malignity were manifest in the flight of the other. Its satyr-like face was twisted in a horrible, never-changing leer, and its lustful eyes were fixed on Nicolette as it hung in air beside the first intruder.

Reynard, as well as the other men, was petrified by a feeling of astonishment and consternation so extreme as almost to preclude terror. Voiceless and motionless, they beheld the demoniac intrusion; and the consternation of Reynard, in particular, was mingled with an element of unspeakable surprise, together with a dreadful recognizance. But the girl Nicolette, with a mad scream of horror, turned and started to flee across the room.

As if her cry had been the one provocation needed, the two demons swooped upon their victims. One, with a ferocious slash of its outstretched claws, tore open the throat of Jean Villom, who fell with a gurgling, blood-choked groan; and then, in the same fashion, it assailed Raoul Coupain. The other, in the meanwhile, had pursued and overtaken the fleeing girl, and had seized her in its bestial forearms, with the ribbed wings enfolding her like a hellish drapery.

The room was filled by a moaning whirlwind, by a chaos of wild cries and tossing struggling shadows. Reynard heard the guttural snarling of the murderous monster, muffled by the body of Coupain, whom it was tearing with its teeth; and he heard the lubricious laughter of the incubus, above the shrieks of the hysterically frightened girl. Then the grotesquely flaring tapers went out in a gust of swirling air, and Reynard received a violent blow in the darkness—the blow of some rushing object, perhaps of a passing wing, that was hard and heavy as stone. He fell, and became insensible.

IV

Dully and confusedly, with much effort, Reynard struggled back to consciousness. For a brief interim, he could not remember where he was nor what had happened. He was troubled by the painful throbbing of his head, by the humming of agitated voices about him, by the glaring of many lights and the thronging of many faces when he opened his eyes; and, above all, by the sense of nameless but grievous calamity and uttermost horror that weighed him down from the first dawning of sentiency.

Memory returned to him, laggard and reluctant; and with it, a full aware-ness of his surroundings and situation. He was lying on the tavern floor, and his own warm, sticky blood was rilling across his face from the wound on his aching head. The long room was half-filled with people of the neighborhood, bearing torches and knives and halberds, who had entered and were peering at the corpses of Villom and Coupain, which lay amid pools of wine-diluted blood and the wreckage of the shattered furniture and table-ware.

Nicolette, with her green gown in shreds, and her body crushed by the embraces of the demon, was moaning feebly while women crowded about her with ineffectual cries and questions which she could not even hear or understand. The two cronies of Villom, horribly clawed and mangled, were dead beside their overturned table.

Stupefied with horror, and still dizzy from the blow that had laid him unconscious, Reynard staggered to his feet, and found himself surrounded at once by inquiring faces and voices. Some of the people were a little sus-picious of him, since he was the sole survivor in the tavern, and bore an ill repute; but his replies to their questions soon convinced them that the new crime was wholly the work of the same demons that had plagued Vyônes in so monstrous a fashion for weeks past.

Reynard, however, was unable to tell them all that he had seen, or to confess the ultimate sources of his fear and stupefaction. The secret of that which he knew was locked in the seething pit of his tortured and devil-ridden soul.

Somehow, he left the ravaged inn, he pushed his way through the gather-ing crowd with its terror-muted murmurs, and found himself alone on the midnight streets. Heedless of his own possible peril, and scarcely knowing where he went, he wandered through Vyônes for many hours; and some-while in his wanderings, he came to his own workshop. With no assignable reason for the act, he entered, and re-emerged with a heavy hammer, which he carried with him during his subsequent peregrinations. Then, driven by his awful and unremissive torture, he went on till the pale dawn had touched the spires and the house-tops with a ghostly glimmering.

By a half-conscious compulsion, his steps had led him to the square before the cathedral. Ignoring the amazed verger, who had just opened the doors, he entered and sought a stairway that wound tortuously upward to the tower on which his own gargoyles were ensconced.

In the chill and livid light of sunless morning, he emerged on the roof; and leaning perilously from the verge, he examined the carven figures. He felt no surprise, only the hideous confirmation of a fear too ghastly to be named, when he saw that the teeth and claws of the malign, cat-headed griffin were stained with darkening blood; and that shreds of apple-green cloth were hanging from the talons of the lustful, bat-winged satyr.

It seemed to Reynard, in the dim ashen light, that a look of unspeakable triumph, of intolerable irony, was imprinted on the face of this latter creature. He stared at it with fearful and agonizing fascination, while impotent rage, abhorrence, and repentance deeper than that of the damned arose within him in a smothering flood. He was hardly aware that he had raised the iron hammer and had struck wildly at the satyr's horned profile, till he heard the sullen, angry clang of impact, and found that he was tottering on the edge of the roof to retain his balance.

The furious blow had merely chipped the features of the gargoyle, and had not wiped away the malignant lust and exultation. Again Reynard raised the heavy hammer.

It fell on empty air; for, even as he struck, the stone-carver felt himself lifted and drawn backward by something that sank into his flesh like many separate knives. He staggered helplessly, his feet slipped, and then he was lying on the granite verge, with his head and shoulders over the dark, deserted street.

Half-swooning, and sick with pain, he saw above him the other gargoyle, the claws of whose right foreleg were firmly embedded in his shoulder. They tore deeper, as if with a dreadful clenching. The monster seemed to tower like some fabulous beast above its prey; and he felt himself slipping dizzily across the cathedral gutter, with the gargoyle twisting and turning as if to resume its normal position over the gulf. Its slow, inexorable movement seemed to be part of his vertigo. The very tower was tilting and revolving beneath him in some unnatural nightmare fashion.

Dimly, in a daze of fear and agony, Reynard saw the remorseless tiger-face bending toward him with its horrid teeth laid bare in an eternal rictus of diabolic hate. Somehow, he had retained the hammer. With an instinctive impulse to defend himself, he struck at the gargoyle, whose cruel features seemed to approach him like something seen in the ultimate madness and distortion of delirium.

Even as he struck, the vertiginous turning movement continued, and he felt the talons dragging him outward on empty air. In his cramped, recumbent position, the blow fell short of the hateful face and came down with a dull clangor on the foreleg whose curving talons were fixed in his shoulder like meat-hooks. The clangor ended in a sharp cracking sound; and the leaning gargoyle vanished from Reynard's vision as he fell. He saw nothing more, except the dark mass of the cathedral tower, that seemed to soar away from him and to rush upward unbelievably in the livid, starless heavens to which the belated sun had not yet risen.

It was the Archbishop Ambrosius, on his way to early Mass, who found the shattered body of Reynard lying face downward in the square. Ambrosius crossed himself in startled horror at the sight; and then, when he saw the object that was still clinging to Reynard's shoulder, he repeated the gesture with a more than pious promptness.

He bent down to examine the thing. With the infallible memory of a true

art-lover, he recognized it at once. Then, through the same clearness of recollection, he saw that the stone foreleg, whose claws were so deeply buried
in Reynard's flesh, had somehow undergone a most unnatural alteration.
The paw, as he remembered it, should have been slightly bent and relaxed;
but now it was stiffly outthrust and elongated, as if, like the paw of a living
limb, it had reached for something, or had dragged a heavy burden with its
ferine talons.

BEYOND THE SINGING FLAME

When I, Philip Hastane, gave to the world the journal of my friend Giles Angarth, I was still doubtful as to whether the incidents related therein were fiction or verity. The trans-dimensional adventures of Angarth and Ebbonly, the city of the Flame with its strange residents and pilgrims, the immolation of Ebbonly, and the hinted return of the narrator himself for a like purpose, after making the last entry in his diary, were very much the sort of thing that Angarth might have imagined in one of the fantastic novels for which he had become so justly famous.

Add to this the seemingly impossible and incredible nature of the whole tale, and my hesitancy in accepting it as veridical will easily be understood.

However, on the other hand, there was the unsolved and eternally recalcitrant enigma offered by the disappearance of the two men. Both were well-known, the one as a writer, the other as an artist; both were in flourishing circumstances, with no serious cares or troubles; and their vanishment, all things considered, was difficult to explain on the ground of any motive less unusual or extraordinary than the one assigned in the journal.

At first, as I have hinted in my foreword to the published diary, I thought that the whole affair might well have been devised as a somewhat elaborate practical joke; but this theory became less and less tenable as weeks and months went by and linked themselves slowly into a year, without the reappearance of the presumptive jokers.

Now, at last, I can testify to the truth of all that Angarth wrote—and more. For I, too, have been in Ydmos, the City of Singing Flame, and have known also the supernal glories and raptures of the Inner Dimension. And of these I must tell, however falteringly and stumblingly, with mere human words, ere the vision fades. For these are things which neither I nor any other shall behold or experience again: since Ydmos itself is now a riven ruin, and the

Temple of the Flame has been blasted to its foundations in the basic rock, and the fountain of singing fire has been stricken at its source, and the Inner Dimension has perished like a broken bubble, in the great war that was made upon Ydmos by the rulers of the Outer Lands....

After editing and publishing Angarth's journal, I was unable to forget the peculiar and tantalizing problems it had raised. The vague but infinitely suggestive vistas opened by the tale were such as to haunt my imagination recurrently with a hint of half-revealed or hidden mysteries; and I was troubled by the possibility of some great mystic meaning behind it all—some cosmic actuality of which the narrator had perceived merely the external veils and fringes.

As time went on, I found myself pondering it perpetually, and more and more I was possessed by an overwhelming wonder, and a sense of something which no mere fiction-weaver would have been likely to invent through the unassisted workings of his own fantasy.

In the early summer of 1931, after finishing a new novel of interplanetary adventure, I felt able for the first time to take the necessary leisure for the execution of a project that had often occurred to me. Putting all my affairs in order, and knitting all the loose ends of my literary labors and correspondence, in case I should not return, I left Auburn ostensibly for a week's vacation, and actually went to Summit with the idea of investigating closely the milieu in which Angarth and Ebbonly had disappeared from human ken.

With strange emotions, I visited the forsaken cabin south of Crater Ridge that had been occupied by Angarth, and saw the rough, home-made table of pine boards upon which my friend had written his journal and had left the sealed package containing it to be forwarded to me after his departure.

There was a weird and brooding loneliness about the place, as if the non-human infinitudes had already claimed it for their own. The unlocked door had sagged inward from the pressure of high-piled winter snows, and fir-needles had sifted across the sill to strew the unswept floor. Somehow, I know not why, the bizarre narrative became more real and more credible to me, while I stood there, as if an occult intimation of all that had happened to its author still lingered around the cabin.

This mysterious intimation grew stronger when I came to visit Crater Ridge itself, and to search amid its miles of pseudo-volcanic rubble for the two boulders so explicitly described by Angarth as having a likeness to the pedestals of ruined columns.

Many of my readers, no doubt, will remember his description of the Ridge; and there is no need to enlarge upon it with reiterative detail, other than that which bears upon my own adventures.

Following the northward path which Angarth must have taken from his cabin, and trying to retrace his wanderings on the long, barren hill, I combed it thoroughly from end to end and from side to side, since he had not specified the location of the boulders. After two mornings spent in this manner without result, I was almost ready to abandon the quest and dismiss the queer, soapy, greenish-grey column-ends as one of Angarth's most provocative and deceptive fictions.

It must have been the formless, haunting intuition of which I have spoken, that made me renew the search on the third morning. This time, after crossing and re-crossing the hill-top for an hour or more, and weaving tortuously to and fro among the cicada-haunted wild currant bushes and sun-flowers on the dusty slopes, I came at last to an open, circular, rock-surrounded space that was totally unfamiliar, and which I had somehow missed in all my previous roamings. It was the place of which Angarth had told; and I saw with an inexpressible thrill the two rounded, worn-looking boulders that were situated in the center of the ring.

I believe that I trembled a little with excitement as I went forward to inspect the curious stones. Bending over, but not daring to enter the bare, pebbly space between them, I touched one of them with my hand, and received a sensation of preternatural smoothness, together with a coolness that was inexplicable, considering that the boulders and the soil about them must have lain unshaded from the sultry August sun for many hours.

From that moment, I became fully persuaded that Angarth's account was no mere fable. Just why I should have felt so certain of this, I am powerless to say. But it seemed to me that I stood on the threshold of an ultramundane mystery, on the brink of uncharted gulfs; and I looked about at the familiar Sierran valleys and mountains, wondering that they still preserved their wonted outlines, and were still unchanged by the contiguity of alien worlds, were still untouched by the luminous glories of arcanic dimensions.

Being convinced that I had indeed found the gateway between the worlds, I was prompted to strange reflections. What, and where, was this other sphere to which my friend had attained entrance? Was it near at hand, like a secret room in the structure of space? Or was it, in reality, millions or trillions of light-years away by the reckoning of astronomic distance, in a planet of some ulterior galaxy? After all, we know little or nothing of the actual nature of space; and perhaps, in some way that we cannot imagine, the infinite is doubled upon itself in places, with dimensional folds and tucks, and short-cuts whereby the distance to Algenib or Aldebaran is but a step. Perhaps, also, there is more than one infinity. The spatial "flaw" into which Angarth had fallen might well be a sort of super-dimension, abridging the cosmic intervals and connecting universe with universe.

However, because of this very certitude that I had found the inter-spheric portals, and could follow Angarth and Ebbonly if I so desired, I hesitated before trying the experiment, mindful of the mystic danger and irrefragable lure that had overcome the others. I was consumed by imaginative curiosity, by an avid, well-nigh feverish longing to behold the wonders of this exotic realm; but I did not purpose to become a victim to the opiate power and fascination of the Singing Flame.

I stood for a long time, eyeing the odd boulders and the barren, pebble-littered spot that gave admission to the unknown. At length, I went away, deciding to defer my venture till the following morn. Visualizing the weird doom to which the others had gone so voluntarily, and even gladly, I must confess that I was afraid. On the other hand, I was drawn by the fateful allurement that leads an explorer into far places... and perhaps by something more than this.

I slept badly that night, with nerves and brain excited by formless, glowing premonitions, by intimations of half-conceived perils and splendors and vastnesses. Early the next morning, while the sun was still hanging above the Nevada Mountains, I returned to Crater Ridge.

I carried a strong hunting-knife and a Colt revolver, and wore a filled cartridge-belt, and also a knapsack containing sandwiches and a thermos bottle of coffee. Before starting, I had stuffed my ears tightly with cotton soaked in a new anaesthetic fluid, mild but efficacious, which would serve to deafen me completely for many hours. In this way, I felt that I should be immune to the demoralizing music of the fiery fountain.

I peered about on the rugged landscape with its varied and far-flung vistas, wondering if I should ever see it again. Then, resolutely, but with the eerie thrilling and shrinking of one who throws himself from a high cliff into some bottomless chasm, I stepped forward into the space between the greyish-green boulders.

My sensations, generally speaking, were similar to those described by Angarth in his diary. Blackness and illimitable emptiness seemed to wrap me round in a dizzy swirl as of rushing wind or milling water, and I went down and down in a spiral descent whose duration I have never been able to estimate. Intolerably stifled, and without even the power to gasp for breath, in the chill, airless vacuum that froze my very muscles and marrow, I felt that I should lose consciousness in another moment, and descend into the greater gulf of death or oblivion.

Something seemed to arrest my fall, and I became aware that I was standing still, though I was troubled for some time by a queer doubt as to whether my position was vertical, horizontal or upside-down in relation to the solid substance that my feet had encountered.

Then the blackness lifted slowly like a dissolving cloud, and I saw the slope of violet grass, the rows of irregular monoliths running downward from where I stood, and the grey-green columns near at hand, and the titan, perpendicular city of red stone that was dominant above the high and multi-colored vegetation of the plain.

It was all very much as Angarth had depicted it; but somehow, even then, I became aware of differences that were not immediately or clearly definable, of scenic details and atmospheric elements for which his account had not prepared me. And, at the moment I was too thoroughly disequilibrated and overpowered by the vision of it all to even speculate concerning the character of these differences.

As I gazed at the city with its crowding tiers of battlements and its multitude of overlooming spires, I felt the invisible threads of a secret attraction, was seized by an imperative longing to know the mysteries hidden behind the massive walls and the myriad buildings. Then, a moment later, my gaze was drawn to the remote, opposite horizon of the plain, as if by some conflicting impulse whose nature and origin were undiscoverable.

It must have been because I had formed so clear and definite a picture of the scene from my friend's narrative, that I was surprised and even a little disturbed as if by something wrong or irrelevant, when I saw in the far distance the shining towers of what seemed to be another city—a city of which Angarth had not written. The towers rose in serried lines, reaching for many miles in a curious arc-like formation, and were sharply defined against a blackish mass of cloud that had reared behind them and was spreading out on the luminous amber sky in sullen webs and sinister, crawling filaments.

Subtle disquietude and repulsion seemed to emanate from the far-off, glittering spires, even as attraction emanated from those of the nearer city. I saw them quiver and pulse with an evil light, like living and moving things, through what I assumed to be some refractive trick of the atmosphere. Then, for an instant, the black cloud behind them glowed with dull, angry crimson throughout its whole mass, and even its questing webs and tendrils were turned into lurid threads of fire.

The crimson faded, leaving the cloud inert and lumpish as before. But from many of the vanward towers, lines of red and violet flame had leaped, like out-thrust lances at the bosom of the plain beneath them, and they were held thus for at least a minute, moving slowly across a wide area, before they vanished. In the spaces between the towers, I now perceived a multitude of gleaming, restless particles, like armies of militant atoms, and wondered if perchance they were living things. If the idea had not appeared so fantastical, I could have sworn even then that the far city had already changed its position and was advancing toward the other on the plain.

Apart from the fulguration of the cloud, and the flames that had sprung from the towers, and the quiverings which I deemed a refractive phenomenon, the whole landscape before and about me was unnaturally still. On the strange amber air, on the Tyrian-tinted grasses, on the proud, opulent foliage of the unknown trees, there lay the dead calm that precedes the stupendous turmoil of typhonic storm or seismic cataclysm. The brooding sky was permeated with intuitions of cosmic menace, was weighed down by a dim, elemental despair.

Alarmed by this ominous atmosphere, I looked behind me at the two pillars which, according to Angarth, were the gateway of return to the human world. For an instant, I was tempted to go back. Then, I turned once more to the nearby city; and the feelings I have mentioned were lost in an oversurging awesomeness and wonder. I felt the thrill of a deep, supernal exaltation before the magnitude of the mighty buildings; a compelling sorcery was laid upon me by the very lines of their construction, by the harmonies of a solemn architectural music. I forgot my impulse to return to Crater Ridge, and started down the slope toward the city.

Soon the boughs of the purple and yellow forest arched above me like the altitudes of Titan-builded aisles, with leaves that fretted the rich heaven in gorgeous arabesques. Beyond them, ever and anon, I caught glimpses of the piled ramparts of my destination; but looking back, in the direction of that other city on the horizon, I found that its fulgurating towers were now lost to view.

I saw, however, that the masses of the great, somber cloud were rising steadily on the sky; and once again they flared to a swart, malignant red, as if with some unearthly form of sheet-lightning; and though I could hear nothing with my deadened ears, the ground beneath me trembled with long vibrations as of thunder. There was a queer quality in the vibrations, that seemed to tear my nerves and set my teeth on edge with its throbbing, lancinating discord, painful as broken glass or the torment of a tightened rack.

Like Angarth before me, I came to the paved, Cyclopean highway. Following it, in the stillness after the unheard peals of thunder, I felt another and subtler vibration, which I knew to be that of the Singing Flame in the temple at the city's core. It seemed to soothe and exalt and bear me on, to erase with soft caresses the ache that still lingered in my nerves from the torturing pulsations of the thunder.

I met no one on the road, and was not passed by any of the trans-dimensional pilgrims such as had overtaken Angarth. And when the accumulated ramparts loomed above the highest trees, and I came forth from the wood in their very shadow, I saw that the great gate of the city was closed, leaving no crevice through which a pygmy like myself might obtain entrance.

Feeling a profound and peculiar discomfiture, such as one would experience in a dream that had gone wrong, I stared at the grim, unrelenting blankness of the gate, which seemed to be wrought from one enormous sheet of somber and lusterless metal. Then I peered upward at the sheerness of the wall, which rose above me like an alpine cliff, and saw that the battlements were seemingly deserted.

Was the city forsaken by its people, by the guardians of the Flame? Was it no longer open to the pilgrims who came from outlying lands to worship the Flame, and to immolate themselves? With a curious reluctance, after lingering there for many minutes in a sort of stupor, I turned away to retrace my steps.

In the interim of my journey, the black cloud had drawn immeasurably nearer, and was now blotting half the heaven with two portentous wing-like formations. It was a sinister and terrible sight; and it lightened again with that ominous, wrathful flaming, with a detonation that beat upon my deaf ears like waves of disintegrative force, and seemed to lacerate the inmost fibers of my body.

I hesitated, fearing that the storm would burst upon me before I could reach the inter-dimensional portals. I saw that I should be exposed to an elemental disturbance of unfamiliar character and supreme violence.

Then, in mid-air, before the imminent, ever-rising cloud, I perceived two flying creatures, whom I can compare only to gigantic moths. With bright, luminous wings, upon the ebon forefront of the storm, they approached me in level but precipitate flight, and would have crashed headlong against the shut gate if they had not checked themselves with sudden and easy poise.

With hardly a flutter, they descended and paused on the ground beside me, supporting themselves on queer, delicate legs that branched at the knee-joints in floating antennae and waving tentacles. Their wings were sumptuously mottled webs of pearl and madder and opal and orange, and their heads were circled by a series of convex and concave eyes, and were fringed with coiling, horn-like organs from whose hollow ends there hung aerial filaments.

I was more than startled, more than amazed by their aspect; but somehow, by an obscure telepathy, I felt assured that their intentions toward me were friendly. I knew that they wished to enter the city, and knew also that they understood my predicament.

Nevertheless, I was not prepared for what happened. With movements of utmost celerity and grace, one of the giant moth-like beings stationed himself at my right hand, and the other at my left. Then, before I could even suspect their intention, they enfolded my limbs and body with their long tentacles, wrapping me round and round as if with powerful ropes; and carrying me between them as if my weight were a mere trifle, they rose in air and soared at the mighty ramparts!

In that swift and effortless ascent, the wall seemed to flow downward beside and beneath us like a wave of molten stone. Dizzily I watched the falling away of the mammoth blocks in endless recession. Then we were level with the broad ramparts, were flying across the unguarded parapets and over a canyon-like space toward the immense rectangular buildings and number-less square towers.

We had hardly crossed the walls, when a weird and flickering glow was cast on the edifices before us by another lightening of the great cloud. The moth-like beings paid no apparent heed, and flew steadily on into the city with their strange faces toward an unseen goal; but, turning my head to peer backward at the storm, I beheld an astounding and appalling spectacle.

Beyond the city ramparts, as if wrought by black magic or the toil of genii, another city had reared, and its high towers were moving swiftly forward beneath the rubescent dome of the burning cloud! A second glance, and I perceived that the towers were identical with those I had beheld afar on the plain. In the interim of my passage through the woods, they had travelled over an expanse of many miles by means of some unknown motive-power, and had closed in on the city of the Flame.

Looking more closely, to determine the manner of their locomotion, I saw that they were not mounted on wheels, but on short, massy legs like jointed columns of metal, that gave them the stride of ungainly colossi. There were six or more of these legs to each tower, and near the tops of the towers were rows of huge eye-like openings, from which issued the bolts of red and violet flame I have mentioned before. The many-colored forest had been burned away by these flames in a league-wide swath of devastation, even to the walls, and there was nothing but a stretch of black, vaporing desert between the mobile towers and the city. Then, even as I gazed, the long, leaping beams began to assail the craggy ramparts, and the topmost parapets were melting like lava beneath them.

It was a scene of utmost terror and grandeur; but, a moment later, it was blotted from my vision by the buildings among which we had now plunged.

The great lepidopterous creatures who bore me went on with the speed of eyrie-questing eagles. In the course of that amazing flight, I was hardly capable of conscious thought or volition; I lived only in the breathless and giddy freedom of aerial movement, of dream-like levitation above the labyrinthine maze of stone immensitudes and marvels.

Also, I was without conscious cognizance of much that I beheld in that stupendous Babel of architectural imageries; and only afterwards, in the more tranquil light of recollection, could I give coherent form and meaning to many of my impressions. My senses were stunned by the vastness and strangeness of it all; and I realized but dimly the cataclysmic ruin that was being loosed upon the city behind us, and the doom from which we were fleeing. I knew that war was being made with unearthly weapons and engineries, by inimical powers that I could not imagine, for a purpose beyond my conception; but to me, it all had the elemental confusion and vague, impersonal horror of some cosmic catastrophe.

We flew deeper and deeper into the city. Broad, platform roofs and terrace-like tiers of balconies flowed away beneath us, and the pavements raced like darkling streams at some enormous depth. Severe cubicular spires and square monoliths were all about and above us; and we saw on some of the roofs the dark, Atlantean people of the city, moving slowly and statuesquely, or standing in attitudes of cryptic resignation and despair, with their faces toward the flaming cloud. All were weaponless, and I saw no engineries anywhere, such as might be used for purposes of military defense.

Swiftly as we flew, the climbing cloud was swifter, and the darkness of its intermittently glowing dome had overarched the town, its spidery filaments had meshed the further heavens and would soon attach themselves to the opposite horizon. The buildings darkened and lightened with the recurrent fulguration; and I felt in all my tissues the painful pulsing of the thunderous vibrations.

Dully and vaguely, I realized that the winged beings who carried me between them were pilgrims to the temple of the Flame. More and more I became aware of an influence that must have been that of the starry music emanating from the temple's heart. There were soft, soothing vibrations in the air, that seemed to absorb and nullify the tearing discords of the unheard thunder. I felt that we were entering a zone of mystic refuge, of sidereal and celestial security; and my troubled senses were both lulled and exalted.

The gorgeous wings of the giant lepidopters began to slant downward. Before and beneath us, at some distance, I perceived a mammoth pile which I knew at once for the temple of the Flame. Down, still down we went, in the awesome space of the surrounding square; and then I was borne in through the lofty, ever-open entrance, and along the high hall with its thousand columns.

It was like some corridor in a Karnak of titan worlds. Pregnant with strange balsams, the dim, mysterious dusk enfolded us; and we seemed to be entering realms of premundane antiquity and transstellar immensity, to be following a pillared cavern that led to the core of some ultimate star.

It seemed that we were the last and only pilgrims; and also that the temple was deserted by its guardians; for we met no one in the whole extent of that column-crowded gloom. After awhile, the dusk began to lighten, and we plunged into a widening beam of radiance, and then into the vast central chamber in which soared the fountain of green fire.

I remember only the impression of shadowy, flickering space, of a vault that was lost in the azure of infinity, of colossal and Memnonian statues that looked down from Himalaya-like altitudes; and, above all, the dazzling jet of flame that aspired from a pit in the pavement and rose in air like the visible rapture of gods.

But all this I saw and knew for an instant only. Then I realized that the beings who bore me were flying straight toward the flame on level wings, without the slightest pause or flutter of hesitation!

There was no room for fear, no time for alarm, in the dazed and chaotic turmoil of my sensations. I was stupefied by all that I had experienced; and, moreover, the drug-like spell of the Flame was upon me, even though I could not hear its fatal singing. I believe that I struggled a little, by some sort of mechanical muscular revulsion, against the tentacular arms that were wound about me. But the lepidopters gave no heed; and it was plain that they were conscious of nothing but the mounting fire and its seductive music.

I remember, however, that there was no sensation of actual heat, such as might have been expected, when we neared the soaring column. Instead, I felt the most ineffable thrilling in all my fibers, as if I were being permeated by waves of celestial energy and demiurgic ecstasy. Then we entered the Flame.

Like Angarth before me, I had taken it for granted that the fate of all those who flung themselves into the Flame was an instant though blissful destruction. I expected to undergo a briefly flaring dissolution, followed by the nothingness of utter annihilation. The thing which really happened was beyond the boldest reach of speculative thought, and to give even the meagerest idea of my sensations would beggar the resources of language.

The Flame enfolded us like a green curtain, blotting from view the great chamber. Then it seemed to me that I was caught and carried to supercelestial heights, in an upward-rushing cataract of quintessential force and deific rapture and all-illuminating light. It seemed that I, and also my companions, had achieved a god-like union with the Flame; that every atom of our bodies had undergone a transcendental expansion, was winged with ethereal lightness; that we no longer existed, except as one divine, indivisible entity, soaring beyond the trammels of matter, beyond the limits of time and space, to attain undreamable shores.

Unspeakable was the joy, and infinite was the freedom of that ascent, in which we seemed to overpass the zenith of the highest star. Then, as if we had risen with the Flame to its culmination, had reached its very apex, we emerged and came to a pause.

My senses were faint with exaltation, my eyes were blind with the glory of the fire; and the world on which I now gazed was a vast arabesque of unfamiliar forms, and bewildering hues from another spectrum than the one to which our eyes are habituated. It swirled before my dizzy eyes like a labyrinth of gigantic jewels, with interweaving rays and tangled lusters; and only by slow degrees was I able to establish order and distinguish detail in the surging riot of my perceptions.

All about me were endless avenues of super-prismatic opal and jacinth, arches and pillars of ultra-violet gems, of transcendent sapphire, of unearthly ruby and amethyst, all suffused with a multi-tinted splendor. I appeared to be treading on jewels; and above me was a jewelled sky.

Presently, with recovered equilibrium, with eyes adjusted to a new range of cognition, I began to perceive the actual features of the landscape. I, with the two moth-like beings still beside me, was standing on a million-flowered grass, among trees of a paradisal vegetation, with fruit, foliage, blossoms and trunks whose very forms were beyond the conception of tri-dimensional life. The grace of their drooping boughs, of their fretted fronds, was inexpressible in terms of earthly line and contour; and they seemed to be wrought of pure, ethereal substance, half-translucent to the empyrean light, which accounted for the gem-like impression I had first received.

I breathed a nectar-laden air; and the ground beneath me was ineffably soft and resilient, as if it were composed of some higher form of matter than ours.

My physical sensations were those of the utmost buoyancy and well-being, with no trace of fatigue or nervousness, such as might have been looked for after the unparalleled and marvellous events in which I had played a part. I felt no sense of mental dislocation or confusion; and apart from my ability to recognize unknown colors and non-Euclidean forms, I began to experience a queer alteration and extension of tactility, through which it seemed that I was able to touch remote objects.

The radiant sky was filled with many-colored suns, like those that might shine on a world of some multiple solar system. But strangely, as I gazed, their glory became softer and dimmer, and the brilliant luster of the trees and grass was gradually subdued, as if by encroaching twilight.

I was beyond surprise, in the boundless marvel and mystery of it all, and nothing, perhaps, would have seemed incredible. But if anything could have amazed me or defied belief, it was the human face—the face of my vanished friend, Giles Angarth, which now emerged from among the waning jewels of the forest, followed by that of another man whom I recognized from photographs I had seen as Felix Ebbonly.

They came out from beneath the gorgeous boughs and paused before me. Both were clad in lustrous fabrics, finer than Oriental silk and of no earthly cut or pattern. Their look was both joyous and meditative; and their faces had taken on a hint of the same translucency that characterized the ethereal fruits and blossoms.

"We have been looking for you," said Angarth. "It occurred to me that after reading my journal, you might be tempted to try the same experiments, if only to make sure whether the account was truth or fiction. This is Felix Ebbonly, whom I believe you have never met."

It surprised me when I found that I could hear his voice with perfect ease and clearness; and I wondered why the effect of the drug-soaked cotton should have died out so soon in my auditory nerves. Yet such details were trivial, in face of the astounding fact that I had found Angarth and Ebbonly; that they, as well as I, had survived the unearthly rapture of the Flame.

"Where are we?" I asked, after acknowledging his introduction. "I confess that I am totally at a loss to comprehend what has happened."

"We are now in what is called the Inner Dimension," explained Angarth. "It is a higher sphere of space and energy and matter than the one into which we were precipitated from Crater Ridge; and the only entrance is through the Singing Flame in the city of Ydmos. The Inner Dimension is born of the fiery fountain, and sustained by it; and those who fling themselves into the Flame are lifted thereby to this superior plane of vibration. For them, the outer worlds no longer exist. The nature of the Flame itself is not known, except that it is a fountain of pure energy, springing from the central rock beneath Ydmos, and passing beyond mortal ken by virtue of its own ardency."

He paused, and seemed to be peering attentively at the winged entities, who still lingered at my side. Then, he continued:

"I haven't been here long enough to learn very much, myself; but I have found out a few things; and Ebbonly and I have established a sort of telepathic communication with the other beings who have passed through the Flame. Many of them have no spoken language, nor organs of speech; and their very methods of thought are basically different from ours, because of their divergent lines of sense-development, and the varying conditions of the worlds from which they come. But we are able to communicate a few images.

"The persons who came with you are trying to tell me something," he went on. "You and they, it seems, are the last pilgrims who will enter Ydmos and attain the Inner Dimension. War is being made on the Flame and its guardians by the rulers of the Outer Lands, because so many of their people have obeyed the lure of the singing fountain and have vanished into the higher sphere; and even now their armies have closed in upon Ydmos, and are blasting the city's ramparts with the force-bolts of their moving towers."

I told him what I had seen, comprehending now much that had been obscure heretofore. He listened gravely; and then said:

"It has long been feared that such war would be made sooner or later. There are many legends in the Outer Lands, concerning the Flame and the fate of those who succumb to its attraction; but the truth is not known, or is guessed only by a few. Many believe, as I did, that the end is destruction; and even by some who suspect its existence, the Inner Dimension is hated, as a thing that lures idle dreamers away from worldly reality. It is regarded as a lethal and pernicious chimera, or a mere poetic dream, or a sort of opium paradise.

"There are a thousand things to tell you, regarding the inner sphere, and the laws and conditions of being to which we are now subject, after the revibration of all our component atoms and electrons in the Flame. But at present there is no time to speak further, since it is highly probable that we are all in grave danger—that the very existence of the Inner Dimension, as well as our own, is threatened by the inimical forces that are destroying Ydmos. There are some who say that the Flame is impregnable, that its pure essence will defy the blasting of all inferior beams, and its source remain impenetrable to the dire lightnings of the Outer Lords. But most are fearful of disaster, and expect the failure of the fountain itself when Ydmos is riven to the central rock.

"Because of this imminent peril, we must not tarry longer. There is a way which affords egress from the inner sphere to another and remoter cosmos in a second infinity—a cosmos unconceived by mundane astronomers, or by the astronomers of the worlds about Ydmos. The majority of the pilgrims, after a term of sojourn here, have gone on to the worlds of this other universe; and Ebbonly and I have waited only for your coming before following them. We must make haste, and delay no more, or doom will overtake us."

Even as he spoke, the two moth-like entities, seeming to resign me to the care of my human friends, arose on the jewel-tinted air and sailed in long, level flight above the paradisal perspectives whose remoter avenues were lost in glory. Angarth and Ebbonly had now stationed themselves beside me; and one took me by the left arm, and the other by the right.

"Try to imagine that you are flying," said Angarth. "In this sphere, levitation and flight are possible through will-power; and you will soon acquire the ability. We shall support and guide you, however, till you have grown accustomed to the new conditions, and are independent of such help."

I obeyed his injunction, and formed a mental image of myself in the act of flying. I was amazed by the clearness and verisimilitude of the thought-picture, and still more by the fact that the picture was becoming an actuality! With little sense of effort, but with exactly the same feeling that characterizes a levitational dream, the three of us were soaring from the jeweled ground, were slanting easily and swiftly upward through the glowing air.

Any attempt to describe the experience would be foredoomed to futility: since it seemed that a whole range of new senses had been opened up in me, together with corresponding thought-symbols for which there are no words in human speech. I was no longer Philip Hastane, but a larger and stronger and freer entity, differing as much from my former self as the personality developed beneath the influence of hashish or kava would differ.

The dominant feeling was one of immense joy and liberation, coupled with a sense of imperative haste, of the need to escape into other realms where the joy would endure eternal and unthreatened. My visual perceptions, as we flew above the burning, lucent woods, were marked by intense aesthetic pleasure, as far above the normal delight afforded by agreeable imagery as the forms and colors of this world were beyond the cognition of normal eyes. Every changing image was a source of veritable ecstasy; and the ecstasy mounted as the whole landscape began to brighten again, and returned to the flashing, scintillating glory it had worn when I first beheld it.

We soared at a lofty elevation, looking down on numberless miles of labyrinthine forest, on long luxurious meadows, on voluptuously folded hills, on palatial buildings, and waters that were clear as the pristine lakes and rivers of Eden. It all seemed to quiver and pulsate like one living, effulgent, ethereal entity: and waves of radiant rapture passed from sun to sun in the splendor-crowded heaven.

As we went on, I noticed again, after an interval, that partial dimming of the light, that somnolent, dreamy saddening of the colors, to be followed by another period of ecstatic brightening. The slow, tidal rhythm of this process appeared to correspond to the rising and falling of the Flame, as Angarth had described it in his journal; and I suspected immediately that there was some connection.

No sooner had I formulated this thought, when I became aware that Angarth was speaking. And yet I am not sure whether he spoke, or whether his worded thought was perceptible to me through another sense than that of physical audition. At any rate, I was cognizant of his comment:

"You are right. The waning and waxing of the fountain and its music is perceived in the Inner Dimension as a clouding and lightening of all visual images."

Our flight began to swiften, and I realized that my companions were employing all their psychic energies in an effort to redouble our speed. The lands below us blurred to a cataract of streaming color, a sea of flowing luminosity; and we seemed to be hurtling onward like stars through the fiery air.

The ecstasy of that endless soaring, the anxiety of that precipitate flight from an unknown doom, are incommunicable. But I shall never forget them, and never forget the state of ineffable communion and understanding that existed between the three of us. The memory of it all is housed in the deepest and most abiding cells of my brain.

Others were flying beside and above and beneath us now, in the fluctuant glory: pilgrims of hidden worlds and occult dimensions, proceeding as we ourselves toward that other cosmos of which the inner sphere was the ante-chamber. These beings were strange and outré beyond belief in their corporeal forms and attributes; and yet I took no thought of their strangeness, but felt toward them the same conviction of fraternity that I felt toward Angarth and Ebbonly.

Now, as we still went on, it appeared to me that my two companions were telling me many things; were communicating, by what means I am not sure, much that they had learned in their new existence. With a grave urgency, as if perhaps the time for imparting this information might well be brief, ideas were expressed and conveyed which I could never have understood amid terrestrial circumstances; and things that were inconceivable in terms of the five senses, or in abstract symbols of philosophic or mathematic thought, were made plain to me as the letters of the alphabet.

Certain of these data, however, are roughly conveyable or suggestible in language. I was told of the gradual process of initiation into the life of the new dimension, of the powers gained by the neophyte during his term of adaptation, of the various recondite aesthetic joys experienced through a mingling and multiplying of all the perceptions: of the control acquired over natural forces and over matter itself, so that raiment could be woven and buildings reared solely through an act of volition.

I learned also of the laws that would control our passage to the further cosmos, and the fact that such passage was difficult and dangerous for anyone who had not lived a certain length of time in the Inner Dimension. Likewise, I was told that no one could return to our present plane from the higher cosmos, even as no one could go backward through the Flame into Ydmos.

Angarth and Ebbonly had dwelt long enough in the Inner Dimension (they said) to be eligible for entrance to the worlds beyond; and they thought that I too could escape through their assistance, even though I had not yet developed the faculty of spatial equilibrium necessary to sustain those who dared the interspheric path and its dreadful sub-jacent gulfs alone.

There were boundless, unforeseeable realms, planet on planet, universe on universe, to which we might attain, and among whose prodigies and marvels we could dwell or wander indefinitely. In these worlds, our brains would be attuned to the comprehension or apprehension of vaster and higher scientific laws, and states of entity beyond those of our present dimensional milieu.

I have no idea of the duration of our flight; since, like everything else, my sense of time was completely altered and transfigured. Relatively speaking, we may have gone on for hours; but it seemed to me that we had crossed an area of that supernal terrain for whose transit many years or centuries might well have been required.

Even before we came within sight of it, a clear pictorial image of our destination had arisen in my mind, doubtless through some sort of thought-transference. I seemed to envision a stupendous mountain-range, with alp on celestial alp, higher than the summer cumuli of earth; and above them all the horn of an ultra-violet peak whose head was enfolded in a hueless and spiral cloud, touched with the sense of invisible chromatic overtones, that seemed to come down upon it from skies beyond the zenith. I knew that the way to the outer cosmos was hidden in the high cloud.

On, on, we soared; and at length the mountain-range appeared on the far horizon, and I saw the paramount peak of ultra-violet with its dazzling crown of cumulus. Nearer still we came, till the strange volutes of cloud were almost above us, towering to the heavens and vanishing among the vari-colored suns. We saw the gleaming forms of pilgrims who preceded us, as they entered the swirling folds.

At this moment, the sky and the landscape had flamed again to their culminating brilliance, they burned with a thousand hues and lusters; so that the sudden, unlooked-for eclipse which now occurred was all the more complete and terrible.

Before I was conscious of anything amiss, I seemed to hear a despairing cry from my friends, who must have felt the oncoming calamity through a subtler sense than any of which I was yet capable.

Then, beyond the high and luminescent alp of our destination, I saw the mounting of a wall of darkness, dreadful and instant and positive and palpable, that rose everywhere and toppled like some Atlantean wave upon the irised suns and the fiery-colored vistas of the Inner Dimension.

We hung irresolute in the shadowed air, powerless and hopeless before the impending catastrophe, and saw that the darkness had surrounded the entire world and was rushing upon us from all sides. It ate the heavens, it blotted the outer suns; and the vast perspectives over which we had flown appeared to shrink and shrivel like a blackened paper. We seemed to wait alone for one terrible instant, in a center of dwindling light on which the cyclonic forces of night and destruction were impinging with torrential rapidity.

The center shrank to a mere point—and then the darkness was upon us like an overwhelming maelstrom—like the falling and crashing of cyclopean walls. I seemed to go down with the wreck of shattered worlds in a roaring sea of vortical space and force, to descend into some infra-stellar pit, some ultimate limbo to which the shards of forgotten suns and systems are flung. Then, after a measureless interval, there came the sensation of violent impact, as if I had fallen among these shards, at the bottom of the universal night.

I struggled back to consciousness with slow, prodigious effort, as if I were crushed beneath some irremovable weight, beneath the lightless and inert débris of galaxies. It seemed to require the labors of a Titan to lift my lids; and my body and limbs were heavy as if they had been turned to some denser element than human flesh; or had been subjected to the gravitation of a grosser planet than the earth.

My mental processes were benumbed and painful and confused to the last degree; but at length I realized that I was lying on a riven and tilted pavement, among gigantic blocks of fallen stone. Above me, the light of a livid heaven came down among overturned and jagged walls that no longer supported their colossal dome. Close beside me, I saw a fuming pit, from which a ragged rift extended through the floor, like the chasm wrought by an earthquake.

I could not recognize my surroundings for a time; but at last, with a toil-some groping of thought, I understood that I was lying in the ruined temple of Ydmos. The pit whose grey and acrid vapors rose beside me was that from which the fountain of singing flame had issued.

It was a scene of stupendous havoc and devastation. The wrath that had been visited upon Ydmos had left no wall nor pylon of the temple stand-ing. I stared at the blighted heavens from an architectural ruin in which the remains of On and Angkor would have been mere rubble-heaps.

With herculean effort, I turned my head away from the smoking pit, whose thin, sluggish fumes curled upward in phantasmal coils where the green ardor of the Flame had soared and sung. Not until then did I perceive my compan-ions. Angarth, still insensible, was lying near at hand; and just beyond him I saw the pale, contorted face of Ebbonly, whose lower limbs and body were pinned down by the rough and broken pediment of a fallen pillar.

Striving as in some eternal nightmare to throw off the leaden-clinging weight of my inertia, and able to bestir myself only with the most painful slowness and laboriousness, I got somehow to my feet and went over to Ebbonly. Angarth, I saw at a glance, was uninjured, and would presently regain consciousness; but Ebbonly, crushed by the monolithic mass of stone, was dying swiftly; and even with the help of a dozen men, I could not have released him from his imprisonment; nor could I have done anything to palliate his agony.

He tried to smile, with gallant and piteous courage, as I stooped above him.

"It's no use—I'm going in a moment," he whispered. "Good-bye, Hastane—and tell Angarth good-bye for me, too." His tortured lips relaxed, his eyelids dropped, and his head fell back on the temple pavement. With an unreal, dream-like horror, almost without emotion, I saw that he was dead. The exhaustion that still beset me was too profound to permit of thought or feeling; it was like the first reaction that follows the awakening from a drug-debauch. My nerves were like burnt-out wires, my muscles dead and unresponsive as clay, my brain was ashen and gutted as if a great fire had burned within it and gone out.

Somehow, after an interval of whose length my memory is uncertain, I managed to revive Angarth, and he sat up dully and dazedly. When I told him that Ebbonly was dead, my words appeared to make no impression upon him; and I wondered for awhile if he had understood. Finally, rousing himself a little with evident labor and difficulty, he peered at the body of our friend, and seemed to realize in some measure the horror of the situation. But I think he would have remained there for hours, or perhaps for all time, in his utter despair and lassitude, if I had not taken the initiative.

"Come," I said, with an attempt at firmness. "We must get out of this."

"Where to?" he queried, dully. "The Flame has failed at its source; and the Inner Dimension is no more. I wish I were dead, like Ebbonly—I might as well be, judging from the way I feel."

"We must find our way back to Crater Ridge," I said. "Surely we can do it, if the inter-dimensional portals have not been destroyed."

Angarth did not seem to hear me, but he followed obediently when I took him by the arm and began to seek an exit from the temple's heart among the roofless halls and overturned columns.

My recollections of our return are dim and confused, and are full of the tediousness of some interminable delirium. I remember looking back at Ebbonly, lying white and still beneath the massive pillar that would serve as an eternal monument for him; and I recall the mountainous ruins of the city, in which it seemed that we were the only living beings—a wilderness of chaotic stone, of fused, obsidian-like blocks, where streams of molten lava still ran in the mighty chasms, or poured like torrents adown unfathomable pits that had opened in the ground. And I remember seeing amid the wreckage the charred bodies of those dark colossi who were the people of Ydmos and the warders of the Flame.

Like pygmies lost in some shattered fortalice of the giants, we stumbled onward, strangling in mephitic and metallic vapors, reeling with weariness, dizzy with the heat that emanated everywhere to surge upon us in buffeting waves. The way was blocked by overthrown buildings, by toppled towers and battlements, over which we climbed precariously and toilsomely; and often we were compelled to divagate from our direct course by enormous rifts that seemed to cleave the foundations of the world.

The moving towers of the wrathful Outer Lords had withdrawn, their armies had disappeared on the plain beyond Ydmos, when we staggered over the riven and shapeless and scoriac crags that had formed the city's ramparts. Before us there was nothing but desolation—a fire-blackened and vapor-vaulted expanse in which no tree or blade of grass remained.

Across this waste we found our way to the slope of violet grass above the plain, which had lain beyond the path of the invader's bolts. There the guiding monoliths, reared by a people of whom we were never to learn even the name, still looked down upon the fuming desert and the mounded wrack of Ydmos. And there, at length, we came once more to the greyish-green columns that were the gateway between the worlds.

SEEDLING OF MARS

It was in the fall of 1947, three days prior to the annual football game between Stanford and the University of California, that the strange visitor from outer space landed in the middle of the huge stadium at Berkeley where the game was to be held.

Descending with peculiar deliberation, it was seen and pointed out by multitudes of people in the towns that border on San Francisco Bay, in Berkeley, Oakland, Alameda, and San Francisco itself. Gleaming with a fiery, copperish-golden light, it floated down from the cloudless autumn azure, dropping in a sort of slow spiral above the stadium. It was utterly unlike any known type of aircraft, and was nearly a hundred feet in length.

The general shape was ovoid, and also more or less angular, with a surface divided into scores of variant planes, and with many diamond ports of purplish material different from that of which the body was constructed. Even at first glance, it suggested the inventive genius and workmanship of some alien world, of a people whose ideas of mechanical symmetry have been conditioned by evolutionary necessities and sense-faculties divergent from ours.

However, when the queer vessel had come to rest in the amphitheater, many conflicting theories regarding its origin and the purpose of its descent were promulgated in the Bay cities. There were those who feared the invasion of some foreign foe, and who thought that the odd ship was the harbinger of a long-plotted attack from the Russian and Chinese Soviets, or even from Germany, whose intentions were still suspected. And many of those who postulated an ultra-planetary origin were also apprehensive, deeming that the visitant was perhaps hostile, and might mark the beginning of some terrible incursion from outer worlds.

In the meanwhile, utterly silent and immobile and without sign of life or occupancy, the vessel reposed in the stadium, where staring crowds began to gather about it. These crowds, however, were soon dispersed by order of the civic authorities, since the nature and intentions of the stranger were alike doubtful and undeclared. The stadium was closed to the public; and, in case of inimical manifestations, machine-guns were mounted on the higher seats with a company of Marines in attendance, and bombing-planes hovered in readiness to drop their lethal freight on the shining, coppery bulk.

The intensest interest was felt by the whole scientific fraternity, and a large group of professors, of chemists, metallurgists, astronomers, astrophysicists and biologists was organized to visit and examine the unknown object. When, on the afternoon following its landing, the local observatories issued a bulletin saying that the vessel had been sighted approaching the earth from translunar space on the previous night, the fact of its nonterrestrial genesis became established beyond dispute in the eyes of most; and controversy reigned as to whether it had come from Venus, Mars, Mercury, or one of the superior planets; or whether, perhaps, it was a wanderer from another solar system than our own.

But of course the nearer planets were favored in this dispute by the majority, especially Mars; for, as nearly as those who had watched it could determine, the line of the vessel's approach would have formed a trajectory with the red planet.

All that day, while argument seethed, while extras with luridly speculative and fantastic headlines were issued by the local papers as well as by the press of the whole civilized world; while public sentiment was divided between apprehension and curiosity, and the guarding Marines and aviators continued to watch for signs of possible hostility, the unidentified vessel maintained its initial stillness and silence.

Telescopes and glasses were trained upon it from the hills above the stadium; but even these disclosed little regarding its character. Those who studied it saw that the numerous ports were made of a vitreous material, more or less transparent; but nothing stirred behind them; and the glimpses of queer machinery which they afforded in the ship's interior were meaningless to the watchers. One port, larger than the rest, was believed to be a sort of door or man-hole; but no one came to open it; and behind it was a weird array of motionless rods and coils and pistons, which debarred the vision from further view.

Doubtless, it was thought, the occupants were no less cautious of their alien milieu than the people of the Bay region were suspicious of the vessel. Perhaps they feared to reveal themselves to human eyes; perhaps they were doubtful of the terrene atmosphere and its effect upon themselves; or perhaps they were merely lying in wait and planning some devilish outburst with unconceived weapons or engineries of destruction.

Apart from the fears felt by some, and the wonderment and speculation of others, a third division of public sentiment soon began to crystallize. In collegiate circles and among sport-lovers, the feeling was that the strange vessel had taken an unwarrantable liberty in pre-empting the stadium, especially at a time so near to the forthcoming athletic event. A petition for its removal was circulated, and presented to the city authorities. The great metallic hull, it was felt, no matter whence it had come or why, should not be allowed to interfere with anything so sacrosanct and of such prime importance as a football game.

However, in spite of the turmoil it had created, the vessel refused to move by so much as the fraction of an inch. Many began to surmise that the occupants had been overcome by the conditions of their transit through space; or perhaps they had died, unable to endure the gravity and atmospheric pressure of the earth.

It was decided to leave the vessel unapproached until morning of the next day, when the committee of investigation would visit it. During that afternoon and night, scientists from many states were speeding toward California by airplane and rocketship, to be on hand in time for this event.

It was felt advisable to limit the number of this committee. Among the fortunate savants who had been selected, was John Gaillard, assistant astronomer at the Mt. Wilson observatory. Gaillard represented the more radical and freely speculative trend of scientific thought, and had become well known for his theories concerning the inhabitability of the inferior planets, particularly Mars and Venus. He had long championed the idea of intelligent and highly organized life on these worlds, and had even published more than one treatise dealing with the subject, in which he had elaborated his theories with much specific detail. His excitement at the news of the strange vessel was intense. He was one of those who had sighted the gleaming and unclassifiable speck far out in space, beyond the orbit of the moon, in the late hours of the previous night; and he had felt even then a premonition of its true character. Others of the party were free and open-minded in their attitude; but no one was more deeply and vitally interested than Gaillard.

Godfrey Stilton, professor of astronomy at the University of California, also on the committee, might have been chosen as the very antithesis of Gaillard in his views and tendencies. Narrow, dogmatic, skeptical of all that could not be proved by line and rule, scornful of all that lay beyond the bourn of a strait empiricism, he was loath to admit the ultra-terrene origin of the vessel, or even the possibility of organic life on any other world than the earth. Several of his confreres belonged to the same intellectual type.

Apart from these two men and their fellow-scientists, the party included three newspaper reporters, as well as the local chief of police, William Polson, and the Mayor of Berkeley, James Gresham, since it was felt that the forces of government should be represented. The entire committee comprised forty men; and a number of expert machinists, equipped with acetylene torches and cutting tools, were held in reserve outside the stadium, in case it should be found necessary to open the vessel by force.

At nine a.m. the investigators entered the stadium and approached the glittering multi-angled object. Many were conscious of the thrill that attends some unforeknowable danger; but more were animated by the keenest curiosity and by feelings of extreme wonderment. Gaillard, in especial, felt himself in the presence of ultramundane mystery and marvelled as he neared the coppery-golden bulk: his feeling amounted almost to an actual vertigo, such as would be experienced by one who gazes athwart unfathomable gulfs upon the arcanic secrets and the wit-transcending wonders of a foreign sphere. It seemed to him that he stood upon the verge between the determinate and the incommensurable, betwixt the finite and the infinite.

Others of the group, in lesser degree, were possessed by similar emotions. And even the hard-headed, unimaginative Stilton was disturbed by a queer uneasiness; which, being minded as he was, he assigned to the weather—or a "touch of liver."

The strange ship reposed in utter stillness, as before. The fears of those who half-expected some deadly ambush were allayed as they drew near; and the hopes of those who looked for a more amicable manifestation of living occupancy were ungratified. The party gathered before the main port, which, like all the others, was made in the form of a great diamond. It was several feet above their heads, in a vertical angle or plane of the hull; and they stood staring through its mauve transparency on the unknown, intricate mechanisms beyond, that were colored as if by the rich panes of some cathedral window.

All were in doubt as to what should be done; for it seemed evident that the occupants of the vessel, if alive and conscious, were in no hurry to reveal themselves to human scrutiny. The delegation resolved to wait a few minutes before calling on the services of the assembled mechanics and their acetylene torches; and while waiting they walked about and inspected the metal of the walls, which seemed to be an alloy of copper and red gold; tempered to a preternatural hardness by some process unfamiliar to telluric metallurgy. There was no sign of jointure in the myriad planes and facets; and the whole enormous shell, apart from its lucid ports, might well have been wrought from a single sheet of the rich alloy.

Gaillard stood peering upward at the main port, while his companions sauntered about the vessel talking and debating among themselves. Somehow, he felt an intuition that something strange and miraculous was about to happen; and when the great port began to open slowly, without visible agency, dividing into two valves that slid away at the sides, the thrill which he experienced was not altogether one of surprise. Nor was he surprised when a sort of metal escalator, consisting of narrow stairs that were little more than rungs, descended step by step from the opening and came down to the ground at his very feet.

The port had opened and the escalator had unfolded in silence, with no faintest creak or clang; but others beside Gaillard had perceived the occurrence, and all hastened in great excitement and gathered before the steps.

Contrary to their not unnatural expectations, no one emerged from the vessel; and they could see little more of the interior than had been visible through the shut valves. They looked for some exotic ambassador from Mars, some gorgeous and bizarre plenipotentiary from Venus to descend the queer steps; and the silence and solitude and mechanical adroitness of it all were uncanny. It seemed that the great ship was a living entity, and possessed a brain and nerves of its own, hidden in the metal-sheathed interior.

The open portal and stairs offered an obvious invitation; and after some hesitancy, the scientists made up their minds to enter. Some were still fearful of a trap; and five of the forty men warily decided to remain without; but all the others were more powerfully drawn by curiosity and investigative ardor; and one by one they climbed the stairs and filed into the vessel.

They found the interior even more provocative of wonder than the outer walls had been. It was quite roomy and was divided into several compartments of ample size, two of which, at the vessel's center, were lined with low couches covered by soft, lustrous, piliated fabrics of opalescent grey. The others, as well as the ante-chamber behind the entrance, were filled with machinery whose motive force and method of operation were alike obscure to the most expert among the investigators.

Rare metals and odd alloys, some of them difficult to classify, had been used in the construction of this machinery. Near the entrance there was a sort of tripodal table or instrument-board whose queer rows of levers and buttons were no less mysterious than the ciphers of some telic cryptogram. The entire ship was seemingly deserted, with no trace of human or extra-planetary life.

Wandering through the apartments and marvelling at the unsolved mechanical enigmas which surrounded them, the delegation-members were not aware that the broad valves of the main port had closed behind them with the same stealthiness and silence that had marked their opening. Nor did they hear the warning shouts of the five men who had remained outside.

Their first intimation of anything untoward came from a sudden lurching and lifting of the vessel. Startled, they looked at the window-like ports, and saw through the violet, vitreous panes the whirling and falling away of those innumerable rows of seats which ringed the immense stadium. The alien spaceship, with no visible hand to control it, was rising rapidly in air with a sort of spiral movement. It was bearing away to some unknown world the entire delegation of hardy scientists that had boarded it, together with the Berkeley Mayor and Chief of Police and the three privileged reporters who had thought to obtain an ultrasensational "scoop" for their respective journals!

The situation was wholly without precedent, and was more than astounding; and the reactions of the various men, though quite divergent in some ways, were all marked by amazement and consternation. Many were too stunned and confounded to realize all the implications or possibilities, others were frankly terrified; and others still were indignant.

"This is an outrage!" thundered Stilton, as soon as he had recovered a little from his primary surprise. There were similar exclamations from others of the same temperament as he, all of whom felt emphatically that something should be done about the situation, and that someone (who, unfortunately, they could not locate or identify) should be made to suffer for such unparalleled audacity.

Gaillard, though he shared in the general amazement, was thrilled to the bottom of his heart by a sense of unearthly and prodigious adventure, by a premonition of interplanetary enterprise. He felt a mystic certainty that he and the others had embarked on a voyage to some world untrodden heretofore by man; that the strange vessel had descended to earth and had opened its port to invite them for this very purpose; that an esoteric and remote power was guiding its every movement and was drawing it to an appointed destination. Vast, inchoate images of unbounded space and splendor and interstellar strangeness filled his mind, and unforelimnable pictures rose to dazzle his vision from an ultratelluric bourn.

In some incomprehensible way, he knew that his life-long desire to penetrate the mysteries of distant spheres would soon be gratified; and he (if not his companions) was resigned from the very first to that bizarre abduction and captivity in the soaring space flier.

Discussing their position with much volubility and vociferousness, the assembled savants rushed to the various ports and stared down at the world they were leaving. In a mere fraction of time, they had risen to a cloud-like altitude. The whole region about San Francisco Bay, as well as the verges of the Pacific ocean, lay stretched below them like an immense relief map; and they could already see the curvature of the horizon, which seemed to reel and dip as they went upward.

It was an awesome and magnificent prospect; but the growing acceleration of the vessel, which had now gained a speed more than equal to that of the rocket-ships which were used at that time for circling the globe in the stratosphere, soon compelled them to relinquish their standing position and seek the refuge of the convenient couches. Conversation also was abandoned, for everyone began to experience an almost intolerable constriction and oppression, which held their bodies as if with clamps of unyielding metal.

However, when they had all laid themselves on the piliated couches, they felt a mysterious relief, whose source they could not ascertain. It seemed that a force emanated from those couches, which alleviated in some way the leaden stress of increased gravity due to the acceleration, and made it possible for the men to endure the terrific speed with which the space-flier was leaving the earth's atmosphere and gravitational zone.

Presently they found themselves able to stand up and walk around once more. Their sensations, on the whole, were almost normal; though, in contra-distinction to the initial crushing weight, there was now an odd lightness which compelled them to shorten their steps to avoid colliding with the walls and machinery. Their weight was less than it would have been on earth, but the loss was not enough to produce discomfort or sickness, and was accompanied by a sort of exhilaration.

They perceived that they were breathing a thin, rarefied and bracing air, not dissimilar to that of terrene mountain-tops, though permeated by one or two unfamiliar elements that gave it a touch of nitric sharpness. This air tended to increase the exhilaration and to quicken their respiration and pulses a little.

"This is damnable!" spluttered the indignant Stilton, as soon as he found that the powers of locomotion and breathing were reasonably subject to control. "It is contrary to all law, decency and order. The U.S. Government should do something about it immediately."

"I fear," observed Gaillard, "that we are now beyond the jurisdiction of the U.S., as well as that of all other mundane governments. No plane or rocket-ship could reach the air-strata through which we are passing; and we will penetrate the interstellar ether in a moment or so. Presumably this vessel is returning to the world from which it came; and we are going with it."

"Absurd! preposterous! outrageous!" Stilton's voice was a roar, slightly subdued and attenuated by the fine atmospheric medium. "I've always maintained that space-travel was utterly chimerical. Even earth-scientists haven't been able to invent a space-ship; and it is ridiculous to assume that highly intelligent life, capable of such invention, could exist on other planets."

"How, then," queried Gaillard, "do you account for our situation?"

"The vessel is of human origin, of course. It must be a new and ultra-powerful type of rocket-ship, devised by the Soviets, and under automatic or radio control, which will probably land us in Siberia after travelling in the highest layers of the stratosphere."

Gaillard, smiling with gentle irony, felt that he could safely abandon the argument. Leaving Stilton to stare wrathfully through a port at the receding bulk of the world, on which the whole of North America, together with Alaska and the Hawaiian Islands, had begun to declare their coastal outlines, he joined others of the party in a renewed investigation of the ship.

Some still maintained that living beings must be hidden on board; but a close search of every apartment, corner and cranny resulted as before. Abandoning this objective, the men began to re-examine the machinery, whose motive-power and method of operation they were still unable to fathom. Utterly perplexed and mystified, they watched the instrument-board, on which certain of the keys would move occasionally, as if shifted by an unseen hand. These changes of alignment were always followed by some change in the vessel's speed, or by a slight alteration of its course, possibly to avoid collision with meteoric fragments.

Though nothing definite could be learned about the propelling mechanism, certain negative facts were soon established. The method of propulsion was plainly non-explosive, for there were no roaring and flaming discharge of rockets. All was silent, gliding, and vibrationless, with nothing to betoken mechanical activity, other than the shifting of the keys and the glowing of certain intricate coils and pistons with a strange blue light. This light, cold as the scintillation of Arctic ice, was not electric in its nature, but suggested rather some unknown form of radio-activity.

After awhile, Stilton joined those who were grouped about the instrument-board. Still muttering his resentment of the unlawful and unscientific indignity to which he had been subjected, he watched the keys for a minute or so, and then, seizing one of them with his fingers, he tried to experiment, with the idea of gaining control of the vessel's movements.

To his amazement and that of his confreres, the key was immovable. Stilton strained till the blue veins stood out on his hand and sweat poured in rills from his baldish brow. Then, one by one, he tried others of the keys, tugging desperately, but always with the same result. Evidently the board was locked against other control than that of the unknown pilot.

Still persisting in his endeavor, Stilton came to a key of large size and different shape from the rest. Touching it, he screamed in agony, and withdrew his fingers from the strange object with some difficulty. The key was cold, as if it had been steeped in the absolute zero of space. It had actually seemed to sear his fingers with its extreme iciness. After that, he desisted, and made no further effort to interfere with the workings of the vessel.

Gaillard, after watching this interlude, had wandered back to one of the main apartments. Peering out once more from his seat on a couch of supernal softness and resilience, he beheld a breathtaking spectacle. The whole world, a great, glowing, many-tinted globe, was swimming abreast of the flier in the black and starlined gulf. The awfulness of the undirectioned deeps, the unthinkable isolation of infinitude rushed upon him, and he felt sick and giddy for a few instants with the shock of realization, and was swept by an overwhelming panic, limitless and without name.

Then, strangely, the terror passed, in a dawning exultation at the prospect of the novel voyage through unsounded heavens and toward untrodden shores. Oblivious of danger, forgetful of the dread alienation from man's accustomed environment, he gave himself up to magical conviction of marvellous adventure and unique destiny to come.

Others, however, were less capable of orientating themselves to these bizarre and terrific circumstances. Pale and horror-stricken, with a sense of irredeemable loss, of all-encompassing peril and giddy confusion, they watched the receding earth from whose comfortable purlieus they had been removed so inexplicably and with such awful suddenness.

Many were speechless with fear, as they realized more clearly their impotence in the grip of an all-powerful and incognizable force.

Some chattered loudly and incoherently, in an effort to conceal their perturbation. The three reporters lamented their inability to communicate with the journals they represented. James Gresham, the Mayor, and William Polson, the Chief of Police, were non-plussed and altogether at a loss as to what to do or think, in circumstances that seemed to nullify completely their wonted civic importance. And the scientists, as might have been expected, were divided into two main camps. The more radical and adventurous were more or less prone to welcome whatever might be in store for the sake of new knowledge; while the others accepted their fate with varying degrees of reluctance, of protest and apprehension.

Several hours went by; and the moon, a ball of dazzling desolation in the great abyss, had been left behind with the waning earth. The flier was speeding alone through the cosmic vastness, in a universe whose grandeur was a revelation even to the astronomers, familiar as they were with the magnitudes and multitudes of suns, nebulae and galaxies. The thirty-five men were being estranged from their natal planet and hurled across unthinkable immensity at a speed far beyond that of any solar body or satellite. It was hard to estimate the precise velocity; but some idea of it could be gained from the rapidity with which the sun and the nearer planets, Mars, Mercury and Venus, changed their relative positions. They seemed almost to fly athwart the heavens like so many jugglers' balls.

It was plain that some sort of artificial gravity prevailed in the ship; for the weightlessness that would otherwise have been inevitable in outer space was not experienced at any time. Also, the scientists found that they were being supplied with air from certain oddly-shapen tanks. Evidently, too, there was some kind of hidden heating-system or mode of insulation against the interspatial zero; for the temperature of the vessel's interior remained constant, at about 65° or 70°.

Looking at their watches, some of the party found that it was now noon by terrestrial time; though even the most unimaginative were impressed by the absurdity of the twenty-four hour division of day and night amid the eternal sunlight of the void.

Many began to feel hungry and thirsty, and to voice their appetence aloud. Not long after, as if in response, like the service given by a good table d'hôte, or restaurant, certain panels in the inner metal wall, hitherto unnoticed by the savants, opened noiselessly before their eyes and revealed a series of long buffets, on which were curious wide-mouthed ewers containing water and deep, tureen-like plates filled to the rim with unknown food-stuffs.

Too astonished to comment at much length on this new miracle, the delegation-members proceeded to sample the viands and beverage thus offered. Stilton, still morosely indignant, refused to taste them but was alone in his abstention.

The water was quite drinkable, though slightly alkaline, as if it had come from desert wells; and the food, a sort of reddish paste, concerning whose nature and composition the chemists were doubtful, served to appease the pangs of hunger even if it was not especially seductive to the palate.

After the earth-men had partaken of this refection, the panels closed as silently and unobtrusively as they had opened. The vessel plunged on through space, hour after hour, till it became obvious to Gaillard and his fellow-astronomers that it was either heading directly for the planet Mars or would pass very close to Mars on its way to some further orb.

The red world, with its familiar markings, which they had watched so often through observatory telescopes, and over whose character and causation they had long puzzled, began to loom before them and swelled upon the heavens with thaumaturgic swiftness. They then perceived a signal deceleration in the speed of the flier, which continued straight on toward the coppery planet, as if its goal were concealed amid the labyrinth of obscure and singular mottlings; and it became impossible to doubt any longer that Mars was their destination.

Gaillard, and those who were more or less akin to him in their interests and proclivities, were stirred by an awesome and sublime expectancy as the vessel neared the alien world. Then it began to float gently down above an exotic landscape in which the well-known "seas" and "canals," enormous with their closeness, could plainly be recognized.

Soon they approached the surface of the ruddy planet, spiraling through its cloudless and mistless atmosphere, while the deceleration slowed to a speed that was little more than that of a falling parachute. Mars surrounded them with its strait, monotonous horizons, nearer than those of earth, and displaying neither mountains nor any salient elevation of hills or hummocks; and soon they hung above it at an altitude of a half-mile or less. Here the vessel seemed to halt and poise, without descending further.

Below them now they saw a desert of low-ridge and yellowish-red sand, intersected by one of the so-called "canals," which ran sinuously away on either side to disappear beyond the horizon.

The scientists studied this terrain in ever-growing amazement and excitement, as the true nature of the veining "canal" was forced upon their perception. It was not water, as many had heretofore presumed, but a mass of pale-green vegetation, of vast and serrate leaves or fronds, all of which seemed to emanate from a single crawling flesh-colored stalk, several hundred feet in diameter and with swollen nodular joints at half-mile intervals! Aside from this anomalous and super-gigantic vine, there was no trace of life, either animal or vegetable, in the whole landscape; and the extent of the crawling stalk, which netted the entire visible terrain but seemed by its form and characteristics to be the mere tendril of some vaster growth, was a thing to stagger the preconceptions of mundane botany.

Many of the scientists were almost stupefied with astonishment as they gazed down from the violet ports on this titanic creeper. More than ever, the journalists mourned the staggering headlines with which they would be unable, under existing circumstances, to endow their respective dailies. Gresham and Polson felt that there was something vaguely illegal about the existence of anything so monstrous in the way of a plant-form; and the scientific disapproval felt by Stilton and his academically minded confreres was most pronounced.

"Outrageous! unheard-of! ludicrous!" muttered Stilton. "This thing defies the most elementary laws of botany. There is no conceivable precedent for it."

Gaillard, who stood beside him, was so wrapt in his contemplation of the novel growth, that he scarcely heard Stilton's comment. The conviction of vast and sublime adventure which had grown upon him ever since the beginning of that bizarre, stupendous voyage, was now confirmed by a clear daylight certitude. He could give no definite form or coherence to the feeling that possessed him; but he was overwhelmed by the intimation of present marvel and future miracle, and the intuition of strange, tremendous revelations to come.

Few of the party cared to speak, or would have been capable of speech. All that had happened to them during the past few hours, and all on which they now gazed, was so far beyond the scope of human action and cognition, that the normal exercise of their faculties was more or less inhibited by the struggle for adjustment to these unique conditions.

After they had watched the gargantuan vine for a minute or two, the savants became aware that the vessel was moving again, this time in a lateral direction. Flying very slowly and deliberately, it followed the course of the creeper toward what seemed to be the west of Mars, above which a small and pallid sun was descending through the dingy, burnt-out sky and casting a thin, chilly light athwart the desolate land.

The men were overpoweringly conscious of an intelligent determination behind all that was occurring; and the sense of this remote, unknowable supervision and control was stronger in Gaillard even than in the others. No one could doubt that every movement of the vessel was timed and predestined; and Gaillard felt that the slowness with which it followed the progress of the great stalk was calculated to give the scientific delegation ample opportunity for the study of their new environment; and, in particular, for observation of the growth itself.

In vain, however, did they watch their shifting milieu for aught that could denote the presence of organic forms of a human, nonhuman or preterhuman type, such as might imaginably exist on Mars. Of course, only such entities, it was thought, could have built, despatched, and guided the vessel in which they were held captive.

The flier went on for at least an hour, traversing an immense territory in which, after many miles, the initial sandy desolation yielded place to a sort of swamp. Here, where sluggish waters webbed the marly soil, the winding creeper swelled to incredible proportions, with lush leaves that embowered the marshy ground for almost a mile on either side of the overlooming stalk.

Here, too, the foliage assumed a richer and more vivid greenness, fraught with sublime vital exuberance; and the stem itself displayed an indescribable succulence, together with a shining and glossy luster, a bloom that was weirdly and incongruously suggestive of well-nourished flesh. The thing seemed to palpitate at regular and rhythmic intervals beneath the eyes of the observers, like a living entity; and in places there were queerly shaped nodes or attachments on the stem, whose purpose no one could imagine.

Gaillard called the attention of Stilton to the strange throbbing that was noticeable in the plant; a throbbing which seemed to communicate itself even to the hundred-foot leaves, so that they trembled like plumes.

"Humph!" said Stilton, shaking his head with an air of mingled disbelief and disgust. "That palpitation is altogether impossible. There must be something wrong with our eyes—some disturbance of focus brought on by the velocity of our voyage, perhaps. Either that, or there is some peculiar refractive quality in the atmosphere, which gives the appearance of movement to stable objects."

Gaillard refrained from calling his attention to the fact that this imputed phenomenon of visual disorder or aerial refraction was confined in its application entirely to the plant and did not extend its range to the bordering landscape.

Soon after this, the vessel came to an enormous branching of the plant; and the earth-men discovered that the stalk they had been following was merely one of three that ramified from a vaster stem to intersect the boggy soil at widely divergent angles and vanish athwart opposing horizons. The junction was marked by a mountainous double node that bore a bizarre likeness to human hips. Here the throbbing was stronger and more perceptible than ever; and odd veinings and mottlings of a reddish color were visible on the pale surface of the stem.

The savants became more and more excited by the unexampled magnitude and singular characteristics of this remarkable growth. But revelations of a still more extraordinary nature were in store. After poising a moment above the monstrous joint, the vessel flew on at a higher elevation with increased speed, along the main stem, which extended for an incalculable distance into the occident of Mars. It revealed fresh ramifications at variable intervals, and growing ever larger and more luxuriant as it penetrated marshy regions which were doubtless the residual ooze of a sunken sea.

"My God! the thing must surround the entire planet," said one of the reporters in an awed voice.

"It looks that way," Gaillard assented gravely. "We must be travelling almost in a line with the equator; and we have already followed the plant for hundreds of miles. From what we have seen, it would seem that the Martian 'canals' are merely its branchings; and perhaps the areas mapped as 'seas' by astronomers are masses of its foliage."

"I can't understand it," grumbled Stilton. "The damned thing is utterly contrary to science, and against nature—it oughtn't to exist in any rational or conceivable cosmos."

"Well," said Gaillard, a little tartly, "it does exist; and I don't see how you are going to get away from it. Apparently, too, it is the only vegetable form on the planet; at least, so far, we have failed to find anything else of the sort. After all, why shouldn't the floral life of Mars be concentrated in a single type? And why shouldn't there be just one example of that type? It shows a marvellous economy on the part of nature. There is no reason at all for assuming that the vegetable or even the animal kingdoms on other worlds would exhibit the same fission and multiplicity that are shown on earth."

Stilton, as he listened to this unorthodox argument, glared at Gaillard like a Mohammedan at some errant infidel, but was either too angry or too disgusted for further speech.

The attention of the scientists was now drawn to a greenish area along the line of their flight, covering many square miles. Here, they saw that the main stem had put out a multitude of tendrils, whose foliage hid the underlying soil like a thick forest. Even as Gaillard had postulated, the origin of the sea-like areas on Mars was now explained.

Forty or fifty miles beyond this mass of foliation, they came to another that was even more extensive. The vessel soared to a great height, and they looked down on the realm-wide expanse of leafage. In its middle they discerned a circular node, leagues in extent, and rising like a rounded alp, from which emanated in all directions the planet-circling stems of the weird growth. Not only the size, but also certain features of the immense node, were provocative of utter dumbfoundment in the beholders. It was like the head of some gargantuan cuttle-fish, and the stalks that ran away on all sides were suggestive of tentacles. And, strangest of all, the men descried in the center of the head two enormous masses, clear and lucent like water, which combined the size of lakes with the form and appearance of optic organs!

The whole plant palpitated like a breathing bosom; and the awe with which the involuntary explorers surveyed it was incommunicable by human words. All were compelled to recognize that even aside from its unparalleled proportions and habit of growth, the thing was in no sense alliable with any mundane botanic genera. And to Gaillard, as well as to others, the thought occurred that it was a sentient organism, and that the throbbing mass on which they now gazed was the brain or central ganglion of its unknown nervous system.

The vast eyes, holding the sunlight like colossal dew-drops, seemed to return their scrutiny with an unreadable and superhuman intelligence: and Gaillard was obsessed by the feeling that preternatural knowledge and wisdom bordering upon omniscience were hidden in those hyaline depths.

The vessel began to descend, and settled vertically down in a sort of valley close to the mountainous head, where the foliation of two departing stems had left a patch of clear land. It was like a forest glade, with impenetrable woods on three sides, and a high crag on the fourth. Here, for the first time during the experience of its occupants, the flier came to rest on the soil of Mars; floating gently down without jar or vibration; and almost immediately after its landing, the valves of the main port unfolded, and the metal stairway descended to the ground, in obvious readiness to disembark the human passengers.

One by one, some with caution and timidity, others with adventuresome eagerness, the men filed out of the vessel and started to inspect their surroundings. They found that the Martian air differed little if at all from that which they had been breathing in the space-flier; and at that hour, with the sun still pouring into the strange valley from the west, the temperature was moderately warm.

It was an outré and fantastic scene; and the details were unlike those of any tellurian landscape. Underfoot was a soft, resilient soil, like a moist loess, wholly devoid of grass, lichens, fungi or any minor plant-forms. The foliage of the mammoth vine, with horizontal fronds of a baroque type, feathery and voluminous, hung about the glade to an altitudinous height like that of ancient evergreens, and quivered in the windless air with the pulsation of the stems.

Close at hand there rose the vast, flesh-colored wall of the central plant-head, which sloped upward like a hill toward the hidden eyes and was no doubt deeply embedded and rooted in the Martian soil. Stepping close to the living mass, the earthmen saw that its surface was netted with millions of wrinkle-like reticulations, and was filled with great pores resembling those of animal skin beneath some extra-powerful microscope. They conducted their inspection in an awe-struck silence; and for some time no one felt able to voice the extraordinary conclusions to which most of them had now been driven.

The emotions of Gaillard were almost religious as he contemplated the scarce-imaginable amplitude of this ultra-terrene life-form, which seemed to him to exhibit attributes nearer to those of divinity than he had found in any other manifestation of the vital principle.

In it, he saw the combined apotheosis of the animal and the vegetable. The thing was so perfect and complete and all-sufficing, so independent of lesser life in its world-enmeshing growth. It poured forth the sense of aeonian longevity, perhaps of immortality. And to what arcanic and cosmic consciousness might it not have attained during the cycles of its development! What super-normal senses and faculties might it not possess! What powers and potentialities beyond the achievement of more limited, more finite forms! In a lesser degree, many of his companions were aware of similar feeling. Almost, in the presence of this portentous and sublime anomaly, they forgot the unsolved enigma of the space-vessel and their voyage across the heretofore unbridged immensities. But Stilton and his brother-conservatives were highly scandalized by the inexplicable nature of it all; and if they had been religiously minded, they would have expressed their sense of violation and outrage by saying that the monstrous plant, as well as the unexampled events in which they had taken an unwilling part, were tainted with the most grievous heresy and flagrant blasphemy. Gresham, who had been eyeing his surroundings with a pompous and puzzled solemnity, was the first to break the silence.

"I wonder where the local Government hangs out?" he queried. "Who the hell is in power here anyway? Hey, Mr. Gaillard, you astronomers know a lot about Mars. Ain't there a U.S. Consulate somewhere in this god-forsaken hole?"

Gaillard was compelled to inform him that there was no consular service on Mars, and also that the form of government on that planet, as well as its official location, was still an open problem.

"However," he went on, "I shouldn't be surprised to learn that we are now in the presence of the sole and supreme ruler of the Martian realms."

"Huh! I don't see anyone," grunted Gresham with a troubled frown, as he surveyed the quivering masses of foliage and the alp-like head of the great plant. The import of Gaillard's observation was too far beyond his intellectual orbit.

Gaillard had been inspecting the flesh-tinted wall of the head with supreme and fascinated interest. At some distance, to one side, he perceived certain peculiar outgrowths, either shrunken or vestigial, like drooping and flaccid horns. They were large as a man's body, and might at some time have been much larger. It seemed as if the plant had put them forth for some unknown purpose, and had allowed them to wither when the purpose had been accomplished. They still retained an uncanny suggestion of semi-human parts and members, of strange appendages, half arms and half tentacles, as if they had been modelled from some exemplar of undiscovered Martian animal life.

Just below them, on the ground, Gaillard noticed a litter of queer metallic tools, with rough sheets and formless ingots of the same coppery material from which the space-flier had been constructed.

Somehow, the spot suggested an abandoned ship-yard; though there were no scaffoldings such as would ordinarily be used in the building of a vessel. An odd inkling of the truth arose in Gaillard's mind as he surveyed the metal remnants, but he was too thoroughly bemused and overawed by the wonder of all that had occurred, as well as by all he had ascertained or surmised, to communicate his inferences to the other savants.

In the meanwhile the entire party had wandered about the glade, which comprised an area of several hundred yards. One of the astronomers, Philip Colton, who had made a side-line of botany, was examining the serried foliage of the super-gigantic creepers with a mingling of utmost interest and perplexity. The fronds or branches were lined with pinnate needles covered by a long, silky pubescence; and each of these needles was four feet in length by three or four inches in thickness, possibly with a hollow and tubular structure. The fronds grew in level array from the main creeper, filling the air like a horizontal forest, and reaching to the very ground in close, imbricated order.

Colton took a jack-knife from his pocket and tried to cut a section from one of the pinnate leaves. At the first touch of the keen blade, the whole frond recoiled violently beyond his reach; and then swinging back, it dealt him a tremendous blow which stretched him on the ground and hurled the knife from his fingers to a considerable distance.

If it had not been for the lesser gravity of Mars, he would have been severely injured by the fall. As it was, he lay bruised and breathless, staring with ludicrous surprise at the great frond, which had resumed its former position among its fellows, and now displayed no other movement than the singular trembling due to the rhythmic palpitation of the stem to which it was attached.

Colton's discomfiture had been noticed by his confreres; and all at once, as if their tongues had been loosed by this happening, a babel of discussion arose among them. It was no longer possible for anyone to doubt the animate or half-animate nature of the growth; and even the outraged and ireful Stilton, who considered that the most sacred laws of scientific probity were being violated, was driven to concede the presence of a biologic riddle not to be explained in terms of orthodox morphology.

Gaillard, who did not care to take any great part in this discussion, preferring his own thoughts and conjectures, continued to watch the throbbing growth. He stood a little apart from the others, and nearer than they to the fleshy and multiporous slope of the huge head; and all at once, as he watched, he saw the sprouting of what appeared to be a new tendril from the surface, at a distance of about four feet above the ground.

The thing grew like something in a slow moving-picture, lengthening out and swelling visibly, with a bulbous knob at the end. This knob soon became a large, faintly convoluted mass, whose outlines puzzled and tantalized Gaillard with their intimation of something he had once seen but could not now remember. There was a bizarre hint of nascent limbs and members, which soon become more definite; and then, with a sort of shock, he saw that the thing resembled a human foetus!

His involuntary exclamation of amazement drew others; and soon the whole delegation was grouped about him, watching the incredible development of the new growth with bated breath. The thing had put forth two well-formed legs, which now rested on the ground, supporting with their five-toed feet the upright body, on which the human head and arms were fully evolved, though they had not yet attained adult size.

The process continued; and simultaneously, a sort of woolly floss began to appear around the trunk, arms and legs, like the rapid spinning of some enormous cocoon. The hands and neck were bare; but the feet were covered with a different material, which took on the appearance of green leather. When the floss thickened and darkened to an iron-grey, and assumed quite modish outlines, it became obvious that the figure was being clothed in garments such as were worn by the earth-men, probably in deference to human ideas of modesty.

The thing was unbelievable; and stranger and more incredible than all else was the resemblance which Gaillard and his companions began to note in the face of the still growing figure. Gaillard felt as if he were looking into a mirror; for in all essential details the face was his own! The garments and shoes were faithful replicas of those worn by himself; and every limb and part of this outré being, even to the finger-tips, were proportioned like his!

The scientists saw that the process of growth was apparently complete. The figure stood with shut eyes and a somewhat blank and expressionless look on its features, like that of a man who has not yet awakened from slumber. It was still attached by a thick tendril to the breathing, mountainous node; and this tendril issued from the base of the brain, like an oddly misplaced umbilical cord.

The figure opened its eyes and stared at Gaillard with a long, level, enigmatic gaze that deepened his sense of shock and stupefaction. He sustained this gaze with the weirdest feeling imaginable—the feeling that he was confronted by his alter ego, by a *doppelgänger* in which was also the soul or intellect of some alien and vaster entity. In the regard of the cryptic eyes, he felt the same profound and sublime mystery that had looked out from the lake-sized orbs of shining dew or crystal in the plant-head.

The figure raised its right hand and seemed to beckon to him. Gaillard went slowly forward till he and his miraculous double stood face to face. Then the strange being placed its hand on his brow; and it seemed to Gaillard that a mesmeric spell was laid upon him from that moment. Almost without his own volition, for a purpose he was not yet permitted to understand, he began to speak; and the figure, imitating his every tone and cadence, repeated the words after him.

It was not till many minutes had elapsed, that Gaillard realized the true bearing and significance of this remarkable colloquy. Then with a start of clear consciousness, he knew that he was giving the figure lessons in the English language! He was pouring forth in a fluent, uninterrupted flood the main vocabulary of the tongue, together with its grammatical rules. And somehow, by a miracle of super-intellect, all that he said was being comprehended and remembered by his interlocutor.

Hours must have gone by during this process; and the Martian sun was now dipping toward the serrate walls of foliage. Dazed and exhausted, Gaillard realized that the long lesson was over; for the being removed its hand from his brow and addressed him in scholarly, well-modulated English:

"Thank you. I have learned all that I need to know for the purposes of linguistic communication. If you and your confreres will now attend me, I shall explain all that has mystified you, and declare the reasons for which you have been brought from your own world to the shores of a foreign planet."

Like men in a dream, barely crediting the fantastic evidence of their senses and yet unable to refute or repudiate it, the earth-men listened while Gaillard's amazing double continued:

"The being through whom I speak, made in the likeness of one of your own party, is a mere special organ which I have developed so that I could communicate with you. I, the informing entity, who combine in myself the utmost genius and energy of those two divisions of life which are known to you as the plant and the animal—I, who possess the virtual omniety and immortality of a god, have had no need of articulate speech or formal language at any previous time in my existence. But since I include in myself all potentialities of evolution, together with mental powers that verge upon omniscience, I have had no difficulty whatever in acquiring this new faculty.

"It was I who constructed, with other special organs that I had put forth for this purpose, the space-flier that descended upon your planet and then returned to me a delegation, most of whom, I have surmised, would represent the scientific fraternities of mankind. The building of the flier, and its mode of control, will be made plain when I tell you that I am the master of many cosmic forces beyond the rays and energies known to tellurian savants. These forces I can draw from the air, the soil or the ether at will, or can even summon from remote stars and nebulae.

"The space-vessel was wrought from metal which I had integrated from molecules floating at random through the atmosphere; and I used the solar rays in concentrated form to create the temperature at which these metals were fused into a single sheet. The power used in propelling and guiding the vessel is a sort of super-electric energy whose exact nature I shall not elucidate, other than to say that it is associated with the basic force of gravity, and also with certain radiant properties of the interstellar ether not detectible by any instruments which you possess. I established in the flier the gravitation of Mars, and supplied it with Martian air and water, and also with chemically created food-stuffs, in order to accustom you during your voyage to the conditions that prevail on Mars.

"I am, as you may have already surmised, the sole inhabitant of this world. I could multiply myself if necessary; but so far, for reasons which you will soon apprehend, I have not felt that this would be desirable. Being complete and perfect in myself, I have had no need of companionship with other entities; and long ago, for my own comfort and security, I was compelled to extirpate certain rival plant-forms, and also certain animals who resembled slightly the mankind of your world; and who, in the course of their evolution, were becoming troublesome and even dangerous to me.

"With my two great eyes, which possess an optic magnifying power beyond that of your strongest telescopes, I have studied Earth and the other planets during the Martian nights, and have learned much regarding the conditions that exist upon each. The life of your world, your history, and the state of your civilization have been in many ways an open book to me; and I have also formed an accurate idea of the geological, faunal and floral phenomena of your globe. I understand your imperfections, your social injustice and maladjustment, and the manifold disease and misery to which you are liable, owing to the dissonant, multiple entities into which the expression of your life-principle has been subdivided.

"From all such evils and error, I am exempt. I have attained to well-nigh absolute knowledge and masterdom; and there is no longer anything in the universe for me to fear, aside from the inevitable process of dehydration and dessication which Mars is slowly undergoing, like all other aging planets.

"This process I am unable to retard, except in a limited and partial manner; and I have already been compelled to tap the artesian waters of the planet in many places. I could live upon sunlight and air alone; but water is necessary to maintain the alimental properties of the atmosphere; and without it, my immortality would fail in the course of time; my giant stems would shrink and shrivel; and my vast innumerable leaves would grow sere for want of the vital humor.

"Your world is still young, with superabundant seas and streams and a moisture-laden air. You have more than is requisite of the element which I lack; and I have brought you here, as representative members of mankind, to propose an exchange which cannot be anything but beneficial to you as well as to myself.

"In return for a modicum of the water of your world, I will offer you the secrets of eternal life and infinite energy, and will teach you to overcome your social imperfections and to master wholly your planetary environment. Because of my great size, my stems and tendrils which girdle the Martian equator and reach even to the poles, it would be impossible for me to leave my natal world; but I will teach you how to colonize the other planets and explore the universe beyond. For these various ends, I suggest the making of an intermundane treaty and a permanent alliance between myself and the peoples of Earth.

"Consider well what I offer you; for the opportunity is without example or parallel. In relation to men, I am like a god in comparison with insects. The benefits which I can confer upon you are inestimable; and in return I ask only that you establish on Earth, under my instruction, certain transmitting stations using a super-potent wave-length, by means of which the essential elements of sea-water, minus the undesirable saline properties, can be teleported to Mars. The amount thus abstracted will make little or no difference in your tide-levels or in the humidity of your air; but for me, it will mean an assurance of everlasting life."

The figure ended its peroration, and stood regarding the earth-men in polite and somewhat inscrutable silence. It waited for their answer.

As might have been expected, the emotions with which the delegation-members had heard this singular address were far from unanimous in their tenor. All the men were beyond mere surprise or astonishment, for miracle had been piled upon miracle till their brains were benumbed with wonder; and they had reached the point where they took the creation of a human figure and its endowment with human utterance wholly for granted. But the proposal made by the plant-entity through its man-like organ was another matter, and it played upon varying chords in the minds of the scientists, the reporters, the Mayor, and the Chief of Police.

Gaillard, who felt himself wholly in accord with this proposition, and more and more thoroughly *en rapport* with the Martian entity, wished to accede at once and to pledge his own support and that of his fellows to a furthering of the suggested treaty and plan of exchange. He was forced to point out to the Martian that the delegation, even if single-minded in its consent, was not empowered to represent the peoples of Earth in forming the projected alliance; that the most it could do would be to lay the offer before the Government of the U.S. and of other terrestrial realms.

Half the scientists, after some deliberation, announced themselves as being in favor of the plan and willing to promote it to the utmost of their ability. The three reporters were also willing to do the same; and they promised, perhaps rashly, that the influence of the world-press would be added to that of the renowned savants.

Stilton and the other dogmatists of the party, however, were emphatically and even rabidly opposed, and declined to consider the Martian's offer for an instant. Any treaty or alliance of the sort, they maintained, would be highly undesirable and improper. It would never do for the nations of Earth to involve themselves in an entanglement of such questionable nature, or to hold commerce of any sort with a being such as the plant-monster, which had no rightful biologic status. It was unthinkable that orthodox and sound-minded scientists should lend their advocacy to anything so dubious. They felt too that there was a savor of deception and trickery about the whole business; and at any rate it was too irregular to be countenanced, or even to be considered with anything but reprehension.

The schism among the savants was rendered final by a hot argument, in which Stilton roundly denounced Gaillard and the other pro-Martians as virtual traitors to humanity, and intellectual Bolshevists whose ideas were dangerous to the integrity of human thought. Gresham and Polson were on the side of mental law and order, being professionally conservative; and thus the party was about evenly divided between those who favored accepting the Martian's offer, and those who spurned it with more or less suspicion and indignation.

During the course of this vehement dispute, the sun had fallen behind the high ramparts of foliage, and an icy chill, such as might well be looked for in a semi-desolate world with attenuating air, had already touched the pale rose twilight. The scientists began to shiver; and their thoughts were distracted from the problem they had been debating by the physical discomfort of which they were increasingly conscious.

They heard the voice of the strange manikin in the dusk:

"I can offer you a choice of shelters for the night and also for the duration of your stay on Mars. You will find the space-flier well-lighted and warmed, with all the facilities which you may require. Also, I can offer you another hospitality. "Look beneath my foliage, a little to your right, where I am now preparing a shelter no less commodious and comfortable than the vessel—a shelter which will help to give you an idea of my varied powers and potentialities."

The earth-men saw that the flier was brilliantly illuminated, pouring out a gorgeous amethystine radiance from its violet ports. Then, beneath the foliage close at hand, they perceived another and stranger luminosity which seemed to be emitted, like some sort of radio-active or noctilucent glow, by the great leaves themselves.

Even where they were standing, they felt a balmy warmth that began to temper the frigid air; and stepping toward the source of these phenomena, they found that the crowded leaves had lifted and arched themselves into a roomy alcove. The ground beneath was lined with a fabric-like substance of soft hues, deep and elastic underfoot, like a fine mattress. Ewers filled with liquids and platters of food-stuffs were disposed on low tables; and the air in the alcove was gentle as that of the spring night in a subtropic land.

Gaillard and the other pro-Martians, filled with profound awe and wonder, were ready to avail themselves at once of the shelter of this thaumaturgic hostelry. But the anti-Martians would have none of it, regarding it as the workmanship of the devil. Suffering keenly from the cold, with chattering teeth and shivering limbs, they promenaded the open glade for some time, and at last were driven to seek the hospitable port of the space-flier, thinking it the lesser of two evils by some queer twist of logic.

The others, after eating and drinking from the mysteriously provided tables, laid themselves down on the mattress-like fabrics. They found themselves greatly refreshed by the liquid in the ewers, which was not water but some kind of roseate, aromatic wine. The food, a literal manna, was more agreeably flavored than that of which they had partaken during their voyage in the space-vessel. In the nerve-wrought and highly excited state that was consequent upon their experiences, none of them had expected to sleep. The unfamiliar air, the altered gravity, the unknown radiations of the exotic soil, as well as their unprecedented journey and the miraculous discoveries and revelations of the day, were all profoundly upsetting and conducive to a severe disequilibration of mind and body.

However, Gaillard and his companions fell into a deep and dreamless slumber as soon as they had laid themselves down. Perhaps the liquid and solid refreshments which they had taken may have conduced to this; or perhaps there was some narcotic or mesmeric influence in the air, falling from the vast leaves or proceeding from the brain of the plant-lord.

The anti-Martians did not fare so well in this respect, and their slumber was restless and broken. Most of them had touched the proffered viands in the space-flier very sparingly; and Stilton, in particular, had refused to eat or drink at all. Doubtless, too, their antagonistic frame of mind was such as to make them more resistant to the hypnotic power of the plant, if such were being exerted. At any rate, they did not share in the benefits conferred upon the others.

A little before dawn, when Mars was still shrouded in crepuscular gloom but slightly lightened by the two small moons, Phobos and Deimos, Stilton arose from the soft couch on which he had tossed in night-long torment, and began to experiment once more, undeterred by his previous failure and discomfiture, with the mechanical controls of the vessel.

To his surprise, he found that the odd-shaped keys were no longer resistant to his fingers. He could move and arrange them at will; and he soon discovered the principle of their working and was able to levitate and steer the flier.

His confreres had now joined him, summoned by his shout of triumph. All were wide-awake, and jubilant with the wild hope of escaping from Mars and the jurisdiction of the plant-monster. Thrilling with this hope, and fearing every moment that the Martian would re-assert its esoteric control of the mechanism, they rose unhindered from the darkling glade to the alien skies and headed toward the brilliant green orb of Earth, descried among the unfamiliar constellations.

Looking back, they saw the vast eyes of the Martian watching them weirdly from the gloom, like pools of clear and bluish phosphorescence; and they shuddered with the dread of being recalled and re-captured. But, for some inscrutable reason, they were permitted to maintain their earthward course without interference. However, the voyage was fraught with a certain amount of disaster; and Stilton's clumsy pilotage hardly formed an ample substitute for the half-divine knowledge and skill of the Martian. More than once, the vessel collided with meteors; none of which, fortunately, were heavy enough to penetrate its hull. And when, after many hours, they approached the earth, Stilton failed to secure the proper degree of deceleration. The flier fell with terrible precipitancy and was saved from destruction only by dropping into the South Atlantic. The jarred mechanism was rendered unworkable by the fall, and most of the occupants were severely bruised and stunned.

After floating at random for days, the coppery bulk was sighted by a northward-going liner and was towed to port in Lisbon. Here the scientists abandoned it, and made their way back to America, after detailing their adventures to representatives of the world-press, and issuing a solemn warning to all the world-peoples against the subversive designs and infamous proposals of the ultra-planetary monster.

The sensation created by their return and by the news they brought was tremendous. A tide of profound alarm and panic, due in part to the immemorial human aversion toward the unknown, swept immediately upon the nations; and immense, formless, exaggerated fears were bred like shadowy hydras in the dark minds of men.

Stilton and his fellow-conservatives continued to foster these fears, and to create with their pronouncements a globe-wide wave of anti-Martian prejudice, of blind opposition and dogmatic animosity. They enlisted on their side as many of the scientific fraternity as they could; that is to say, all those who were minded like themselves, as well as others overawed or subdued by the pressure of authority. They sought also, with much success, to marshal the political powers of the world in a strong league that would ensure the repudiation of any further offers of alliance from the Martian.

In all this gathering of inimical forces, this regimenting of earthly conservation and insularity and ignorance, the religious factor, as was inevitable, soon asserted itself. The claim to divine knowledge and power made by the Martian, was seized upon by all the various mundane hierarchies, by Christian and Muhammadan, by Buddhist and Parsee and Voodoist alike, as forming a supremely heinous blasphemy. The impiety of such claims, and the menace of a non-anthropomorphic god and type of worship that might be introduced on earth, could not be tolerated for a moment. Khalif and Pope, lama and imaum, parson and mahatma, all made common cause against this ultra-terrestrial invader.

Also, the reigning political powers felt that there might be something Bolshevistic behind the offer of the Martian to promote an Utopian state of society on earth. And the financial, commercial, and manufacturing interests likewise thought that it might imply a threat to their welfare or stability. In short, every branch of human life and activity was well represented in the anti-Martian movement.

In the interim, on Mars, Gaillard and his companions had awakened from their sleep to find that the luminous glow of the arching leaves had given place to the ardent gold of morn. They discovered that they could venture forth with comfort from the alcove; for the air of the glade without had grown swiftly warm beneath the rising sun.

Even before they had noticed the absence of the coppery flier, they were apprised of its departure by the man-organ of the great plant. This being, unlike its human prototypes, was exempt from fatigue; and it had remained standing or reclining all night against the fleshy wall to which it was attached. It now addressed the earth-men thus:

"For reasons of my own, I have made no attempt to prevent the flight of your companions, who with their blindly hostile attitude, would be worse than useless to me, and whose presence could only hinder the rapport which should exist between you and myself. They will reach the earth, and will try to warn its peoples against me and to poison their minds against my beneficent offer. Such an outcome, alas, cannot be avoided, even if I were to bring them back to Mars or divert their flight by means of my control and send them speeding forever through the void beyond the worlds. I perceive that there is much ignorance and dogmatism and blind self-interest to be overcome, before the excelling light which I proffer can illumine the darkness of earthly minds.

"After I have kept you here for a few days, and have instructed you thoroughly in the secrets of my transcendent wisdom, and have imbued you with surprising powers that will serve to demonstrate my omnivalent superiority to the nations of Earth, I shall send you back to Earth as my ambassadors, and though you will meet with much opposition from your fellows, my cause will prevail in the end, beneath the infallible support of truth and science."

Gaillard and the others received this communication as well as the many that followed it, with supreme respect and semi-religious reverence. More and more they became convinced that they stood in the presence of a higher and ampler entity than man; that the intellect which thus discoursed to them through the medium of a human form was well-nigh inexhaustible in its range and depth, and possessed many characteristics of infinitude and more than one attribute of deity.

Agnostic though most of them were by nature or training, they began to accord a certain worship to this amazing plant-lord; and they listened with an attitude of complete submission if not of abjection, to the outpourings of cycle-gathered lore, and immortal secrets of cosmic law and life and energy, in which the great being proceeded to instruct them.

The illumination thus accorded them was both simple and esoteric. The plant-lord began by dwelling at some length upon the monistic nature of all phenomena, of matter, light, color, sound, electricity, gravity, and all other forms of irradiation, as well as time and space; which, it said, were only the various perceptual manifestations of a single underlying principle or substance.

The listeners were then taught the evocation and control, by quite rudimentary chemical media, of many forces and rates of energy that had hitherto lain beyond the detection of human senses or instruments. They were taught also the terrific power obtainable by refracting with certain sensitized elements the ultraviolet and infra-red rays of the spectrum; which, in a highly concentrated form, could be used for the disintegration and rebuilding of the molecules of matter.

They learned how to make engines that emitted beams of destruction and transmutation; and how to employ these unknown beams, more potent even than the so-called "cosmic rays," in the renewal of human tissues and the conquest of disease and old age.

Simultaneously with this tuition, the plant-lord carried on the building of a new space-car, in which the earth-men were to return to their own planet and preach the Martian evangel. The construction of this car, whose plates and girders seemed to materialize out of the void air before their very gaze, was a practical lesson in the use of arcanic natural forces. Atoms that would form the requisite alloys were brought together from space by the play of invisible magnetic beams, were fused by concentrated solar heat in a specially refractive zone of atmosphere, and were then moulded into the desired form as readily as the bottle that shapes itself from the pipe of the glass-blower.

Equipped with this new knowledge and potential masterdom, with a cargo of astounding mechanisms and devices made for their use by the plant-lord, the pro-Martians finally embarked on their earthward voyage.

A week after the abduction of the thirty-five earth-men from the stadium at Berkeley, the space-car containing the Martian's proselytes landed at noon in this same stadium. Beneath the infinitely skillful and easy control of the far-off plant-being, it came down without accident, lightly as a bird; and as soon as the news of its arrival had spread, it was surrounded by a great throng, in which the motives of hostility and curiosity were almost equally paramount.

Through the denunciation of the dogmatists led by Stilton, the savants and the three reporters beneath the leadership of Gaillard had been internationally outlawed before their arrival. It was expected that they would return sooner or later through the machinations of the plant-lord; and a special ruling that forbade them to land on terrene soil, under penalty of imprisonment, had been made by all the Governments.

Ignorant of this, and ignorant also of how wide-spread and virulent was the prejudice against them, they opened the vessel's port and stood in readiness to emerge.

Gaillard, going first, paused at the head of the metal stairway, and something seemed to arrest him as he looked down on the milling faces of the mob that had gathered with incredible swiftness. He saw enmity, fear, hatred, suspicion, in many of these faces; and in others a gaping and zany-like inquisitiveness, such as might be shown before the freaks of some travelling circus. A small corps of policemen, elbowing and thrusting the rabble aside with officious rudeness, was pushing toward the front; and cries of derision and hatred, gathering by two and threes and uniting to a rough roar, were now hurled at the occupants of the car.

"Damn the pro-Martians! Down with the dirty traitors! Hang the——dogs!"

An overripe tomato, large and dripping, sailed toward Gaillard and splashed on the steps at his feet. Hisses and hoots and cat-calls added to the roaring bedlam, but above it all, he and his comrades heard a quiet voice that spoke within the car; the voice of the Martian, borne across inestimable miles of ether:

"Beware, and defer your landing. Resign yourselves to my guidance, and all will be well."

Gaillard stepped back as he heard this minatory voice, and the valvular port closed quickly behind the folded stairs, just as the policemen who had come to arrest the vessel's occupants broke from the forefront of the throng.

Peering out on those hateful faces, Gaillard and his brother-savants beheld an astounding manifestation of the Martian's power. A wall of violet flame, descending from the remote heavens to the ground, seemed to intervene between the car and the crowd, and the policemen, bruised and breathless but uninjured, were hurled backward as if by a great wave. This flame, whose color changed to blue and green and yellow and scarlet like a sort of aurora, played for hours about the vessel and rendered it impossible for anyone to approach. Retreating to a respectful distance, awe-struck and terrified, the crowd looked on in silence; and the police waited in vain for a chance to fulfill their commission. After awhile, the flame became white and misty, and upon it, as upon the bosom of a cloud, a bizarre and mirage-like scene was imprinted, visible alike to the occupants of the car and the throng without. This scene was the Martian landscape in which the central brain of the plant-lord was located; and the crowd gasped with astonishment as it met the gaze of the enormous telescopic eyes, and saw the unending stems and league-wide masses of sempervirent foliage.

Other scenes and demonstrations followed, all of which were calculated to impress upon the throng the wonder-working powers and marvellous faculties of this remote being.

Pictures that illustrated the historic life of the Martian, as well as the various arcanic natural energies subject to its dominion, followed each other in rapid succession. The purpose of the desired alliance with Earth, and the benefits which would accrue thereby to humanity, were also depicted. The divine benignity and wisdom of this puissant being, its superior organic nature, and its vital and scientific supremacy, were made plain to the dullest observer.

Many of those who had come to scoff, or had been prepared to receive the pro-Martians and their evangel with scorn and hate and violence, became converted to the alien cause forthwith by these sublime demonstrations.

However, the more dogmatic scientists, the true "die-hards" as represented by Godfrey Stilton, maintained an adamantine obstructionism, in which they were supported by the officers of law and government, as well as by the presbyters of the various religions. The world-wide dissidence of opinion which soon resulted, became the cause of many civil wars or revolutions, and, in one or two cases, ended in actual warfare between nations.

Numerous efforts were made to apprehend or destroy the Martian space-car, which, beneath the guidance of its ultra-planetary master, appeared in many localities all over the world, descending suddenly from the stratosphere to perform incredible scientific miracles before the eyes of astonished multitudes. In all quarters of the globe, the mirage-like pictures were flashed on the screen of cloudy fire, and more and more people went over to the new cause.

Bombing planes pursued the vessel and sought to drop their deadly freight upon it, but without success; for whenever the car was endangered, the auroral flames intervened, deflecting and hurling back the exploded bombs, often to the detriment of their launchers.

Gaillard and his confreres, with leonine boldness, emerged many times from the car, to display before crowds or selected bodies of savants the marvellous inventions and chemical thaumaturgies with which they had been endowed by the Martian. Everywhere the police sought to arrest them, maddened mobs endeavored to do them violence, armed regiments tried to surround them and cut them off from the car. But with an adroitness that seemed no less than supernatural, they contrived always to elude capture; and often they discomfited their pursuers by astonishing displays or evocations of esoteric force, temporarily paralyzing the civic officers with unseen rays, or creating about themselves a defensive zone of intolerable heat or trans-arctic cold.

In spite of all these myriad demonstrations, however, the citadels of human ignorance and insularity remained impregnable in many places. Deeply alarmed by this ultra-terrene menace to their stability, the governments and religions of Earth, as well as the more conservative scientific elements, rallied their resources in a most heroic and determined effort to stem the incursion. Men of all ages, everywhere, were conscripted for service in the national armies; and even women and children were equipped with the deadliest weapons of the age for use against the pro-Martians, who, with their wives and families, were classed as infamous renegades to be hunted down and killed without ceremony like dangerous beasts.

The internecine warfare that ensued was the most terrible in human history. Class became divided against class and family against family. New and more lethal gases than any heretofore employed, were devised by chemists, and whole cities or territories were smothered beneath their agonizing pall. Others were blown into skyward-flying fragments by single charges of superpotent explosives; and war was carried on by planes, by rocket-ships, by submarine, by dreadnaughts, by tanks, by every vehicle and engine of death or destruction that the homicidal ingenuity of man had yet created.

The pro-Martians, who had won several victories at first, were gravely outnumbered; and the tide of battle began to turn against them. Scattered in many lands, they found themselves unable to unite and organize their forces to the same degree as those of their official opponents. Though Gaillard and his devoted confreres went everywhere in the space-vessel, aiding and abetting the radicals, and instructing them in the use of new weapons and cosmic energies, the party suffered great reverses through the sheer brute preponderance of its foes. More and more it became split up into small bands, hunted and harried, and driven to seek refuge in the wilder or less explored sections of the earth.

In North America, however, a large army of the scientific rebels, whose families had been compelled to join them, contrived to hold the antagonists at bay for awhile. Surrounded at last, and faced by overwhelming odds, this army was on the verge of a crushing defeat.

Gaillard, hovering above the black, voluminous clouds of the battle, in which poisonous gases mingled with the fumes of high explosives, felt for the first time the encroachment of actual despair. It seemed to him, and also to his companions, that the Martian had abandoned them, disgusted perhaps with the bestial horror of it all and the hateful, purblind narrowness and fanatic nescience of mankind.

Then, through the smoke-smothered air, a fleet of coppery-golden cars descended, to land on the battle-front among the Martian adherents. There were thousands of these cars; and from all the entrance-ports, which had opened simultaneously, there issued the voice of the planet-lord, summoning its supporters and bidding them enter the vessels.

Saved from annihilation by this act of Martian providence, the entire army obeyed the command; and as soon as the last man, woman and child had gone aboard, the ports closed again, and the fleet of space-cars, wheeling in graceful and derisive spirals above the heads of the baffled conservatives, soared from the battle-clouds like a flock of reddish-golden birds and vanished in the noon-tide heavens, led by the car containing Gaillard's party.

At the same time, in all portions of the world where the little bands of heroic radicals had been cut off and threatened with capture or destruction, other cars descended in like manner and carried away the pro-Martians and their families even to the last unit. These vessels joined the main fleet in mid-space; and then all continued their course beneath the mysterious piloting of the plant-lord, flying at super-cosmic velocity through the star-surrounded gulf.

Contrary to the anticipations of the mundane exiles, the vessels were not drawn toward Mars; and it soon became evident that their objective was the planet Venus. The voice of the Martian, speaking athwart the eternal ether, made the following announcement:

"In my infinite wisdom, my supreme foreprescience, I have removed you from the hopeless struggle to establish on Earth the sovereign light and truth which I offer. You alone I have found worthy; and the moiety of mankind, who have refused salvation with hatred and contumely, preferring the natal darkness of death and disease and ignorance in which they were born, must be left henceforward to their inevitable fate.

"You, as my loyal and well-trusted servants, I am sending forth to colonize beneath my tutelage a great continent on the planet Venus, and to found amid the primal exuberance of this new world a super-scientific nation."

The fleet soon approached Venus, and circled the equator for a great distance in the steam-thick atmosphere, through which nothing could be descried other than a hot and over-fuming ocean, close to the boiling-point, which seemed to cover the entire planet. Here, beneath the never-setting sun, intolerable temperatures prevailed everywhere, such as would have parboiled the flesh of a human being exposed directly to the semi-aqueous air. Suffering even in their insulated cars from this terrific heat, the exiles wondered how they were to exist in such a world.

At last, however, their destination came in view and their doubts were resolved. Nearing the nightward side of Venus which is never exposed to daylight, in a latitude where the sun slanted far behind them as over arctic realms, they beheld through thinning vapors an immense tract of land, the sole continent amid the planetary sea. This continent was covered by rich jungles, containing a flora and fauna similar to those of pre-glacial eras on the earth. Calamites and cycads and fern-plants of unbelievable luxuriance revealed themselves to the earth-men; and they saw everywhere the great, brainless reptiles, the megalosaurs, plesiosaurs, labyrinthodons and pterodactyls of Jurassic times.

Beneath the instruction of the Martian, before landing, they slew these reptiles, incinerating them completely with infra-red beams, so that not even their carcasses would remain to taint the air with putrefactive effluvia. When the whole continent had been cleared of its noxious life, the cars descended; and emerging, the colonists found themselves in a terrain of unequalled fertility, whose very soil seemed to pulsate with primordial vigors, and whose air was rich with ozone and oxygen and nitrogen.

Here the temperature, though still sub-tropic, was agreeable and balmy; and through the use of protective fabrics provided by the Martian, the earth-men soon accustomed themselves to the eternal sunlight and intense ultra-violet radiation. With the super-knowledge at their disposal, they were able to combat the unknown, highly pernicious bacteria peculiar to Venus, and even to exterminate such bacteria in the course of time. They became the lords of a salubrious climate, dowered with four mild and equable seasons by the slight annual rotation of the planet; but having one eternal day, like the mythic Isles of the Blest beneath a low and undeparting sun.

Beneath the leadership of Gaillard, who remained in close rapport and continual communication with the plant-lord, the great forests were cleared in many places. Cities of lofty and ethereal architecture, lovely as those of some trans-stellar Eden, builded by the use of force-beams, began to rear their graceful turrets and majestic cumuli of domes above the gigantic calamites and ferns.

Through the labors of the terrene exiles, a truly Utopian nation was established, giving allegiance to the plant-lord as to some tutelary deity; a nation devoted to cosmic progress, to scientific knowledge, to spiritual tolerance and freedom; a happy, law-abiding nation, blest with millennial longevity, and exempt from sorrow and disease and error.

Here, too, on the shores of the Venusian sea, were builded the great transmitters that sent through interplanetary space, in ceaseless waves of electronic radiation, the water required to replenish the dehydrated air and soil of Mars, and thus to ensure for the plant-being a perpetuity of god-like existence.

In the meanwhile, on earth, unknown to Gaillard and his fellow-exiles, who had made no effort to communicate with the abandoned world, an amazing thing had occurred; a final proof of the virtual omnipotence and all-inclusive sapience of the Martian.

In the great vale of Kashmeer, in Northern India, there descended one day from the clear heavens a mile-long seed, flashing like a huge meteor, and terrifying the superstitious Asian peoples, who saw in its fall the portent of some tremendous disaster. The seed rooted itself in this valley; and before its true nature had been ascertained, the supposed meteorite began to sprout and send forth on all sides a multitude of mammoth tendrils which burst immediately into leaf. It covered both the southward plains and the eternal snows and rock of the Hindu Kush and Himalayas with their gigantic verdure.

Soon the Afghan mountaineers could hear the explosion of its leaf-buds amid their passes, echoing like distant thunder; and, at the same time, it rushed like a Juggernaut upon Central India. Spreading in all directions, and growing with the speed of express-trains, the tendrils of the mighty vine proceeded to enmesh the Asian realms. Overshadowing vales, peaks, hills, plateaus, deserts, cities and sea-boards with its titan leaves, it invaded Europe and Africa; and then, bridging the Bering Straits, it entered North America and ran southward, ramifying on all sides till the whole continent, and also South America even to Tierra de Fuego, had been buried beneath the masses of insuperable foliage.

Frantic efforts to stay the progress of the plant were made by armies with bombs and cannons, with lethal sprays and gases; but all in vain. Everywhere humanity was smothered beneath the vast leaves, like those of some omnipresent upas, which emitted a stupefying and narcotic odor that conferred upon all who inhaled it a swift euthanasia.

Soon the plant had netted the whole globe; for the seas offered little or no barrier to its full-grown stems and tendrils. When the process of growth was complete, the anti-Martian moiety of the human race had joined the uncouth monsters of pre-historic time in that limbo of oblivion to which all superseded and out-dated genera have gone. But, through the divine clemency of the plant-lord, the final death that overtook the "die-hards" was no less easy than irresistible.

Stilton and a few of his associates contrived to evade the general doom for awhile by fleeing in a rocket-ship to the Antarctic plateau. Here, as they were congratulating themselves on their escape, they saw far-off on the horizon the rearing of the swift stems, beneath whose foliage the ice and snow appeared to melt away in rushing torrents. These torrents soon became a diluvial sea, in which the last dogmatists were drowned. Only in this way did they elude the euthanasia of the great leaves, which had overtaken all their fellows.

THE VAULTS OF YOH-VOMBIS

Preface

As an interne in the terrestrial hospital at Ignarh, I had charge of the singular case of Rodney Severn, the one surviving member of the Octave Expedition to Yoh-Vombis, and took down the following story from his dictation. Severn had been brought to the hospital by the Martian guides of the Expedition. He was suffering from a horribly lacerated and inflamed condition of the scalp and brow, and was wildly delirious part of the time and had to be held down in his bed during recurrent seizures of a mania whose violence was doubly inexplicable in view of his extreme debility.

The lacerations, as will be learned from the story, were mainly self-inflicted. They were mingled with numerous small round wounds, easily distinguished from the knife-slashes, and arranged in regular circles, through which an unknown poison had been injected into Severn's scalp. The causation of these wounds was difficult to explain; unless one were to believe that Severn's story was true, and was no mere figment of his illness. Speaking for myself, in the light of what afterwards occurred, I feel that I have no other recourse than to believe it. There are strange things on the red planet; and I can only second the wish that was expressed by the doomed archaeologist in regard to future explorations.

The night after he finished telling me his story, while another doctor than myself was supposedly on duty, Severn managed to escape from the hospital, doubtless in one of the strange seizures at which I have hinted: a most astonishing thing, for he had seemed weaker than ever after the long strain of his terrible narrative, and his demise had been hourly expected. More astonishing still, his bare footsteps were found in the desert, going toward Yoh-Vombis, till they vanished in the path of a light sandstorm; but no trace of Severn himself has yet been discovered.

The Narrative of Rodney Severn

If the doctors are correct in their prognostication, I have only a few Martian hours of life remaining to me. In those hours I shall endeavor to relate, as a warning to others who might follow in our footsteps, the singular and frightful happenings that terminated our researches among the ruins of Yoh-Vombis. Somehow, even in my extremity, I shall contrive to tell the story; since there is no one else to do it. But the telling will be toilsome and broken; and after I am done, the madness will recur, and several men will restrain me, lest I should leave the hospital and return across many desert leagues to those abominable vaults beneath the compulsion of the malignant and malevolent virus which is permeating my brain. Perhaps death will release me from that abhorrent control, which would urge me down to bottomless underworld warrens of terror for which the saner planets of the solar system can have no analogue. I say *perhaps*... for, remembering what I have seen, I am not sure that even death will end my bondage....

There were eight of us, professional archaeologists with more or less terrene and interplanetary experience, who set forth with native guides from Ignarh, the commercial metropolis of Mars, to inspect that ancient, aeon-deserted city. Allan Octave, our official leader, held his primacy by virtue of knowing more about Martian archaeology than any other Terrestrial on the planet; and others of the party, such as William Harper and Jonas Halgren, had been associated with him in many of his previous researches. I, Rodney Severn, was more of a newcomer, having spent but a few months on Mars; and the greater part of my own ultra-terrene delvings had been confined to Venus.

I had often heard of Yoh-Vombis, in a vague and legendary sort of manner, and never at first hand. Even the ubiquitous Octave had never seen it. Builded by an extinct people whose history has been lost in the latter, decadent eras of the planet, it remains a dim and fascinating riddle whose solution has never been approached... and which, I trust, may endure forevermore unsolved by man. Certainly I hope that no one will ever follow in our steps....

Contrary to the impression we had received from Martian stories, we found that the semi-fabulous ruins lay at no great distance from Ignarh with its terrestrial colony and consulates. The nude, spongy-chested natives had spoken deterringly of vast deserts filled with ever-swirling sand-storms, through which we must pass to reach Yoh-Vombis; and in spite of our munificent offers of payment, it had been difficult to secure guides for the journey. We had provisioned ourselves amply and had prepared for all emergencies that might eventuate during a long trip. Therefore, we were pleased as well as surprised when we came to the ruins after seven hours of plodding across the flat, treeless, orange-yellow desolation to the south-west of Ignarh. On account of the lesser gravity, the journey was far less tiring than one who is unfamiliar with Martian conditions might expect. But because of the thin, Himalaya-like air, and the possible strain on our hearts, we had been careful not to hasten.

Our coming to Yoh-Vombis was sudden and spectacular. Climbing the low slope of a league-long elevation of bare and deeply eroded stone, we saw before us the shattered walls of our destination, whose highest tower was notching the small, remote sun that glared in stifled crimson through the floating haze of fine sand. For a little, we thought that the domeless, three-angled towers and broken-down monoliths were those of some unlegended city, other than the one we sought. But the disposition of the ruins, which lay in a sort of arc for almost the entire extent of the low and gneissic elevation, together with the type of architecture, soon convinced us that we had found our goal. No other ancient city on Mars had been laid out in that manner; and the strange, many-terraced buttresses of the thick walls, like the stairways of forgotten Anakim, were peculiar to the prehistoric race that had built Yoh-Vombis. Moreover, Yoh-Vombis was the one remaining example of this architecture, aside from a few fragments in the neighborhood of Ignarh, which we had previously examined.

I have seen the hoary, sky-confronting walls of Macchu Pichu amid the desolate Andes, and the teocallis that are buried in the Mexican jungles. And I have seen the frozen, giant-builded battlements of Uogam on the glacial tundras of the nightward hemisphere of Venus. But these were as things of yesteryear, bearing at least the memory or the intimation of life, compared with the awesome and lethiferous antiquity, the cycle-enduring doom of a petrified sterility, that seemed to invest Yoh-Vombis. The whole region was far from the life-giving canals beyond whose environs even the more noxious flora and fauna are seldom found; and we had seen no living thing since our departure from Ignarh. But here, in this place of eternal bareness and solitude, it seemed that life could never have been. The stark, eroded stones were things that might have been reared by the toil of the dead, to house the monstrous ghouls and demons of primal desolation.

I think we all received the same impression as we stood staring in silence while the pale, sanies-like sunset fell on the dark and megalithic ruins. I remember gasping a little, in an air that seemed to have been touched by the irrespirable chill of death; and I heard the same sharp, laborious intake of breath from others of our party.

"That place is deader than an Egyptian morgue," observed Harper.

"Certainly it is far more ancient," Octave assented. "According to the most reliable legends, the Yorhis, who built Yoh-Vombis, were wiped out by the present ruling race at least forty thousand years ago."

"There's a story, isn't there," said Harper, "that the last remnant of the Yorhis was destroyed by some unknown agency—something too horrible and outré to be mentioned even in a myth?"

"Of course, I've heard that legend," agreed Octave. "Maybe we'll find evidence among the ruins, to prove or disprove it. The Yorhis may have been cleaned out by some terrible epidemic, such as the Yashta pestilence, which was a kind of green mould that ate all the bones of the body, starting with the teeth and nails. But we needn't be afraid of getting it, if there are any mummies in Yoh-Vombis—the bacteria will all be dead as their victims, after so many cycles of planetary desiccation. Anyway, there ought to be a lot for us to learn. The Aihais have always been more or less shy of the place. Few have ever visited it: and none, as far as I can find, have made a thorough examination of the ruins."

The sun had gone down with uncanny swiftness, as if it had disappeared through some sort of prestigitation rather than the normal process of setting. We felt the instant chill of the blue-green twilight: and the ether above us was like a huge, transparent dome of sunless ice, shot with a million bleak sparklings that were the stars. We donned the coats and helmets of Martian fur, which must always be worn at night; and going on to westward of the walls, we established our camp in their lee, so that we might be sheltered a little from the *jaar*, that cruel desert wind that always blows from the east before dawn. Then, lighting the alcohol lamps that had been brought along for cooking purposes, we huddled around them while the evening meal was prepared and eaten.

Afterwards, for comfort rather than because of weariness, we retired early to our sleeping-bags; and the two Aihais, our guides, wrapped themselves in the cerement-like folds of grey *bassa*-cloth which are all the protection their leathery skins appear to require even in sub-zero temperatures.

Even in my thick, double-lined bag, I still felt the rigor of the night air; and I am sure it was this, rather than anything else, which kept me awake for a long while and rendered my eventual slumber somewhat restless and broken. Of course, the strangeness of our situation, and the weird proximity of those aeonian walls and towers may in some measure have contributed to my unrest. But at any rate, I was not troubled by even the least presentiment of alarm or danger; and I should have laughed at the idea that anything of peril could lurk in Yoh-Vombis, amid whose undreamable and stupefying antiquities the very phantoms of its dead must long since have faded into nothingness.

I remember little, however, except the feeling of interminable duration that often marks a shallow and interrupted sleep. I recall the marrow-piercing wind that moaned above us toward midnight, and the sand that stung my face like a fine hail as it passed, blowing from desert to immemorial desert; and I recall the still, inflexible stars that grew dim for awhile with that fleeing ancient dust. Then the wind went by; and I drowsed again, with starts of semi-wakefulness. At last, in one of these, I knew vaguely that the small twin moons, Phobos and Deimos, had risen and were making huge and spectral shadows with the ruins and were casting an ashen glimmer on the shrouded forms of my companions.

I must have been half-asleep; for the memory of that which I saw is doubtful as any dream. I watched beneath drooping lids the tiny moons that had topped the domeless triangular towers; and I saw the far-flung shadows that almost touched the bodies of my fellow-archaeologists.

The whole scene was locked in a petrific stillness; and none of the sleepers stirred. Then, as my lids were about to close, I received an impression of movement in the frozen gloom; and it seemed to me that a portion of the foremost shadow had detached itself and was crawling toward Octave, who lay nearer to the ruins than we others.

Even through my heavy lethargy, I was disturbed by a warning of something unnatural and perhaps ominous. I started to sit up; and even as I moved, the shadowy object, whatever it was, drew back and became merged once more in the greater shadow. Its vanishment startled me into full wakefulness; and yet I could not be sure that I had actually seen the thing. In that brief, final glimpse, it had seemed like a roughly circular piece of cloth or leather, dark and crumpled, and twelve or fourteen inches in diameter, that ran along the ground with the doubling movement of an inch-worm, causing it to fold and unfold in a startling manner as it went.

I did not go to sleep again for nearly an hour; and if it had not been for the extreme cold, I should doubtless have gotten up to investigate and make sure whether I had really beheld an object of such bizarre nature or had merely dreamt it. I lay staring at the deep ebon shadow in which it had disappeared, while a series of fanciful wonderings followed each other in antic procession through my mind. Even then, though somewhat perturbed, I was not aware of any actual fear or intuition of possible menace. And more and more I began to convince myself that the thing was too unlikely and fantastical to have been anything but the figment of a dream. And at last I nodded off into light slumber.

The chill, demoniac sighing of the *jaar* across the jagged walls awoke me, and I saw that the faint moonlight had received the hueless accession of early dawn. We all arose, and prepared our breakfast with fingers that grew numb in spite of the spirit-lamps. Then, shivering, we ate, while the sun leapt over the horizon like a juggler's ball. Enormous, gaunt, without gradations of shadow or luminosity, the ruins beetled before us in the thin light, like the mausolea of primordial giants, that abide from darkness-eaten aeons to confront the last dawn of an expiring orb.

My queer visual experience during the night had taken on more than ever a fantasmagoric unreality; and I gave it no more than a passing thought and did not speak of it to the others. But, even as the faint, distorted shadows of slumber often tinge one's waking hours, it may have contributed to the nameless mood in which I found myself: a mood in which I felt the unhuman alienage of our surroundings and the black, fathomless antiquity of the ruins like an almost unbearable oppression. The feeling seemed to be made of a million spectral adumbrations that oozed unseen but palpable from the great, unearthly architecture; that weighed upon me like tomb-born incubi, but were void of form and meaning such as could be comprehended by human thought. I appeared to move, not in the open air, but in the smothering gloom of sealed sepulchral vaults; to choke with a death-fraught atmosphere, with the miasmata of aeon-old corruption.

My companions were all eager to explore the ruins; and of course it was impossible for me to even mention the apparently absurd and baseless shadows of my mood. Human beings on other worlds than their own are often subject to nervous and psychic symptoms of this sort, engendered by the unfamiliar forces, the novel radiations of their environment. But, as we approached the buildings in our preliminary tour of examination, I lagged behind the others, seized by a paralyzing panic that left me unable to move or breathe for a few moments. A dark, freezing clamminess seemed to pervade my brain and muscles and suspend their inmost working. Then it lifted; and I was free to go on and follow the others.

Strangely, as it seemed, the two Martians refused to accompany us. Stolid and taciturn, they gave no explicit reason; but evidently nothing would induce them to enter Yoh-Vombis. Whether or not they were afraid of the ruins, we were unable to determine: their enigmatic faces, with the small oblique eyes and huge, flaring nostrils, betrayed neither fear nor any other emotion intelligible to man. In reply to our questions, they merely said that no Aihai had set foot among the ruins for ages. Apparently there was some mysterious tabu in connection with the place.

For equipment in that preliminary tour, we took along only a crowbar and two picks. Our other tools, and some cartridges of high explosives, we left at our camp, to be used later if necessary, after we had surveyed the ground. One or two of us owned automatics: but these also were left behind; for it seemed absurd to imagine that any form of life would be encountered among the ruins.

Octave was visibly excited as we began our inspection, and maintained a running-fire of exclamatory comment. The rest of us were subdued and silent; and I think that my own feeling, in a measure, was shared by many of the others. It was impossible to shake off the somber awe and wonder that fell upon us from those megalithic stones.

I have no time to describe the ruins minutely, but must hasten on with my story. There is much that I could not describe anyway; for the main area of the city was destined to remain unexplored.

We went on for some distance among the triangular, terraced buildings, following the zig-zag streets that conformed to this peculiar architecture. Most of the towers were more or less dilapidated; and everywhere we saw the deep erosion wrought by cycles of blowing wind and sand, which, in many cases, had worn into roundness the sharp angles of the mighty walls. We entered some of the towers through high, narrow doorways, but found utter emptiness within. Whatever they had contained in the way of furnishings must long ago have crumbled into dust; and the dust had been blown away by the searching desert gales. On some of the outer walls, there was evidence of carving or lettering; but all of it was so worn down and obliterated by time that we could trace only a few fragmentary outlines, of which we could make nothing.

At length we came to a wide thoroughfare, which ended in the wall of a vast terrace, several hundred yards long by perhaps forty in height, on which the central buildings were grouped like a sort of citadel or acropolis. A flight of broken steps, designed for longer limbs than those of men or even the gangling modern Martians, afforded access to the terrace, which had seemingly been hewn from the plateau itself.

Pausing, we decided to defer our investigation of the higher buildings, which, being more exposed than the others, were doubly ruinous and dilapidated, and in all likelihood would offer little for our trouble. Octave had begun to voice his disappointment over our failure to find anything in the nature of artifacts or carvings that would throw light on the history of Yoh-Vombis.

Then, a little to the right of the stairway, we perceived an entrance in the main wall, half-choked with ancient debris. Behind the heap of detritus, we found the beginning of a downward flight of steps. Darkness poured from the opening like a visible flood, noisome and musty with primordial stagnancies of decay; and we could see nothing below the first steps, which gave the appearance of being suspended over a black gulf.

O ctave and myself and several others had brought along electric torches, in case we should need them in our explorations. It had occurred to us that there might be subterranean vaults or catacombs in Yoh-Vombis, even as in the latter-day cities of Mars, which are often more extensive underground than above; and such vaults would be the likeliest place in which to look for vestiges of the Yorhi civilization.

Throwing his torch-beam into the abyss, Octave began to descend the stairs. His eager voice called us to follow.

Again, for an instant, the unknown, irrational panic froze my faculties, and I hesitated while the others pressed forward behind me. Then, as before, the terror passed; and I wondered at myself for being overcome by anything so absurd and unfounded. I followed Octave down the steps, and the others came trooping after me.

At the bottom of the high, awkward steps, we found ourselves in a long and roomy vault, like a subterranean hallway. Its floor was deep with siftings of immemorial dust; and in places there were heaps of a coarse grey powder, such as might be left by the decomposition of certain fungi that grow in the Martian catacombs, under the canals. Such fungi, at one time, might conceivably have existed in Yoh-Vombis; but, owing to the prolonged and excessive dehydration, they must have died out long ago. Nothing, surely, not even a fungus, could have lived in those arid vaults for many aeons past.

The air was singularly heavy, as if the lees of an ancient atmosphere, less tenuous than that of Mars today, had settled down and remained in that stagnant darkness. It was harder to breathe than the outer air; it was filled with unknown effluvia; and the light dust arose before us at every step, diffusing a faintness of bygone corruption, like the dust of powdered mummies.

At the end of the vault, before a strait and lofty doorway our torches revealed an immense shallow urn or pan, supported on short cube-shaped legs, and wrought from a dull blackish-green material which suggested some bizarre alloy of metal and porcelain. The thing was about four feet across, with a thick rim adorned by writhing indecipherable figures, deeply etched as if by acid. In the bottom of the bowl we perceived a deposit of dark and cinder-like fragments, which gave off a slight but disagreeable pungence, like the phantom of some more powerful odor. Octave, bending over the rim began to cough and sneeze as he inhaled it.

"That stuff, whatever it was, must have been a pretty strong fumigant," he observed. "The people of Yoh-Vombis may have used it to disinfect the vaults."

The doorway beyond the shallow urn admitted us to a larger chamber, whose floor was comparatively free of dust. We found that the dark stone beneath our feet was marked off in multiform geometric patterns, traced with ochreous ore, amid which, as in Egyptian cartouches, hieroglyphics and highly formalized drawings were enclosed. We could make little from most of them; but the figures in many were doubtless designed to represent the Yorhis themselves. Like the Aihais, they were tall and angular, with great bellows-like chests; and they were depicted as possessing a supplementary third arm, which issued from the bosom; a characteristic which, in vestigial form, sometimes occurs among the Aihais. The ears and nostrils, as far as we could judge, were not so huge and flaring as those of the modern Martians. All of these Yorhis were represented as being nude; but in one of the cartouches, done in a far hastier style than the others, we perceived two figures whose high, conical craniums were wrapped in what seemed to be a sort of turban, which they were about to remove or adjust. The artist seemed to have laid a peculiar emphasis on the odd gesture with which the sinuous, four-jointed fingers were plucking at these head-dresses; and the whole posture was unexplainably contorted.

From the second vault, passages ramified in all directions, leading to a veritable warren of catacombs. Here, enormous pot-bellied urns of the same material as the fumigating-pan, but taller than a man's head and fitted with angular-handled stoppers, were ranged in solemn rows along the walls, leaving scant room for two of us to walk abreast. When we succeeded in removing one of the huge stoppers, we saw that the jar was filled to the rim with ashes and charred fragments of bone. Doubtless (as is still the Martian custom) the Yorhis had stored the cremated remains of whole families in single urns.

Even Octave became silent as we went on; and a sort of meditative awe seemed to replace his former excitement. We others, I think, were utterly weighed down to a man by the solid gloom of a concept-defying antiquity, into which it seemed that we were going further and further at every step.

The shadows fluttered before us like the monstrous and misshapen wings of phantom bats. There was nothing anywhere but the atom-like dust of ages, and the jars that held the ashes of a long-extinct people. But, clinging to the high roof in one of the further vaults, I saw a dark and corrugated patch of circular form, like a withered fungus. It was impossible to reach the thing; and we went on after peering at it with many futile conjectures. Oddly enough, I failed to remember at that moment the crumpled, shadowy object I had seen or dreamt the night before.

I have no idea how far we had gone, when we came to the last vault; but it seemed that we had been wandering for ages in that forgotten underworld. The air was growing fouler and more irrespirable, with a thick, sodden quality, as if from a sediment of material rottenness; and we had about decided to turn back. Then, without warning, at the end of a long, urn-lined catacomb, we found ourselves confronted by a blank wall.

Here, we came upon one of the strangest and most mystifying of our discoveries—a mummified and incredibly desiccated figure, standing erect against the wall. It was more than seven feet in height, of a brown, bituminous color, and was wholly nude except for a sort of black cowl that covered the upper head and drooped down at the sides in wrinkled folds. From the three arms, and general contour, it was plainly one of the ancient Yorhis—perhaps the sole member of this race whose body had remained intact.

We all felt an inexpressible thrill at the sheer age of this shrivelled thing, which, in the dry air of the vault, had endured through all the historic and geologic vicissitudes of the planet, to provide a visible link with lost cycles.

Then, as we peered closer with our torches, we saw *why* the mummy had maintained an upright position. At ankles, knees, waist, shoulders and neck it was shackled to the wall by heavy metal bands, so deeply eaten and embrowned with a sort of rust that we had failed to distinguish them at first sight in the shadow. The strange cowl on the head, when closelier studied, continued to baffle us. It was covered with a fine, mould-like pile, unclean and dusty as ancient cobwebs. Something about it, I know not what, was abhorrent and revolting.

"By Jove! this is a real find!" ejaculated Octave, as he thrust his torch into the mummified face, where shadows moved like living things in the pit-deep hollows of the eyes and the huge triple nostrils and wide ears that flared upward beneath the cowl.

Still lifting the torch, he put out his free hand and touched the body very lightly. Tentative as the touch had been, the lower part of the barrel-like torso, the legs, the hands and forearms all seemed to dissolve into powder, leaving the head and upper body and arms still hanging in their metal fetters. The progress of decay had been queerly unequal, for the remnant portions gave no sign of disintegration.

Octave cried out in dismay, and then began to cough and sneeze, as the cloud of brown powder, floating with airy lightness, enveloped him. We others all stepped back to avoid the powder. Then, above the spreading cloud, I saw an unbelievable thing. The black cowl on the mummy's head began to curl and twitch upward at the corners, it writhed with a verminous motion, it fell from the withered cranium, seeming to fold and unfold convulsively in mid-air as it fell. Then it dropped on the bare head of Octave who, in his disconcertment at the crumbling of the mummy, had remained standing close to the wall. At that instant, in a start of profound terror, I remembered the thing that had inched itself from the shadows of Yoh-Vombis in the light of the twin moons, and had drawn back like a figment of slumber at my first waking movement.

Cleaving closely as a tightened cloth, the thing enfolded Octave's hair and brow and eyes, and he shrieked wildly, with incoherent pleas for help, and tore with frantic fingers at the cowl, but failed to loosen it. Then his cries began to mount in a mad crescendo of agony, as if beneath some instrument of infernal torture; and he danced and capered blindly about the vault, eluding us with strange celerity as we all sprang forward in an effort to reach him and release him from his weird incumbrance. The whole happening was mysterious as a nightmare; but the thing that had fallen on his head was plainly some unclassified form of Martian life, which, contrary to all the known laws of science, had survived in those primordial catacombs. We must rescue him from its clutches if we could.

We tried to close in on the frenzied figure of our chief—which, in the far from roomy space between the last urns and the wall, should have been an easy matter. But, darting away, in a manner doubly incomprehensible because of his blindfolded condition, he circled about us and ran past, to disappear among the urns toward the outer labyrinth of intersecting catacombs.

"My God! What has happened to him?" cried Harper. "The man acts as if he were possessed."

There was obviously no time for a discussion of the enigma, and we all followed Octave as speedily as our astonishment would permit. We had lost sight of him in the darkness, and when we came to the first division of the vaults, we were doubtful as to which passage he had taken, till we heard a shrill scream, several times repeated, in a catacomb on the extreme left. There was a weird, unearthly quality in those screams, which may have been due to the long-stagnant air or the peculiar acoustics of the ramifying caverns. But somehow I could not imagine them as issuing from human lips—at least not from those of a living man. They seemed to contain a soulless, mechanical agony, as if they had been wrung from a devil-driven corpse.

Thrusting our torches before us into the lurching, fleeing shadows, we raced along between rows of mighty urns. The screaming had died away in sepulchral silence; but far off we heard the light and muffled thud of running feet. We followed in headlong pursuit; but, gasping painfully in the vitiated, miasmal air, we were soon compelled to slacken our pace without coming in sight of Octave. Very faintly, and further away than ever, like the tomb-swallowed steps of a phantom, we heard his vanishing footfalls. Then they ceased; and we heard nothing, except our own convulsive breathing, and the blood that throbbed in our temple-veins like steadily beaten drums of alarm.

We went on, dividing our party into three contingents when we came to a triple branching of the caverns. Harper and Halgren and myself took the middle passage; and after we had gone on for an endless interval without finding any trace of Octave, and had threaded our way through recesses piled to the roof with colossal urns that must have held the ashes of a hundred generations, we came out in the huge chamber with the geometric floor-designs. Here, very shortly, we were joined by the others, who had likewise failed to locate our missing leader.

It would be useless to detail our renewed and hour-long search of the myriad vaults, many of which we had not hitherto explored. All were empty, as far as any sign of life was concerned. I remember passing once more through the vault in which I had seen the dark, rounded patch on the ceiling, and noting with a shudder that the patch was gone. It was a miracle that we did not lose ourselves in that underworld maze; but at last we came back to the final catacomb in which we had found the shackled mummy.

We heard a measured and recurrent clangor as we neared the place—a most alarming and mystifying sound under the circumstances. It was like the hammering of ghouls on some forgotten mausoleum. When we drew nearer, the beams of our torches revealed a sight that was no less unexplainable than unexpected. A human figure, with its back toward us and the head concealed by a swollen black object that had the size and form of a sofa cushion, was standing near the remains of the mummy and was striking at the wall with a pointed metal bar. How long Octave had been there, and where he had found the bar, we could not know. But the blank wall had crumbled away beneath his furious blows, leaving on the floor a pile of cement-like fragments; and a small, narrow door, of the same ambiguous material as the cinerary urns and the fumigating-pan, had been laid bare.

Amazed, uncertain, inexpressibly bewildered, we were all incapable of action or volition at that moment. The whole business was too fantastic and too horrifying, and it was plain that Octave had been overcome by some sort of madness. I, for one, felt the violent upsurge of sudden nausea when I had identified the loathsomely bloated thing that clung to Octave's head and drooped in obscene tumescence on his neck. I did not dare to surmise the causation of its bloating.

Before any of us could recover our faculties, Octave flung aside the metal bar and began to fumble for something in the wall. It must have been a hidden spring; though how he could have known its location or existence is beyond all legitimate conjecture. With a dull, hideous grating, the uncovered door swung inward, thick and ponderous as a mausolean slab, leaving an aperture from which the nether midnight seemed to well like a flood of aeon-buried foulness. Somehow, at that instant, our electric torches appeared to flicker and grow dim; and we all breathed a suffocating fetor, like a draft from inner worlds of immemorial putrescence.

Octave had turned toward us now, and he stood in an idle posture before the open door, like one who has finished some ordained task. I was the first of our party to throw off the paralyzing spell; and pulling out a clasp-knife—the only semblance of a weapon which I carried—I ran over to him. He moved back, but not quickly enough to evade me, when I stabbed with the four-inch blade at the black, turgescent mass that enveloped his whole upper head and hung down upon his eyes.

What the thing was, I should prefer not to imagine—if it were possible to imagine. It was formless as a great slug, with neither head nor tail nor apparent organs—an unclean, puffy, leathery thing, covered with that fine, mould-like fur of which I have spoken. The knife tore into it as if through rotten parchment, making a long gash, and the horror appeared to collapse like a broken bladder. Out of it there gushed a sickening torrent of human blood, mingled with dark, filiated masses that may have been half-dissolved hair, and floating gelatinous lumps like molten bone, and shreds of a curdy white substance. At the same time, Octave began to stagger, and went down at full length on the floor. Disturbed by his fall, the mummy-dust arose about him in a curling cloud, beneath which he lay mortally still.

Conquering my revulsion, and choking with the dust, I bent over him and tore the flaccid, oozing horror from his head. It came with unexpected ease, as if I had removed a limp rag: but I wish to God that I had let it remain. Beneath, there was no longer a human cranium, for all had been eaten away, even to the eyebrows, and the half-devoured brain was laid bare as I lifted the cowl-like object. I dropped the unnamable thing from fingers that had grown suddenly nerveless, and it turned over as it fell, revealing on the nether side many rows of pinkish suckers, arranged in circles about a pallid disk that was covered with nerve-like filaments, suggesting a sort of plexus.

My companions had pressed forward behind me; but, for an appreciable interval, no one spoke.

"How long do you suppose he has been dead?" It was Halgren who whispered the awful question, which we had all been asking ourselves. Apparently no one felt able or willing to answer it; and we could only stare in horrible, timeless fascination at Octave.

At length I made an effort to avert my gaze; and turning at random, I saw the remnants of the shackled mummy, and noted for the first time, with mechanical, unreal horror, the half-eaten condition of the withered head. From this, my gaze was diverted to the newly opened door at one side, without perceiving for a moment what had drawn my attention. Then, startled, I beheld beneath my torch, far down beyond the door, as if in some nether pit, a seething, multitudinous, worm-like movement of crawling shadows. They seemed to boil up in the darkness; and then, over the broad threshold of the vault, there poured the verminous vanguard of a countless army: things that were kindred to the monstrous, diabolic leech I had torn from Octave's eaten head. Some were thin and flat, like writhing, doubling disks of cloth or leather, and others were more or less poddy, and crawled with glutted slowness. What they had found to feed on in the sealed, eternal midnight I do not know; and I pray that I never shall know.

I sprang back and away from them, electrified with terror, sick with loathing, and the black army inched itself unendingly with nightmare swiftness from the unsealed abyss, like the nauseous vomit of horror-sated hells. As it poured toward us, burying Octave's body from sight in a writhing wave, I saw a stir of life from the seemingly dead thing I had cast aside, and saw the loathly struggle which it made to right itself and join the others.

But neither I nor my companions could endure to look longer. We turned and ran between the mighty rows of urns, with the slithering mass of demon leeches close upon us, and scattered in blind panic when we came to the first division of the vaults. Heedless of each other or of anything but the urgency of flight, we plunged into the ramifying passages at random. Behind me, I heard someone stumble and go down, with a curse that mounted to an insane shrieking; but I knew that if I halted and went back, it would be only to invite the same baleful doom that had overtaken the hindmost of our party.

Still clutching the electric torch and my open clasp-knife, I ran along a minor passage which, I seemed to remember, would conduct with more or less directness upon the large outer vault with the painted floor. Here I found myself alone. The others had kept to the main catacombs; and I heard far off a muffled babel of mad cries, as if several of them had been seized by their pursuers.

It seemed that I must have been mistaken about the direction of the passage; for it turned and twisted in an unfamiliar manner, with many intersections, and I soon found that I was lost in the black labyrinth, where the dust had lain unstirred by living feet for inestimable generations. The cinerary warren had grown still once more; and I heard my own frenzied panting, loud and stertorous as that of a Titan in the dead silence.

Suddenly, as I went on, my torch disclosed a human figure coming toward me in the gloom. Before I could master my startlement, the figure had passed me with long, machine-like strides, as if returning to the inner vaults. I think it was Harper, since the height and build were about right for him; but I am not altogether sure, for the eyes and upper head were muffled by a dark, inflated cowl, and the pale lips locked as if in a silence of tetanic torture—or death. Whoever he was, he had dropped his torch; and he was running blindfold, in utter darkness, beneath the impulsion of that unearthly vampirism, to seek the very fountain-head of the unloosed horror. I knew that he was beyond human help; and I did not even dream of trying to stop him.

Trembling violently, I resumed my flight, and was passed by two more of our party, stalking by with mechanical swiftness and sureness, and cowled with those Satanic leeches. The others must have returned by way of the main passages; for I did not meet them; and was never to see them again.

The remainder of my flight is a blur of pandemonian terror. Once more, after thinking that I was near the outer cavern, I found myself astray, and fled through a ranged eternity of monstrous urns, in vaults that must have extended for an unknown distance beyond our explorations. It seemed that I had gone on for years; and my lungs were choking with the aeon-dead air, and my legs were ready to crumble beneath me, when I saw far off a tiny point of blessed daylight. I ran toward it, with all the terrors of the alien darkness crowding behind me, and accursed shadows flittering before, and saw that the vault ended in a low, ruinous entrance, littered by rubble on which there fell an arc of thin sunshine.

It was another entrance than the one by which we had penetrated this lethal underworld. I was within a dozen feet of the opening when, without sound or other intimation, something dropped upon my head from the roof above, blinding me instantly and closing upon me like a tautened net. My brow and scalp, at the same time, were shot through with a million needle-like pangs—a manifold, ever-growing agony that seemed to pierce the very bone and converge from all sides upon my inmost brain.

The terror and suffering of that moment were worse than aught which the hells of earthly madness or delirium could ever contain. I felt the foul, vampiric clutch of an atrocious death—and of more than death.

I believe that I dropped the torch: but the fingers of my right hand had still retained the open knife. Instinctively—since I was hardly capable of conscious volition—I raised the knife and slashed blindly, again and again, many times, at the thing that had fastened its deadly folds upon me. The blade must have gone through and through the clinging monstrosity, to gash my own flesh in a score of places; but I did not feel the pain of those wounds in the million-throbbing torment that possessed me.

At last I saw light, and saw that a black strip, loosened from above my eyes and dripping with my own blood, was hanging down my cheek. It writhed a little, even as it hung, and I ripped it away, and ripped the other remnants of the thing, tatter by oozing, bloody tatter, from off my brow and head. Then I staggered toward the entrance; and the wan light turned to a far, receding, dancing flame before me as I lurched and fell outside the cavern—a flame that fled like the last star of creation above the yawning, sliding chaos and oblivion into which I descended....

I am told that my unconsciousness was of brief duration. I came to myself, with the cryptic faces of the two Martian guides bending over me. My head was full of lancinating pains, and half-remembered terrors closed upon my mind like the shadows of mustering harpies. I rolled over, and looked back toward the cavern-mouth, from which the Martians, after finding me, had seemingly dragged me for some little distance. The mouth was under the terraced angle of an outer building, and within sight of our camp.

I stared at the black opening with hideous fascination, and descried a shadowy stirring in the gloom—the writhing, verminous movement of things that pressed forward from the darkness but did not emerge into the light. Doubtless they could not endure the sun, those creatures of ultramundane night and cycle-sealed corruption.

It was then that the ultimate horror, the beginning madness, came upon me. Amid my crawling revulsion, my nausea-prompted desire to flee from that seething cavern-mouth, there rose an abhorrently conflicting impulse to return; to thread my backward way through all the catacombs, as the others had done; to go down where never men save they, the inconceivably doomed and accursed, had ever gone; to seek beneath that damnable compulsion a nether world that human thought can never picture. There was a black light, a soundless calling, in the vaults of my brain: the implanted summons of the Thing, like a permeating and sorcerous poison. It lured me to the subterranean door that was walled up by the dying people of Yoh-Vombis, to immure those hellish and immortal leeches, those dark parasites that engraft their own abominable life on the half-eaten brains of the dead. It called me to the depths beyond, where dwell the noisome, necromantic Ones, of whom the leeches, with all their powers of vampirism and diabolism, are but the merest minions....

It was only the two Aihais who prevented me from going back. I struggled, I fought them insanely as they strove to retard me with their spongy arms; but I must have been pretty thoroughly exhausted from all the superhuman adventures of the day; and I went down once more, after a little, into fathomless nothingness, from which I floated out at long intervals, to realize that I was being carried across the desert toward Ignarh.

Well, that is all my story. I have tried to tell it fully and coherently, at a cost that would be unimaginable to the sane... to tell it before the madness falls upon me again, as it will very soon—as it is doing now.... Yes, I have told my story... and you have written it all out, haven't you? Now I must go back to Yoh-Vombis—back across the desert and down through all the catacombs to the vaster vaults beneath. Something is in my brain, that commands me and will direct me... I tell you, I must go....

The Eternal World

C hristopher Chandon went to his laboratory window for a last look at the mountain solitude about him, which, in all likelihood, he would never see again. With no faltering of his determination, and yet not wholly without regret, he stared at the rugged gully beneath, where the Gothic shade of firs and hemlocks was threaded by the brawling silver of a tiny stream. He saw the granite-sheeted slope beyond, and the two nearer peaks of the Sierras, whose slaty azure was tipped by the first autumn snow; and saw the pass between them that lay in a line with his apparent route through the space-time continuum.

Then he turned to the strange apparatus whose completion had cost him so many years of toil and experiment. On a raised platform in the center of the room, there stood a large cylinder, not without resemblance to a diving-bell. Its base and lower walls were of metal, its upper half was made wholly of indestructible glass. A hammock, inclined at an angle of forty degrees, was slung between its sides. In this hammock, Chandon meant to lash himself securely, to insure as much protection as would be feasible against the unknown velocities of his proposed flight. Gazing through the clear glass, he could watch with comfort whatever visual phenomena the journey might offer.

The cylinder had been set directly in front of an enormous disk, ten feet in diameter, with a hundred perforations in its silvery surface. Behind it were ranged a series of dynamos, designed for the development of an obscure power, which, for want of a better name, Chandon had called the negative *time-force*. This power he had isolated with infinite labors from the positive energy of time, that fourth-dimensional gravity which causes and controls the rotation of events. The negative power, amplified a thousand-fold by the dynamos, would remove to an incalculable distance in contemporary time

95

and space anything that stood in its path. It would not permit of travel into the past or future, but would cause an instant projection *across* the temporal stream that enfolds the entire cosmos in its endless, equal flowing.

Unfortunately, Chandon had not been able to construct a mobile machine, in which he could travel as in a rocket-ship and perhaps return as to his starting-point. He must plunge boldly and forever into the unknown. But he had furnished the cylinder with an oxygen-apparatus, with electric light and heat, and a month's supply of food and water. Even if his flight should end in empty space, or in some world whose conditions would render human survival impossible, he would at least live long enough to make a thorough observation of his surroundings.

He had a theory, however, that his journey would not terminate in the midst of mere ether; that the cosmic bodies were neuclei of the time-gravity, and that the weakening of the propulsive force would permit the cylinder to be drawn to one of them.

The hazards of his venture were past foreseeing; but he preferred them to the safe, monotonous certitudes of earthly life. He had always chafed beneath a feeling of limitation, had longed only for the unexplored vastnesses. He could not brook the thought of any horizons, other than those which have never been overpassed by man.

With a strange thrilling in his heart, he turned from the alpine landscape and proceeded to lock himself in the cylinder. He had installed a timing-device, which would automatically start the dynamos at a given hour.

Lying in the hammock beneath leather straps that he had buckled about his waist, ankles and shoulders, he still had a minute or so to wait before the turning-on of the power. In those moments, for the first time, there swept upon him in an unleashed flood the full terror and peril of his experiment; and he was almost tempted to unbind himself and leave the cylinder before it was too late. He had all the sensations of one who is about to be blown from a cannon's mouth.

Suspended in a weird silence, from which all sounds had been excluded by the air-tight walls, he resigned himself to the unknown, with many conflicting surmises as to what would occur. He might or might not survive the passage through unfamiliar dimensions, at speed to which the velocity of light would be laggardly. But if he did survive, he might reach the farthest galaxies in a mere flash.

His fears and surmises were terminated by something that came with the suddenness of sleep—or death. Everything seemed to dissolve and vanish in a bright flare; and then there passed before him a swarming, broken panorama, a babel of impressions, ineffably various and multiplied. It seemed to him that he possessed a thousand eyes with which to apprehend in one instant the flowing of many aeons, the passing of countless worlds.

The cylinder seemed no longer to exist; and he did not appear to be moving. But all the systems of time were going by him, and he caught the scraps and fragments of a million scenes: objects, faces, forms, angles, and colors which he recalled later as one recalls the deliriously amplified and distorted visions of certain drugs.

He saw the giant evergreen forests of lichen, the continents of Brobding-nagian grasses, in planets remoter than the systems of Hercules. Before him there passed, like an architectural pageant, the mile-high cities that wear the sumptuous aerial motley of rose and emerald and Tyrian, wrought by the tangent beams of triple suns. He beheld unnamable things in spheres unlisted by astronomers. There crowded upon him the awful and limitless evolution-ary range of transtellar life, the cyclorama of teeming morphologies.

It seemed as if the barriers of his brain had been extended to include the whole of the cosmic flux; that his thought, like the web of some mammoth and divine arachnidan, had woven itself from world to world, from galaxy to galaxy, above the dread gulfs of the infinite continuum.

Then, with the same suddenness that had marked its beginning, the vi-sion came to an end and was replaced by something of a totally different character.

It was only afterwards that Chandon could figure out what had occurred, and divine the nature and laws of the new environment into which he had been projected. At the time (if one can use a word so inaccurate as time) he was wholly incapable of anything but a single contemplative visual impression—the strange world upon which he looked through the clear wall of the cylinder: a world that might have been the dream of some geo-metrician mad with infinity.

It was like some planetary glacier, fretted into shapes of ordered grotes-query, filled with a white, unglittering light, and obeying the laws of other perspectives than those of our own world. The distances on which he gazed were literally interminable; there was no horizon; and yet nothing seemed to dwindle in size or definitude, whatever its remoteness. Part of the impression received by Chandon was that this world arched back upon itself, like the interior surface of a hollow sphere; that the pale vistas returned overhead after they had vanished from his view.

Nearer to him than any other object in the scene, and preserving the same relative distance as in his laboratory, he perceived a large circular section of rough planking—that portion of the laboratory wall which had lain in the path of the negative beam. It hung motionless in air, as if suspended by a field of invisible ice.

The foreground beyond the planking was thronged by innumerable rows of objects that were suggestive both of statues and of crystalloid formations. Wan as marble or alabaster, each of them presented a mélange of simple curves and symmetric angles, which somehow seemed to include the latency of almost endless geometrical development. They were gigantic, with a rudimentary division into head, limbs and body, as if they were living things. Behind them, at indefinite distances, were other forms that might have been the blind buds or frozen blossoms of unknown vegetable growths.

Chandon had no sense of the passing of time as he peered from the cylinder. He could remember nothing, could imagine nothing. He was unaware of his body, or the hammock in which he lay, except as a half-seen image on the rim of vision.

Somehow, in that strange, frozen impression, he felt the inert dynamism of the forms about him: the silent thunder, the unlaunched lightnings, as of cataleptic gods; the atom-folded heat and flame, as of unlit suns. Inscrutably they brooded before him, as they had done from all eternity and would continue to do forever. In this world, there could be no change, no event: all things must preserve the same aspect and the same attitude.

As he realized later, his attempt to change his own position in the time-stream had led to an unforeseen result. He had projected himself *beyond time* into some further cosmos where the very ether, perhaps, was a non-conductor of the time-force, and in which, therefore, the phenomena of temporal sequence were impossible.

The sheer velocity of his flight had lodged him on the verge of this eternity, like some Arctic explorer caught in everlasting ice. There, obedient to the laws of timelessness, he seemed fated to remain. Life, as we know the term, was impossible for him; and yet—since death would involve a time-sequence—it was equally impossible for him to die. He must maintain the position in which he had landed, must hold the breath he had been breathing at the moment of his impact against the eternal. He was fixed in a catalepsy of the senses; in a bright Nirvana of contemplation.

It would seem, according to all logic, that there was no escape from his predicament. However, I must now relate the strangest thing of all; the thing that was seemingly unaccountable; that defied the proven laws of the time-less sphere.

Into the glacial field of Chandon's vision, athwart the horizonless ranks of immutable figures, there came an intruding object; a thing that drifted as if through aeons; that grew upon the scene with the slowness of some millennial coral reef in a crystal sea.

Even from its first appearance, the object was plainly alien to the scene; was obviously, like Chandon's cylinder and the wall-section, of non-eternal origin. It was black and unlustrous, with more than the blackness of infrastellar space or of metals locked from light in the core of planets. It forced itself upon the sight with ultra-material solidity; and yet it seemed to refuse the crystal daylight, to insulate itself from the never-varying splendor.

The thing disclosed itself as a sharp and widening wedge, driven upon the adamantine ether, and forming, by the same violent act of irruption, a new visual image in Chandon's paralytic eyes. In defiance of the mental laws of his surroundings, it caused him to form an idea of duration and movement.

Seen in its entirety, the thing was a large, spindle-shaped vessel, dwarfing Chandon's cylinder like an ocean-liner beside a ship's dinghy. It floated aloof and separate—a seamless mass of unbroken ebon, swelling to an orb-like equator, and dwindling to a point at each end. The form was such as might have been calculated to pierce some obdurate medium.

The substance of which it had been wrought, and its motive power, were destined to remain unknown to Chandon. Perhaps it was driven by some tremendous concentration of the time-force with which he had played so ignorantly and ineptly.

The intruding vessel, wholly stationary, hung now above the rows of statu-esque entities that were foremost in his field of vision. By infinite gradations, a huge circular door seemed to open in its bottom; and from the opening there issued a crane-like arm, of the same black material as the vessel. The arm ended in numerous pendent bars, that somehow gave the idea of finger-like suppleness.

It descended upon the head of one of the strange geometric images; and the myriad bars, bending and stretching with slow but limitless fluidity, wrapped themselves like a net of chains about the crystalloid body. Then the figure was dragged upward as if with herculean effort, and vanished at length, together with the shortening arm, in the vessel's interior.

Again the arm emerged, to repeat the bizarre, impossible abduction, and draw another of the enigmatic things from its everlasting station. And once more the arm descended, and a third entity was taken, like the theft of still another marble god from its marble heaven.

All this was done in profound silence—the immeasurable slowness of motion being muffled by the ether, and creating nothing that Chandon's ear could apprehend as sound.

After the third disappearance with its strange prey, the arm returned, extending itself diagonally and to greater length than before, till the black fingers barred the glass of Chandon's cylinder and closed upon it with their irresistible clutch.

He was scarcely aware of any movement; but it seemed to him that the ranks of white figures, the unhorizoned and never-dwindling vistas, were sinking slowly from his ken, like a foundering world. He saw the ebon bulk of the great vessel, toward which he was drawn by the shortening arm, till it filled his entire vision. Then the cylinder was lifted into the night-black opening, where it seemed that light was powerless to follow.

Chandon could see nothing; he was aware of nothing but solid darkness, enfolding the cylinder even as it had been enfolded by the white, achromatic light of timelessness. He felt about him the sense of long, tremendous vibra-tion; a soundless pulsing that seemed to spread in circles from some dynamic center; to pass over and beyond him through aeons, as if from some Titanic heart whose beats defied the environing eternity.

Simultaneously, he realized that his own heart was beating again, with the same protraction as this unknown pulse; that he drew breath and exhaled it in obedience to the cyclical vibration. In his benumbed brain, there grew the nascent idea of wonder; the first beginning of a natural thought-sequence. His body and mind were beginning to function once more, beneath the influence of the power that had been strong enough to intrude upon the timeless universe and pluck him from that petrifying ether.

The vibration began to swiften, spreading outward in mighty ripples. It became audible as a cyclopean pounding; and Chandon somehow conceived the idea of giant-built machinery, turning and throbbing in an underworld prison. The vessel seemed to be forging onward with resistless power through some material barrier. Doubtless it was wrenching itself free from the eternal dimension, was tearing its way back into time.

The blackness had persisted for awhile, like a positive radiation rather than the mere absence of light. Now it cleared away and was replaced by an all-revealing, ruddy illumination. At the same time, the loud, engine-like vibration died to a muted throbbing. Perhaps the darkness had been in some manner associated with the full development of the strange force that had enabled the vessel to move and function in that ultra-temporal medium. With the return into time, and the diminishment of the power, it had vanished.

The faculties of thought, feeling, cognition and movement, under their normal time-aspects, all came back to Chandon like the loosing of a dammed-up flood. He was able to co-relate all that had occurred to him, and infer in some measure the meaning of his unique experiences. With growing awe and astonishment, he studied the scene that was visible from his position in the hammock.

The cylinder, with the weird, crystalloid figures looming near at hand, was reposing in a huge room, probably the main hold of the vessel. The interior of this room was curved like a sphere; and all about and above, gigantic, unfamiliar machineries were disposed. Not far away, he saw the retracted crane or arm. It seemed that the force of gravitation inhered everywhere in the vessel's inner surface; for certain peculiar beings passed before Chandon as he watched, and ran upward on the walls till they hung inverted from the ceiling with the nonchalance of flies.

There were perhaps a dozen of these beings within sight. No one with earthly biological prepossessions could even have imagined them very readily. Each of them possessed a roughly globular body with the upper hemisphere swelling mid-way between pole and equator to form two neckless, conical heads. The lower hemisphere terminated in many limbs and appendages, some of which were used for walking and others solely for prehension.

The heads were featureless, but a glittering, web-like membrane hung between them, trembling continually. Certain of the nether appendages, waving like inquisitive tentacles, were tipped with organs that may have served for eyes, ears, nostrils and mouths.

These creatures shone with a silvery light and appeared to be almost translucent. In the center of the pointed heads, a spot of coal-bright crimson glowed and faded with pulse-like regularity; and the spherical bodies darkened and lightened as if with the rhythmic interchange of rib-like zones of shadow beneath their surfaces. Chandon felt that they were formed of some non-protoplasmic substance, perhaps a mineral that had organized itself into living cells. Their movements were very quick and dexterous, with an inhuman poise; and they seemed able to perform many different motions with perfect simultaneity.

The earth-man was stricken to renewed immobility by the strangeness of it all. With vain, fantastical surmises, he sought to fathom the mystery. Who were these creatures, and what had been their purpose in penetrating the eternal dimension? Why had they removed certain of its inhabitants, together with himself? Whither was the vessel bound? Was it returning, somewhere in time and space, to the planetary world from which it had set forth on its weird voyage?

He could be sure of nothing; but he knew that he had fallen into the hands of super-scientific beings, who were expert navigators of space-time. They had been able to build a vessel such as he had merely dreamt of building; and perhaps they had explored and charted all the unknown deeps, and had deliberately planned their incursion into the frozen world beyond.

If they had not come to rescue him, he would never have escaped from the doom of timelessness, into which he had been hurled by his own clumsy effort to cross the secular stream.

Pondering, he turned to the giant things that were his companions. He could scarcely recognize them in the red glow: their pallid planes and angles seemed to have undergone a subtle re-arrangement; and the light quivered upon them in bloody lusters, conferring an odd warmth, a suggestion of awaking life. More than ever, they gave the impression of latent power, of frozen dynamism.

Then, suddenly, he saw an unmistakable movement from one of the statue-like entities, and realized that the thing had begun to alter its shape! The cold, marble substance seemed to flow like quicksilver. The rudimentary head assumed a stern, many-featured form, such as might belong to the demi-god of some foreign world. The limbs lengthened, and new members of indeterminate use were put forth. The simple curves and angles multiplied themselves with mysterious complexity. A diamond-shaped eye, glowing with blue fire, appeared in the face and was quickly followed by other eyes. The thing seemed to be undergoing, in a few moments, the entire process of some long-suspended evolution.

Chandon saw that the other figures were displaying singular alterations, though in each case the ensuing development was wholly individual. The geometric facets began to swell like opening buds, and flowed into lines of celestial beauty and grandeur. The boreal pallor was suffused with unearthly iridescence, with opal tones that raced and trembled in ever-living patterns, in belted arabesques, in rainbow hieroglyphs.

The human watcher felt the insurgence of a measureless *èlan*, of a super-stellar intellection, in these remarkable beings. A thrill of terror, electric, eerie, ran through him. The process he had just seen was too incalculable, too tremendous. Who, or what, could limit and control the unsealed activities of these Eternal Ones, aroused from their slumber? Surely he was in the presence of beings akin to gods, to the demons or genii of myth. That which he beheld was like the opening of the sea-recovered jars of Solomon.

He saw that the marvellous transformation had also been perceived by the owners of the vessel. These creatures, thronging from all parts of the spheroid interior, began to crowd around the timeless entities. Their mechanical, darting motions, the lifting and levelling of certain members that ended in eye-shaped organs, betrayed an unhuman excitement and curiosity. They seemed to be inspecting the transfigured forms with the air of learned biologists who had been prepared for such an event and were gratified by its consummation.

The Timeless Ones, it appeared, were also curious regarding their captors. Their flaming eyes returned the stare of the periscopic tentacles, and certain odd horn-shaped appendages of their lofty crowns began to quiver inquisitively, as if with the reception of unknown sense-impressions. Then, suddenly, each of the three put forth a single, jointless arm, emitting in mid-air seven long, fan-like rays of purple light in lieu of a hand.

These rays, no doubt, were capable of receiving and conveying tactile impressions. Slowly and deliberately, like groping fingers, they reached out, and each of the fans, curving fluctuantly where it encountered a rounded surface, began to play with a rhythmic flaring about the foremost of the double-headed creatures.

These beings, as if in alarm or discomfort, drew back and sought to elude the searching rays. The purple fingers lengthened, encircled them, held them helpless, ran about them in broadening, clinging zones, as if to explore their whole anatomy. From the two heads to the disk-like pads that served them for feet, the beings were swathed around with flowing rings and ribbons of light.

Others of the vessel's crew, beyond reach of the curious beams, had darted back to a more secure distance. One of them lifted certain of his members in a swift, emphatic gesture. As far as Chandon could see, the being had not touched any of the vessel's machinery. But as if in obedience to the gesture, a huge, round, mirror-like mechanism overhead began to revolve in its frame on massive pivots.

The mechanism appeared to be made of some pale, lucid substance, neither glass nor metal. Ceasing its rotation, as if the desired focus had been secured, the mighty lens emitted a beam of hueless light, which somehow reminded Chandon of the chill, frozen radiance of the eternal world. This beam, falling on the timeless entities, was plainly repressive in its effect. Immediately the finger-like rays relinquished their quarry, and faded back to the jointless arms, which were then retracted. The eyes closed like hidden jewels, the opal patterns grew cold and dull, and the strange, half-divine beings appeared to lose their complex angles, to regain their former quiescence, like devolving crystals. Yet, somehow, they were still alive, they still retained the nascent lines of their preternatural efflorescence.

In his awe and wonder before this miraculous tableau, Chandon had automatically freed himself from the leather bands, had risen from the hammock, and was standing with his face pressed against the wall of the cylinder. His change of position was noted by the vessel's crew, and their eye-tentacles were all raised and levelled upon him for a moment, following the devolution of the Timeless Ones.

Then, in response to another enigmatic gesture from one of their number, the giant lens rotated a little further, and the glacial beam began to shift and widen, till it played upon the cylinder though still including in its hueless range the dynamic figures.

The earth-man had the sensation of being caught in a motionless flood of something that was inexpressibly thick and viscid. His body seemed to congeal, his thoughts crawled with painful slowness through some obstructing medium that had permeated his very brain. It was not the complete arrest of all the life-processes that had been entailed by his impingement upon eternity. Rather, it was a deceleration of these processes; a subjection to some unthinkably retarded rhythm of time-movement and sequence.

Whole years seemed to intervene betwixt the beats of Chandon's heart. The crooking of his little finger would have required lustrums. Through tediously elongated time, his brain strove to form a single thought: the suspicion that his captors had been alarmed by his change of posture, and had apprehended some troublous demonstration of power from him, as from the Timeless Ones. Then, through further decades, he conceived another thought: that he himself was perhaps regarded as one of the god-like beings by these alien time-voyagers. They had found him in eternity, amid the measureless ranks; and how were they to know that he, like themselves, had come originally from a temporal world.

With his altered sense of duration, the earth-man could form no proper conception of the length of the voyage in time-space. To him, it was almost another eternity, punctuated at lustrum-long intervals by the humming vibration of the machinery. To his delayed visual perception, the crew of the vessel seemed to move with incredible sluggishness, by imperceptible gradations. He, with his weird companions, had been set apart by the chill beam in a prison of slow time, while the ship itself was plunging through fathomless dimensions of secular and cosmic infinitude!

At last the voyage came to an end. Chandon felt the gradual dawning of an all-pervasive light that drowned the vessel's ruddy glow in fierce whiteness. By infinite degrees, the walls became perfectly transparent, together with the machinery, and he realized that the light was coming from a world without. Immense images, multiform and intricate, began to crowd with the slowness of creation itself upon the glaring splendor. Then—doubtless to permit the removal of the guarded captives—the retarding ray was switched off, and Chandon recovered his normal powers of cognition and movement.

He beheld an awesome vision through the clear wall, whose transparence was perhaps due to the complete turning-off of the vessel's motive-power. He saw that the vessel was reposing in a diamond-shaped area, surrounded with architectural piles whose very magnitude imposed itself like an irremovable weight upon his senses.

Far up, in a fiery orange sky, he saw the looming of bulbous Atlantean pillars with platform capitals; the thronging of strange cruciform towers; of unnatural cupolas that were like inverted pyramids. He saw the spiral pinnacles that seemed to support an unbelievable burden of terraces; the slanting walls, like fluted mountain-scarps, that formed the base of imagineless cumuli. All were wrought of some shining, night-black stone, like a marble quarried from an ultra-cosmic Erebus. They interposed their heavy, lowering, malignant masses between Chandon and the flames of a hidden sun that was incomparably more brilliant than our own.

Blinded by the glare and dizzied by those lofty piles; aware also of a queer heaviness in all his bodily sensations, doubtless due to an increased gravity, the earth-man turned his attention to the foreground. The diamond area, he now saw, was thronged with people similar to the crew of the time-vessel. Like giant, silvery, globular-bodied insects, they came hurrying from all directions on the dark pavement. Arranged in a ring about the vessel, were colossal mounted mirrors, of the same type that had emitted the retarding ray. The gathering people stopped at some little distance, leaving a clear space between the ray-machines and the ship, as if for the landing of the crew and captives.

Now, as if in response to some hidden mechanism, a huge, circular door was opened in the seamless wall. The folded crane began to lengthen, and covered one of the timeless beings with its mesh of tentacles. Then the mysterious entity, still quiet and unresisting, was lifted through the aperture and deposited on the pavement outside.

The arm returned, and repeated this procedure with the second figure, which, in the meanwhile, had apparently realized the cessation of the retarding beam, and was less submissive than its fellow had been. It offered a rather tentative resistance, and began to swell as the tentacles enfolded it, and to put forth pseudopodic members and finger-like rays that plucked gently at the tightening mesh. However, in a few moments, the second being had joined its companion in the world without.

At the same time, a startling change had begun to manifest itself in the third figure. Chandon felt as if he were present at the epiphany of some aeon-veiled and secluded god, revealing himself in his true likeness from the molten chrysalis of matter. The transformation that occurred was as if some chill stalagmite should burgeon forth in a thousand-featured shape of cloud and fire. In one apocalyptic moment, the thing seemed to expand, to rush upward, to change its entire substance, to develop organs and attributes such as could belong only to a super-material stage of evolution. Aeons of star-life, of world-life, of the slow alchemy of atoms, were abridged in that instant.

Chandon could form no clear conception of what was happening. The metamorphosis was too far beyond the normal interpretative range of human senses. He saw something that towered before him, filling the vessel to its roof and pressing terribly against the curved transparent surface. Then, with inestimable violence, the entire vessel broke in a thousand flying, glittering, glass-like fragments, that shrieked with the high, thin note of tortured things as they hurtled and fell in all directions.

Before the last fragments had fallen, the time-cylinder was caught and drawn upward from the wreck as if by some mighty hand. Whether the looming giant had reached down with one of its non-human members, or whether the cylinder had been lifted by magnetic force, was never wholly clear to Chandon. All he could remember afterwards was the light, aerial soaring, in which he experienced a sudden and complete relief from the heavy gravitation of that unknown planet. He seemed to float very swiftly to an elevation hard to estimate, from the absence of familiar scale; and then the cylinder came to rest on the cloud-like shoulder of the Timeless One, and clung there as securely as if it had landed on the shore of some far-off, separate world, aloof in space.

He was beyond awe or surprise or bewilderment. As if in some cataclysmic dream, he resigned himself to the unfolding of the swift miracle. He peered out from his airy vantage, and saw above him, like the topmost crag of a lofty cumulus, with stormy suns for eyes, the head of the being who had shattered the alien time-vessel and had risen above its ruins like a loosed and rebellious genie.

Far down, he beheld the black diamond area that swarmed with the silvery people. Then, from the pavement, there rushed heavenward, like the pillared fumes of a monstrous explosion, the mounting and waxing forms of the other Timeless Ones. Tumultuous, awful, cyclonic, they rose beside the first, to complete that rebel trinity. Yet, vast and tall as they had grown, the pylons around them were taller; the terrace-bearing pinnacles, the topsy-turvy pyramids, the cruciform towers, still frowned upon them from the glowing, coal-bright air like the dark, colossal guardians of a transgalactic hell.

Chandon was aware of a thousand impressions. He felt the divine and limitless energies, waked from eternal sleep, that were flowering with such dynamic violence in time. And he felt, warring with these, endeavoring to subdue and constrain them, the jarring radiations and malignly concentered powers of the new world. The very light was inimical and tyrannous in its fiery beating; the blackness of the lowering domes and prostyles was like the crushing fall of a thousand muffled maces, swung by sullen, cruel, silent Anakim. The lens-machines, revolving, glared upward like the eyes of boreal Cyclops, and turned their frosted beams on the cloudy giants. At intervals, the sky lightened with a white-hot flaring, like the reflex of a million remote furnaces; and Chandon was aware of surly, infra-bass, reverberant, bell-toned clangors, of drum-notes loud as beaten worlds, that impinged upon him from all quarters of the throbbing air.

The environing piles appeared to darken, as if they had gathered to themselves a more evil and positive ebon, and were raying it forth to stupefy the senses. But beyond this, beyond all physical perceptions, Chandon felt the black magnetism that surged in never-ceasing waves; that clamored before the barriers of his will, that sought to usurp his mind, to wrest and shape his very thoughts into forms of monstrous thralldom. Wordless, and conveyed in thronging images of terrible strangeness, he caught the biddings of inhuman bane, of transtellary hatred. The very stones of the massive buildings were joined with the brains of that exotic people in an effort to resume control of Chandon and the three Eternal Ones!

Darkly, the earthman understood. He must not only submit to the silvery beings, he must do their will in all things. He and his companions had been brought from eternity for a purpose—to aid their captors in some stupendous war with a rival people of the same world. Even as mankind employs in warfare explosives of titanic potency, the silver creatures had desired to employ the time-loosed energies of the Eternal Ones against their otherwise equally matched foes! They had known the route through secret dimensions from time into timelessness. With well-nigh demoniac audacity, they had planned and executed the weird abduction; and they had assumed that Chandon was one of the eternal entities, with latencies of immense *élan* and god-like power.

The waves of evil monition rose ever higher. Chandon felt himself inundated, swamped. With televisic clearness, there grew in his mind a picture of the foe against whom he was being adjured to go forth. He saw the glaring perspectives of remote, unearthly lands, the mightily swarming piles of unhuman cities, lying beneath an incandescent sun that was vaster than Antares. For a moment, he felt himself hating these lands and cities with the cold, imagineless rancor of an otherworld psychology.

Then, as if he had been lifted above it by the giant upon whose shoulder he rode, Chandon knew that the black sea was no longer beating upon him. He was free from the clutching mesmerism, he could no longer conceive the alien emotions and pictures that had invaded his mind. Miraculous ease and sublime security enveloped him; he was the center of a sphere of resistant and resilient force, which nothing could subdue or penetrate.

Sitting as if on a mountain-throne, he saw that the demiurgic triad, contemptuous and defiant of the pygmies beneath, had resumed their magic growth and were shooting upward to attain and surpass the level of the topmost piles. A moment more, and he peered across the Babelian tiers of sullen stone, crowded with the silver people, and saw the outer avenues of a mammoth metropolis; and beyond these, the far-flung horizons of the unnamed planet.

He seemed to know the thoughts of the Timeless Ones as they looked forth on this world whose impious people had dreamt to enslave their illimitable essence. He knew that they saw and comprehended it all in a glance. He felt them pause in momentary curiosity; and felt the swift, relentless anger, the irrevocable decision, that followed,

Then, very tentatively and deliberately, as if they were testing their untried powers, the three beings began to destroy the city. From the head of Chandon's white, supernal bearer, there issued a circle of ruby flame, to detach itself, to spin and broaden in a great wheel as it slanted down and settled on one of the higher piles. Beneath that burning crown, the unnatural-angled domes and inverse pyramids began to quiver, and seemed to expand like a dark vapor. They lost their solid outlines, they lightened, they took on the patterns of shaken sand, they shuddered skyward in rhythmic circles of somber, deathly iris, paling and vanishing upon the intolerable glare.

From the other Timeless Ones, there emanated the visible and invisible agencies of annihilation; slowly at first, and then with cyclonic acceleration, as if their anger were mounting or they were becoming more engrossed in the awful and god-like game.

From out their celestial bodies, as from high crags, there leaped living rivers and raging cataracts of energy; there descended bolts, orbs, ellipsoid wheels of white or vari-colored fire, to fall on the doomed city like a rain of ravening meteors. The builded cumuli dissolved into molten slag, the columns and piled terraces passed in driven wraiths of steam, under the burning tempest. The city ran in swift torrents of lava; it quivered away in spirals of spectral dust; it rose in black flames, in sullen auroras.

Over its ruins, there moved the Eternal Ones, clearing for themselves an instant way. Behind them, in the black and clean-swept levels whereon they had trodden, foci of dissolution appeared, and the very soil and stone dissolved in ever-spinning, widening vortices, that ate the surface of the planet and bored down upon its core. As if they had taken into their own substance the molecules and electrons of all that they had destroyed, the Eternal Ones grew ever taller and vaster.

Chandon beheld it all from his fantastic eyrie with supernal remoteness and detachment. Enisled in a moving zone of inviolate peace, he saw the fiery rain that consumed the ultra-galactic Sodom; he saw the belts of devastation that ran and radiated, broadening ever, to the four quarters; he peered from an ever-loftier height upon vast horizons, that fled as in reeling terror before the timeless giants.

Faster and faster played the lethal orbs and beams. They spawned in mid-air, they gave birth to countless others. They were sown abroad like the dragon's teeth of fable, to follow the longitudes of the great planet to its poles. The stricken city was soon left behind, and the giants marched on monstrous seas and deserts, on broad plains and high mountain-walls, where other cities shone far down like littered pebbles.

There were tides of atomic fire that went before to wash down the prodigious Alps. There were vengeful, flying globes that turned the seas into instant vapor, that smote the deserts to molten, stormy oceans. There were arcs, circles, quadrilaterals of annihilation, growing always, that sank downwards through the basic stone.

The fire-bright noon was muffled with chaotic murk. A bloody Cyclops, a red Laocoön, battling with serpent-coils of cloud and shadow, the mighty sun seemed to stagger in mid-heaven, to rush dizzily to and fro as the world reeled beneath that intolerable trampling of macrocosmic Titans. The lands below were veiled by mephitic fumes, riven momentarily to disclose the heaving and foundering continents.

Now to that stupendous chaos the very elements of the doomed world were adding their unleashed energies. Clouds that were black Himalayas with realm-wide lightning, followed behind the destroyers. The ground crumbled to release the central fires in volcanic geysers, in skyward-flowing cataracts. The seas ebbed, revealing dismal peaks and long-submerged ruins, as they roared in their nether channels to be sucked down through earthquake-riven beds to feed the boiling cauldrons of internal disruption.

The air went mad with thunders as of Typhon breaking forth from his underworld dungeon; with roaring as of spire-tongued fires in the red pits of a crumbling inferno; with moaning and whining as of djinns trapped by the fall of mountains in some unscalable abyss; with howling as of frantic demons, loosed from primordial tombs.

Above the tumult, higher and higher, Chandon was borne, till he looked down from the calm altitude of ether; till he gazed from a sun-like vantage upon the seething and shattered orb, and saw the huge sun itself from an equal height in space. The cataclysmic moan, the mad thunder, seemed to die away. The seas of catastrophic ruin eddied like a shallow backwash about the feet of the Timeless Ones. The furious, all-devouring maelstroms were no more than some ephemeral puff of dust, stirred by the casual step of a passer-by.

Then, beneath him, there was no longer even the nebulous wrack of a world. The being upon whose shoulder he still clung, like an atom to some planetary parapet, was striding through cosmic emptiness; and spurned by its departure, the ruinous ball was flung abyssward after the receding sun around which it had revolved with all its vanished enigmas of alien life and civilization.

Dimly the earth-man saw the inconceivable vastness to which the Eternal Ones had attained. He beheld their glimmering outlines, the vague masses of their forms, with stars behind them, seen as through the luminous veil of comets. He was perched on a nebular thing, huge as the orbit of systems, and moving with more than the velocity of light, that strode through unnamed galaxies, through never-charted dimensions of space and time. He felt the immeasurable eddying of ether, he saw the labyrinthine swirling of stars, that formed and faded and were replaced by the fleeing patterns of other stellar mazes. In sublime security, in his sphere of dream-like ease and miraculous volancy, Chandon was borne on without knowing why or whither; and, like the participant of some prodigious dream, he did not even ask himself such questions as these.

After infinities of flying light, of whirling and falling emptiness; after the transit of many skies, of unnumbered systems, there came to him the sense of a sudden pause. For one moment, from the still gulf, he gazed on a tiny sun with its entourage of nine planets, and wondered vaguely if the sun were some familiar astronomic body.

Then, with ineffable lightness and velocity, it seemed to him that he was falling toward one of the nearer worlds. The blurred and broadening mass of its seas and continents surged up to meet him; he seemed to descend, meteor-like, on a region of rough mountains sharp with snowy pinnacles that rose above somber spires of pine.

There, as if he had been deposited by some all-mighty hand, the cylinder came to rest; and Chandon peered out with the eerie startlement of an awakened dreamer, to see around him the walls of his own Sierran laboratory! The Timeless Ones, omniscient, by some benignant whim, had returned him to his own station in time and space; and then had gone on, perhaps to the conquest of other universes; perhaps to find again the white, eternal world of their origin and to fold themselves anew in the pale Nirvana of immutable contemplation.

THE DEMON OF THE FLOWER

Lying one summer night below the stars, when the Milky Way was spanning the sapphire zenith, and the wind had fallen asleep in the high, somber pines, I heard this tale as a whispering borne from strange worlds beyond the Scorpion:

Not as the plants and flowers of earth, growing peacefully beneath a simple sun, were the blossoms of the planet Lophai. Coiling and uncoiling in double dawns; tossing tumultuously to enormous suns of jade green and balas-ruby orange; swaying and weltering in rich twilights, they resembled fields of rooted servants that dance eternally to an otherworldly music.

Many were small and furtive, and crept in the fashion of vipers on the low ground. Others were tall as pythons, rearing proudly to the jewelled light in hieratic postures. Some were like abdominous wyverns with long, slender throats and coronals of scroll-shaped antennae. And some bore the far-off likeness of pygmy cockadrills with high, carmine-tinted combs.

The flowers grew with single or double stems that burgeoned into hydra heads; or triple or quadruple stems that joined again to put forth a single blossom. They were frilled and festooned with varicolored leaves, that suggested the wings of flying lizards, the pennons of faery lances, the phylacteries of an alien sacerdotalism. They bloomed with petals that issued like flaming tongues from ebon mouths; or curled in scarlet wattles as of wild dragons turned to plants by a wizard spell; or floated on the air in deep reticulations as of fleshy nets of madder and rose; or hung aloft like bucklers of exotic war.

They were armed with venomous darts, with deadly fangs; and many possessed the power of fatal constriction. All were weirdly alive and sentient, were malignly restless and alert, save in the irregular, infrequent winters when Lophai hung at its twofold aphelion. Then they ceased their perennial

111

tossing in a brief torpor, and folded their monstrous petals beneath the rays that fall obliquely from remote poles.

The flowers were the lords of Lophai, and all other life existed only by their sufferance. The people of the world had been their inferiors from unrecorded cycles; and even in the oldest myths there was no suggestion that any other order of things had ever prevailed. And the plants themselves, together with the fauna and mankind of Lophai, gave immemorial obeisance to that supreme and terrible flower known as the Voorqual, in which a tutelary demon, more ancient than the twin suns, was believed to have made its immortal avatar.

The Voorqual was served by a human priesthood, chosen from amid the royalty and aristocracy of Lophai. In the heart of the chief city, Lospar, in an equatorial realm, it had grown from antiquity on the summit of a high pyramid of sable terraces that overloomed the town like the hanging gardens of some greater Babylon, crowded with the lesser but deadly floral forms. At the center of the broad apex, the Voorqual stood alone in a basin level with the surrounding platform of black mineral. The basin was filled with a compost in which the dust of royal mummies formed an essential ingredient.

The tall, demonian flower sprang from a bulb so old, so encrusted with the growth of centuries that it resembled an urn of stone. Above this, there rose the gnarled and mighty stalk that had displayed in earlier times the bifurcation of a mandrake, but whose halves had now grown together into a scaly, furrowed thing like the tail of some mythic sea-monster. The stalk was variegated with hues of greening bronze, of antique copper, with the sere yellows and burnt madders of tropic autumn, the livid blues and deathly purples of carnal corruption. It ended in a crown of stiff, blackish leaves, banded and spotted with poisonous, metallic white, and edged with sharp serrations as of savage weapons. From below the crown, there issued a long, sinuous arm, scaled like the main stem, and serpentining downward and outward to terminate in the huge upright bowl of a bizarre blossom—as if the arm, in sardonic fashion, should hold out a hellish beggar's cup.

Abhorrent and monstrous was the bowl—which, like the leaves, was legended to renew itself at intervals of a thousand years. It smouldered at the base with sullen ruby steeped in sepulchral shadow; it lightened into zones of sultry dragon's blood, into belts of the rose of infernal sunset, on the fluted, swelling sides; and it flamed at the rim to a yellowish nacarat red, like the ichor of salamandrine devils. To one who dared to peer within, the deep grail was lined with funereal violet, blackening toward the bottom, pitted with myriad pores, and striated with turgescent veins of sulphurous green.

Swaying slowly, in a weird, lethal hypnotic rhythm, with a deep and solemn sibilation, the Voorqual dominated the city of Lospar and the world Lophai. Below, on the tiers of the pyramid, the thronged ophidian plants kept time to this rhythm in their tossing and hissing. And far beyond Lospar, to the poles of the planet and in all its longitudes, the fields of living blossoms obeyed the sovereign tempo of the Voorqual.

Boundless was the power exercised by this being over the people who, for want of a better name, I have called the humankind of Lophai. Many and frightful were the legends that had gathered through aeons about the Voorqual. And dire was the sacrifice demanded each year at the summer solstice by the demon; the filling of its proffered cup with the life-blood of a priest or priestess, chosen from amid the assembled hierophants who passed before the Voorqual till the poised cup, inverted and empty, descended like a devil's miter on the hapless head of one of their number.

Lunithi, king of the realms about Lospar, and high-priest of the Voorqual, was the last if not the first of his race to rebel against this singular and sinister domination. There were doubtful myths of some primordial ruler who had dared to refuse the required sacrifice; and whose people, in consequence, had been decimated by a mortal war with the serpentine plants which, obeying the angry demon, had uprooted themselves everywhere from the soil and had marched on the cities of Lophai, slaying or vampirizing all who fell in their way. Lunithi, from childhood, had obeyed implicitly and without question the will of the floral overlord; had offered the stated worship, had performed the necessary rites. To withhold them would have been blasphemy. He had not dreamt of rebellion till, at the time of the annual choosing of the victim, and thirty suns before the date of his nuptials with Nala, priestess of the Voorqual, he saw the hesitant, inverted grail come down in deathly crimson on the fair head of his betrothed.

A mute and sorrowful consternation, a sullen, recalcitrant dismay which he sought to smother even in his own heart, was experienced by Lunithi. Nala, dazed and resigned, in a mystic inertia of despair, accepted her doom without question; but a blasphemous doubt formed itself surreptitiously in the mind of the king. Scarcely he dared admit the thought to full consciousness, lest the demon should know by means of its telepathic powers and visit him some baleful retribution.

Trembling with his own impiety, he asked himself if there was not some way in which he could save Nala from the sacrificial knife, could cheat the demon of its ghastly tribute. To do this, and escape with impunity to himself and his subjects, he knew infallibly that he must strike at the very life of the monster, which was believed to be deathless and invulnerable. It seemed impious even to wonder concerning the truth of this unanimous belief, which had long assumed the force of a religious tenet among the peoples of Lophai.

Amid such reflections as these, Lunithi remembered an old myth about the existence of a neutral and independent being known as the Occlith: a demon coeval with the Voorqual, and allied neither to man nor to the flower creatures. This being was said to dwell beyond the desert of Aphom, in the otherwise unpeopled mountains of white stone that are never visited by snow and which lie above the habitat of the ophidian blossoms. In latter days, at least, no man had seen the Occlith, for the journey through Aphom was a thing not lightly to be undertaken. But this entity was supposed to be immortal; and it lived apart and alone, meditating upon all things and interfering never with their processes. However, it was said to have given, in earlier times, valuable advice concerning affairs of state to a certain king who had gone forth from Lospar to its lair among the white crags.

In his grief and desperation, Lunithi resolved to seek the Occlith and to question it anent the possibility of slaying the Voorqual. If, by any mortal means, the demon could be destroyed, he would remove from Lophai the long-established tyranny whose shadow fell upon all things from the sable pyramid.

It was necessary for him to proceed with utmost caution, to confide in no one, to veil his very thoughts at all times from the occult scrutiny of the Voorqual. In the interim of five days between the choosing of the victim and the consummation of the sacrifice, he must carry out his mad plan.

Unattended, and disguised as a simple herder, Lunithi left his palace during the brief night of universal three-hour slumber, and stole forth toward the desert through fields comparatively free of the serpentine growths. In the dawn of the balas-ruby sun, he had reached the pathless waste, and was toiling painfully over its knife-sharp ridges of dark stone, like the waves of a mounting ocean petrified in storm.

Soon the rays of the green sun were added to those of the other, and Aphom became a painted inferno through which Lunithi dragged his way, crawling from scarp to glassy scarp and resting at whiles in the colored shadows. There was no water anywhere; but swift mirages gleamed and faded; and the sifting sand appeared to run like rills in the bottom of deep, flaming valleys.

At setting of the first sun, Lunithi came within sight of the pale mountains beyond Aphom, towering like a precipice of frozen foam above the desert's darker sea. They were tinged with evanescent lights of azure and jade and orange in the going of the yellow-red orb and the westward slanting of its binary. Then the lights melted into tourmaline and beryl, and the green sun was regnant over all, till it too went down, leaving a twilight whose colors were those of shoaling sea-water. In the gloom, Lunithi reached the foot of the lower crags; and there, exhausted, he slept till the second dawn.

Rising, he began his escalade of the white mountains, which rose bleak and terrible before him against the hidden suns, with cliffs that were sheer as the terraces of Titans. Like the king who had gone before in the ancient myth, he found the precarious way that led upward through narrow, broken chasms. At last he came to the vaster fissure, riving the heart of the white range, by which it was possible to reach the legendary lair of the Occlith.

The beetling walls of the chasm rose higher and higher above him, shutting out the double daylight but creating with their pallor a wan and deathly glimmer to illumine his way through the dusk. The fissure was such as might have been cloven by the sword of a macrocosmic giant. It led downward, steepening ever, like a wound that pierced the heart of Lophai.

Lunithi, like all of his race, was able to exist for prolonged periods without other nutriment than sunlight and water. He had brought with him a metal flask, filled with the aqueous element of Lophai, from which he drank sparingly as he descended along the chasm; for, like Aphom itself, the white mountains were waterless; and he feared to touch the rills and pools of unknown fluids upon which he came at intervals in the gloom. There were sanguine-colored springs that bubbled from the walls, to vanish in fathomless rifts; and sluggish brooklets of mercurial metal, green, blue, or amber, that wound beside him like liquescent serpents and then disappeared mysteriously in dark caverns. Acrid metallic vapors rose from clefts in the chasm-floor; and Lunithi felt himself among strange alchemies and chemistries of nature. In this fantastic world of stone, which the plants of Lophai could never invade, he seemed to have gone beyond the Satanic tyranny of the Voorqual.

At last he came to a clear, hueless pool, that almost filled the entire width of the chasm, leaving on one side a narrow, insecure ledge along which he was forced to scramble. A fragment of the marble stone, loosened by his passing, fell into the pool as he gained the opposite edge; and the clear liquid foamed and hissed like a thousand vipers. Wondering as to its properties, and fearful of the virulent hissing, which did not subside for some time, Lunithi hurried on, and came after an interval to the end of the fissure.

Here he emerged in the huge crater-like pit that was the home of the Occlith. Fluted and columned walls went up to an overwhelming height on all sides; and the sun of orange ruby, now at zenith, was pouring down a vertical cataract of gorgeous fires and shadows.

Addorsed against the further wall of the pit, Lunithi beheld that fabulous being known as the Occlith, which had the likeness of a high cruciform pillar of blue mineral, shining with its own esoteric luster. Going forward, he prostrated himself before the pillar; and then, in accents that quavered with a deep awe, he ventured to ask the desired oracle.

For awhile the Occlith maintained its aeonian silence. Peering timidly, the king perceived the twin lights of mystic silver that brightened and faded with a slow, regular pulsation in the arms of the blue cross. Then, from the lofty, shining thing, by means of no visible organ, there issued a voice that was like the tinkling of mineral fragments lightly clashed together, but which somehow shaped itself into articulate words.

"It is possible," said the Occlith, "to slay the plant known as the Voorqual, in which an elder demon has its habitation. Though the flower has attained millennial age, it is not necessarily immortal: for all things have their proper term of existence and decay; and nothing has been created without its corresponding agency of death…. I do not advise you to slay the plant… but

I can furnish you with the information which you desire. In the mountain chasm through which you came to seek me, there flows a hueless spring of mineral poison, deadly to all the ophidian plantlife of this world..."

The Occlith went on, and told Lunithi the manner in which the poison should be prepared and administered. The chill, toneless, tinkling voice concluded:

"I have answered your question. If there is anything more that you wish to learn, it would be well to ask me now."

Prostrating himself again, Lunithi gave thanks to the Occlith; and, considering that he had learned all that was requisite in regard to the Voorqual, he did not avail himself of the opportunity to question further the strange entity of living stone. And the Occlith, cryptic and aloof in its termless, impenetrable meditation, apparently saw fit to vouchsafe nothing more except in answer to a direct query.

Withdrawing from the marble-walled abyss, Lunithi returned in haste along the narrow chasm; till, reaching the clear pool of which the Occlith had spoken, he paused to empty his water-flask and fill it with the angry, hissing liquid. Then he resumed his journey.

At the end of two days, after incredible fatigues and torments in the blazing hell of Aphom, he reached Lospar in the time of darkness and slumber, as when he had departed. Since his absence had been unannounced, it was supposed by everyone that he had retired to the underground adyta below the pyramid of the Voorqual for purposes of prolonged meditation, as was sometimes his wont.

In fearful hope and trepidation, dreading the miscarriage of his plan, and shrinking still from its audacious impiety, Lunithi awaited the night preceding that double dawn of summer solstice when, in a secret room of the black pyramid, the monstrous offering was to be prepared. Nala would be slain by a fellow-priest or priestess, chosen by lot, and her life-blood would drip from the channeled altar into a great cup; and the cup would then be borne with solemn rites to the Voorqual and its contents poured into the evilly supplicative bowl of the sanguinated blossom.

He saw little of Nala during that brief interim. She was more withdrawn than ever, and seemed to have consecrated herself wholly to the coming doom. To no one—and least of all to his beloved—did Lunithi dare to hint a possible prevention of the sacrifice.

There came the dreaded eve, with its swiftly changing twilight of jewelled hues and its darkness hung with auroral flames. Lunithi stole across the sleeping city and entered the pyramid whose massive blackness towered amid the frail and open architecture of buildings that were little more than canopies and lattices of stone. With infinite caution, hiding his real intention in the nethermost crypts of his mind, he made the preparations prescribed by the Occlith. Into the huge sacrificial cup of black metal, in a room eternally lit with stored sunlight, he emptied the seething, sibilant poison he had brought with him from the white mountains. Then, opening with surgical adroitness a vein in one of his arms, he added a certain amount of his own life-fluid to the lethal potion. The blood appeared to quiet that angry venom, above whose foaming crystal it floated like a magic oil, without mingling; so that the entire cup, to all appearance, was filled with the liquid most acceptable to the Satanic blossom.

Bearing in his hands the black grail, Lunithi mounted a coiling stairway that led to the Voorqual's presence. His heart quailing within him, his senses swooning in chill gulfs of superstitious terror, he emerged on the lofty sable summit above the shadowy town.

In a luminous azure gloom, against the weird and iridescent streamers of light that foreran the double dawn, he saw the dreamy swaying of the monstrous plant, and heard its somnolent hissing that was answered drowsily by innumerable blossoms on the terraces below. A nightmare oppression, black and tangible, seemed to flow from the pyramid and to lie in stagnant shadow on all the lands of Lophai.

Aghast at his own temerity, and deeming that his shrouded thoughts would surely be understood as he drew nearer, or that the Voorqual would be suspicious of an offering brought before the customary hour, Lunithi made obeisance to his floral overlord. The Voorqual vouchsafed no sign that it had deigned to perceive his presence; but the great flower-cup, with its flaring crimsons dulled to garnet and purple in the twilight, was held forward as if in readiness to receive the hideous gift.

Breathless, and fainting with religious fear, in a moment of suspense that seemed eternal, Lunithi poured the blood-mantled poison into the yawning cup. The venom boiled and hissed like a wizard's brew as the thirsty flower drank it up; and Lunithi saw the coiling arm draw back in sudden doubt and tilt its demonian grail quickly, as if to repudiate the sacrificial draft.

It was too late; for the poison had been absorbed by the blossom's porous lining. The tilting motion changed in midair to an agonized writhing of the serpentine arm; and then the Voorqual's huge, scaly stalk and serrate leaf-crown began to toss in a frenetic dance of death, waving darkly against the auroral curtains of morn. Its deep, solemn hissing sharpened to an insupportable note, fraught with the pain of a dying devil; and looking down from the platform edge on which he crouched to avoid the swaying growth, Lunithi saw that the lesser plants on all the black terraces beneath were tossing in mad unison with their master. Like noises in an evil dream, he heard the chorus of their tortured sibilations.

He dared not look again at the Voorqual, till he became aware of a strange, unnatural silence, and saw that the blossoms below had ceased to writhe and were drooping limply on their stems. Then, incredulous, he knew that the Voorqual was dead.

Turning, in mingled horror and triumph, he beheld the flaccid stalk that had fallen prone on its bed of unholy compost. He saw the sudden withering of the stiff, sworded leaves, of the gross and hellish flower. Even the stony bulb appeared to collapse and crumble before his eyes. The entire stem, with its evil colors fading swiftly, shrank and fell in upon itself like a sere and empty serpent-skin.

At the same time, in some obscure manner, Lunithi was still aware of a presence that brooded above the pyramid. Even in the death of the Voorqual, it seemed to him that he was not alone. Then, as he stood and waited, fearing he knew not what, he felt the passing of a cold and unseen thing in the azure gloom—a thing that flowed across his body like the coils of some enormous python, without sound, in dark and clammy undulations. A moment more and it was gone; and Lunithi no longer felt the brooding presence.

He turned to go; and it seemed that the dying night was ominous of an unconceived terror that gathered before him as he went down the long volutes of somber stairs. Slowly he descended; and a weird despair was upon him. He had slain the Voorqual, had seen it wither in death; so Nala should be saved from the morrow's sacrifice. Yet he could not believe the thing he had done; the lifting of the ancient doom was still no more than an idle myth.

The twilight had begun to brighten as he passed through the slumbering city. According to custom of Lophai, no one would be abroad for another hour. Then the priests of the Voorqual would gather for the annual rite of blood-offering.

Midway between the pyramid and his own palace, Lunithi was more than startled to meet the maiden Nala. Pale and ghostly, she glided by him with a swift and swaying movement almost serpentine, which differed strangely from her habitual languor. Lunithi dared not accost her when he saw her shut, unheeding eyes, like those of a somnambulist; and he was deeply awed and troubled by the serpentine ease, the unnatural surety of her motion. It reminded him of something which he feared to remember. In a turmoil of fantastic doubt and apprehension, he followed her.

Threading the exotic maze of Lospar with the fleet and sinuous glide of a homing serpent, Nala entered the sacred pyramid. Lunithi, less swift than the maiden, had fallen behind; and he knew not where she had gone in the myriad vaults and interior chambers; but a strange and fearsome intuition drew his steps without delay to the platform of the summit.

He knew not what he should find; but his heart was drugged with an esoteric hopelessness; and he was aware of no surprise when he came forth in the many-colored dawn and beheld the thing which awaited him.

The maiden Nala—or that which he knew to be Nala—was standing in the basin of evil soil, above the withered remains of the Voorqual. She had undergone—was still undergoing—a monstrous and diabolic transformation. Her frail, slight body had assumed a long and dragon-like form, and the tender skin was marked off in incipient scales that darkened momentarily with a mottling of baleful hues. Her head was no longer recognizable as such, and the human lineaments were flaring into a weird semi-circle of pointed leaf-buds. Her lower limbs had joined together, had rooted themselves in the ground. One of her arms was becoming a part of the ophidian bole; and the other was lengthening into a scaly stem that bore the dark-red bud of a sinister blossom.

More and more the monstrosity took on the similitude of the Voorqual; and Lunithi, crushed by the ancient awe and dark, terrible faith of his ancestors, could feel no longer any doubt of its true identity. Soon there was no trace of Nala in the thing before him, which began to sway with a dreamy, python-like rhythm, and to utter a deep and measured sibilation, to which the plants on the lower tiers responded. He knew then that the Voorqual had returned to claim its sacrifice and preside forever above the city Lospar and the world Lophai.

THE NAMELESS OFFSPRING

Many and multiform are the dim horrors of Earth, infesting her ways from the prime. They sleep beneath the unturned stone; they rise with the tree from its roots; they move beneath the sea and in subterranean places; they dwell unchallenged in the inmost adyta; they emerge betimes from the shutten sepulcher of haughty bronze and the low grave that is sealed with clay. There be some that are long known to man, and others as yet unknown that abide the terrible latter days of their revealing. Those which are the most dreadful and the loathliest of all are haply still to be declared. But among those that have revealed themselves aforetime and have made manifest their veritable presence, there is one which may not openly be named for its exceeding foulness. It is that spawn which the hidden dweller in the vaults has begotten upon mortality.
—From the *Necronomicon* of Abdul Alhazred.

In a sense, it is fortunate that the story I must now relate should be so largely a thing of undetermined shadows, of half-shaped hints and forbidden inferences. Otherwise, it could never be written by human hand or read by human eye. My own slight part in the hideous drama was limited to its last act; and to me its earlier scenes were merely a remote and ghastly legend. Yet, even so, the broken reflex of its unnatural horrors has crowded out in perspective the main events of normal life; has made them seem no more than frail gossamers, woven on the dark, windy verge of some unsealed abyss, some deep, half-open charnel, wherein earth's nethermost corruptions lurk and fester.

The legend of which I speak was familiar to me from childhood, as a theme of family whispers and head-shakings, for Sir John Tremoth had been a school-mate of my father's. But I had never met Sir John, had never visited Tremoth Hall, till the time of those happenings which formed the final tragedy. My father had taken me from England to Canada when I was a small infant; he had prospered in Manitoba as an apiarist; and after his death the bee-ranch had kept me too busy for years to execute a long-cherished dream of visiting my natal land and exploring its rural by-ways.

When, finally, I set sail, the story was pretty dim in my memory; and Tremoth Hall was no conscious part of my itinerary when I began a motor-cycle tour of the English counties. In any case, I should never have been drawn to the neighborhood out of morbid curiosity, such as the frightful tale might possibly have evoked in others. My visit, as it happened, was purely accidental. I had forgotten the exact location of the place, and did not even dream that I was in its vicinity. If I had known, it seems to me that I should have turned aside, in spite of the circumstances that impelled me to seek shelter, rather than intrude upon the almost demoniacal misery of its owner.

When I came to Tremoth Hall, I had ridden all day, in early autumn, through a rolling country-side with leisurely, winding thoroughfares and lanes. The day had been fair, with skies of pale azure above noble parks that were tinged with the first amber and crimson of the mellowing year. But toward the middle of the afternoon, a mist had come in from the hidden ocean across low hills and had closed me about with its moving phantom circle. Somehow, in that deceptive fog, I managed to lose my way, to miss the mile-post that would have given me my direction to the town where I had planned to spend the ensuing night.

I went on for awhile, at random, thinking that I should soon reach another cross-road. The way that I followed was little more than a rough lane and was singularly deserted. The fog had darkened and drawn closer, obliterating all horizons; but from what I could see of it, the country was one of heath and boulders, with no sign of cultivation. I topped a level ridge and went down a long, monotonous slope as the mist continued to thicken with twilight. I thought that I was riding toward the west; but before me, in the wan dusk, there was no faintest gleaming or flare of color to betoken the drowned sunset. A dank odor that was touched with salt, like the smell of sea-marshes, came to meet me.

The road turned at a sharp angle, and I seemed to be riding between downs and marshland. The night gathered with an almost unnatural quickness, as if in haste to overtake me; and I began to feel a sort of dim concern and alarm, as if I had gone astray in regions that were more dubious than an English county. The fog and twilight seemed to withhold a silent landscape of chill, deathly, disquieting mystery.

Then, to the left of my road and a little before me, I saw a light that some-how suggested a mournful and tear-dimmed eye. It shone among blurred, uncertain masses that were like trees from a ghostland wood. A nearer mass, as I approached it, was resolved into a small lodge-building, such as would guard the entrance of some estate. It was dark and apparently unoccupied. Pausing and peering, I saw the outlines of a wrought-iron gate in a hedge of untrimmed yew.

It all had a desolate and forbidding air; and I felt in my very marrow the brooding chillness that had come in from the unseen marsh in that dismal, ever-coiling fog. But the light was promise of human nearness on the lonely downs; and I might obtain shelter for the night, or at least find someone who could direct me to a town or inn.

Somewhat to my surprise, the gate was unlocked. It swung inward with a rusty grating sound, as if it had not been opened for a long time; and pushing my motor-cycle before me, I followed a weed-grown drive toward the light. The rambling mass of a large manor-house disclosed itself, among trees and shrubs whose artificial forms, like the hedge of ragged yew, were assuming a wilder grotesquery than they had received from the hand of the topiary.

The fog had turned into a bleak drizzle. Almost groping in the gloom, I found a dark door, at some distance from the window that gave forth the solitary light. In response to my thrice-repeated knock, I heard at length the muffled sound of slow, dragging footfalls. The door was opened with a gradualness that seemed to indicate caution or reluctance, and I saw before me an old man, bearing a lighted taper in his hand. His fingers trembled with palsy or decrepitude, and monstrous shadows flickered behind him in a dim hallway, and touched his wrinkled features as with the flitting of ominous, bat-like wings.

"What do you wish, sir?" he asked. The voice, though quavering and hesitant, was far from churlish and did not suggest the attitude of suspicion and downright inhospitality which I had begun to apprehend. However, I sensed a sort of irresolution or dubiety; and as the old man listened to my account of the circumstances that had led me to knock at that lonely door, I saw that he was scrutinizing me with a keenness that belied my first impression of extreme senility.

"I knew you were a stranger in these parts," he commented when I had finished. "But might I inquire your name, sir?"

"I am Henry Chaldane."

"Are you not the son of Mr. Arthur Chaldane?"

Somewhat mystified, I admitted the ascribed paternity.

"You resemble your father, sir. Mr. Chaldane and Sir John Tremoth were great friends, in the days before your father went to Canada. Will you not come in, sir? This is Tremoth Hall. Sir John has not been in the habit of receiving guests for a long time; but I shall tell him that you are here; and it may be that he will wish to see you."

Startled, and not altogether agreeably surprised at the discovery of my whereabouts, I followed the old man to a book-lined study whose furnishings bore evidence of luxury and neglect. Here he lit an oil-lamp of antique fashion, with a dusty, painted shade, and left me alone with the dustier volumes and furniture.

I felt a queer embarrassment, a sense of actual intrusion, as I waited in the wan yellow lamplight. There came back to me the details of the strange, horrific, half-forgotten story I had overheard from my father in childhood years.

Lady Agatha Tremoth, Sir John's wife, in the first year of their marriage, had become the victim of cataleptic seizures. The third seizure had apparently terminated in death, for she did not revive after the usual interval, and displayed all the familiar marks of the *rigor mortis*. Lady Agatha's body was placed in the family vaults, which were of almost fabulous age and extent, and had been excavated in the hill behind the manor-house. On the day following the interment, Sir John, troubled by a queer, insistent doubt as to the finality of the medical verdict, had re-entered the vaults in time to hear a wild cry, and had found Lady Agatha sitting up in her coffin. The nailed lid was lying on the stone floor, and it seemed impossible that it could have been removed by the struggles of the frail woman. However, there was no other plausible explanation, though Lady Agatha herself could throw little light on the circumstances of her strange resurrection.

Half-dazed, and almost delirious, in a state of dire terror that was easily understandable, she told an incoherent tale of her experience. She did not seem to remember struggling to free herself from the coffin, but was troubled mainly by recollections of a pale, hideous, unhuman face which she had seen in the gloom on awakening from her prolonged and death-like sleep. It was the sight of this face, stooping over her as she lay in the *open* coffin, that had caused her to cry out so wildly. The thing had vanished before Sir John's approach, fleeing swiftly to the inner vaults; and she had formed only a vague idea of its bodily appearance. She thought, however, that it was large and white, and ran like an animal on all fours, though its limbs were semi-human.

Of course, her tale was regarded as a sort of dream, or a figment of delirium induced by the awful shock of her experience, which had blotted out all recollection of its true terror. But the memory of the horrible face and figure had seemed to obsess her permanently, and was plainly fraught with associations of mind-unhinging fear. She did not recover from her illness, but lived on in a shattered condition of brain and body; and nine months later she died, after giving birth to her first child.

Her death was a merciful thing; for the child, it seemed, was one of those appalling monsters that sometimes appear in human families. The exact nature of its abnormality was not known, though frightful and divergent rumors had purported to emanate from the doctor, nurses and servants who had seen it. Some of the latter had left Tremoth Hall and had refused to return, after a single glimpse of the monstrosity.

After Lady Agatha's death, Sir John had withdrawn from society: and little or nothing was divulged in regard to his doings or the fate of the horrible infant. People said, however, that the child was kept in a locked room with iron-barred windows, which no one but Sir John himself had ever entered. The tragedy had blighted his whole life, and he had become a recluse, living alone with one or two faithful servants, and allowing his estate to decline grievously through neglect.

Doubtless, I thought, the old man who had admitted me was one of the remaining servitors. I was still reviewing the dreadful legend, still striving to recollect certain particulars that had almost passed from memory, when I heard the sound of footsteps which, from their slowness and feebleness, I took to be those of the returning man-servant.

However, I was mistaken; for the person who entered was plainly Sir John Tremoth himself. The tall, slightly bent figure, the face that was lined as if by the trickling of some corrosive acid, were marked with a dignity that seemed to triumph over the double ravages of mortal sorrow and illness. Somehow (though I could have calculated his real age) I had expected an old man; but he was scarcely beyond middle life. His cadaverous pallor and feeble, tottering walk were those of a man who is stricken with some fatal malady.

His manner, as he addressed me, was impeccably courteous and even gracious. But the voice was that of one to whom the ordinary relations and actions of life had long since become meaningless and perfunctory.

"Harper tells me that you are the son of my old school-friend, Arthur Chaldane," he said. "I bid you welcome to such poor hospitality as I am able to offer. I have not received guests for many years, and I fear you will find the Hall pretty dull and dismal and will think me an indifferent host. Nevertheless, you must remain, at least for the night. Harper has gone to prepare dinner for us."

"You are very kind," I replied. "I fear, however, that I am intruding. If—"

"Not at all," he countered firmly. "You must be my guest. It is miles to the nearest inn, and the fog is changing into a heavy rain. Indeed, I am glad to have you. You must tell me all about your father and yourself at dinner. In the meanwhile, I'll try to find a room for you, if you'll come with me."

He led me to the second floor of the manor-house and down a long hall with beams and panels of ancient oak. We passed several doors which were doubtless those of bed-chambers. All were closed, and one of the doors was re-enforced with iron bars, heavy and sinister as those of a dungeon-cell. Inevitably, I surmised that this was the chamber in which the monstrous child had been confined; and also I wondered if the abnormality still lived, after a lapse of time that must have been nearly thirty years. How abysmal, how abhorrent, must have been its departure from the human type, to necessitate an immediate removal from the sight of others! And what characteristics of its further development could have rendered necessary the massive bars on an oaken door which, by itself, was strong enough to have resisted the assaults of any common man or beast?

Without even glancing at the door, my host went on, carrying a taper that scarcely shook in his feeble fingers. My curious reflections, as I followed him, were interrupted with nerve-shattering suddenness by a loud cry that seemed to issue from the barred room. The sound was a long, ever-mounting ululation, infra-bass at first like the tomb-muffled voice of a demon, and rising through abominable degrees to a shrill, ravenous fury, as if the demon had emerged by a series of underground steps to the open air. It was neither human nor bestial, it was wholly preternatural, hellish, macabre; and I shuddered with an insupportable eeriness, that still persisted when the demon voice, after reaching its culmination, had returned by reverse degrees to a profound sepulchral silence.

Sir John had given no apparent heed to the awful sound, but had gone on with no more than his usual faltering. He had reached the end of the hall, and was pausing before the second chamber from the one with the sealed door.

"I'll let you have this room," he said. "It's just beyond the one that I occupy." He did not turn his face toward me as he spoke; and his voice was unnaturally toneless and restrained. I realized with another shudder that the chamber he had indicated as his own was adjacent to the room from which the frightful ululation had appeared to issue.

The chamber to which he now admitted me had manifestly not been used for years. The air was chill, stagnant, unwholesome, with an all-pervading mustiness, and the antique furniture had gathered the inevitable increment of dust and cobwebs. Sir John began to apologize.

"I didn't realize the condition of the room," he said. "I'll send Harper after dinner, to do a little dusting and clearing, and put fresh linen on the bed."

I protested, rather vaguely, that there was no need for him to apologize. The unhuman loneliness and decay of the old manor-house, its lustrums and decades of neglect, and the corresponding desolation of its owner, had impressed me more painfully than ever. And I dared not speculate overmuch concerning the ghastly secret of the barred chamber, and the hellish howling that still echoed in my shaken nerves. Already I regretted the singular fortuity that had drawn me to that place of evil and festering shadows. I felt an urgent desire to leave, to continue my journey even in the face of the bleak autumnal rain and wind-blown darkness. But I could think of no excuse that would be sufficiently tangible and valid. Manifestly, there was nothing to do but remain.

Our dinner was served in a dismal but stately room, by the old man whom Sir John had referred to as Harper. The meal was plain but substantial and well-cooked; and the service was impeccable. I had begun to infer that Harper was the only servant—a combination of valet, butler, housekeeper and chef.

In spite of my hunger, and the pains taken by my host to make me feel at ease, the meal was a solemn and almost funereal ceremony. I could not forget my father's story; and still less could I forget the sealed door and the baleful ululation. Whatever it was, the monstrosity still lived; and I felt a complex mingling of admiration, pity and horror as I looked at the gaunt and gallant face of Sir John Tremoth, and reflected upon the life-long hell to which he had been condemned, and the apparent fortitude with which he had borne its unthinkable ordeals.

A bottle of excellent sherry was brought in. Over this, we sat for an hour or more. Sir John spoke at some length concerning my father, of whose death he had not previously heard; and he drew me out in regard to my own affairs with the subtle adroitness of a polished man of the world. He said little about himself; and not even by hint or inference did he refer to the tragic history which I have outlined.

Since I am rather abstemious, and did not empty my glass with much frequency, the major part of the heavy wine was consumed by my host. Toward the end, it seemed to bring out in him a curious vein of confidentiality; and he spoke for the first time of the ill-health that was all too patent in his appearance. I learned that he was subject to that most painful form of heart disease, angina pectoris, and had recently recovered from an attack of unusual severity.

"The next one will finish me," he said. "And it may come at any time—perhaps tonight." He made the announcement very simply, as if he were voicing a commonplace or venturing a prediction about the weather. Then, after a slight pause, he went on, with more emphasis and weightiness of tone:

"Maybe you'll think me queer, but I have a fixed prejudice against burial or vault-interment. I want my remains to be thoroughly cremated, and have left careful directions to that end. Harper will see to it that they are fulfilled. Fire is the cleanest and purest of the elements; and it cuts short all the damnable processes between death and ultimate disintegration. I can't bear the idea of some mouldy, worm-infested tomb."

He continue to discourse on the subject for some time, with a singular elaboration and tenseness of manner that showed it to be a familiar theme of thought, if not an actual obsession. It seemed to possess a morbid fascination for him; and there was a painful light in his hollow, haunted eyes, and a touch of rigidly subdued hysteria in his voice, as he spoke. I remembered the interment of Lady Agatha, and her tragic resurrection, and the dim, delirious horror of the vaults, that had formed an inexplicable and vaguely disturbing part of her story. It was not hard to understand Sir John's aversion to burial; but I was far from suspecting the full terror and ghastliness on which his repugnance had been founded.

Harper had disappeared after bringing the sherry; and I surmised that he had been given orders for the renovation of my room. We had now drained our last glasses; and my host had ended his peroration. The wine, which had animated him briefly, seemed to die out, and he looked more ill and haggard than ever. Pleading my own fatigue, I expressed a wish to retire; and he, with his invariable courtliness, insisted on seeing me to my chamber and making sure of my comfort, before seeking his own bed.

In the hall above, we met Harper, who was just descending from a flight of stairs that must have led to an attic or third floor. He was carrying a heavy iron pan, in which a few scraps of meat remained; and I caught an odor of pronounced gaminess, almost of virtual putrescence, from the pan as he went by. I wondered if he had been feeding the unknown monstrosity, and if perhaps its food were supplied to it through a trap in the ceiling of the barred room. The surmise was reasonable enough, but the odor of the scraps, by a train of remote, half-literary association, had begun to suggest other surmises which, it would seem, were beyond the realm of possibility and reason. Certain evasive, incoherent hints appeared to join themselves suddenly to an atrocious and abhorrent whole. With imperfect success, I assured myself that the thing I had fancied was incredible to science; was a mere creation of superstitious diablerie. No, it could not be... here in England, of all places... that corpse-devouring demon of Arabesque tales and legends... the *ghoul.*

Contrary to my fears, there was no repetition of the fiendish howling as we passed the secret room. But I thought that I heard a measured crunching, such as a large animal would make in devouring its food.

My room, though still drear and dismal enough, had been cleared of its accumulated dust and matted gossamers. After a personal inspection, Sir John left me and retired to his own chamber. I was struck by his deathly pallor and weakness, as he said good-night to me; and felt guiltily apprehensive that the strain of receiving and entertaining a guest might have aggravated the dire disease from which he suffered. I seemed to detect actual pain and torment beneath his careful armor of urbanity; and wondered if the urbanity had not been maintained at an excessive cost.

The fatigue of my day-long journey, together with the heavy wine I had drunk, should have conduced to early slumber. But though I lay with tightly closed lids in the darkness, I could not dismiss those evil shadows, those black and charnel larvae, that swarmed upon me from the ancient house. Insufferable and forbidden things besieged me with filthy talons, brushed me with noisome coils, as I tossed through eternal hours and lay staring at the grey square of the storm-darkened window. The dripping of the rain, the sough and moan of the wind, resolved themselves to a dread mutter of half-articulate voices that plotted against my peace and whispered loathfully of nameless secrets in demonian language.

At length, after the seeming lapse of nocturnal centuries, the tempest died away, and I no longer heard the equivocal voices. The window lightened a little in the black wall; and the terrors of my night-long insomnia seemed to withdraw partially, but without bringing the surcease of slumber. I became aware of utter silence; and then, in the silence, of a queer, faint, disquieting sound whose cause and location baffled me for many minutes.

The sound was muffled and far-off at times; then it seemed to draw near, as if it were in the next room. I began to identify it as a sort of scratching, such as would be made by the claws of an animal on solid woodwork. Sitting up in bed, and listening attentively, I realized with a fresh start of horror that it came from the direction of the barred chamber. It took on a strange resonance; then it became almost inaudible; and suddenly, for awhile, it ceased. In the interim, I heard a single groan, like that of a man in great agony or terror. I could not mistake the source of the groan, which had issued from Sir John Tremoth's room; nor was I doubtful any longer as to the causation of the scratching.

The groan was not repeated; but the damnable clawing sound began again and was continued till daybreak. Then, as if the creature that had caused the noise were wholly nocturnal in its habits, the faint, vibrant rasping ceased and was not resumed. In a state of dull, nightmarish apprehension, drugged with weariness and want of sleep, I had listened to it with intolerably straining ears. With its cessation, in the hueless livid dawn, I slid into a deep slumber, from which the muffled and amorphous specters of the old Hall were unable to detain me any longer.

I was awakened by a loud knocking on my door—a knocking in which even my sleep-confused senses could recognize the imperative and urgent. It must have been close upon mid-day; and feeling guilty at having overslept so egregiously, I ran to the door and opened it. The old man-servant, Harper, was standing without; and his tremulous, grief-broken manner told me before he spoke that something of dire import had occurred.

"I regret to tell you, Mr. Chaldane," he quavered, "that Sir John is dead. He did not answer my knock as usual; so I made bold to enter his room. He must have died early this morning."

Inexpressibly shocked by his announcement, I recalled the single groan I had heard in the grey beginning of dawn. My host, perhaps, had been dying at that very moment. I recalled, too, the detestable nightmare scratching. Unavoidably, I wondered if the groan had been occasioned by fear as well as by physical pain. Had the strain and suspense of listening to that abhorrent sound brought on the final paroxysm of Sir John's malady? I could not be sure of the truth; but my brain seethed with awful and ghastly conjectures.

With the futile formalities that one employs on such occasions, I tried to condole with the aged servant, and offered him such assistance as I could in making the necessary arrangements for the disposition of his master's remains. Since there was no telephone in the house, I volunteered to find a doctor who would examine the body and sign the death-certificate. The old man seemed to feel a singular relief and gratitude.

"Thank you, sir," he said fervently. Then, as if in explanation: "I don't want to leave Sir John—I promised him that I'd keep a close watch over his body." He went on to speak of Sir John's desire for cremation. It seemed that the baronet had left explicit directions for the building of a pyre of driftwood on the hill behind the Hall, the burning of his remains on this pyre, and the sowing of his ashes on the fields of the estate. These directions he had enjoined and empowered the servant to carry out as soon after death as possible. No one was to be present at the ceremony, except Harper and the hired pall bearers; and Sir John's nearer relatives (none of whom lived in the vicinity) were not to be informed of his demise till all was over.

I refused Harper's offer to prepare my breakfast, telling him that I would obtain a meal in the neighboring village. There was a strange uneasiness in his manner; and I realized, with thoughts and emotions not to be specified in this narrative, that he was anxious to begin his promised vigil beside Sir John's corpse.

It would be tedious and unnecessary to detail the funereal afternoon that followed. The heavy sea-fog had returned; and I seemed to grope my way through a sodden but unreal world as I sought the nearby town. I succeeded in locating a doctor and also in securing several men to build the pyre and act as pall bearers. I was met everywhere with an odd taciturnity, and no one seemed willing to comment on Sir John's death or to speak of the dark legendry that was attached to Tremoth Hall.

Harper, to my amazement, had proposed that the cremation should take place at once. This, however, proved to be impracticable. When all the formalities and arrangements had been completed, the fog turned into a steady, everlasting downpour which rendered impossible the lighting of the pyre; and we were compelled to defer the ceremony. I had promised Harper that I should remain at the Hall till all was done; and so it was that I spent a second night beneath that roof of accurst and abominable secrets.

The darkness came on betimes. After a last visit to the village, in which I procured some sandwiches for Harper and myself, in lieu of dinner, I returned to the lonely Hall. I was met by Harper on the stairs, as I ascended to the death-chamber. There was an increased agitation in his manner, as if something had happened to frighten him.

"I wonder if you'd keep me company tonight, Mr. Chaldane," he said. "It's a gruesome watch that I'm asking you to share, and it may be a dangerous one. But Sir John would thank you, I am sure. If you have a weapon of any sort, it will be well to bring it with you."

It was impossible to refuse his request, and I assented at once. I was unarmed; so Harper insisted on equipping me with an antique revolver, of which he himself carried the mate.

"Look here, Harper," I said bluntly, as we followed the hall to Sir John's chamber. "What are you afraid of?"

He flinched visibly at the question and seemed unwilling to answer. Then, after a moment, he appeared to realize that frankness was necessary.

"It's the thing in the barred room," he explained. "You must have heard it, sir. We've had the care of it, Sir John and I, these eight-and-twenty years; and we've always feared that it might break out. It never gave us much trouble... as long as we kept it well-fed. But for the last three nights, it has been scratching at the thick oaken wall of Sir John's chamber, which is something it never did before. Sir John thought it knew that he was going to die, and that it wanted to reach his body—being hungry for other food than we had given it. That's why we must guard him closely tonight, Mr. Chaldane. I pray to God that the wall will hold; but the thing keeps on clawing and clawing, like a demon; and I don't like the hollowness of the sound—as if the wood were getting pretty thin."

Appalled by this confirmation of my own most repugnant surmise, I could offer no rejoinder, since all comment would have been infinitely futile. With Harper's open avowal, the inferred abnormality took on a darker and more encroaching shadow, a more potent and tyrannic menace. Willingly would I have foregone the promised vigil... but this, of course, was impossible to do.

The bestial, diabolic scratching, louder and more frantic than before, assailed my ears as we passed the barred room. All too readily, I understood the nameless fear that had impelled the old man to request my company. The sound was inexpressibly alarming and nerve-sapping, with its grim, macabre insistence, its intimation of ghoulish hunger. It became even plainer, with a hideous, tearing vibrancy, when we entered the room of death.

During the whole course of that funeral day, I had refrained from visiting this chamber, since I am lacking in the morbid curiosity which impels many to gaze upon the dead. So it was that I beheld my host for the second and last time. Fully dressed and prepared for the pyre, he lay on the chill white bed whose heavily figured, arras-like curtains had been drawn back. The room was lit by several tall tapers, arranged on a little table in curious brazen candelabras that were greened with antiquity; but the light seemed to afford only a doubtful, dolorous glimmering in the drear spaciousness and mortuary shadows.

Somewhat against my will, I gazed on the dead features, and averted my eyes very hastily. I was prepared for the stony pallor and rigor, but not for the full betrayal of that hideous revulsion, that inhuman terror and horror, which must have corroded the man's heart through infernal years; and which, with almost superhuman control, he had masked from the casual beholder in life. The revelation was too painful, and I could not look at him again. In a sense, it seemed that he was not dead; that he was still listening with agonized attention to the dreadful sounds that might well have served to precipitate the final attack of his malady.

There were several chairs, dating, I think, like the bed itself, from the seventeenth century. Harper and I seated ourselves near the small table and between the death-bed and the panelled wall of blackish wood from which the ceaseless clawing sound appeared to issue. In tacit silence, with drawn and cocked revolvers, we began our ghastly vigil.

Abhorrently, but irresistibly, as we sat and waited, I was driven to picture the unnamed monstrosity; and formless or half-formed images of charnel nightmare pursued each other in chaotic succession through my mind. An atrocious curiosity, to which I should normally have been a stranger, prompted me to question Harper; but I was restrained by an even more powerful inhibition. On his part, the old man volunteered no information or comment whatever, but watched the wall with fear-bright eyes that did not seem to waver in his palsy-nodding head.

It would be impossible to convey the unnatural tension, the macabre suspense and baleful expectation of the hours that followed. The woodwork must have been of great thickness and hardness, such as would have defied the assaults of any normal creature equipped only with talons or teeth; but in spite of such obvious arguments as these, I thought momently to see it crumble inward. The scratching noise went on eternally; and to my febrile fancy, it grew sharper and nearer every instant. At recurrent intervals, I seemed to hear a low, eager, dog-like whining, such as a ravenous animal would make when it neared the goal of its burrowing.

Neither of us had spoken of what we should do, in case the monster should attain its objective; but there seemed to be an unvoiced agreement. However, with a superstitiousness of which I should not have believed myself capable, I began to wonder if the monster possessed enough of humanity in its composition to be vulnerable to mere revolver bullets. To what extent would it display the traits of its unknown and fabulous paternity? I tried to convince myself that such questions and wonderings were patently absurd; but was drawn to them again and again, as if by the allurement of some forbidden gulf.

The night wore on, like the flowing of a dark, sluggish stream; and the tall, funereal tapers had burned to within an inch of their verdigris-eaten sockets. It was this circumstance alone that gave me an idea of the passage of time; for I seemed to be drowning in a black eternity, motionless beneath the crawling and seething of blind horrors. I had grown so accustomed to the clawing noise in the woodwork, and the sound had gone on so long, that I deemed its ever-growing sharpness and hollowness a mere hallucination; and so it was that the end of our vigil came without apparent warning.

Suddenly, as I stared at the wall and listened with frozen fixity, I heard a harsh, splintering sound, and saw that a narrow strip had broken loose and was hanging from the panel. Then, before I could collect myself or credit the awful witness of my senses, a large semi-circular portion of the wall collapsed in many splinters beneath the impact of some ponderous body.

Mercifully, perhaps, I have never been able to recall with any degree of distinctness the hellish thing that issued from the panel. The visual shock, by its own excess of horror, has almost blotted the details from memory. I have, however, the blurred impression of a huge, whitish, hairless and semi-quadruped body, of canine teeth in a half-human face, and long hyena nails at the end of forelimbs that were both arms and legs. A charnel stench preceded the apparition, like a breath from the den of some carrion-eating animal; and then, with a single nightmare leap, the thing was upon us.

I heard the staccato crack of Harper's revolver, sharp and vengeful in the closed room; but there was only a rusty click from my own weapon. Perhaps the cartridge was too old; at any rate, it had misfired. Before I could press the trigger again, I was hurled to the floor with terrific violence, striking my head against the heavy base of the little table. A black curtain, spangled with countless fires, appeared to fall upon me and to blot the room from sight. Then all the fires went out, and there was only darkness.

Again, slowly, I became conscious of flame and shadow; but the flame was bright and flickering, and seemed to grow ever more brilliant. Then my dull, doubtful senses were sharply revived and clarified by the acrid odor of burning cloth. The features of the room returned to vision, and I found that I was lying huddled against the overthrown table, gazing toward the death-bed. The guttering candles had been hurled to the floor. One of them was eating a slow circle of fire in the carpet beside me; and another, spreading, had ignited the bed curtains, which were flaring swiftly upward to the great canopy. Even as I lay staring, huge, ruddy tatters of the burning fabric fell upon the bed in a dozen places, and the body of Sir John Tremoth was ringed about with starting flames.

I staggered heavily to my feet and giddy with the fall that had hurled me into oblivion. The room was empty, except for the old man-servant, who lay near the door, moaning indistinctly. The door itself stood open, as if someone—or something—had gone out during my period of unconsciousness.

I turned again to the bed, with some instinctive, half-formed intention of trying to extinguish the blaze. The flames were spreading rapidly, were leaping higher, but they were not swift enough to veil from my sickened eyes the hands and features (if one could any longer call them such) of that which had been Sir John Tremoth. Of the last horror that had overtaken him, I must forbear explicit mention; and I would that I could likewise avoid the remembrance.... All too tardily had the monster been frightened away by the fire.

There is little more to tell. Looking back once more, as I reeled from the smoke-laden room with Harper in my arms, I saw that the bed and its canopy had become a mass of mounting flames. The unhappy baronet had found in his own death-chamber the funeral pyre for which he had longed with such dreadful ardor.

It was nearly dawn when we emerged from the doomed manor-house. The rain had ceased, leaving a heaven lined with high and dead-grey clouds. The chill air appeared to revive the aged man-servant; and he stood feebly beside me, uttering not a word, as we watched an ever-climbing spire of flame that broke from the somber roof of Tremoth Hall and began to cast a sullen glare on the unkempt hedges and dishevelled trees.

In the combined light of the fireless dawn and the lurid conflagration, we both saw at our feet the semi-human, monstrous footprints, with their mark of long and canine nails, that had been trodden freshly and deeply in the rain-wet soil. They came from the direction of the manor-house, and ran toward the heath-clad hill that rose behind it.

Still without speaking, we followed the steps. Almost without interruption, they led to the entrance of the ancient family vaults, to the heavy iron door in the hillside that had been closed for a full generation by Sir John Tremoth's order. The door itself swung open, and we saw that its rusty chain and lock had been shattered by a strength that was more than the strength of man or beast. Then, peering within, we saw the clay-touched outline of the unreturning footprints that went downward into mausolean darkness on the stone stairs.

We were both weaponless, having left our revolvers behind us in the death-chamber; but we did not hesitate long. Harper possessed a liberal supply of matches; and looking about, I found a heavy billet of water-soaked wood, which might serve in lieu of a cudgel. In grim silence, with tacit determination, and forgetful of any danger, we conducted a thorough search of the well-nigh interminable vaults, striking match after match as we went on in the musty shadows.

The traces of ghoulish footsteps grew fainter as we followed them into those black recesses; and we found nothing anywhere but noisome dampness and undisturbed cobwebs and the countless coffins of the dead. The thing that we sought had vanished utterly, as if swallowed up by the subterranean walls.

At last we returned to the entrance. There, as we stood blinking in the full daylight, with grey and haggard faces, Harper spoke for the first time, saying in his slow, tremulous voice:

"Many years ago—soon after Lady Agatha's death—Sir John and I searched the vaults from end to end; but we could find no trace of the thing we suspected. Now, as then, it is useless to seek. There are mysteries which, God helping, will never be fathomed. We know only that the offspring of the vaults has gone back to the vaults. There may it remain."

Silently, in my shaken heart, I echoed his last words and his wish.

A VINTAGE FROM ATLANTIS

I thank you, friend, but I am no drinker of wine, not even if it be the rarest Canary or the oldest Amontillado. Wine is a mocker, strong drink is raging… and more than others, I have reason to know the truth that was writ by Solomon the Jewish king. Give ear, if ye will, and I shall tell you a story such as would halt the half-drained cup on the lips of the hardiest bibber.

We were seven-and-thirty buccaneers, who raked the Spanish Main under Barnaby Dwale, he that was called Red Barnaby for the spilling of blood that attended him everywhere. Our ship, the *Black Falcon*, could outfly and outstrike all other craft that flew the Jolly Roger. Full often, Captain Dwale was wont to seek a remote isle on the eastward verge of the West Indies, and lighten the vessel of its weight of ingots and doubloons.

The isle was far from the common course of maritime traffic, and was not known to maps or other mariners; so it suited our purpose well. It was a place of palms and sand and cliffs, with a small harbor sheltered by the curving outstretched arms of rugged reefs, on which the dark ocean climbed and gnashed its fangs of white foam without troubling the tranquil waters beyond. I know not how many times we had visited the isle; but the soil beneath many a coco tree was heavy with our hidden trove. There we had stored the loot of bullion-laden ships, the massy plate and jewels of cathedral towns.

Even as to all mortal things, an ending came at last to our visits. We had gathered a goodly cargo of loot, but might have stayed longer on the open main where the Spaniards passed, if a tempest had not impended. We were near the secret isle, as it chanced, when the skies began to blacken; and wallowing heavily in the rising seas, we fled to our placid harbor, reaching it by night-fall. Before dawn the hurricane had blown by; and the sun came up in cloudless amber and blue. We proceeded with the landing and burying of our chests of coin and gems and ingots, which was a task of some length;

and afterwards we refilled our water-casks at a cool sweet spring that ran from beneath the palmy hill not far inland.

It was now mid-afternoon. Captain Dwale was planning to weigh anchor shortly and follow the westering sun toward the Caribbees. There were nine of us, loading the last barrels into the boats, with Red Barnaby looking on and cursing us for being slower than mud-turtles; and we were bending knee-deep in the tepid, lazy water, when suddenly the Captain ceased to swear, and we saw that he was no longer watching us. On the contrary, he had turned his back and was stooping over a strange object that must have drifted in with the tide, after the storm: a huge and barnacle-laden thing that lay on the sand, half in and half out of the shoaling water. Somehow, none of us had perceived it heretofore.

Red Barnaby was not silent long.

"Come here, ye chancre-eaten coistrels," he called to us. We obeyed willingly enough, and gathered around the beached object, which our Captain was examining with much perplexity. We too were greatly bewondered when we saw the thing more closely; and none of us could name it off-hand or with certainty.

The object had the form of a great jar, with a tapering neck and a deep, round, abdominous body. It was wholly encrusted with shells and corals that had gathered upon it as if through many ages in the ocean deeps, and was festooned with weeds and sea-flowers such as we had never before beheld; so that we could not determine the substance of which it was made.

At the order of Captain Dwale, we rolled it out of the water and beyond reach of the tide, into the shade of nearby palms; though it required the efforts of four men to move the unwieldy thing, which was strangely ponderous. We found that it would stand easily on end, with its top reaching almost to the shoulders of a tall man. While we were handling the great jar, we heard a swishing noise from within, as if it were filled with some sort of liquor.

Our Captain, as it chanced, was a learned man.

"By the communion-cup of Satan!" he swore. "If this thing is not an antique wine-jar, then I am a Bedlamite. Such vessels—though mayhap they were not so huge—were employed by the Romans to store the goodly vintages of Falernus and Cecuba. Indeed, there is today a Spanish wine—that of Valdepenas—which is kept in earthen jars. But this, if I mistake not, is neither from Spain nor olden Rome. It is ancient enough, by its look, to have come from that long-sunken isle, the Atlantis whereof Plato speaks. Truly, there should be a rare vintage within, a wine that was mellowed in the youth of the world, before the founding of Rome and Athens; and which, perchance, has gathered fire and strength with the centuries. Ho! my rascal sea-bullies! We sail not from this harbor till the jar is broached. And if the liquor within be sound and potable, we shall make holiday this evening on the sands."

"Belike, 'tis a funeral urn, full of plaguey cinders and ashes," said the mate, Roger Aglone, who had a gloomy turn of thought.

Red Barnaby had drawn his cutlass and was busily prying away the crust of barnacles and quaint fantastic coral-growths from the top of the jar. Layer on layer of them he removed, and swore mightily at this increment of forgotten years. At last a great stopper of earthen-ware, sealed with a clear wax that had grown harder than amber, was revealed by his prying. The stopper was graven with queer letters of an unknown language, plainly to be seen; but the wax refused the cutlass-point. So, losing all patience, the Captain seized a mighty fragment of stone, which a lesser man could scarce have lifted, and broke therewith the neck of the jar.

Now even in those days, I, Stephen Magbane, the one Puritan amid that Christless crew, was no bibber of wine or spirituous liquors, but a staunch Rechabite on all occasions. Therefore I held back, feeling little concern other than that of reprobation, while the others pressed about the jar and sniffed greedily at the contents. But, almost immediately with its opening, my nostrils were assailed by an odor of heathen spices, heavy and strange, together with a powerful vinulence; and the very inhalation thereof caused me to feel a sort of giddiness, so that I thought it well to retreat still further. But the others were eager as midges around a fermenting-vat in autumn.

"'Sblood! 'Tis a royal vintage!" roared the Captain, after he had dipped a forefinger in the jar and sucked the purple drops that dripped from it. "Avast, ye slumdegullions! Stow the water-casks on board, and summon all hands ashore, leaving only a watch there to ward the vessel. We'll have a gala night before we sack any more Spaniards."

We obeyed his order; and there was much rejoicing amid the crew of the *Black Falcon* at the news of our find and the postponement of the voyage. Three men, grumbling sorely at their absence from the revels, were left on board; though, in that tranquil harbor, such vigilance was virtually needless. We others returned to the shore, bringing a supply of pannikins in which to serve the wine, and provisions for a feast. Then we gathered pieces of drift with which to build a great fire, and caught several huge tortoises along the sands, and unearthed their hidden eggs, so that we might have an abundance and variety of victuals.

In these preparations, I took part with no special ardor. Knowing my habit of abstention, and being of a somewhat malicious and tormenting humor, Captain Dwale had expressly commanded my presence at the feast. However, I anticipated nothing more than a little ribaldry at my expense, as was customary at such times; and being partial to fresh tortoise-meat, I was not wholly unresigned to my lot as a witness of the Babylonian inebrieties of the others.

At nightfall, the feasting and drinking began; and the fire of driftwood, with eerie witch-colors of blue and green and white amid the flame, leapt high in the dusk while the sunset died to a handful of red embers far on purpling seas.

It was a strange wine that the crew and Captain swilled from their pannikins. I saw that the stuff was thick and dark, as if it had been mingled with blood; and the air was filled with the reek of those pagan spices, hot and rich and unholy, that might have poured from a broken tomb of antique emperors. And stranger still was the intoxication of that wine; for those who drank it became still and thoughtful and sullen; and there was no singing of lewd songs, no playing of apish antics.

Red Barnaby had been drinking longer than the others, having begun to sample the vintage while the crew were making ready for their revel. To our wonderment, he ceased to swear at us after the first cupful, and no longer ordered us about or paid us any heed, but sat peering into the sunset with eyes that held the dazzlement of unknown dreams. And one by one, as they began to drink, the others were likewise affected, so that I marvelled much at the unwonted power of the wine. I had never before beheld an intoxication of such nature; for they spoke not nor ate, and moved only to re-fill their cups from the mighty jar.

The night had grown dark as indigo beyond the flickering fire; and there was no moon; and the firelight blinded the stars. But one by one, after an interval, the drinkers rose from their places and stood staring into the darkness toward the sea. Unquietly they stood, and strained forward, peering intently as men who behold some marvellous thing; and queerly they muttered to one another, with unintelligible words. I knew not why they stared and muttered thus, unless it were because of some madness that had come upon them from the wine; for naught was visible in the dark, and I heard nothing, save the low murmur of wavelets lapping on the sand.

Louder grew the muttering; and some raised their hands and pointed seaward, babbling wildly as if in delirium. Noting their demeanor, and doubtful as to what further turn their madness might take, I bethought me to withdraw along the shore. But when I began to move away, those who were nearest me appeared to waken from their dream, and restrained me with rough hands. Then, with drunken, gibbering words, of which I could make no sense, they held me helpless while one of their number forced me to drink from a pannikin filled with the purple wine.

I fought against them, doubly unwilling to quaff that nameless vintage, and much of it was spilled. The stuff was sweet as liquid honey to the taste, but burned like hell-fire in my throat. I turned giddy; and a sort of dark confusion possessed my senses by degrees; and I seemed to hear and see and feel as in the mounting fever of calenture.

The air about me seemed to brighten, with a redness of ghostly blood that was everywhere; a light that came not from the fire nor from the nocturnal heavens. I beheld the faces and forms of the drinkers, standing without shadow, as if mantled with a rosy phosphorescence. And beyond them, where they stared in troubled and restless wonder, the darkness was illumed with the strange light.

Mad and unholy was the vision that I saw: for the harbor waves no longer lapped on the sand, and the sea had wholly vanished. The *Black Falcon* was gone, and where the reefs had been, great marble walls ascended, flushed as if with the ruby of lost sunsets. Above them were haughty domes of heathen temples, and spires of pagan palaces; and beneath were mighty streets and causeys where people passed in a never-ending throng. I thought that I gazed upon some immemorial city, such as had flourished in Earth's prime; and I saw the trees of its terraced gardens, fairer than the palms of Eden. Listening, I heard the sound of dulcimers that were sweet as the moaning of women; and the cry of horns that told forgotten glorious things; and the wild sweet singing of people who passed to some hidden, sacred festival within the walls.

I saw that the light poured upward from the city, and was born of its streets and buildings. It blinded the heavens above; and the horizon beyond was lost in a shining mist. One building there was, a high fane above the rest, from which the light streamed in a ruddier flood; and from its open portals music came, sorcerous and beguiling as the far voices of bygone years. And the revellers passed gayly into its portals forever; but none came forth. The weird music seemed to call me and entice me; and I longed to tread the streets of the alien city; and a deep desire was upon me to mingle with its people and pass into the glowing fane.

Verily I knew why the drinkers had stared at the darkness and had muttered among themselves in wonder. I knew that they also longed to descend into the city. And I saw that a great causey, built of marble and gleaming with the red luster, ran downward from their very feet over meadows of unknown blossoms to the foremost buildings.

Then, as I watched and listened, the singing grew sweeter, the music stranger; and the rosy luster brightened, fair as the gleaming of lost suns recalled by necromancy from eternal night. Then, with no backward glance, no word or gesture of injunction to his men, Captain Dwale went slowly forward, treading the marble causey like a dreamer who walks in his dream. And after him, one by one, Roger Aglone and the crew followed in the same manner, going toward the city.

Haply I too should have followed, drawn by the witching music. For truly it seemed that I had trod the ways of that city in former time, and had known the things whereof the music told and the voices sang. Well did I remember why the people passed eternally into the fane, and why they came not forth; and there, it seemed, I should meet familiar and beloved faces, and take part in mysteries recalled from the foundered years.

All this, which the wine had remembered through its sleep in the ocean depths, was mine to behold and conceive for a moment. And well it was that I had drunk less of that evil and pagan vintage than the others, and was less besotted than they with its luring vision. For, even as Captain Dwale and his crew went toward the city, it appeared to me that the rosy glow began to fade a little. The walls took on a wavering thinness, and the domes grew insubstantial. The rose departed, the light was pale as a phosphor of the tomb; and the people went to and fro like phantoms, with a thin crying of ghostly horns and a ghostly singing. Dimly above the sunken causey the harbor waves returned; and Red Barnaby and his men walked down beneath them. Slowly the waters darkened above the fading spires and walls; and the midnight blackened upon the sea; and the city was lost even as the vanished bubbles of wine.

A terror came upon me, knowing the fate of those others. I fled swiftly, stumbling in darkness toward the palmy hill that crowned the isle. No vestige remained of the rosy light; and the sky was filled with returning stars. And looking oceanward as I climbed the hill, I saw a lantern that burned on the *Black Falcon* in the harbor, and discerned the embers of our fire that smouldered on the sands. Then, praying with a fearful fervor, I waited for dawn.

THE WEIRD OF AVOOSL WUTHOQQUAN

I

"**G**ive, give, O magnanimous and liberal lord of the poor," cried the beggar.

Avoosl Wuthoqquan, the richest and most avaricious money-lender in all Commoriom, and, by that token, in the whole of Hyperborea, was startled from his train of reverie by the sharp, eerie, cicada-like voice. He eyed the supplicant with acidulous disfavor. His meditations, as he walked homeward that evening, had been splendidly replete with the shining of costly metals, with coins and ingots and gold-work and argentry, and the flaming or sparkling of many-tinted gems in rills, rivers and cascades, all flowing toward the coffers of Avoosl Wuthoqquan. Now the vision had flown; and this untimely and obstreperous voice was imploring for alms.

"I have nothing for you." His tones were like the grating of a shut clasp.

"Only two *pazoors*, O generous one, and I will prophesy."

Avoosl Wuthoqquan gave the beggar a second glance. He had never seen so disreputable a specimen of the mendicant class in all his wayfarings through Commoriom. The man was preposterously old, and his mummy-brown skin, wherever visible, was webbed with wrinkles that were like the heavy weaving of some giant jungle spider. His rags were no less than fabulous; and the beard that hung down and mingled with them was hoary as the moss of a primeval juniper.

"I do not require your prophecies."

"One *pazoor* then."

"No."

The eyes of the beggar became evil and malignant in their hollow sockets, like the heads of two poisonous little pit-vipers in their holes.

"Then, O Avoosl Wuthoqquan," he hissed, "I will prophesy gratis. Harken to your weird: the godless and exceeding love which you bear to all material

141

things, and your lust therefor, shall lead you on a strange quest and bring you to a doom whereof the stars and the sun will alike be ignorant. The hidden opulence of earth shall allure you and ensnare you; and earth itself shall devour you at the last."

"Begone," said Avoosl Wuthoqquan. "The weird is more than a trifle cryptic in its earlier clauses; and the final clause is somewhat platitudinous. I do not need a beggar to tell me the common fate of mortality."

II

It was many moons later, in that year which became known to pre-glacial historians as the year of the Black Tiger.

Avoosl Wuthoqquan sat in a lower chamber of his house, which was also his place of business. The room was obliquely shafted by the brief, aerial gold of the reddening sunset, which fell through a crystal window, lighting a serpentine line of irised sparks in the jewel-studded lamp that hung from copper chains, and touching to fiery life the tortuous threads of silver and similor in the dark arrases. Avoosl Wuthoqquan, seated in an umber shadow beyond the lane of light, peered with an austere and ironic mien at his client, whose swarthy face and somber mantle were gilded by the passing glory.

The man was a stranger; possibly a travelling merchant from outland realms, the usurer thought—or else an outlander of more dubious occupation. His narrow, slanting, beryl-green eyes, his bluish, unkempt beard, and the uncouth cut of his sad raiment, were sufficient proof of his alienage in Commoriom.

"Three hundred *djals* is a large sum," said the money-lender thoughtfully. "Moreover, I do not know you. What security have you to offer?"

The visitor produced from the bosom of his garment a small bag of tiger-skin, tied at the mouth with sinew, and opening the bag with a deft movement, poured on the table before Avoosl Wuthoqquan two uncut emeralds of immense size and flawless purity. They flamed at the heart with a cold and ice-green fire as they caught the slanting sunset; and a greedy spark was kindled in the eyes of the usurer. But he spoke coolly and indifferently.

"It may be that I can loan you one hundred and fifty *djals*. Emeralds are hard to dispose of; and if you should not return to claim the gems and pay me the money, I might have reason to repent my generosity. But I will take the hazard."

"The loan I ask is a mere tithe of their value," protested the stranger. "Give me two hundred and fifty *djals*.... There are other money-lenders in Commoriom, I am told."

"Two hundred *djals* is the most I can offer. It is true that the gems are not without value. But you may have stolen them. How am I to know? It is not my habit to ask indiscreet questions."

"Take them," said the stranger, hastily. He accepted the silver coins which

Avoosl Wuthoqquan counted out, and offered no further protest. The usurer watched him with a sardonic smile as he departed, and drew his own inferences. He felt sure that the jewels had been stolen, but was in no wise perturbed or disquieted by this fact. No matter who they had belonged to, or what their history, they would form a welcome and valuable addition to the coffers of Avoosl Wuthoqquan. Even the smaller of the two emeralds would have been absurdly cheap at three hundred *djals*; but the usurer felt no apprehension that the stranger would return to claim them at any time.... No, the man was plainly a thief, and had been glad to rid himself of the evidence of his guilt. As to the rightful ownership of the gems—that was hardly a matter to arouse the concern or the curiosity of the money-lender. They were his own property now, by virtue of the sum in silver which had tacitly been regarded by himself and the stranger as a price rather than a mere loan.

The sunset faded swiftly from the room and a brown twilight began to dull the metal broideries of the curtains and the colored eyes of the gems. Avoosl Wuthoqquan lit the fretted lamp; and then, opening a small brazen strong-box, he poured from it a flashing rill of jewels on the table beside the emeralds. There were pale and ice-clear topazes from Mhu Thulan, and gorgeous crystals of tourmaline from Tscho Vulpanomi; there were chill and furtive sapphires of the north, and arctic carnelians like frozen blood, and southern diamonds that were hearted with white stars. Red, unblinking rubies glared from the coruscating pile, chatoyants shone like the eyes of tigers, garnets and alabraundines gave their somber flames to the lamplight amid the restless hues of opals. Also, there were other emeralds, but none so large and flawless as the two that he had acquired that evening.

Avoosl Wuthoqquan sorted out the gems in gleaming rows and circles, as he had done so many times before; and he set apart all the emeralds with his new acquisitions at one end, like captains leading a file. He was well pleased with his bargain, well satisfied with his overflowing caskets. He regarded the jewels with an avaricious love, a miserly complacence; and one might have thought that his eyes were little beads of jasper, set in his leathery face as in the smoky parchment cover of some olden book of doubtful magic. Money and precious gems—these things alone, he thought, were immutable and non-volatile in a world of never-ceasing change and fugacity.

His reflections, at this point, were interrupted by a singular occurrence. Suddenly and without warning—for he had not touched or disturbed them in any manner—the two large emeralds started to roll away from their companions on the smooth, level table of black ogga-wood; and before the startled money-lender could put out his hand to stop them, they had vanished over the opposite edge and had fallen with a muffled rattling on the carpeted floor.

Such behavior was highly eccentric and peculiar, not to say unaccountable; but the usurer leapt to his feet with no other thought save to retrieve the jewels. He rounded the table in time to see that they had continued their mysterious rolling and were slipping through the outer door, which the stranger in departing had left slightly a-jar. This door gave on a courtyard; and the courtyard, in turn, opened on the streets of Commoriom.

Avoosl Wuthoqquan was deeply alarmed, but was more concerned by the prospect of losing the emeralds than by the eeriness and mystery of their departure. He gave chase with an agility of which few would have believed him capable, and throwing open the door, he saw the fugitive emeralds gliding with an uncanny smoothness and swiftness across the rough, irregular flags of the courtyard. The twilight was deepening to a nocturnal blue; but the jewels seemed to wink derisively with a strange phosphoric luster as he followed them. Clearly visible in the gloom, they passed through the unbarred gate that gave on a principal avenue, and disappeared.

It began to occur to Avoosl Wuthoqquan that the jewels were bewitched; but not even in the face of an unknown sorcery was he willing to relinquish anything for which he had paid the munificent sum of two hundred *djals*. He gained the open street with a running leap, and paused only to make sure of the direction in which his emeralds had gone.

The dim avenue was almost entirely deserted; for the worthy citizens of Commoriom, at that hour, were pre-occupied with the consumption of their evening meal. The jewels, gaining momentum, and skimming the ground lightly in their flight, were speeding away on the left toward the less reputable suburbs and the wild, luxuriant jungle beyond. Avoosl Wuthoqquan saw that he must redouble his pursuit if he were to overtake them.

Panting and wheezing valiantly with the unfamiliar exertion, he renewed the chase; but in spite of all his efforts, the jewels ran always at the same distance before him, with a maddening ease and eerie volitation, tinkling musically at whiles on the pavement. The frantic and bewildered usurer was soon out of breath; and being compelled to slacken his speed, he feared to lose sight of the eloping gems; but strangely, thereafterward, they ran with a slowness that corresponded to his own, maintaining ever the same interval.

The money-lender grew desperate. The flight of the emeralds was leading him into an outlying quarter of Commoriom where thieves and murderers and beggars dwelt. Here he met a few passers, all of dubious character, who stared in stupefaction at the fleeing stones but made no effort to stop them. Then the foul tenements among which he ran became smaller, with wider spaces between; and soon there were only sparse huts, where furtive lights gleamed out in the full-grown darkness, beneath the lowering frondage of high palms.

Still plainly visible, and shining with a mocking phosphorescence, the jewels fled before him on the dark road. It seemed to him, however, that he was gaining upon them a little. His flabby limbs and pursy body were faint with fatigue, and he was grievously winded; but he went on in renewed hope, gasping with eager avarice. A full moon, large and amber-tinted, rose beyond the jungle and began to light his way.

Commoriom was far behind him now; and there were no more huts on the lonely forest road, nor any other wayfarers. He shivered a little—either with fear or the chill night air; but did not relax his pursuit. He was closing in on the emeralds, very gradually but surely; and he felt that he would recapture them soon. So engrossed was he in the weird chase, with his eyes on the ever-rolling gems, that he failed to perceive that he was no longer following an open highway. Somehow, somewhere, he had taken a narrow path that wound among monstrous trees whose foliage turned the moonlight to a mesh of quicksilver with heavy, fantastic raddlings of ebony. Crouching in grotesque menace, like giant retiarii, they seemed to close in upon him from all sides. But the money-lender was oblivious of their shadowy threats, and heeded not the sinister strangeness and solitude of the jungle path, nor the dank odors that lingered beneath the trees like unseen pools.

Nearer and nearer he came to the fleeing gems, till they ran and flickered tantalizingly a little beyond his reach, and seemed to look back at him like two greenish, glowing eyes, filled with allurement and mockery. Then, as he was about to fling himself forward in a last and supreme effort to secure them, they vanished abruptly from view, as if they had been swallowed by the forest shadows that lay like sable pythons athwart the moonlit way.

Baffled and disconcerted, Avoosl Wuthoqquan paused and peered in bewilderment at the place where they had disappeared. He saw that the path ended in a cavern-mouth, yawning blackly and silently before him, and leading to unknown subterranean depths. It was a doubtful and suspicious-looking cavern, fanged with sharp stones and bearded with queer grasses; and Avoosl Wuthoqquan, in his cooler moments, would have hesitated a long while before entering it. But just then he was capable of no other impulse than the fervor of the chase and the prompting of avarice.

The cavern that had swallowed his emeralds in a fashion so nefarious was a steep incline, running swiftly down into darkness. It was low and narrow, and slippery with noisome oozings; but the money-lender was heartened as he went on by a glimpse of the glowing jewels, which seemed to float beneath him in the black air, as if to illuminate his way. The incline led to a level, winding passage, in which Avoosl Wuthoqquan began to overtake his elusive property once more; and hope flared high in his panting bosom.

The emeralds were almost within reach; then, with sleightful suddenness, they slipped from his ken beyond an abrupt angle of the passage; and following them, he paused in wonder, as if halted by an irresistible hand. He was half-blinded for some moments by the pale, mysterious, bluish light that poured from the roof and walls of the huge cavern into which he had emerged; and he was more than dazzled by the multi-tinted splendor that flamed and glowed and glistened and sparkled at his very feet.

He stood on a narrow ledge of stone; and the whole chamber before and beneath him, almost to the level of this ledge, was filled with jewels even as a granary is filled with grain! It was as if all the rubies, opals, beryls, diamonds, amethysts, emeralds, chrysolites, and sapphires of the world had been gathered together and poured into an immense pit. He thought that he saw his own emeralds, lying tranquilly and decorously in a nearer mound of the undulant mass; but there were so many others of like size and flawlessness that he could not be sure of them.

For awhile, he could hardly believe the ineffable vision. Then, with a single cry of ecstasy, he leapt forward from the ledge, sinking almost to his knees in the shifting and tinkling and billowing gems. In great double handfuls, he lifted the flaming and scintillating stones and let them sift between his fingers, slowly and voluptuously, to fall with a light clash on the monstrous heap. Blinking joyously, he watched the royal lights and colors run in spreading or narrowing ripples; he saw them burn like steadfast coals and secret stars, or leap out in blazing eyes that seemed to catch fire from each other.

In his most audacious dreams, the usurer had never even suspected the existence of such riches. He babbled aloud in a rhapsody of delight, as he played with the numberless gems; and he failed to perceive that he was sinking deeper with every movement into the unfathomable pit. The jewels had risen above his knees, were engulfing his pudgy thighs, before his avaricious rapture was touched by any thought of peril.

Then, startled by the realization that he was sinking into his new-found wealth as into some treacherous quicksand, he sought to extricate himself and return to the safety of the ledge. He floundered helplessly; for the moving gems gave way beneath him, and he made no progress but went deeper still, till the bright, unstable heap had risen to his waist.

Avoosl Wuthoqquan began to feel a frantic terror amid the intolerable irony of his plight. He cried out; and as if in answer, there came a loud, unctuous, evil chuckle from the cavern behind him. Twisting his fat neck with a painful effort, so that he could peer over his shoulder, he saw a most peculiar entity that was couching on a sort of shelf above the pit of jewels. The entity was wholly and outrageously unhuman; and neither did it resemble any species of animal, or any known god or demon of Hyperborea. Its aspect was not such as to lessen the alarm and panic of the money-lender; for it was very large and pale and squat, with a toad-like face and a swollen, squidgy body and numerous cuttle-fish limbs or appendages. It lay flat on the shelf, with its chinless head and long slit-like mouth overhanging the pit , and its cold, lidless eyes peering obliquely at Avoosl Wuthoqquan. The usurer was not reassured when it began to speak in a thick and loathsome voice, like the molten tallow of corpses dripping from a wizard's kettle.

"Ho! what have we here?" it said. "By the black altar of Tsathoggua, 'tis a fat money-lender, wallowing in my jewels like a lost pig in a quagmire!"

"Help me!" cried Avoosl Wuthoqquan. "See you not that I am sinking?"

The entity gave its oleaginous chuckle. "Yes, I see your predicament, of course…. What are you doing here?"

"I came in search of my emeralds—two fine and flawless stones for which I have just paid the sum of two hundred *djals*."

"*Your* emeralds?" said the entity. "I fear that I must contradict you. The jewels are mine. They were stolen not long ago from this cavern, in which I have been wont to gather and guard my subterranean wealth for many ages. The thief was frightened away… when he saw me… and I suffered him to go. He had taken only the two emeralds; and I knew that they would return to me—as my jewels always return—whenever I choose to call them. The thief was lean and bony, and I did well to let him go: for now, in his place, there is a plump and well-fed usurer."

Avoosl Wuthoqquan, in his mounting terror, was barely able to comprehend the words or to grasp their implications. He had sunk slowly but steadily into the yielding pile, and green, yellow, red and violet gems were blinking gorgeously about his bosom and sifting with a light tinkle beneath his arm-pits.

"Help! help!" he wailed. "I shall be engulfed!"

Grinning sardonically, and showing the cloven tip of a fat white tongue, the singular entity slid from the shelf with boneless ease; and spreading its flat body on the pool of gems, into which it hardly sank, it slithered forward to a position from which it could reach the frantic usurer with its octopus-like members. It dragged him free with a single motion of incredible celerity. Then, without pause or preamble or further comment, in a leisurely and methodical manner, it began to devour him.

THE INVISIBLE CITY

"Confound you," said Langley, in a hoarse whisper that came with effort through swollen lips, blue-black with thirst. "You've gulped about twice your share of the last water in the Lob-nor Desert." He shook the canteen which Furnham had just returned to him, and listened with a savage frown to the ominously light gurgling of its contents.

The two surviving members of the Furnham Archaeological Expedition eyed each other with new-born but rapidly growing disfavor. Furnham, the leader, flushed with dark anger beneath his coat of deepening dust and sunburn. The accusation was unjust, for he had merely moistened his parched tongue from Langley's canteen. His own canteen, which he had shared equally with his companion, was now empty.

Up to that moment, the two men had been the best of friends. Their months of association in a hopeless search for the ruins of the semi-fabulous city of Kobar had given them abundant reason to respect each other. Their quarrel sprang from nothing else than the mental distortion and morbidity of sheer exhaustion, and the strain of a desperate predicament. Langley, at times, was even growing a trifle light-headed after their long ordeal of wandering on foot through a land without wells, beneath a sun whose flames poured down upon them like molten lead.

"We ought to reach the Tarim River pretty soon," said Furnham stiffly, ignoring the charge and repressing a desire to announce in mordant terms his unfavorable opinion of Langley.

"If we don't, I guess it will be your fault," the other snapped. "There's been a jinx on this expedition from the beginning; and I shouldn't wonder if the jinx were you. It was your idea to hunt for Kobar anyway. I've never believed there was any such place."

Furnham glowered at his companion, too near the breaking point himself

149

to make due allowance for Langley's nerve-wrought condition, and then turned away, refusing to reply. The two plodded on, ignoring each other with sullen ostentatiousness.

The expedition, consisting of five Americans in the employ of a New York museum, had started from Khotan two months before to investigate the archaeological remains of Eastern Turkestan. Ill-luck had dogged them continually; and the ruins of Kobar, their main objective, said to have been built by the ancient Uighurs, had eluded them like a mirage. They had found other ruins, had exhumed a few Greek and Byzantine coins, and a few broken Buddhas; but nothing of much novelty or importance, from a museum viewpoint.

At the very outset, soon after leaving the oasis of Tchertchen, one member of the party had died from gangrene caused by the vicious bite of a Bactrian camel. Later on, a second, seized by a cramp while swimming in the shallow Tarim River, near the reedy marshes of Lob-nor, that strange remnant of a vast inland sea, had drowned before his companions could reach him. A third had died of some mysterious fever. Then in the desert south of the Tarim, where Furnham and Langley still persisted in a futile effort to locate the lost city, their Mongol guides had deserted them, taking all the camels and most of the provisions, and leaving to the two men only their rifles, their canteens, their other personal belongings, the various antique relics they had amassed, and a few tins of food.

The desertion was hard to explain, for the Mongols had heretofore shown themselves reliable enough. However, they had displayed a queer reluctance on the previous day, had seemed unwilling to venture further among the endless undulations of coiling sand and pebbly soil.

Furnham, who knew the language better than Langley, had gathered that they were afraid of something, were deterred by superstitious legends concerning this portion of the Lob-nor Desert. But they had been strangely vague and reticent as to the object of their fear; and Furnham had learned nothing of its actual nature.

Leaving everything but their food, water and rifles to the mercy of the drifting sands, the men had started northward toward the Tarim, which was sixty or seventy miles away. If they could reach it, they would find shelter in one of the sparse settlements of fishermen along its shores; and could eventually make their way back to civilization.

It was now afternoon of the second day of their wanderings. Langley had suffered most, and he staggered a little as they went on beneath the eternally cloudless heavens, across the glaring desolation of the dreary landscape. His heavy Winchester had become an insufferable burden, and he had thrown it away in spite of the remonstrance of Furnham, who still retained his own weapon.

The sun had lowered a little, but burned with gruelling rays, tyrannically torrid, through the bright inferno of stagnant air. There was no wind, except for brief and furious puffs that whirled the light sand in the faces of the men, and then died as suddenly as they had risen. The ground gave back the heat and glare of the heavens in shimmering, blinding waves of refraction.

Langley and Furnham mounted a low, gradual ridge, and paused in sweltering exhaustion on its rocky spine. Before them was a broad, shallow valley, at which they stared in a sort of groggy wonderment, puzzled by the level and artificial-looking depression, perfectly square, and perhaps a third of a mile wide, which they descried in its center. The depression was bare and empty, with no sign of ruins, but was lined with numerous pits that suggested the ground-plan of a vanished city.

The men blinked, and both were prompted to rub their eyes as they peered through flickering heat-waves; for each had received a momentary impression of flashing light, broken into myriad spires and columns, that seemed to fill the shallow basin and fade like a mirage.

Still mindful of their quarrel, but animated by the same unspoken thought, they started down the long declivity, heading straight toward the depression. If the place were the site of some ancient city, they might possibly hope to find a well or water-spring.

They approached the basin's edge, and were puzzled more and more by its regularity. Certainly it was not the work of nature; and it might have been quarried yesterday, for seemingly there were no ravages of wind and weather in the sheer walls; and the floor was remarkably smooth, except for the multitude of square pits that ran in straight, intersecting lines, like the cellars of destroyed or unbuilt houses. A growing sense of strangeness and mystery troubled the two men; and they were blinded at intervals by the flash of evanescent light that seemed to overflow the basin with phantom towers and pillars.

They paused within a few feet of the edge, incredulous and bewildered. Each began to wonder if his brain had been affected by the sun. Their sensations were such as might mark the incipience of delirium. Amid the blasts of furnace-like heat, a sort of icy coolness appeared to come upon them from the broad basin. Clammy but refreshing, like the chill that might emanate from walls of sunless stone, it revived their fainting senses and quickened their awareness of unexplained mystery.

The coolness became even more noticeable when they reached the very verge of the precipice. Here, peering over, they saw that the sides fell unbroken at all points for a depth of twenty feet or more. In the smooth bottom, the cellar-like pits yawned darkly and unfathomably. The floor about the pits was free of sand, pebbles or detritus.

"Christ! What do you make of that?" muttered Furnham to himself rather than to Langley. He stooped over the edge, staring down with feverish and inconclusive speculations. The riddle was beyond his experience—he had met nothing like it in all his researches. His puzzlement, however, was partly submerged in the more pressing problem of how he and Langley were to descend the sheer walls. Thirst—and the hope of finding water in one of the pits—were more important at that moment than the origin and nature of the square basin.

Suddenly, in his stooping position, a kind of giddiness seized him, and the earth seemed to pitch deliriously beneath his feet. He staggered, he lost his balance, and fell forward from the verge.

Half-fainting, he closed his eyes against the hurtling descent and the crash twenty feet below. Instantly, it seemed, he struck bottom. Amazed and incomprehending, he found that he was lying at full length, prone on his stomach in mid-air, upborne by a hard, flat, invisible substance. His outflung hands encountered an obstruction, cool as ice and smooth as marble; and the chill of it smote through his clothing as he lay gazing down into the gulf. Wrenched from his grasp by the fall, his rifle hung beside him.

He heard the startled cry of Langley, and then realized that the latter had seized him by the ankles and was drawing him back to the precipice. He felt the unseen surface slide beneath him, level as a concrete pavement, glib as glass. Then Langley was helping him to his feet. Both, for the nonce, had forgotten their misunderstanding.

"Say, am I bughouse?" cried Langley. "I thought you were a goner when you fell. What have we stumbled on, anyhow?"

"Stumbled is good," said Furnham reflectively, as he tried to collect himself. "That basin is floored with something solid, but transparent as air—something unknown to geologists or chemists. God knows what it is, or where it came from or who put it there. We've found a mystery that puts Kobar in the shade. I move that we investigate."

He stepped forward, very cautiously, still half-fearful of falling, and stood suspended over the basin.

"If you can do it, I guess I can," said Langley, as he followed. With Furnham in the lead, the two began to cross the basin, moving slowly and gingerly along the invisible pavement. The sensation of peering down as if through empty air was indescribably weird.

They had started midway between two rows of the dark pits, which lay about fifty feet apart. Somehow, it was like following a street. After they had gone some little distance from the verge, Furnham deviated to the left, with the idea of looking directly down into one of these mysterious pits. Before he could reach a vertical vantage-point, he was arrested by a smooth, solid wall, like that of a building.

"I think we've discovered a city," he announced. Groping his way along the air-clear wall, which seemed free of angles or roughness, he came to an open doorway. It was about five feet wide and of indeterminable height. Fingering the wall like a blind man, he found that it was nearly six inches thick. He and

Langley entered the door, still walking on a level pavement, and advanced without obstruction, as if in a large empty room.

For an instant, as they went forward, light seemed to flash above them in great arches and arcades, touched with evanescent colors like those in fountain-spray. Then it vanished, and the sun shone down as before from a void and desert heaven. The coolness emanating from the unknown substance was more pronounced than ever; and the men almost shivered. But they were vastly refreshed, and the torture of their thirst was somewhat mitigated.

Now they could look perpendicularly into the square pit below them in the stone floor of the excavation. They were unable to see its bottom, for it went down into shadow beyond the westering sun-rays. But both could see the bizarre and inexplicable object which appeared to float immobile in air just below the mouth of the pit. They felt a creeping chill that was more insidious, more penetrant than the iciness of the unseen walls.

"Now I'm seeing things," said Langley.

"Guess I'm seeing them too," added Furnham.

The object was a long, hairless, light-grey body, lying horizontally, as if in some invisible sarcophagus or tomb. Standing erect, it would have been fully nine feet in height. It was vaguely human in its outlines, and possessed two legs and two arms; but the head was quite unearthly. The thing seemed to have a double set of high, concave ears, lined with perforations; and in place of nose, mouth and chin, there was a long, tapering trunk which lay coiled on the bosom of the monstrosity like a serpent. The eyes—or what appeared to be such—were covered by leathery, lashless and hideously wrinkled lids.

The thing lay rigid; and its whole aspect was that of a well-preserved corpse or mummy. Half in light and half in shadow, it hung amid the funereal, fathomless pit; and beneath it, at some little distance, as their eyes became accustomed to the gloom, the men seemed to perceive another and similar body.

Neither could voice the mad, eerie thoughts that assailed them. The mystery was too macabre and overwhelming and impossible. It was Langley who spoke at last.

"Say, do you suppose they are *all* dead?"

Before Furnham could answer, he and Langley heard a thin, shrill, exiguous sound, like the piping off some unearthly flute whose notes were almost beyond human audition. They could not determine its direction; for it seemed to come from one side and then from another as it continued. Its degree of apparent nearness or distance was also variable. It went on ceaselessly and monotonously, thrilling them with an eeriness as of untrod worlds, a terror as of uncharted dimensions. It seemed to fade away in remote ultramundane gulfs; and then, louder and clearer than before, the piping came from the air beside them.

Inexpressibly startled, the two men stared from side to side in an effort to locate the source of the sound. They could find nothing. The air was clear and still about them; and their view of the rocky slopes that rimmed the basin was blurred only by the dancing haze of heat.

The piping ceased, and was followed by a dead, uncanny silence. But Furnham and Langley had the feeling that someone—or something—was near them—a stealthy presence that lurked and crouched and drew closer till they could have shrieked aloud with the terror of suspense. They seemed to wait amid the unrealities of delirium and mirage, haunted by some elusive, undeclared horror.

Tensely they peered and listened, but there was no sound or visual ostent. Then Langley cried out, and fell heavily to the unseen floor, borne backward by the onset of a cold and tangible thing, resistless as the launching coils of an anaconda. He lay helpless, unable to move, beneath the dead and fluid weight of the unknown incubus, which crushed down his limbs and body and almost benumbed him with an icy chill as of etheric space. Then something touched his throat, very lightly at first, and then with a pressure that deepened intolerably to a stabbing pain, as if he had been pierced by an icicle.

A black faintness swept upon him, and the pain seemed to recede as if the nerves that bore it to his brain were spun like lengthening gossamers across gulfs of anesthesia.

Furnham, in a momentary paralysis, heard the cry of his companion, and saw Langley fall and struggle feebly, to lie inert with closing eyes and whitening face. Mechanically, without realizing for some moments what had happened, he perceived that Langley's garments were oddly flattened and pressed down beneath an invisible weight. Then, from the hollow of Langley's neck, he saw the spurting of a thin rill of blood, which mounted straight in air for several inches, and vanished in a sort of red mist.

Bizarre, incoherent thoughts arose in Furnham's mind. It was all too incredible, too unreal. His brain must be wandering, it must have given way entirely... but something was attacking Langley—an invisible vampire of this invisible city.

He had retained his rifle. Now he stepped forward and stood beside the fallen man. His free hand, groping in the air, encountered a chill, clammy surface, rounded like the back of a stooping body. It numbed his finger-tips even as he touched it. Then something seemed to reach out like an arm and hurl him violently backward.

Reeling and staggering, he managed to retain his balance, and returned more cautiously. The blood still rose in a vanishing rill from Langley's throat. Estimating the position of the unseen attacker, Furnham raised his rifle and took careful aim, with the muzzle less than a yard away from its hidden mark.

The gun roared with deafening resonance, and its sound died away in slow echoes, as if repeated by a maze of walls. The blood ceased to rise from

Langley's neck, and fell to a natural trickle. There was no sound, no manifestation of any kind from the thing that had assailed him. Furnham stood
in doubt, wondering if his shot had taken effect. Perhaps the thing had been
frightened away, perhaps it was still close at hand, and might leap upon him
at any moment, or return to its prey.

He peered at Langley, who lay white and still. The blood was ceasing to
flow from the tiny puncture. He stepped toward him, with the idea of trying to revive him, but was arrested by a strange circumstance. He saw that
Langley's face and upper body were blurred by a grey mist that seemed to
thicken and assume palpable outlines. It darkened apace, it took on solidity
and form; and Furnham beheld the monstrous thing that lay prone between
himself and his companion, with part of its fallen bulk still weighing upon
Langley. From its inertness, and the bullet-wound in its side, whence oozed
a viscid purple fluid, he felt sure that the thing was dead.

The monster was alien to all terrene biology—a huge, invertebrate body,
formed like an elongated starfish, with the points ending in swollen tentacular
limbs. It had a round, shapeless head with the curving, needle-tipped bill
of some mammoth insect. It must have come from other planets or dimensions than ours. It was wholly unlike the mummified creature that floated in
the pit below, and Furnham felt that it represented an inferior animal-like
type. It was evidently composed of an unknown order of organic matter that
became visible to human eyes only in death.

His brain was swamped by the mad enigma of it all. What was this place
upon which he and Langley had stumbled? Was it an outpost of worlds
beyond human knowledge or observation? What was the material of which
these buildings had been wrought? Who were their builders? Whence had
they come? And what had been their purpose? Was the city of recent date?
Or was it, perhaps, a sort of ruin, whose builders lay dead in its vaults—a
ruin haunted only by the vampire monster that had assailed Langley?

Shuddering with repulsion at the dead monster, he started to drag the still
unconscious man from beneath the loathsome mass. He avoided touching
the dark, semi-translucent body, which lapsed forward, quivering like a stiff
jelly when he had pulled his companion away from it.

Like something very trivial and far away, he remembered the absurd quarrel
which Langley had picked with him, and remembered his own resentment
as part of a doubtful dream, now lost in the extra-human mystery of their
surroundings. He bent over his comrade, anxiously, and saw that some of the
natural tan was returning to the pale face and that the eyelids were beginning
to flutter. The blood had clotted on the tiny wound. Taking Langley's canteen,
he poured the last of its contents between the owner's teeth.

In a few moments, Langley was able to sit up. Furnham helped him to his
feet, and the two began to grope their way from the crystal maze.

They found the doorway; and Furnham, still supporting the other, decided to retrace their course along the weird street by which they had started to cross the basin. They had gone but a few paces, when they heard a faint, almost inaudible rustling in the air before them, together with a mysterious grating noise. The rustling seemed to spread and multiply on every hand, as if an invisible crowd were gathering; but the grating soon ceased.

They went on, slowly and cautiously, with a sense of imminent, uncanny peril. Langley was now strong enough to walk without assistance; and Furnham held his cocked rifle ready for instant use. The vague rustling sounds receded, but still encircled them.

Midway between the underlying rows of pits, they moved on toward the desert precipice, keeping side by side. A dozen paces on the cold, solid pavement, and then they stepped into empty air and landed several feet below, with a terrific jar, on another hard surface. It must have been the top of a flight of giant stairs; for, losing their balance, they both lurched and fell, and rolled downward along a series of similar surfaces, and lay stunned at the bottom.

Langley had been rendered unconscious by the fall; but Furnham was vaguely aware of several strange, dream-like phenomena. He heard a faint, ghostly, sibilant rustling, he felt a light and clammy touch upon his face, and smelt an odor of suffocating sweetness, in which he seemed to sink as into an unfathomable sea. The rustling died to a vast and spatial silence; oblivion darkened above him; and he slid swiftly into nothingness.

It was night when Furnham awoke. His first impression was the white dazzle of a full moon, shining in his eyes. Then he became aware that the circle of the great orb was oddly distorted and broken, like a moon in some cubistic painting. All around and above him were bright, crystalline angles, crossing and intermingling—the outlines of a translucent architecture, dome on dome and wall on wall. As he moved his head, showers of ghostly iris—the lunar yellow and green and purple—fell in his eyes from the broken orb and vanished.

He saw that he was lying on a glass-like floor, which caught the light in moving sparkles. Langley, still unconscious, was beside him. Doubtless they were still in the mysterious oubliette down whose invisible stairs they had fallen. Far off to one side, through a mélange of the transparent partitions, he could see the vague rocks of the Gobi, twisted and refracted in the same manner as the moon.

Why, he wondered, was the city now visible? Was its substance rendered perceptible, in a partial sort of way, by some unknown ray which existed in moonlight but not in the direct beams of the sun? Such an explanation sounded altogether too unscientific; but he could not think of any other, at the moment.

Rising on his elbow, he saw the glassy outlines of the giant stairs down which he and Langley had plunged. A pale, diaphanous form, like a phantom of the mummified creature they had seen in the pit, was descending the stairs. It moved forward with fleet strides, longer than those of a man, and stooped above Furnham with its spectral trunk waving inquisitively and poising an inch or two from his face. Two round, phosphorescent eyes, emitting perceptible beams like lanterns, glowed solemnly in its head above the beginning of the proboscis.

The eyes seemed to transfix Furnham with their unearthly gaze. He felt that the light they emitted was flowing in a ceaseless stream into his own eyes—into his very brain. The light seemed to shape itself into images, formless and incomprehensible at first, but growing clearer and more coherent momently. Then, in some indescribable way, the images were associated with articulate words, as if a voice were speaking: words that he understood as one might understand the language of dreams.

"We mean you no harm," the voice seemed to say. "But you have stumbled upon our city; and we cannot afford to let you escape. We do not wish to have our presence known to men.

"We have dwelt here for many ages. The Lob-nor desert was a fertile realm when we first established our city. We came to your world as fugitives from a great planet that once formed part of the solar system—a planet composed entirely of ultra-violet substances, which was destroyed in a terrible cataclysm. Knowing the imminence of the catastrophe, some of us were able to build a huge space-flier, in which we fled to the Earth. From the materials of the flier, and other materials we had brought along for the express purpose, we built our city, whose name, as well as it can be conveyed in human phonetics, is Ciis.

"The things of your world have always been plainly visible to us; and, in fact, due to our immense scale of perceptions, we probably see much that is not manifest to you. Also, we have no need of artificial light at any time. We discovered, however, at an early date, that we ourselves and our buildings were invisible to men. Strangely enough, our bodies undergo in death a degradation of substance which brings them within the infra-violet range; and thus within the scope of your visual cognition."

The voice seemed to pause, and Furnham realized that it had spoken only in his thoughts by a sort of telepathy. In his own mind, he tried to shape a question:

"What do you intend to do with us?"

Again he heard the still, toneless voice:

"We plan to keep you with us permanently. After you fell through the trapdoor we had opened, we overpowered you with an anesthetic; and during your period of unconsciousness, which lasted many hours, we injected into your bodies a drug which has already affected your vision, rendering visible, to a certain degree, the ultra-violet substances that surround you. Repeated injections, which must be given slowly, will make these substances no less plain and solid to you than the materials of your own world. Also, there are other processes to which we intend to subject you… processes that will serve to adjust and acclimate you in all ways to your new surroundings."

Behind Furnham's weird interlocutor, several more phantasmal figures had descended the half-visible steps. One of them was stooping over Langley, who had begun to stir and would recover full consciousness in a few instants. Furnham sought to frame other questions, and received an immediate reply.

"The creature that attacked your companion was a domestic animal. We were busy in our laboratories at the time, and did not know of your presence till we heard the rifle-shots.

"The flashes of light which you saw among our invisible walls on your arrival were due to some queer phenomenon of refraction. At certain angles the sunlight was broken or intensified by the molecular arrangement of the unseen substance."

At this juncture Langley sat up, looking about him in a bewildered fashion.

"What the hell is all this? And where the hell are we?" he inquired as he peered from Furnham to the people of the city.

Furnham proceeded to explain, repeating the telepathic information he had just received. By the time he had ceased speaking, Langley himself appeared to become the recipient of some sort of mental reassurance from the phantom-like creature who had been Furnham's interlocutor; for Langley stared at this being with a mixture of enlightenment and wonder in his expression.

Once more, there came the still, super-auditory voice, fraught now with imperious command.

"Come with us. Your initiation into our life is to begin immediately. My name is Aispha—if you wish to have a name for me in your thoughts. We ourselves, communicating with each other without language, have little need for names; and their use is a rare formality among us. Our generic name, as a people, is the Tiisins."

Furnham and Langley arose with an unquestioning alacrity, for which afterwards they could hardly account, and followed Aispha. It was as if a mesmeric compulsion had been laid upon them. Furnham noted, in an automatic sort of way, as they left the oubliette, that his rifle had vanished. No doubt it had been carefully removed during his period of insensibility.

He and Langley climbed the high steps with some difficulty. Queerly enough, considering their late fall, they found themselves quite free of stiffness and bruises; but at the time they felt no surprise—only a drugged acquiescence in all the marvels and perplexities of their situation.

They emerged on the outer pavement, amid the bewildering outlines of the luminous buildings, which towered above them with intersections of multiform crystalline curves and angles. Aispha went on without pause, leading them toward the fantastic serpentine arch of an open doorway in one of the tallest of these edifices, whose pale domes and pinnacles were heaped in immaterial splendor athwart the zenith-nearing moon.

Four of the ultra-violet people—the companions of Aispha—brought up the rear. Aispha was apparently unarmed; but the others carried weapons like heavy-bladed and blunt-pointed sickles of glass or crystal. Many others of this incredible race, intent on their own enigmatic affairs, were passing to and fro in the open street and through the portals of the unearthly buildings. The city was a place of silent and phantasmal activity.

At the end of the street they were following, before they passed through the arched entrance, Furnham and Langley saw the rock-strewn slope of the Lob-nor, which seemed to have taken on a queer filminess and insubstantiality in the moon-light. It occurred to Furnham, with a sort of weird shock, that his visual perception of earthly objects, as well as of the ultra-violet city, was being affected by the injections of which Aispha told him.

The building they now entered was full of apparatuses made in the form of distorted spheres and irregular disks and cubes, some of which seemed to change their outlines from moment to moment in a confusing manner. Certain of them appeared to concentrate the moonlight like ultra-powerful lenses, turning it to a fiery, blinding brilliance. Neither Furnham nor Langley could imagine the purpose of these devices; and no telepathic explanation was vouchsafed by Aispha or any of his companions.

As they went on into the building, there was a queer sense of some importunate and subtle vibration in the air, which affected the men unpleasantly. They could not assign its source nor could they be sure whether their own perception of it was purely mental or came through the avenues of one or more of the physical senses. Somehow it was both disturbing and narcotic; and they sought instinctively to resist its influence.

The lower story of the edifice was seemingly one vast room. The strange apparatuses grew taller about them, rising as if in concentric tiers, as they went on. In the huge dome above them, living rays of mysterious light appeared to cross and re-cross at all angles of incidence, weaving a bright, ever-changing web that dazzled the eye.

They emerged in a clear, circular space at the center of the building. Here ten or twelve of the ultra-violet people were standing about a slim column, perhaps five feet high, that culminated in a shallow basin-like formation. There was a glowing oval-shaped object in the basin, large as the egg of some extinct bird. From this object, numerous spokes of light extended horizontally in all directions, seeming to transfix the heads and bodies of those who stood in a loose ring about the pillar. Furnham and Langley became aware of a high, thin, humming noise which emanated from the glowing egg and was somehow inseparable from the spokes of light, as if the radiance had become audible.

Aispha paused, facing the men; and a voice spoke in their minds.

"The glowing object is called the Dōir. An explanation of its real nature and origin would be beyond your present comprehension. It is allied, however, to that range of substances which you would classify as minerals; and is one of a number of similar objects which existed in our former world. It generates a mighty force which is intimately connected with our life-principle; and the rays emanating from it serve us in place of food. If the Dōir were lost or destroyed, the consequences would be serious; and our life-term, which, normally, is many thousand years, would be shortened for want of the nourishing and revivifying rays."

Fascinated, Furnham and Langley stared at the egg-shaped orb. The humming seemed to grow louder; and the spokes of light lengthened and increased in number. The men recognized it now as the source of the vibration that had troubled and oppressed them. The effect was insidious, heavy, hypnotic, as if there were a living brain in the object that sought to overcome their volition and subvert their senses and their minds in some unnatural thralldom.

They heard the mental command of Aispha:

"Go forward and join those who partake of the luminous emanations of the Dōir. We believe that by so doing you will, in course of time, become purged of your terrestrial grossness; that the very substance of your bodies may eventually be transformed into something not unlike that of our own; and your senses raised to a perceptional power such as we possess."

Half unwillingly, with an eerie consciousness of compulsion, the men started forward.

"I don't like this," said Furnham in a whisper to Langley. "I'm beginning to feel queer enough already." Summoning his utmost will-power, he stopped short of the emanating rays and put out his hand to arrest Langley.

With dazzled eyes, they stood peering at the Dōir. A cold, restless fire, alive with some nameless evil that was not akin to the evil of Earth, pulsated in its heart; and the long, sharp beams, quivering slightly, passed like javelins into the semi-crystalline bodies of the beings who stood immobile around the column.

"Hasten!" came the unvocal admonition of Aispha. "In a few moments the force in the Dōir, which has a regular rhythm of ebb and flow, will begin to draw back upon itself. The rays will be retracted; and you will have to wait for many minutes before the return of the emanation."

A quick, daring thought had occurred to Furnham. Eyeing the Dōir closely, he had been impressed by its seeming fragility. The thing was evidently not attached to the basin in which it reposed; and in all likelihood, it would shatter like glass if hurled or even dropped on the floor. He tried to suppress his thought, fearing that it would be read by Aispha or others of the ultra-violet people. At the same time, he sought to phrase, as innocently as possible, a mental question:

"What would happen if the Dōir were broken?"

Instantly, he received an impression of anger, turmoil and consternation in the mind of Aispha. His question, however, was apparently not answered; and it seemed that Aispha did not want to answer it—that he was concealing something too dangerous and dreadful to be revealed. Furnham felt, too, that Aispha was suspicious, had received an inkling of his own repressed thought.

It occurred to him that he must act quickly, if at all. Nerving himself, he leapt forward through the ring of bodies about the Dōir. The rays had already begun to shorten slightly; but he had the feeling of one who hurls himself upon an array of lance-points. There was an odd, indescribable sensation, as if he were being pierced by something that was both hot and cold; but neither the warmth nor the chill was beyond endurance. A moment, and he stood beside the column, lifting the glowing egg in his hands and poising it defiantly as he turned to face the ultra-violet people.

The thing was phenomenally light; and it seemed to burn his fingers and to freeze them at the same time. He felt a strange vertigo, an indescribable confusion; but he succeeded in mastering it. The contact of the Dōir might be deadlier to the human tissues than that of radium, for aught he knew. He would have to take his chances. At any rate, it would not kill him immediately; and if he played his cards with sufficient boldness and skill, he could make possible the escape of Langley—if not his own escape.

The ring of ultra-violet beings stood as if stupefied by his audacity. The retracting spokes of light were slowly drawing back into the egg; but Furnham himself was still impaled by them. His fingers seemed to be growing translucent where they clutched the weird ball.

He met the phosphoric gaze of Aispha, and heard the frantic thoughts that were pouring into his mind, not only from Aispha but from all the partakers of the Dōir's luminous beams. Dread, unhuman threats, desperate injunctions to return the Dōir to its pedestal, were being laid upon him. Rallying all his will, he defied them.

"Let us go free," he said mentally, addressing Aispha. "Give me back my weapon and permit my companion and me to leave your city. We wish you no harm; but we cannot allow you to detain us. Let us go—or I will shatter the Dōir—will smash it like an egg on the floor."

At the shaping of his destructive thought, a shudder passed among the semi-spectral beings; and he felt the dire fear that his threat had aroused in them. He had been right: the Dōir *was* fragile; and some awful catastrophe, whose nature he could not quite determine, would ensue instantly upon its shattering.

Step by step, glancing frequently about to see that no one approached him by stealth from behind, Furnham returned to Langley's side. The Tiisins drew back from him in evident terror. All the while, he continued to issue his demands and comminations:

"Bring the rifle quickly... the weapon you took from me... and give it into my companion's hands. Let us go without hindrance or molestation—or I will drop the Dōir. When we are outside the city, one of you—one only—shall be permitted to approach us, and I will deliver the Dōir to him."

One of the Tiisins left the group, to return in less than a minute with Furnham's Winchester. He handed it to Langley, who inspected the weapon carefully and found that it had not been damaged or its loading or mechanism tampered with in any way. Then, with the ultra-violet creatures following them in manifest perturbation, Furnham and Langley made their way from the building and started along the open street in the general direction (as Langley estimated from the compass he carried) of the Tarim River.

They went on amid the fantastic towering of the crystalline piles; and the people of the city, called as if by some unworded summons, poured from the doorways in an ever-swelling throng and gathered behind them. There was no active demonstration of any overt kind; but both the men were increasingly aware of the rage and consternation that had been aroused by Furnham's audacious theft of the Dōir—a theft that seemed to be regarded in the light of actual blasphemy. The hatred of the Tiisins, like a material radiation, dark, sullen, stupefying, stultifying, beat upon them at every step. It seemed to clog their brains and their feet like some viscid medium of nightmare; and their progression toward the Gobi slope became painfully slow and tedious.

Before them, from one of the buildings, a tentacled, star-fish monster, like the thing that had assailed Langley, emerged and lay crouching in the street as if to dispute their passage. Raising its evil beak, it glared with filmy eyes, but slunk away from their approach, as if at the monition of its owners.

Furnham and Langley, passing it with involuntary shivers of repugnance, went on. The air was oppressed with alien, unformulable menace. They felt an abnormal drowsiness creeping upon them at whiles. There was an un-heard, narcotic music, which sought to overcome their vigilance, to beguile them into slumber.

Furnham's fingers grew numb with the unknown radiations of the Dōir; though the sharp beams of light, by accelerative degrees, had withdrawn into its center, leaving only a formless misty glow that filled the weird orb. The thing seemed latent with terrible life and power. The bones of his transparent hand were outlined against it like those of a skeleton.

Looking back, he saw that Aispha followed closely, walking in advance of the other Tiisins. He could not read the thoughts of Aispha as formerly. It was as if a blank, dark wall had been built up. Somehow, he had a premo-nition of evil—of danger and treachery in some form which he could not understand or imagine.

He and Langley came to the end of the street, where the ultra-violet pave-ment joined itself to the desert acclivity. As they began their ascent of the slope, both men realized that their visual powers had indeed been affected by the injective treatment of the Tiisins: for the soil seemed to glow beneath them, faintly translucent; and the boulders were like semi-crystalline masses, whose inner structure they could see dimly.

Aispha followed them on the slope; but the other people of Ciis, as had been stipulated by Furnham, paused at the juncture of their streets and buildings with the infra-violet substances of Earth.

After they had gone perhaps fifty yards on the gentle acclivity, Furnham came to a pause and waited for Aispha, holding out the Dōir at arm's length. Somehow, he had a feeling that it was unwise to return the mystic egg; but he would keep his promise, since the people of Ciis had kept their part of the bargain so far.

Aispha took the Dōir from Furnham's hands; but his thoughts, whatever they were, remained carefully shrouded. There was a sense of something ominous and sinister about him as he turned and went back down the slope with the fiery egg shining through his body like a great watchful eye. The beams of light were beginning to emanate from its center once more.

The two men, looking back ever and anon, resumed their journey. Ciis glimmered below them like the city of a mirage in the moonlit hollow. They saw the ultra-violet people crowding to await Aispha at the end of their streets.

Then, as Aispha neared his fellows, two rays of cold, writhing fire leaped forth from the base of a tower that glittered like glass at the city's verge. Clinging to the ground, the rays ran up the slope with the undulant motion of pythons, following Langley and Furnham at a speed that would soon overtake them.

"They're double-crossing us!" warned Furnham. He caught the Winchester from Langley, dropped to his knees and aimed carefully, drawing a bead on the luminous orb of the Dōir through the spectral form of Aispha, who had now reached the city and was about to enter the waiting throng.

"Run!" he called to Langley. "I'll make them pay for their treachery; and perhaps you can get away in the meanwhile."

He pulled the trigger, missing Aispha but dropping at least two of the Tiisins who stood near the Dōir. Again, steadily, he drew bead, while the rays from the tower serpentined onward, pale, chill and deadly-looking, till they were almost at his feet. Even as he aimed, Aispha took refuge in the foremost ranks of the crowd, through whose filmy bodies the Dōir still glowed.

This time, the high-powered bullet found its mark, though it must have passed through more than one of the ultra-violet beings before reaching Aispha and the mystic orb.

Furnham had hardly known what the result would be; but he had felt sure that some sort of catastrophe would ensue the destruction of the Dōir. What really happened was incalculable and almost beyond description.

Before the Dōir could fall from the hands of its stricken bearer, it seemed to expand in a rushing wheel of intense light, revolving as it grew and blotting out the forms of the ultra-violet people in the foreground. With awful velocity, the wheel struck the nearer buildings, which appeared to soar and vanish like towers of fading mirage. There was no audible explosion—no sound of any kind—only that silent, ever-spinning, ever-widening disk of light that threatened to involve by swift degrees the whole extent of Ciis.

Gazing spell-bound, Furnham had almost forgotten the serpentine rays. Too late, he saw that one of them was upon him. He leapt back, but the thing caught him, coiling about his limbs and body like an anaconda. There was a sensation of icy cold, of horrible constriction; and then, helpless, he found that the strange beam of force was dragging him back down the slope toward Ciis, while its fellow went on in pursuit of the fleeing Langley.

In the meanwhile, the spreading disk of fire had reached the tower from which the rays emanated. Suddenly Furnham was free—the serpentine beams had both vanished. He stood rooted to the spot in speechless awe; and Langley, returning to his aid, also paused, watching the mighty circle of light that seemed to fill the entire basin at their feet with a soundless vortex of destruction.

"My God!" cried Furnham, after a brief interval. "Look what's happening to the slope."

As if the force of the uncanny explosion were now extending beyond Ciis, boulders and masses of earth began to rise in air before the white, glowing maelstrom, and sailed in slow, silent levitation toward the men.

Furnham and Langley started to run, stumbling up the slope, and were overtaken by something that lifted them softly, buoyantly, irresistibly, with a strange feeling of utter weightlessness, and bore them like wind-wafted leaves or feathers through the air. They saw the bouldered crest of the acclivity flowing far beneath them; and then they were floating, floating, ever higher in the moonlight, above leagues of dim desert. A faintness came upon them both—a vague nausea—an illimitable vertigo—and slowly, somewhere in that incredible flight, they lapsed into unconsciousness.

The moon had fallen low, and its rays were almost horizontal in Furnham's eyes when he awoke. An utter confusion possessed him at first; and his circumstances were more than bewildering. He was lying on a sandy slope, among scattered shrubs, meager and stunted; and Langley was lying not far away. Raising himself a little, he saw the white and reed-fringed surface of a river—which could be none other than the Tarim—at the slope's bottom. Half- incredulous, doubting his own senses, he realized that the force of the weird explosion had carried Langley and himself many miles and had deposited them, apparently unhurt, beside the goal of their desert wanderings!

Furnham rose to his feet, feeling a queer lightness and unsteadiness. He took a tentative step—and landed four or five feet away. It was as if he had lost half his normal weight. Moving with great care he went over to Langley, who had now started to sit up. He was reassured to find that his eye-sight was becoming normal again; for he perceived merely a faint glowing in the objects about him. The sand and boulders were comfortably solid; and his own hands were no longer translucent.

"Gosh!" he said to Langley, "That was some explosion. The force that was liberated by the shattering of the Dōir must have done something to the gravity of all surrounding objects. I guess the city of Ciis and its people have gone back into outer space; and even the infra-violet substances about the city must have been more or less degravitated. But I guess the effect is wearing off, as far as you and I are concerned—otherwise we'd be travelling still."

Langley got up and tried to walk, with the same disconcerting result that had characterized Furnham's attempt. He mastered his limbs and his equilibrium after a few experiments.

"I still feel like a sort of dirigible," he commented. "Say, I think we'd better leave this out of our report to the museum. A city, a people, all invisible, in the heart of the Lob-nor—that would be too much for scientific credibility."

"I agree with you," said Furnham—"the whole business would be too fantastic, outside of a super-scientific story. In fact," he added a little maliciously, "it's even more incredible than the existence of the ruins of Kobar."

THE IMMORTALS OF MERCURY

I

Cliff Howard's first sensation, as he came back to consciousness, was one of well-nigh insufferable heat. It seemed to beat upon him from all sides in a furnace-like blast and to lie upon his face, limbs and body with the heaviness of molten metal. Then, before he had opened his eyes, he became aware of the furious light that smote upon his lids, turning them to a flame-red curtain. His eyeballs ached with the muffled radiation; every nerve of his being cringed from the pouring sea of incalescence; and there was a dull throbbing in his scalp, which might have been either headache induced by the heat, or the pain of a somewhat recent blow.

He recalled, very dimly, that there had been an expedition—somewhere—in which he had taken part; but his efforts to remember the details were momentarily distracted by new and inexplicable sensations. He felt now that he was moving swiftly, borne on something that pitched and bounded against a high wind that seared his face like the breath of hell.

He opened his eyes, and was almost blinded when he found himself staring at a whitish heaven where blown columns of steam went by like spectral genii. Just below the rim of his vision, there was something vast and incandescent, toward which, instinctively, he feared to turn. Suddenly he knew what it was, and began to realize his situation. Memory came to him in a tumbling torment of images; and with it, a growing wonder and alarm.

He recalled the ramble he had taken, alone, amid the weird and scrubby jungles of the twilight zone of Mercury—that narrow belt, warm and vaporous, lying between the broiling deserts on which an enormous sun glares perpetually, and the heaped and mountainous glaciers of the planet's nightward side.

He had not gone far from the rocket-ship—a mile at most, toward the sulphurous, fuming afterglow of the sun, now wholly hidden by the planet's libration. Johnson, the head of that first scientific expedition to Mercury, had warned him against these solitary excursions; but Howard, a professional botanist, had been eager to hasten his investigations of the unknown world, in which they had now sojourned for a week of terrestrial time.

Contrary to expectation, they had found a low, thin, breathable atmosphere, fed by the melting of ice in the variable twilight belt—an air that was drawn continually in high winds toward the sun; and the wearing of special equipment was unnecessary. Howard had not anticipated any danger; for the shy, animal-like natives had shown no hostility and had fled from the earth-men whenever approached. The other life-forms, as far as had been determined, were of low, insensitive types, often semi-vegetative, and easily avoided when poisonous or carnivorous.

Even the huge, ugly, salamander-like reptiles who seemed to roam at will from the twilight zone to the scalding deserts beneath an eternal day, were seemingly quite inoffensive.

Howard had been examining a queer, unfamiliar growth resembling a large truffle, which he had found in an open space, among the pale, poddy, wind-bowed shrubs. The growth, when he touched it, had displayed signs of sluggish animation and had started to conceal itself, burrowing into the boggy soil. He was prodding the thing with the sponge-like branch of a dead shrub, and was wondering how to classify it, when, looking up, he had found himself surrounded by the Mercutian savages. They had stolen upon him noiselessly from the semi-fungoid thickets; but he was not alarmed at first, thinking merely that they had begun to overcome their shyness and show their barbaric curiosity.

They were gnarled and dwarfish creatures, who walked partially erect at most times; but ran upon all fours when frightened. The earth-men had named them the Dlukus, because of the clucking sounds resembling this word which they often made. Their skins were heavily scaled, like those of reptiles; and their small, protruding eyes appeared to be covered at all times with a sort of thin film. Anything ghastlier or more repulsive than these beings could hardly have been found on the inner planets. But when they closed in upon Howard, walking with a forward crouch and clucking incessantly, he had taken their approach for a sort of overture and had neglected to draw his *tonanite* pistol. He saw that they were carrying rough pieces of some blackish mineral, and had surmised, from the way in which their webbed hands were held toward him, that they were bringing him a gift or peace-offering.

Their savage faces were inscrutable; and they had drawn very close before he was disillusioned as to their intent. Then, without warning, in a cool, orderly manner, they had begun to assail him with the fragments of the mineral they carried. He had fought them; but his resistance had been cut short by a violent blow from behind, which had sent him reeling into oblivion.

All this he remembered clearly enough; but there must have been an indefinite blank, following his lapse into insensibility. What, he wondered, had happened during this interim, and where was he going? Was he a captive among the Dlukus? The glaring light and scorching heat could mean only one thing—that he had been carried into the sunward lands of Mercury. That incandescent thing toward which he dared not look was the sun itself, looming in a vast arc above the horizon.

He tried to sit up, but succeeded merely in raising his head a little. He saw that there were leathery thongs about his chest, arms and legs, binding him tightly to some mobile surface that seemed to heave and pant beneath him. Slewing his head to one side, he found that this surface was horny, rounded and reticulated. It was like something he had seen.

Then, with a start of horror, he recognized it. He was bound, Mazeppa-like, to the back of one of those salamandrine monsters to which the earth-scientists had given the name of "heat-lizards." These creatures were large crocodiles, but possessed longer legs than any terrestrial saurian. Their thick hides were apparently, to an amazing extent, non-conductors of heat, and served to insulate them against temperatures that would have parboiled any other known form of life.

The exact range of their habitat had not yet been learned; but they had been seen from the rocket-ship, during a brief sunward dash, in deserts where water was perpetually at the boiling point; where rills and rivers, flowing from the twilight zone, wasted themselves in heavy vapors from terrible cauldrons of naked rock.

Howard's consternation, as he realized his plight and his probable fate, was mingled with a passing surprise. He felt sure that the Dlukus had bound him to the monster's back, and wondered that beings so low in the evolutionary scale should have been intelligent enough to know the use of thongs. Their act showed a certain power of calculation, as well as a devilish cruelty. It was obvious that they had abandoned him deliberately to an awful doom.

However, he had little time for reflection. The heat-lizard, with an indescribable darting and running motion, went swiftly onward into the dreadful hell of writhing steam and heated rock. The great ball of intolerable whiteness seemed to rise higher momently and to pour its beams upon Howard like the flood of an opened furnace. The horny mail of the monster was like a hot gridiron beneath him, scorching through his clothes; and his wrists and neck and ankles were seared by the tough leather cords as he struggled madly and uselessly against them.

Turning his head from side to side, he saw dimly the horned rocks that leaned toward him from curtains of hellish mist. His head swam deliriously, and the very blood appeared to simmer in his veins. He lapsed at intervals into deadly faintness: a black shroud seemed to fall upon him, but his vague senses were still oppressed by the crushing, searing radiation. He seemed to descend into bottomless gulfs, pursued by unpitying cataracts of fire and seas of molten heat. The darkness of his swoon was turned to immitigable light.

At times, Howard came back to full consciousness, and was forced to grit his teeth to avoid screaming with agony. His eyelids seemed to scorch his eyes, as he blinked in the blinding refraction; and he saw his surroundings in broken glimpses, through turning wheels of fire and blots of torrid color, like scenes from a mad kaleidoscope.

The heat-lizard was following a tortuous stream that ran in hissing rapids, among twisted crags and chasm-riven scarps. Rising in sheets and columns, the steam of the angry water was blown at intervals toward the earth-man, scalding his bare face and hands. The thongs cut into his flesh intolerably, when the monster leapt across mighty fissures that had been made by the cracking of the super-heated stone.

Howard's brain seemed to broil in his head, and his blood was a fiery torrent in his roasted body. He fought for breath—and the breath seared his lungs. The vapors eddied about him in deepening swirls, and he heard a muffled roaring whose cause he could not determine. He became aware that the heat-lizard had paused; and moving his head a little, saw that it was standing on the rocky verge of a great gulf, into which the waters fell to an unknown depth, amid curtains of steam.

His heart and his senses failed him, as he struggled like a dying man to draw breath from the suffocating air. The precipice and the monster seemed to pitch and reel beneath him, the vapors swayed vertiginously, and he thought that he was plunging with his weird steed into the unfathomably shrouded gulf.

Then, from the burning mist, the hooded forms of white and shining devils appeared to rise up and seize him, as if to receive him into their unknown hell. He saw their strange, unhuman faces; he felt the touch of their fingers, with a queer and preternatural coolness, on his seared flesh; and then all was darkness....

II

Howard awoke under circumstances that were novel and inexplicable. Instantly, with great clearness, he remembered all that had occurred prior to his final lapse, but could find no clue to his present situation.

He was lying on his back in a green radiance—a soft and soothing light that reminded him of the verdant grass and emerald seawater of the far-off Earth. The light was all about him, it seemed to flow beneath and above him, laving his body with cool ripples that left a sense of supreme well-being.

He saw that he was quite naked; and he had the feeling of immense buoyancy, as if he had been rendered weightless. Wondering, he saw that his skin was entirely free of burns, and realized that he felt no pain, no ill-effects of any kind, such as would have seemed inevitable after his dread ordeal in the Mercutian desert.

For awhile, he did not associate the green luminosity with any idea of spatial limitation; for he seemed to be floating in a vast abyss. Then, suddenly, he perceived his error. Putting out his hands, he touched on either side the wall of a narrow vault, and saw that its roof was only a few feet above him. The floor lay at an equal distance beneath; and he himself, without visible support, was reclining in mid-air. The green light, streaming mysteriously from all the sides of the vault, had given him the illusion of unbounded space.

Abruptly, at his feet, the end of the vault seemed to disappear in a white glory like pure sunlight. Long, sinuous, six-fingered hands reached out from the glow, grasped him about the ankles, and drew him gently from the green-lit space in which he floated. Weight seemed to return to him as his limbs and body entered the dazzling whiteness; and a moment later, he found himself standing erect in a large chamber, lined with some sort of pale, shimmering metal. Beside him, a strange, unearthly being was closing the panel-like door through which he had been drawn from the emerald-litten vault; and beyond this being, there were two others of the same type, one of whom was holding Howard's garments in his arms.

In growing astonishment, Howard gazed at these incredible entities. Each of them was about the height of a tall man, and the physical conformation was vaguely similar to that of mankind, but was marked by an almost god-like beauty and grace of contour, such as could hardly have been found in the most perfect of antique marbles.

Nostrils, ears, lips, hands, and all other features and members, were carven with well-nigh fantastic delicacy; and the skin of these beings, none of whom wore any sort of raiment, was white and translucent, and seemed to shine with an internal radiance. In place of hair, the full, intellectual heads were crowned with a mass of heavy flesh-like filaments, hued with changing iridescence, and tossing and curling with a weird, restless life, like the serpent locks of Medusa. The feet were like those of men, except for long, horny spurs that protruded from the heels.

The three entities returned the earth-man's gaze with unreadable eyes, brilliant as diamonds and cold as far-off stars. Then, to complete his amazement, the being who had just closed the door of the vault began to address him in high, flute-sweet tones, which baffled his ears at first, but after a little, became recognizable as flawless English.

"We trust," said the being, "that you have recovered wholly from your late experience. It was fortunate that we were watching you through our televisors when you were seized by the savages and were bound to the back of the *groko*—that creature known to you as the 'heat-lizard.' These beasts are often tamed by the savages, who, being ignorant of the use of artificial heat, make a strange use of the *groko*'s proclivities for ranging the terrible sunward deserts. Captives caught from rival tribes—and sometimes even their own kin—are tied to the monsters, who carry them through oven-like temperatures till the victims are thoroughly roasted—or, as you would say, done to a turn. Then the *grokos* return to their masters—who proceed to feast on cooked meat.

"Luckily we were able to rescue you in time; for the *groko*, in its wanderings, approached one of our cavern-exits in the great desert. Your body was covered with enormous burns when we found you; and you would assuredly have died from the effects, if we had not exposed you to the healing ray in the green vault. This ray, like many others, is unknown to your scientists; and it has, among other things, the peculiar power of nullifying gravity. Hence your sensation of weightlessness under its influence."

"Where am I? And who are you?" cried Howard.

"You are in the interior of Mercury," said the being. "I am Agvur, a savant, and a high noble of the ruling race of this world." He went on in a tone of half-disdainful explanation, as if lecturing to a child: "We call ourselves the Oumnis; and we are an old people, wise and erudite in all the secrets of nature. To protect ourselves from the intense radiations of the sun, which of course are more powerful on Mercury than on the further planets, we dwell in caverns lined with a metallic substance of our own composition. This substance, even in thin sheets, excludes all the harmful rays, some of which can pierce all other forms of matter to any depth. When we emerge to the outer world, we wear suits of this metal, whose name in our language is *mouffa*.

"Being thus insulated at all times, we are practically immortal, as well as exempt from disease; for all death and decay, in the course of nature, are caused by certain solar rays whose frequency is beyond detection of your instruments. The metal does not exclude the radiations that are beneficial and necessary to life; and by means of an apparatus similar in its principle to radio, our underworld is illumined with transmitted sunlight."

Howard began to express his thanks to Agvur. His brain was giddy with wonder, and his thoughts whirled in a maze of astounding speculations.

Agvur, with a swift and graceful gesture, seemed to wave aside his expression of gratitude. The being who bore Howard's garments came forward, and helped him, in a deft, valet-like fashion, to put them on.

Howard wanted to ask a hundred questions; for the very existence of intelligent, highly evolved beings such as the Oumnis on Mercury had been unsuspected by earth-scientists. Above all, he was curious regarding the mastery of human language displayed by Agvur. His question, as if divined by a sort of telepathy, was forestalled by the Mercutian.

"We are possessed of many delicate instruments," said Agvur, "which enable us to see and hear—and even to pick up other sense-impressions—at immense distances. We have long studied the nearer planets, Venus, Earth and Mars, and have often amused ourselves by listening to human conversations. Our brain-development, which is vastly superior to yours, has made it a simple matter for us to learn your speech; and of course the science, history and sociology of your world is an open book to us. We watched the approach of your ether-ship from space; and all the movements of your party since landing have been observed by us."

"How far am I from the rocket-ship?" asked Howard. "I trust you can help me to get back."

"You are now a full mile beneath the surface of Mercury," said Agvur, "and the part of the twilight zone in which your vessel lies is about five miles away and could readily be reached by an incline leading upward to a small exit in a natural cavern within sight of the ship. Doubtless some of the members of your party have seen the cavern and have assumed that it was a mere animal-den. When your vessel landed, we took care to block the exit with a few loose boulders and fragments of detritus, easily removable.

"As to rejoining your comrades—well, I fear that it will scarcely be practicable. You must be our guest—perhaps indefinitely." There was a kind of brusqueness in his tone as he concluded:

"We do not want our existence known to terrestrial explorers. From what we have seen of your world, and your dealings with the peoples of Mars and Venus, whose territories you have begun to arrogate, we think it would be unwise to expose ourselves to human curiosity and rapacity. We are few in number, and we prefer to remain in peace—undisturbed."

Before Howard could frame any sort of protest, there came a singular interruption. Loud and imperious, with clarion-like notes, a voice rang out in the empty air between Agvur and the earth-man. Howard was ungovernably startled; and the three Mercutians all seemed to stiffen with rapt attention. The voice went on for nearly a minute, speaking rapidly, with accents of arrogant command. Howard could make nothing of the words, whose very phonetic elements were strange and unfamiliar. But a chill ran through him at something which he sensed in the formidable voice—a something that told of relentless, implacable power.

The voice ended on a high, harsh note, and the listening Mercutians made a queer gesture with their heads and hands, as if to indicate submission to a superior will.

"Our temporal ruler and chief scientist, Ounavodo," said Agvur, "has just spoken from his hall in the lower levels. After hours of deliberation, he has reached a decision regarding your fate. In a sense, I regret the decision, which seems a trifle harsh to me; but the mandates of the Shol, as we call our ancient ruler, are to be obeyed without question. I must ask you to follow me; and I shall explain as we go along. The order must be executed without delay."

In perplexity not unmingled with consternation, Howard was led by Agvur to a sort of inclined hall or tunnel, on which the chamber opened. The tunnel was seemingly interminable, and was lit by brilliant and apparently sourceless light—the transmitted sun-rays of which the Mercutian had spoken. Like the chamber, it was lined with a pale metallic substance.

An odd machine, shaped like a small open boat, and mounted on little wheels or castors, stood before the door, on the easy monotonous grade. Agvur stationed himself in its hollow prow, motioning Howard to follow. When the other Oumnis had placed themselves behind Howard, Agvur pulled a sort of curving lever, and the machine began to glide rapidly, in perfect silence, down the interminable hall.

"This tunnel," said Agvur, "runs upward to the exit near your vessel; and it leads down to the heart of our underworld realms. If the worst happens—as I fear it may—you will see only the antechambers of our labyrinth of caverns, in which we have dwelt, immune to disease and old age, for so many centuries. I am sorry; for I had hoped to take you to my own laboratories, in the nether levels. There you might have served me... in certain biologic tests.

"Ounavodo," he went on, in calm explanatory tones, "has ordered the fusing and casting of a certain quantity of the *mouffa*-alloy, to be used in the making of new garments. This alloy, invented aeons ago by our metallurgists, is a compound of no less than six elements, and is made in two grades, one for the lining of our caverns, and the other exclusively for raiment.

"Both, for their perfection, require a seventh ingredient—a small admixture of living, protoplasmic matter, added to the molten metal in the furnace. Only thus—for a reason that is still mysterious to our savants—can the *mouffa* acquire its full power of insulation against the deadly solar rays.

"The *mouffa* used in comparatively heavy sheets for cavern-lining needs only the substance of inferior life-forms, such as the *grokos*, the half-animal savages of the twilight zone, and various creatures which we catch or breed in our underworld tunnels. But the higher grade of *mouffa*, employed in light, flexible sheets for suiting, requires the protoplasm of superior life.

"Regretfully, at long intervals, we have been compelled to sacrifice one of our own scanty number in the making of new metal to replace that which has become outworn. Whenever possible, we select those who in some manner have offended against our laws; but such infringements are rare, and commonly the victim has been chosen by a sort of divination.

"After studying you closely in his televisic mirror, Ounavodo has decided that you are sufficiently high in the evolutionary scale to provide the protoplasmic element in the next lot of *mouffa*. At least, he thinks that the test is worth trying, in the interests of science."

"However, in order that you should not feel that you are being discriminated against or treated unjustly, you will merely take your chance of being chosen from among many others. The method of selection will be revealed to you in due time."

While Agvur was speaking, the vehicle had sped swiftly down the endless incline, passing several other barge-shaped cars driven by the white, naked Immortals, whose serpentine locks flowed behind them on the air. Occasionally there were openings in the tunnel wall, leading no doubt to side-caverns;

and after a mile or two, they came to a triple branching, where caverns ran upward at reverse angles from the main passage. Horrified and shaken as he was by Agvur's disclosure, Howard took careful note of the route they were following.

He made no reply to the Mercutian. He felt his helplessness in the hands of an alien, extra-human race, equipped, it would seem, with scientific knowledge and power to which humanity had not yet attained. Thinking with desperate quickness, he decided that it would be better to pretend resignation to the will of his captors. His hand stole instinctively to the pocket in which he had carried the little *tonanite* pistol with its twelve charges of deadly heat-producing explosive; and he was dismayed, though hardly surprised, to find that the weapon was gone.

His movement was noted by Agvur; and a strange sardonic smile flickered across the unhumanly intellectual face of the savant. In his desperation, Howard thought of leaping from the car; but to do this would have meant death or serious injury at the high speed of their descent.

He became aware that the incline had ended in a large level cavern with numerous side-openings where multitudes of Oumnis were passing in and out. Here they left the boat-like vehicle; and Howard was led by Agvur through one of the side-exits, into another vast chamber, where perhaps fifty of the white people were standing in silent, semi-circular rows.

These beings were all fronting toward the opposite wall; but many of them turned to watch the earth-man with expressions of unreadable curiosity or disdain, as Agvur drew him forward to the first of the waiting ranks and motioned him to take his place at the end.

Now, for the first time, Howard saw the singular object which the Oumnis were facing. Apparently it was some sort of rootless plant-growth, with a swollen, yellowish bole or body like that of a barrel-cactus. From this body, tall as a man, leafless branches of vivid arsenic green, fringed with a white hispidity, trailed in limp, sinuous masses on the cavern-floor.

Agvur spoke in a piercing whisper: "The plant is called the Roccalim, and we employ it to choose, from a given quota, the person who shall be cast into the furnace of molten *mouffa*. You will perceive that, including yourself, there are about fifty candidates for this honor—all of whom, for one reason or another, in varying degrees, have incurred the displeasure of Ounavodo, or have given rise to doubt regarding their social usefulness. One by one, you are to walk about the Roccalim in a complete circle, approaching well within reach of the sensitive, mobile branches; and the plant will indicate the destined victim by touching him with the tips of these branches."

Howard felt, as Agvur spoke, the chill of a sinister menace; but in the weirdness of the ceremony that followed, he almost lost his apprehension of personal peril.

One by one, from the further end of the row in which he was standing, the silent Oumnis went forward and circled the strange plant, walking slowly within a few feet of the inert branches of poisonous green that resembled sleepy, half-coiled serpents. The Roccalim preserved a torpid stillness, without the least sign of animation, as Oumni after Oumni finished his perilous circuit and retired to the further side of the room, there to stand and watch the perambulations of the others.

About twenty of the white Immortals had undergone this ordeal, when Howard's turn came. Resolutely, with a sense of unreality and grotesquery rather than actual danger, he stepped forward and began his circuit of the living plant. The Oumnis looked on like alabaster statues; and all was utterly still and silent, except for a muffled, mysterious throbbing as of underworld machinery at a distance.

Howard moved on in an arc, watching the green branches with a growing tenseness. He had gone half the required distance when he felt, rather than saw, a flash of swift, intense light that appeared to stab downward from the cavern roof and strike the lumpish yellow bole of the Roccalim. The light faded in the merest fraction of time, leaving Howard in doubt as to whether he had really seen it.

Then, as he went on, he perceived with startled horror that the trailing tentacular boughs had begun to twitch and quiver, and were lifting slowly from the floor and waving toward him. On and on they came, rising and straightening, like a mass of ropy kelp that flows in an ocean-stream. They reached him, they slithered with reptilian ease about his body, and touched his face with their venomous-looking tips, clammy and inquisitive.

Howard drew back, wrenching himself away from the waving mass, and found Agvur at his elbow. The face of the Mercutian was touched with an unearthly gloating; and his iridescent locks floated upward, quivering with weird restlessness, like the Roccalim branches.

At that moment, it came to Howard that his fate had been predetermined from the beginning; that the swift, evanescent flash of light, proceeding from an unknown source, had perhaps served in some manner to irritate the living plant and provoke the action of its tentacular limbs.

Swift anger flared in the earth-man, but he repressed it. He must be cautious, must watch for an opportunity—even the slimmest—of escape. By giving the impression that he was resigned, he might throw his captors off their guard.

He saw that a number of new Mercutians, equipped with long glittering tubes like blow-pipes, had entered the cavern and were surrounding him. The companions of his late ordeal had begun to disperse in various directions.

"I am sorry," said Agvur, "that the choice should have fallen upon you. But your death will be swift—and the time is near at hand. The fusing must be completed, and the metal must be poured off and cast in thin, malleable sheets, before the next term of darkness and slumber, which will occur in little more than an hour. During this term—three hours out of every thirty-six—the transmitted sunlight is excluded from all our chambers and passages; and most of our machinery, which derives its power from light, is rendered inactive."

III

In mingled horror and dumbfoundment, Howard was taken through an opposite entrance of the Roccalim's cavern and along a sort of hall which appeared to run parallel with the one in which the incline had ended. Agvur walked at his side; and the Oumni guards were grouped before and behind him. He surmised that the glittering, hollow tubes they carried were weapons of some novel type.

As they went on, the mysterious throbbing noise drew steadily nearer. Howard saw that the far end of the corridor was illumined with a fiery red light. The air was touched with queer metallic odors; and the temperature, which had heretofore been one of unobtrusive warmth, seemed to rise slightly.

At one side, through an open door in the passage wall, as they neared the source of the red light, Howard saw a large room whose further end was filled with lofty banks of shining cylinder-shaped mechanisms. In front of these mechanisms, a solitary Mercutian stood watching an immense pivot-mounted ball which appeared to be filled nearly to the top with liquid blackness, leaving a crescent of bright crystal. Near the ball, there was a sort of inclined switchboard, from which arose many rods and levers, made of some transparent material.

"The lighting apparatus of all our caverns is controlled from that room," said Agvur, with a sort of casual boastfulness. "When the ball has turned entirely black, the sunlight will be turned off for the three-hour period, which gives us all the sleep and rest we require."

A moment more, and the party reached the end of the passage. Howard stood blinking and breathless with wonder when he saw the source of the dazzling red light.

He was on the threshold of a cavern so enormous that its roof was lost in luminosity and gave the effect of a natural sky. Titanic machines of multiform types, some squat and ungainly and others like prodigious bulbs or huge inverted funnels, crowded the cavern-floor; and in the center, towering above the rest was a double, terrace-like platform of sable stone, thirty feet in height, with many pipes of dark metal that ramified from its two tiers to the floor, like the legs of some colossal spider. From the middle of the summit, the ruddy light arose in a great pillar. Gleaming strangely against the fiery glow, the forms of Oumnis moved like midges.

Just within the entrance of the Cyclopean room, there stood a sort of rack, from which hung a dozen suits of the *mouffa*-metal. Their construction was very simple, and they closed and opened at the breast, with odd dove-tailings.

The head was a loose, roomy hood; and the metal had somehow been rendered transparent in a crescent-like strip across the eyes.

The suits were donned by Agvur and the guards; and Howard noticed that they were extremely light and flexible. He himself, at the same time, was ordered to disrobe.

"The *mouffa* mixture, during the process of fusing, gives off some dangerous radiations," said Agvur. "These will hardly matter in your case; and the suits of finished metal will protect my companions and me against them, even as against the deadly solar rays."

Howard had now removed all his clothes, which he left lying near the rack. Still pretending his resignation, but thinking desperately all the while and observing closely the details of his situation, he was led along the crowded floor, amid the sinister throbbing and muttering of the strange engines. Steep, winding stairs gave access to the terraced mass of dark stone. The earth-man saw as he went upward, that the lower tier was fitted with broad, shallow moulds, in which doubtless the metal would run off from the furnace to cool in sheets.

Howard felt an almost overpowering heat when he stood on the upper platform; and the red glare blinded him. The furnace itself, he now saw, was a circular crater, fifteen feet across, in the black stone. It was filled nearly to the rim with the molten metal, which eddied with a slow maelstrom-like movement, agitated by some unknown means, and glowing unbearably. The black stone must have been a non-conductor of heat, for it was cool beneath Howard's bare soles.

On the broad space about the furnace, a dozen Oumnis, all sheathed in the glittering *mouffa*, were standing. One of them was turning a small, complicated-looking wheel, mounted obliquely on a miniature pillar; and as if he were regulating the temperature of the furnace, the metal glowed more brightly and eddied with new swiftness in its black crater.

Apart from this wheel, and several rods that protruded from long, notched grooves in the stone, there was no visible machinery on the platform. The stone itself was seemingly all one block, except for a slab, ten feet long and two feet wide, which ran to the crater's verge. Howard was directed to stand on this slab, at the end opposite to the furnace.

"In another minute," said Agvur, "the slab will begin to move, will tilt, and precipitate you into the molten *mouffa*. If you wish, we can administer to you a powerful narcotic, so that your death will be wholly free of fear or pain."

Overcome by an unreal horror, Howard nodded his head in mechanical assent, snatching hopelessly at the momentary reprieve. Perhaps... even yet... there might be a chance; though he could have laughed at himself for the impossible notion.

Peering again toward the awful furnace, he was startled to see an inexplicable thing. Foot by foot, from the solid stone of the crater's further lip, there rose the figure of a Mercutian, till it stood with haughty features, very tall and pale and wholly naked upon the platform. Then, as Howard gasped with incredulous awe, the figure seemed to step in a stately manner from the verge, and hang suspended in air above the glowing cauldron.

"It is the Shol, Ounavodo," said Agvur in reverent tones, "though he is now many miles away in the nether caverns, he has projected his televisual image to attend the ceremony."

One of the Mercutian guards had come forward, bearing in his hands a heavy, shallow bowl of some bronze-like substance, filled with a hueless liquid. This he proffered to the earth-man.

"The narcotic acts immediately," said Agvur, as if in reassurance.

Giving a quick, unobtrusive glance about him, Howard accepted the bowl and raised it to his lips. The narcotic was odorless as well as colorless, and had the consistency of a thick, sluggish oil.

"Be quick," admonished Agvur. "The slab responds to a timing mechanism; and already it starts to move."

Howard saw that the slab was gliding slowly, bearing him as on a great protruding tongue toward the furnace. It began to tilt a little beneath his feet.

Tensing all his muscles, he leapt from the slab and hurled the heavy bowl in the face of Agvur, who stood close by. The Mercutian staggered, and before he could regain his balance, Howard sprang upon him, and lifting him bodily, flung him across the rising, sliding slab, which bore Agvur along in its accelerated movement. Stunned by the fall, and unable to recover himself, he rolled from the tilting stone into the white-hot maelstrom and disappeared with a splash. The liquid seethed and eddied with a swifter motion than before.

For a moment, the assembled Oumnis stood like metal statues; and the televisual image of the Shol, standing inscrutable and watchful above the furnace, had not stirred. Leaping at the foremost guards, Howard flung them aside as they started to lift their tubular weapons. He gained the platform's railless verge, but saw that several Oumnis had run to intercept him before he could reach the stairs. It was a twelve-foot drop to the second platform, and he feared to leap with bare feet. The strange curving pipes which ran from the upper platform to the main cavern-floor, offered his only possible means of escape.

These pipes were of darkish metal, perfectly smooth and jointless, and were about ten inches thick. Straddling the nearest one, where it entered the black stone just below the verge, Howard began to slide as quickly as he could toward the floor.

His captors had followed him to the platform-edge; and facing them as he slid, the earth-man saw two of the Immortals aim their weapons at him. From the hollow tubes, there issued glowing balls of yellow fire which came flying toward Howard. One of them fell short, striking the side of the great pipe, and causing it to melt away like so much solder. He saw the dripping of the molten metal as he ducked to avoid the second ball.

Others of the Oumnis were levelling their weapons; and a rain of the terrible fire-globes fell about Howard as he slid along the pipe's lower portion, where it curved sharply toward the floor. One of the balls brushed his right arm and left an agonizing burn.

He reached the floor, and saw that a dozen Immortals were descending the platform-stairs in great bounds. The main cavern, fortunately, was deserted. The earth-man leapt for the shelter of a huge rhomboidal machine, and heard the hiss and drip of liquid metal as the fire-balls struck behind him.

Threading his way among the looming mechanisms, and interposing their bulks as much as possible between himself and his pursuers, Howard made for the entrance through which he had been conducted to the furnace by Agvur. There were other exits from the immense cavern; but these would have led him deeper into the unknown labyrinth. He had no clearly formulated plan, and his ultimate escape was more than problematical; but his instincts bade him to go on as long as he could before being recaptured.

He heard the mysterious pounding of the untended mechanisms all about him; but there was no sound from his pursuers, who came on in grim silence, with incredible leaps, gaining visibly upon him.

Then, startlingly, as he rounded one of the machines, he found himself confronted by the televisual phantom of the Shol, standing in an attitude of menace, and waving him back with imperious gestures. He felt the awful burning gaze of eyes that were hypnotic with age-old wisdom and immemorial power; and he seemed to hurl himself against an unseen barrier, as he sprang at the formidable image. He felt a slight electric shock that jarred his entire body; but apparently the phantom was capable of little more than visual manifestation. It seemed to melt away; and then it was hovering above and a little before him, pointing out his line of flight to the pursuing Oumnis.

Passing a huge squat cylinder, he came to the rack on which the suits of *mouffa* had hung. Two of them still remained. Disregarding his own garments, which lay in a heap nearby, he snatched one of the metal suits from its place and rolled the thin, marvellously flexible stuff into a bundle as he continued his flight. Perhaps, somewhere, he would have a chance to put it on; and thus disguised, might hope to prolong his freedom—or even to find his way from this tremendous underworld.

There was a broad open space between the rack and the cavern exit. Howard's pursuers emerged from the medley of towering mechanisms before he could reach the doorway, and he was forced to dodge another fusillade of the fire-balls, which splattered in white-hot fury all around him. Before him, the menacing phantom of the Shol still hovered.

Now he had gained the corridor beyond the exit. He meant to retrace the route by which he had come with Agvur, if possible. But as he neared the door through which he had seen the watcher of the darkening globe, and the light-controlling mechanisms, he perceived that a number of Mercutians, armed with fire-tubes, were coming to intercept his flight in the corridor. Doubtless they had been summoned through some sort of teleaudition by the furnace-tenders.

Looking back, he saw that his former guards were closing upon him. In a few moments, he would be surrounded and trapped. With no conscious idea, other than the impulse to flee, he darted through the open door of the cavern of light-machines.

The solitary watcher still stood beside the massive ball with his back toward the earth-man. The crystal crescent on the dark globe had narrowed to a thin horn, like the bow of a dying moon.

A mad, audacious inspiration came to Howard, as he recalled what Agvur had told him about the control of the lighting-system. Quickly and silently he stole toward the watcher of the ball.

Again the vengeful image of the Shol stood before him, as if to drive him back; and as he neared the unsuspecting watcher, it rose in air and poised above the ball, warning the Oumni with a loud, harsh cry. The watcher turned, snatching up a heavy metal rod that lay on the floor, and leapt to meet Howard, raising his weapon for a ferocious blow.

Before the rod could descend, the earth-man's fist had caught the Mercutian full in the face, driving him back upon the slanting dial of regulative levers beside the pivot-mounted ball. There was a shivering crash as he fell among the curving crystalline rods; and at the same instant, utter overwhelming darkness rushed upon the room and blotted out the banks of gleaming mechanism, the fallen Oumni, and the phantom of Shol.

IV

Standing uncertain and bewildered, the earth-man heard a low moaning from the injured Mercutian, and a loud wail of consternation from the corridor without, where the two groups of his pursuers had found themselves overtaken by darkness. The wailing ceased abruptly; and except for the moaning near at hand, which still went on, there was absolute silence. Howard realized that he no longer heard the mutter of the strange engines in the furnace-room. Doubtless their operation had in some manner been connected with the lighting system, and had ceased with darkness.

Howard still retained the suit of *mouffa*. Groping about, he found the metal rod that had dropped from the hand of the watcher. It would make a highly serviceable weapon. Grasping it firmly, he started in what he surmised to be the direction of the door. He went slowly and cautiously, knowing that his pursuers would have gathered to await him, or might even be creeping toward him.

Listening intently, he heard a faint metallic rustle. Some of the Oumnis, clothed in *mouffa*, were coming to seek him in the darkness. His own bare feet were soundless; and stepping to one side, he heard the rustling pass. With redoubled caution, he stole on toward the door, stretching one hand before him.

Suddenly his fingers touched a smooth surface, which he knew to be the wall. He had missed the door in his groping. Listening again, he seemed to hear a faint sound on the left, as if he were being followed; and moving in the opposite direction, along the wall, he encountered empty space and saw a dim glimmer of seemingly sourceless light.

His eyes were growing accustomed to the darkness, and he made out a mass of dubious shadows against the glimmering. He had found the door, which was lined with waiting Oumnis.

Lifting his bar, he rushed upon the shadows, striking blow after blow, and stumbling over the bodies that fell before his onslaught. There were shrill cries about him, and he broke from chill, *mouffa*-sheathed fingers that sought to clutch him in the gloom. Then, somehow, he had broken through, and was in the corridor.

The glimmering, he saw, came from the cavern of machines, where the hidden furnace still burned. Into the dying glow that lit the entrance, there came hurrying figures, each of which appeared to have an enormous Cyclopean eye of icy green. Howard realized that more Mercutians, bearing artificial lights, were coming to join the pursuit.

Keeping close to the corridor wall, he ran as fast as he dared in the solid blackness, toward the cavern of the Roccalim. He heard a stealthy metallic rustling, as the foremost Oumnis followed; and glancing back, saw them dimly outlined against the remote glow. They came on in a cautious, lagging manner, as if they were waiting for the new contingent with the green lights. After a little, he saw that the two parties had united and were following him steadily.

Fingering the wall at intervals as he ran, Howard reached the entrance of the large chamber in whose center stood the Roccalim. The lights were gaining upon him rapidly. Calculating in his mind, as well as he could, the direction of the opposite doorway, giving on the main tunnel that led to the incline, he started toward it. As he went on, he veered a little, thinking to avoid the monstrous plant-growth. It was like plunging into a blind abyss; and he seemed to wander for an immense distance, feeling sure that he would reach the opposite wall at any moment.

Suddenly his feet tripped on an unknown obstruction, and he fell at full length, landing on what seemed to be a tangle of great hairy ropes that pricked his bare skin in a thousand places. Instantly, he knew that he had collided with the Roccalim.

The mass of python-like branches lay inert beneath him, without a quiver of animation. Doubtless, in the absence of light, the queer, semi-animal growth was torpid.

Pulling himself from the spiny couch on which he had fallen, Howard looked back and perceived the thronging of green lights, cold and malignant as the eyes of boreal dragons. His pursuers were entering the cavern, and would overtake him in a few instants.

Still clutching the *mouffa* garments and the metal bar, he groped across the tangle of branches, pricking his feet painfully at every step. Suddenly he plunged through to the floor, and found that he was standing in an open space where the heavy creepers, descending from the bole, had parted on either side. Crouching down, as the lights approached him, he found a low, hollow place into which he could crawl beneath the branches, close to the cactus-like stem.

The creepers were thick enough to conceal him from casual scrutiny. Lying there, with their prickly weight upon him, he saw through narrow rifts the passing of the green lights toward the outer cavern. Apparently none of the Mercutians had thought of pausing to examine the mass of Roccalim branches.

Emerging from his fantastic hiding-place, after all the Oumnis had gone past, Howard followed them boldly. He saw the vanishing of their icy lamps as they entered the outside tunnel. Moving again in utter darkness, he found the exit. There he recovered the running pencils of light, cast by the hurrying lamps as their bearers went toward the incline.

Following, Howard stumbled against an unseen object, which was either the vehicle used by Agvur, or another of the same type. Probably, in the shutting-off of power, these vehicles were now useless: otherwise, some of them might have been employed by the earth-man's pursuers. Hunters and hunted were on an equal footing; and realizing this, Howard felt for the first time an actual thrill of hope.

Going on, with the lights moving steadily before him, he started up the interminable incline which led—perhaps—to freedom. The tunnel was deserted, except for the hunters and their human quarry; and it seemed as if the multitude of Oumnis seen by Howard on his arrival with Agvur had all retired with the falling of darkness. Perhaps they had to for the usual three-hour term of night and repose.

The light-bearers appeared to disregard all the side passages that ran from the main tunnel. It occurred to Howard that they were hastening toward the surface exits, with the idea of cutting off his possible escape. Afterward they would hunt him down at leisure.

The incline ran straight ahead; and there was little danger of losing sight of the lights. Howard paused an instant to slip on the suit of *mouffa*, hoping that it might serve to deceive or baffle his hunters later on. The raiment was easily donned, and fitted him quite loosely; but the unfamiliar intricate method of fastening eluded his untaught fingers. He could not remember quite how it had been done; so he went on with the strange garment open at the breast. The queer elongated heels, made to accommodate the spurs of the Immortals, flapped behind him.

He kept as much as possible the same relative distance between himself and the Oumnis. Glancing back, after awhile, he was horrified to see, far down, the tiny green eyes of another group of lights following him. Evidently others had rallied to the pursuit.

It was a long, interminably tedious climb—mile after mile of that monotonous tunnel whose gloom was relieved only by the sinister points of green light. The Mercutians went on at a tireless pace, unhuman and implacable; and only by ceaseless exertion, half walking, half running, could the earthman maintain his position midway between the companies of lamps.

He panted heavily, and a faintness came upon him at times, in which the lights seemed to blur. A great weariness clogged his limbs and his brain. How long it was since he had eaten, he could not know. He was not aware of hunger or thirst; but he seemed to fight an ever-growing weakness. The corridor became a black eternity, haunted by the green eyes of cosmic demons.

Hour after hour he went on, through a cycle of sunless night. He lost the sense of time, and his movements became a sort of automation. His limbs were numb and dead, and it was only his relentless will that lived and drove him on. Almost, at times, he forgot where he was going—forgot everything but the blind, primitive impulse of flight. He was a nameless thing, fleeing from anonymous terror.

At last, through the crushing numbness of his fatigue, there dawned the realization that he was gaining a little on the group of lights ahead. Possibly their bearers had paused in doubt or debate. Then, suddenly, he saw that the lights were spreading out, were diverging and vanishing on either hand, till only four of them remained.

Dimly puzzled, he went on, and came to that triple division of the tunnel which he remembered passing with Agvur. He saw now that the party of Oumnis had divided into three contingents, following all the branches. Doubtless each tunnel led to a separate exit.

Recalling what Agvur had said, he kept to the middle passage. This, if Agvur had spoken truly, would lead to an exit in the twilight zone, not far from the rocket-ship. The other tunnels would lead he knew not where—perhaps to the terrible deserts of heat and the piled, chaotic glaciers of the nightward hemisphere. The one he was following, with luck, would enable him to rejoin his comrades.

A sort of second wind came to Howard now—as if hope had revived his swooning faculties. More clearly than before, he became conscious of the utter silence and profound mystery of this underworld empire, of which he had seen—was to see—so little. His hope quickened when he looked back and saw that the lights behind him had diminished in number, as if the second party had likewise separated to follow all three of the tunnels. It was obvious that there was no general pursuit. In all likelihood the smashing of the transmission levers had deranged all the machineries of the Immortals, even to their system of communication. Howard's escape, doubtless, was known only to those who had been present or near at the time. He had brought chaos and demoralization upon this super-scientific people.

V

Mile after mile of that monotone of gloom. Then, with a start of bewilderment, the earth-man realized that the four lights in front had all disappeared. Looking back, he saw that the lamps which followed him had similarly vanished. About, before and behind there was nothing but a solid, tomb-like wall of darkness.

Howard felt a strange disconcertment, together with the leaden, crushing return of his weariness. He went on with doubtful, slackening steps, following the right hand wall with cautious fingers. After awhile he turned a sharp corner; but he did not recover the lost lights. There was a drafty darkness in the air, and odors of stone and mineral, such as he had not met heretofore in the *mouffa*-lined caverns. He began to wonder if he had somehow gone astray: there might have been other branchings of the tunnel, which he had missed in his groping. In a blind surge of alarm, he started to run, and crashed headlong against the angular wall of another turn in the passage.

Half-stunned, he picked himself up. He hardly knew, henceforth, whether he was maintaining the original course of his flight or was doubling on his own steps. For aught that he could tell, he might be lost beyond all redirection in a cross-labyrinth of caverns. He stumbled and staggered along, colliding many times with the tunnel-sides, which seemed to have closed in upon him and to have grown rough with flinty projections.

The draft in his face grew stronger, with a smell of water. Presently the blindfold darkness before him melted into a chill, bluish glimmering, which revealed the rugate walls and boulder-flanged roof of the natural passage he was following.

He came out in a huge, chamber-like cave of some marble-pallid stone with twisted columnar forms. The glimmering, he saw, was a kind of phosphorescence emitted by certain vegetable growths, probably of a thallophytic nature, which rose in thick clusters from the floor, attaining the height of a tall man. They were flabby and fulsome-looking, with abortive branches, and pendulous fruit-shaped nodes of etiolated purple along their puffy, whitish-blue stems. The phosphorescence, which issued equally from all portions of these plants, served to light the gloom for some distance around, and brought out dimly the columnated character of the cavern's further walls.

Howard saw, as he passed among them, that the plants were rootless. It seemed that they would topple at a touch; but happening to stumble against one of the clumps, he found that they supported his weight with resilient solidity. No doubt they were attached firmly by some sort of suction to the smooth stone.

In the middle of the cave, behind a lofty fringing of these luminous fungi, he discovered a pool of water, fed by a thin trickle that descended through the gloom from a high vault that the phosphorescence could not illumine. Impelled by a sudden, furious thirst, he slid back the *mouffa*-hood and drank recklessly, though the fluid was sharp and bitter with strange minerals. Then, with the ravening hunger of one who has not eaten for days, he began to eye the pear-shaped nodes of the tall thallophytes. He broke one of them from its parent stem, tore off the glimmering rind, and found that it was filled with a meaty pulp. A savorous, peppery odor tempted him to taste the pulp. It was not unpleasant, and forgetting all caution (possibly he had become a little mad from his extra-human ordeals) he devoured the stuff in hasty mouthfuls.

The node must have contained a narcotic principle; for almost immediately he was overpowered by an insuperable drowsiness. He fell back and lay where he had fallen, in a deep sodden sopor without dreams, for a length of time which, as far as he could know, might have been the interim of death between two lives. He awoke with violent nausea, a racking headache, and a feeling of hopeless, irredeemable confusion.

He drank again from the bitter pool, and then began to hunt with cloudy senses and feeble, uncertain steps for another exit than the tunnel by which he had entered. His mind was dull and heavily drugged, as if from the lingering of the unknown narcotic, and he could formulate no conscious plan of action but was led only by an animal-like impulse of flight.

He discovered a second opening, low, and fanged with broken-off pillar formations, in the opposite wall of the cavern. It was filled with Stygian darkness; and before entering it, he tore a lumpy branch from one of the phosphorescent fungi, to serve him in lieu of other light.

His subsequent wanderings were nightmarish and interminable. He seemed to have gotten into some tremendous maze of natural caverns, varying greatly in size, and intersecting each other in a bewildering honeycomb fashion: an underworld that lay beyond the metal-insulated realm of the Oumnis.

There were long, tediously winding tunnels that went down into Cimmerian depth, or climbed at acclivitous angles. There were strait cubby-holes, dripping with unknown liquid ores, through which he crawled like a lizard on his belly; and Dantean gulfs that he skirted on slippery, perilous, broken ledges, hearing far below him the sullen sigh or the weirdly booming roar of sub-Mercutian waters.

For awhile, his way led mainly downward, as if he were plunging to the bowels of the planet. The air became warmer and more humid. He came at last to the sheer brink of an incommensurable abyss, where noctilucent fungi, vaster than any he had yet seen, grew tall as giant trees along the precipice that he followed for miles.

They were like fantastic monolithic tapers; but their luminosity failed to reveal the giddy depth above and beneath.

He met none of the Oumnis in this inexhaustible world of night and silence. But after he had rounded the great gulf, and had started to re-ascend in smaller caverns, he began to encounter, at intervals, certain blind, white, repulsive creatures the size of an overgrown rat, but without even the rudiments of tail or legs. In his demoralized condition of mind and body, he felt a primitive fear of these things, rather than the mere repugnance which their aspect would normally have aroused. However, they were non-aggressive and shrank sluggishly away from him. Once, he trod inadvertently on one of the creatures and leapt away, howling with fright, when it squirmed nauseously beneath his heel. Finding he had crushed its head, he took courage and began to belabor the flopping abnormality with the metal rod which he still carried. He mashed it into an oozy pulp—a pulp that still quivered with life; and then, overcome by bestial, atavistic hunger, and forgetting all the painfully acquired prejudices of civilized man, he knelt down and devoured the pulp with shameless greed. Afterward, replete, he stretched himself out and slept for many hours.

VI

He awoke with renewed physical strength, but with nerves and mind that were still partially shattered by his experiences. Like a savage who awakens in some primordial cave, he felt the irrational terror of darkness and mystery. His memories were dazed and broken, and he could recall the Oumnis only as a vague and almost supernatural source of fear, from which he had fled.

The fungus-bough, which had served him in lieu of a torch or lantern, was lying beside him in the darkness. With the bough in one hand and the metal rod in the other, he resumed his wanderings. He met more of the white, legless creatures; but he had conquered his fear of them now, and looked upon them only as a possible source of food. He proceeded to kill and eat one of them anon, relishing the worm-soft flesh as an aborigine would have relished a meal of grubs or white ants.

He had lost all notion of the passing of time or its measurement. He was a thing that clambered endlessly on Tartarean cavern-slopes or along the brink of lightless rivers and pools and chasms, killing when he was hungry, sleeping when his weariness became too urgent. Perhaps he went on for days; perhaps for many weeks, in a blind, instinctive search for light and outer air.

The flora and fauna of the caverns changed. He dragged himself through passages that were wholly lined with bristling, glowing thallophytes, some of which were tough and sharp as if fibered with iron. He came to tepid lakes whose waters were infested by long, agile, hydra-bodied creatures, divided into tapeworm segments, that rose to dispute his way but were powerless to harm his *mouffa*-covered limbs with their toothless, pulpy mouths.

For awhile, he seemed to be passing through a zone of unnatural warmth, due, no doubt, to the presence of hidden volcanic activity. There were hot geysers, and gulfs from which sultry vapors rose, filling the air with queer, metallic-smelling gases that seemed to burn corrosively in his nostrils and lungs. Some remnant of his former scientific knowledge caused him to recoil from such neighborhoods and retrace his footsteps into caverns free of these gases.

Fleeing from one of the mephitic-laden caves, he found himself in a mile-wide chamber, lined with fungi of uncommon exuberance, amid whose luminiferous growths he met with one of his most terrible adventures. A vast and semi-ophidian monster, white as the other life-forms he had met, and equally legless but owning a single, Cyclopean, phosphoric eye, leapt upon him from the unearthly vegetation and hurled him to the ground with the ram-like impact of its blunt, shapeless head. He lay half-stunned, while the monster began to ingest him in its enormous maw, starting with his feet. Seemingly the metal which he wore was no barrier to its appetite. The creature had swallowed him nearly to the hips, when he recovered his senses and realized his frightful predicament.

Smitten with hideous terror, howling and gibbering like a caveman, he lifted the metal rod, which his clutching fingers had somehow retained, and struck frantically at the awful head into whose mouth he was being drawn by inches. The blows made little or no impression on the great rubbery mass; and soon he was waist-deep in the monstrous maw. In his dire need, a trace of reasoning-power returned to him; and using the rod like a rapier he thrust it into the immense, glaring eye, burying it to his hand, and probably penetrating whatever rudimentary semblance of brain the animal possessed. A pale and egg-like fluid oozed from the broken eye, and the slobbering lips tightened intolerably upon Howard, almost crushing him in what proved to be the death-spasm. The white, swollen barrel-thick body tossed for many minutes; and during its convulsions, Howard was knocked insensible. When he came to again, the creature was lying comparatively still; and the sack-like mouth had begun to relax, so that he was able to extricate himself from the dreadful gorge.

The shock of this experience completed his mental demoralization and drove him even further into primitive brutehood. At times, his brain was almost a blank; and he knew nothing, remembered nothing but the blind horror of those infra-planetary caverns and the dumb instinct that still impelled him to seek escape.

Several times, as he continued his way through the thickets of fungi, he was forced to flee or hide from other monsters of the same type as the one that had so nearly ingested him. Then he entered a region of steep acclivities that took him ever upward. The air became chill and the caverns were seemingly void of vegetable or animal life. He wondered dully as to the reason of the growing cold; but his broken mind could suggest no explanation.

Before entering this realm, he had supplied himself with another fragment of luminiferous fungus to light his way. He was groping through a mountain-like wilderness of chasms and riven scarps and dolomites, when, at some distance above, he saw with inexpressible fright a glimmering as of two cold green eyes that moved among the crags. He had virtually forgotten the Oumnis and their lamps; but something—half intuition, half memory—warned him of direr peril than any he had hitherto met in the darkness.

He dropped his luminous torch and concealed himself behind one of the dolomitic formations. From his hiding-place, he saw the passing of two of the Immortals, clad in silvery *mouffa*, who descended the scarp and vanished in the craggy gulfs below. Whether or not they were hunting for him, he could not know; but when they had gone from sight, he resumed his climb, hurrying at breakneck speed and feeling that he must get as far away as possible from the bearers of those icy green lights.

The dolomites dwindled in size, and the steep chamber narrowed like the neck of a bottle and closed in upon him presently from all sides, till it was only a narrow, winding passage. The floor of the passage became fairly level. Anon, as he followed it, he was startled and blinded by a glare of light directly ahead—a light that was brilliant as pure sunshine. He cowered and stepped back, shielding his eyes with his hands till they became somewhat tempered to the glare. Then, stealthily, with a mingling of confused fears and dim, unworded hopes, he crept toward the light and came out in an endless metal hall, apparently deserted but filled as far as eye could see with the apparently sourceless brilliance.

The mouth of the rough natural passage from which he had emerged was fitted with a sort of valve, which had been left open, doubtless by the Immortals he had seen among the nether crags. The boat-shaped vehicle they had used was standing in the hall. This vehicle, and the hall itself, were familiar to him, and he began to recollect, in a partial way, the ordeals he had undergone among the Oumnis before his flight into outer darkness.

The hall was slightly inclined; and he seemed to remember that the upward grade would presumably lead to a lost world of freedom. Apprehensively and furtively, he began to follow it, loping like an animal.

After he had gone for perhaps a mile, the floor became perfectly level, but the hall itself started to turn in a sort of arc. He was unable to see very far ahead. Then, so abruptly that he could not check his headlong flight, he came in view of three Oumnis, clothed in metal, who were all standing with their backs to him. A boat-vehicle was near at hand. One of the Immortals was tugging at a huge, capstan-like bar that protruded from the wall of the passage; and as if in response to the bar, a sort of gleaming metal valve was descending slowly from the roof. Inch by inch, it came down like a mighty curtain; and soon it would close the entire passage and render impossible the earth-man's egress.

Somehow, it did not occur to Howard that the tunnel beyond the valve might lead to other realms than the outer air for which he longed so desperately. As if by a miracle, something of his former courage and resourcefulness had returned to him; and he did not turn and flee incontinently at sight of the Immortals, as he would have done a short time before. He felt that now or never was his opportunity to escape from the sub-Mercutian levels.

Leaping forward on the unsuspecting Oumnis, all of whom were intent on the closing of the valve, he struck at the foremost with his metal bar. The Mercutian toppled and went down with a clattering of *mouffa* on the floor. The one who was operating the lever continued his task, and Howard had no time to strike him down, for the remaining Immortal, with tigerish agility, had sprung back and was levelling the deadly fire-tube which he carried.

Howard saw that the great valve was still descending—was barely two feet above the cavern floor. He made a flying dive for the opening, sprawling on all fours and then crawling prone on his stomach beneath the terrible curtain of metal.

Struggling to rise, he found himself impeded and held back. He was in utter darkness now; but getting to his knees and groping about, he determined the cause of his retardation. The fallen valve had caught the loose elongated heel of the *mouffa* on his right foot. He had all the sensations of a trapped animal as he sought to wrench himself free. The tough *mouffa* held, weighed down by the enormous valve; and it seemed that there was no escape.

Then, amid his desperation, he somehow remembered that the *mouffa*-armor was open at the breast. Awkwardly and painfully, he managed to crawl forth from it, leaving it there like a discarded lizard-skin.

Getting to his feet, he raced on in the darkness. He was without light, for he had dropped the phosphorescent bough in his dive under the closing valve. The cavern was rough and flinty to his naked feet; and he felt an icy wind, bleak as the breath of glaciers, that blew upon him as he went. The floor sloped upward, and in places it was broken into stair-like formations against which he stumbled and fell, bruising himself severely. Then he cut his head cruelly on a sharp stone that projected from the low roof. The wet, warm blood flowed down across his brow and into his eyes.

The passage steepened and the air took on a terrible frigidity. There was no sign of pursuit from the Oumnis; but fearing they would raise the valve and follow him, the earth-man hastened on. He was puzzled by the growing Arctic cold, but the suppositional reason seemed to elude him. His naked limbs and torso were studded with goose-flesh; and he began to shiver with violent ague, in spite of the high speed at which he ran and climbed.

Now the cavern-stairs were more regular and defined. They seemed to mount forever in the darkness; and growing accustomed to them he was able to grope his way from step to step with no more than an occasional fall or stumble. His feet were cut and bleeding; but the cold had begun to numb them and he felt little pain.

He saw a dim, circular patch of light far above him, and gasping with the icy air, which appeared to grow thinner and more irrespirable, he rushed toward it. Hundreds, thousands of those black, glaciated steps he seemed to climb before he neared the light. He came out beneath a sable heaven crowded with chill, pulseless, glaring stars, in a sort of valley-bottom among drear unending scarps and pinnacles, still and silent as a frozen dream of death. They gleamed in the starlight with reflections of myriad-angled ice; and the valley-bottom itself was lit by patches of a leprous whiteness. One of these patches fringed the mouth of the incline on whose topmost step the earth-man was standing.

He fought agonizingly for breath in the tenuous infra-zero air and his body stiffened momently with a permeating rigor as he stood and peered in numb bewilderment at the icy, mountainous chaos of the landscape in which he had emerged. It was like a dead crater in a world of unspeakable and perpetual desolation, where life could never have been.

The flowing blood had congealed upon his brow and cheeks. With glazing eyes, he saw, in a nearby cliff, the continuation of the cavern-steps. Hewn for some unimaginable purpose by the Immortals, they ran upward in the ice toward the higher summits.

It was not the familiar twilight zone of Mercury in which he had come forth—it was the bleak, nightward side, eternally averted from the sun, and blasted with the frightful cold of cosmic space. He felt the pinnacles and chasms close him in, relentless and rigid, like some hyperborean hell. Then the realization of his plight became something very remote and recessive, a dim thought that floated above his ebbing consciousness. He fell forward on the snow with limbs already stiff and unbending; and the mercy of the final numbness grew complete.

THE EMPIRE OF THE NECROMANCERS

The legend of Mmatmuor and Sodosma shall arise only in the latter cycles of Earth, when the glad legends of the prime have been forgotten. Before the time of its telling, many epochs shall have passed away, and the seas shall have fallen in their beds, and new continents shall have come to birth. Perhaps, in that day, it will serve to beguile for a little the black weariness of a dying race, grown hopeless of all but oblivion. I tell the tale as men shall tell it in Zothique, the last continent, beneath a dim sun and sad heavens where the stars come out in terrible brightness before eventide.

I

Mmatmuor and Sodosma were necromancers who came from the dark isle of Naat, to practise their baleful arts in Tinarath, beyond the shrunken seas. But they did not prosper in Tinarath: for death was deemed a holy thing by the people of that grey country; and the nothingness of the tomb was not lightly to be desecrated; and the raising up of the dead by necromancy was held in abomination.

So, after a short interval, Mmatmuor and Sodosma were driven forth by the anger of the inhabitants, and were compelled to flee toward Cincor, a desert of the south, which was peopled only by the bones and mummies of a race that the pestilence had slain in former time.

The land into which they went lay drear and leprous and ashen below the huge, ember-colored sun. Its crumbling rocks and deathly solitudes of sand would have struck terror to the hearts of common men; and since they had been thrust out in that barren place without food or sustenance, the plight of the sorcerers might well have seemed a desperate one. But, smiling secretly, with the air of conquerors who tread the approaches of a long-coveted realm, Sodosma and Mmatmuor walked steadily on into Cincor.

Unbroken before them, through fields devoid of trees and grass, and across the channels of dried-up rivers, there ran the great highway by which travellers had gone formerly between Cincor and Tinarath. Here they met no living thing; but soon they came to the skeletons of a horse and its rider, lying full in the road, and wearing still the sumptuous harness and raiment which they had worn in the flesh. And Mmatmuor and Sodosma paused before the piteous bones, on which no shred of corruption remained; and they smiled evilly at each other.

"The steed shall be yours," said Mmatmuor, "since you are a little the elder of us two, and are thus entitled to precedence; and the rider shall serve us both and be the first to acknowledge fealty to us in Cincor."

Then, in the ashy sand by the wayside, they drew a threefold circle; and standing together at its center, they performed the abominable rites that compel the dead to arise from tranquil nothingness and obey henceforward, in all things, the dark will of the necromancer. Afterwards, they sprinkled a pinch of magic powder on the nostril-holes of the man and the horse; and the white bones, creaking mournfully, rose up from where they had lain and stood in readiness to serve their masters.

So, as had been agreed between them, Sodosma mounted the skeleton steed and took up the jewelled reins, and rode in an evil mockery of Death on his pale horse; while Mmatmuor trudged on beside him, leaning lightly on an ebon staff; and the skeleton of the man, with its rich raiment flapping loosely, followed behind the two like a servitor.

After a while, in the grey waste, they found the remnants of another horse and rider, which the jackals had spared and the sun had dried to the leanness of old mummies. These also they raised up from death; and Mmatmuor bestrode the withered charger; and the two magicians rode on in state, like errant emperors, with a lich and a skeleton to attend them. Other bones and charnel remnants of men and beasts, to which they came anon, were duly resurrected in like fashion; so that they gathered to themselves an ever-swelling train in their progress through Cincor.

Along the way, as they neared Yethlyreom, which had been the capital, they found numerous tombs and necropoli, inviolate still after many ages, and containing swathed mummies that had scarcely withered in death. All these they raised up and called from sepulchral night to do their bidding. Some they commanded to sow and till the desert fields and hoist water from the sunken wells; others they left at divers tasks, such as the mummies had performed in life. The century-long silence was broken by the noise and tumult of myriad activities; and the lank liches of weavers toiled at their shuttles; and the corpses of plowmen followed their furrows behind carrion oxen.

Weary with their strange journey and their oft-repeated incantations, Mmatmuor and Sodosma saw before them at last, from a desert hill, the lofty spires and fair, unbroken domes of Yethlyreom, steeped in the darkening stagnant blood of ominous sunset.

"It is a goodly land," said Mmatmuor, "and you and I will share it between us, and hold dominion over all its dead, and be crowned as emperors on the morrow in Yethlyreom."

"Aye," replied Sodosma, "for there is none living to dispute us here; and those that we have summoned from the tomb shall move and breathe only at our dictation, and may not rebel against us."

So, in the blood-red twilight that thickened with purple, they entered Yethlyreom and rode on among the lofty, lampless mansions, and installed themselves with their grisly retinue in that stately and abandoned palace, where the dynasty of Nimboth emperors had reigned for two thousand years with dominion over Cincor.

In the dusty golden halls, they lit the empty lamps of onyx by means of their cunning sorcery, and supped on royal viands, provided from past years, which they evoked in like manner. Ancient and imperial wines were poured for them in moonstone cups by the fleshless hands of their servitors; and they drank and feasted and revelled in phantasmagoric pomp, deferring till the morrow the resurrection of those who lay dead in Yethlyreom.

They rose betimes, in the dark crimson dawn, from the opulent palace-beds in which they had slept; for much remained to be done. Everywhere in that forgotten city, they went busily to and fro, working their spells on the people that had died in the last year of the pest and had lain unburied. And having accomplished this, they passed beyond Yethlyreom into that other city of high tombs and mighty mausoleums, in which lay the Nimboth emperors and the more consequential citizens and nobles of Cincor.

Here, they bade their skeleton slaves to break in the sealed doors with hammers; and then, with their sinful, tyrannous incantations, they called forth the imperial mummies, even to the eldest of the dynasty, all of whom came walking stiffly, with lightless eyes, in rich swathings sewn with flame-bright jewels. And also later they brought forth to a semblance of life many generations of courtiers and dignitaries.

Moving in solemn pageant, with dark and haughty and hollow faces, the dead emperors and empresses of Cincor made obeisance to Mmatmuor and Sodosma, and attended them like a train of captives through all the streets of Yethlyreom. Afterwards, in the immense throne-room of the palace, the necromancers mounted the high double throne, where the rightful rulers had sat with their consorts. Amid the assembled emperors, in gorgeous and funereal state, they were invested with sovereignty by the sere hands of the mummy of Hestaiyon, earliest of the Nimboth line, who had ruled in half-mythic years. Then all the descendants of Hestaiyon, crowding the room in a great throng, acclaimed with toneless, echo-like voices the dominion of Mmatmuor and Sodosma.

Thus did the outcast necromancers find for themselves an empire and a subject people in the desolate, barren land where the men of Tinarath had driven them forth to perish. Reigning supreme over all the dead of Cincor, by virtue of their malign magic, they exercised a baleful despotism. Tribute was borne to them by fleshless porters from outlying realms; and plague-eaten corpses, and tall mummies scented with mortuary balsams, went to and fro upon their errands in Yethlyreom, or heaped before their greedy eyes, from inexhaustible vaults, the cobweb-blackened gold and dusty gems of antique time.

Dead laborers made their palace-gardens to bloom with long-perished flowers; liches and skeletons toiled for them in the mines, or reared superb, fantastic towers to the dying sun. Chamberlains and princes of old time were their cupbearers; and stringed instruments were plucked for their delight by the slim hands of empresses with golden hair that had come forth untarnished from the night of the tomb. Those that were fairest, whom the plague and the worm had not ravaged overmuch, they took for their lemans and made to serve their necrophilic lust.

II

In all things, the people of Cincor performed the actions of life at the will of Mmatmuor and Sodosma. They spoke, they moved, they ate and drank as in life. They heard and saw and felt with a similitude of the senses that had been theirs before death; but their brains were enthralled by a dreadful necromancy. They recalled but dimly their former existence; and the state to which they had been summoned was empty and troublous and shadow-like. Their blood ran chill and sluggish, mingled with water of Lethe; and the vapors of Lethe clouded their eyes.

Dumbly they obeyed the dictates of their tyrannous lords, without rebellion or protest, but filled with a vague, illimitable weariness such as the dead must know, when having drunk of eternal sleep, they are called back once more to the bitterness of mortal being. They knew no passion or desire or delight, only the black languor of their awakening from Lethe, and a grey, ceaseless longing to return to that interrupted slumber.

Youngest and last of the Nimboth emperors was Illeiro, who had died in the first month of the plague, and had lain in his high-built mausoleum for two hundred years before the coming of the necromancers.

Raised up with his people and his fathers to attend the tyrants, Illeiro had resumed the emptiness of existence without question and had felt no surprise. He had accepted his own resurrection and that of his ancestors as one accepts the indignities and marvels of a dream. He knew that he had come back to a faded sun, to a hollow and spectral world, to an order of things in which his place was merely that of an obedient shadow. But at first he was troubled only, like the others, by a dim weariness and a pale hunger for the lost oblivion.

Drugged by the magic of his overlords, weak from the age-long nullity of death, he beheld like a somnambulist the enormities to which his fathers were subjected. Yet, somehow, after many days, a feeble spark awoke in the sodden twilight of his mind.

Like something lost and irretrievable, lying beyond prodigious gulfs, he recalled the pomp of his reign in Yethlyreom, and the golden pride and exultation that had been his in youth. And recalling it, he felt a vague stirring of revolt, a ghostly resentment against the magicians who had haled him forth to this calamitous mockery of life. Darkly he began to grieve for his fallen state, and the mournful plight of his ancestors and his people.

Day by day, as a cupbearer in the halls where he had ruled aforetime, Illeiro saw the doings of Mmatmuor and Sodosma. He saw their caprices of cruelty and lust, their growing drunkenness and gluttony. He watched them wallow in their necromantic luxury, and become lax with indolence, gross with indulgence. They neglected the study of their art, they forgot many of their spells. But still they ruled, mighty and formidable; and, lolling on couches of purple and rose, they planned to lead an army of the dead against Tinarath.

Dreaming of conquest, and of vaster necromancies, they grew fat and slothful as worms that have installed themselves in a charnel rich with corruption. And pace by pace with their laxness and tyranny, the fire of rebellion mounted in the shadowy heart of Illeiro, like a flame that struggles with Lethean damps. And slowly, with the waxing of his wrath, there returned to him something of the strength and firmness that had been his in life. Seeing the turpitude of the oppressors, and knowing the wrong that had been done to the helpless dead, he heard in his brain the clamor of stifled voices demanding vengeance.

Among his fathers, through the palace-halls of Yethlyreom, Illeiro moved silently at the bidding of the masters, or stood awaiting their command. He poured in their cups of onyx the amber vintages, brought by wizardry from hills beneath a younger sun; he submitted to their contumelies and insults. And night by night he watched them nod in their drunkenness, till they fell asleep, flushed and gross, amid their arrogated splendor.

There was little speech among the living dead; and son and father, daughter and mother, lover and beloved, went wearily to and fro without sign of recognition, making no comment on their evil lot. But at last, one midnight, when the tyrants lay in slumber, and the flames wavered in the necromantic lamps, Illeiro took counsel with Hestaiyon, his eldest ancestor, who had been famed as a great wizard in fable and was reputed to have known the secret lore of antiquity.

Hestaiyon stood apart from the others, in a corner of the shadowy hall. He was brown and withered in his crumbling mummy-cloths; and his lightless obsidian eyes appeared to gaze still upon nothingness. He seemed not to have heard the questions of Illeiro; but at length, in a dry, rustling whisper, he responded:

"I am old, and the night of the sepulcher was long, and I have forgotten much. Yet, groping backward across the void of death, it may be that I shall retrieve something of my former wisdom; and between us we shall devise a mode of deliverance." And Hestaiyon searched among the shreds of memory, as one who reaches into a place where the worm has been and the hidden archives of old time have rotted between their covers. Till at last he remembered, and said:

"I recall that I was once a mighty wizard; and among other things, I knew the spells of necromancy but employed them not, deeming their use and the raising up of the dead an abhorrent act. Also, I possessed other knowledge; and perhaps, among the remnants of that ancient lore, there is something which may serve to guide us now. For I recall a dim, dubitable prophecy, made in the primal years, at the founding of Yethlyreom and the empire of Cincor. The prophecy was, that an evil greater than death would befall the emperors and the people of Cincor in future times; and that the first and the last of the Nimboth dynasty, conferring together, would effect a mode of release and the lifting of the doom. The evil was not named in the prophecy; but it was said that the two emperors would learn the solution of their problem by the breaking of an ancient clay image that guards the nethermost vault below the imperial palace in Yethlyreom."

Then, having heard this prophecy from the faded lips of his forefather, Illeiro mused a while, and said:

"I remember now an afternoon in early youth, when searching idly through the unused vaults of our palace, as a boy might do, I came to the last vault and found therein a dusty, uncouth image of clay, whose form and countenance were strange to me. And, knowing not the prophecy, I turned away in disappointment, and went back as idly as I had come, to seek the moted sunlight."

Then, stealing away from their heedless kinfolk, and carrying jewelled lamps they had taken from the hall, Hestaiyon and Illeiro went downward by subterranean stairs beneath the palace; and, threading like implacable furtive shadows the maze of nighted corridors, they came at last to the lowest crypt.

Here, in the black dust and clotted cobwebs of an immemorial past, they found, as had been decreed, the clay image, whose rude features were those of a forgotten earthly god. And Illeiro shattered the image with a fragment of stone; and he and Hestaiyon took from its hollow center a great sword of unrusted steel, and a heavy key of untarnished bronze, and tablets of bright brass on which were inscribed the various things to be done, so that Cincor should be rid of the dark reign of the necromancers and the people should win back to oblivious death.

So, with the key of untarnished bronze, Illeiro unlocked, as the tablets had instructed him to do, a low and narrow door at the end of the nethermost vault, beyond the broken image; and he and Hestaiyon saw, as had been prophesied, the coiling steps of somber stone that led downward to an undiscovered abyss, where the sunken fires of earth still burned. And leaving Illeiro to ward the open door, Hestaiyon took up the sword of unrusted steel in his thin hand, and went back to the hall where the necromancers slept, lying a-sprawl on their couches of rose and purple, with the wan, bloodless dead about them in patient ranks.

Upheld by the ancient prophecy and the lore of the bright tablets, Hestaiyon lifted the great sword and struck off the head of Mmatmuor and the head of Sodosma, each with a single blow. Then, as had been directed, he quartered the remains with mighty strokes. And the necromancers gave up their unclean lives, and lay supine, without movement, adding a deeper red to the rose and a brighter hue to the sad purple of their couches.

Then, to his kin, who stood silent and listless, hardly knowing their liberation, the venerable mummy of Hestaiyon spoke in sere murmurs, but authoritatively, as a king who issues commands to his children. The dead emperors and empresses stirred, like autumn leaves in a sudden wind, and a whisper passed among them and went forth from the palace, to be communicated at length, by devious ways, to all the dead of Cincor.

All that night, and during the blood-dark day that followed, by wavering torches or the light of the failing sun, an endless army of plague-eaten liches, of tattered skeletons, poured in a ghastly torrent through the streets of Yethlyreom and along the palace-hall where Hestaiyon stood guard above the slain necromancers. Unpausing, with vague, fixed eyes, they went on like driven shadows, to seek the subterranean vaults below the palace, to pass through the open door where Illeiro waited in the last vault, and then to wend downward by a thousand thousand steps to the verge of that gulf in which boiled the ebbing fires of earth. There, from the verge, they flung themselves to a second death and the clean annihilation of the bottomless flames.

But, after all had gone to their release, Hestaiyon still remained, alone in the fading sunset, beside the cloven corpses of Mmatmuor and Sodosma. There, as the tablets had directed him to do, he made trial of those spells of elder necromancy which he had known in his former wisdom, and cursed the dismembered bodies with that perpetual life-in-death which Mmatmuor and Sodosma had sought to inflict upon the people of Cincor. And maledictions came from the pale lips, and the heads rolled horribly with glaring eyes, and the limbs and torsos writhed on their imperial couches amid clotted blood. Then, with no backward look, knowing that all was done as had been ordained and predicted from the first, the mummy of Hestaiyon left the necromancers to their doom, and went wearily through the nighted labyrinth of vaults to rejoin Illeiro.

So, in tranquil silence, with no further need of words, Illeiro and Hestaiyon passed through the open door of the nether vault, and Illeiro locked the door behind them with its key of untarnished bronze. And thence, by the coiling stairs, they wended their way to the verge of the sunken flames and were one with their kinsfolk and their people in the last, ultimate nothingness.

But of Mmatmuor and Sodosma, men say that their quartered bodies crawl to and fro to this day in Yethlyreom, finding no peace or respite from their doom of life-in-death, and seeking vainly through the black maze of nether vaults the door that was locked by Illeiro.

THE SEED FROM THE SEPULCHER

"**Y**es, I found the place," said Falmer. "It's a queer sort of place, pretty much as the legends describe it." He spat quickly into the fire, as if the act of speech had been physically distasteful to him, and, half averting his face from the scrutiny of Thone, stared with morose and somber eyes into the jungle-matted Venezuelan darkness.

Thone, still weak and dizzy from the fever that had incapacitated him for continuing their journey to its end, was curiously puzzled. Falmer, it seemed to him, had undergone an inexplicable change during the three days of his absence—a change so elusive and shadowy in some of its phases that Thone was unable to delimit it fully in his thoughts.

Other phases, however, were all too obvious. Falmer, even during extreme hardship or jungle illness, had been heretofore unquenchably loquacious and cheerful. Now he seemed sullen, uncommunicative, as if his mind were preoccupied with far-off things of disagreeable import. His bluff face had grown hollow—even pointed—and his eyes had narrowed to secretive slits. Thone was troubled by these changes, though he tried to dismiss his impressions as mere distempered fancies due to the influence of the ebbing fever.

"But can't you tell me what the place was like?" he persisted.

"There isn't much to tell," said Falmer, in a queer grumbling tone. "Just a few crumbling walls overgrown and half-displaced by the forest trees, and a few falling pillars netted with lianas."

"But didn't you find the burial-pit of the Indian legend, where the gold was supposed to be?"

"Oh, yes, I found it. The place has started to cave in from above, so there wasn't much difficulty about that—but there was no treasure." Falmer's voice had taken on a forbidding surliness; and Thone decided to refrain from further questioning.

"I guess," he commented lightly, "that we had better stick to orchid-hunting. Treasure trove doesn't seem to be in our line. By the way, did you find any unusual flowers or plants during the trip?"

"Hell, no," Falmer snapped. His face had gone suddenly ashen in the firelight, and his eyes had assumed a set glare that might have meant either fear or anger. "Shut up, can't you? I don't want to talk. I've had a headache all day—some damned Venezuelan fever coming on, I suppose. We'd better head for the Orinoco tomorrow, even if we are both sick. I've had all I want of this trip."

James Falmer and Roderick Thone, professional orchid-hunters, with two Indian guides, had been following an obscure tributary of the upper Orinoco. The country was rich in rare flowers; and, beyond its floral wealth, they had been drawn by vague but persistent rumors among the local tribes concerning the existence of a ruined city somewhere on this tributary: a city that contained a burial-pit in which vast treasures of gold, silver and jewels had been interred together with the dead of some nameless people. These rumors were never first hand, but the two men had thought it worthwhile to investigate them. Thone had fallen sick while they were still a full day's journey from the supposed site of the ruins, and Falmer had gone on in a canoe with one of the Indians, leaving the other to attend to Thone. He had returned at nightfall of the third day following his departure.

Thone decided after a while, as he lay staring at his companion, that the latter's taciturnity and moroseness were perhaps due to disappointment over his failure to find the treasure. It must have been that—together with some tropical infection working in his blood. However, he admitted doubtfully to himself, it was not like Falmer to be disappointed or downcast under such circumstances. Greediness for mere wealth, as far as he had occasion to observe, was not in the man's nature.

Falmer did not speak again, but sat glaring before him as if he saw something invisible to others beyond the labyrinth of fire-touched boughs and lianas in which the whispering, stealthy darkness crouched. Somehow, there was a shadowy fear in his aspect. Thone continued to watch him, and saw that the Indians, impassive and cryptic, were also watching him, as if with some obscure expectancy. The riddle was too much for Thone, and he gave it up after a while, lapsing into restless, fever-turbulent slumber, from which he awakened at intervals to see the set face of Falmer, dimmer and more distorted each time with the slowly dying fire. At last it became a half-human thing, devoured by inhuman shadows and twisted by the ever-changing horror of those febrile dreams.

Thone felt stronger in the morning: his brain was clear, his pulse tranquil once more; and he saw with mounting concern the mysterious indisposition of Falmer, who seemed to rouse and exert himself with great difficulty, speaking hardly a word and moving with singular stiffness and sluggishness. He appeared to have forgotten his announced project of returning toward the Orinoco, and Thone took entire charge of the preparations for departure. His companion's condition puzzled him more and more: the signs were not born of any malady with which he was familiar. There was no fever and the symptoms were wholly obscure and ambiguous. However, on general principles, he administered a stiff dose of quinine to Falmer before they started.

The paling saffron of a sultry dawn sifted upon them through the jungle-tops as they loaded their belongings into the dugouts and pushed off down the slow current. Thone sat near the bow of one of the boats, with Falmer in the rear, and a large bundle of orchid roots and part of their equipment filling the middle. The two Indians, taciturn and stolid, occupied the other boat, together with the rest of the supplies.

It was a monotonous journey. The river wound like a sluggish olive snake between dark, interminable walls of forest, from which, at intervals, the goblin faces of orchids leaned and leered. There were no sounds other than the splash of paddles, the furious chattering of monkeys and petulant cries of strange, fiery-colored birds. The sun rose above the jungle and poured down a waveless tide of torrid brilliance.

Thone rowed steadily, looking back over his shoulder at times to address Falmer with some casual remark or friendly question. The latter, with dazed eyes and features that were queerly pale and pinched in the sunlight, sat dully erect and made no effort to use his paddle, seeming to lack both the strength and the inclination. He offered no reply to the solicitous queries of Thone, but shook his head at intervals with a sort of shuddering motion that was plainly automatic and involuntary, rather than the expression of common negation. After a while he began to moan thickly, as if in pain or delirium.

They went on in this manner for several hours; the heat grew more oppressive between the stifling, airless walls of jungle. Thone became aware of a shriller cadence in the moans of his sick companion. Looking back, he saw that Falmer had removed his sun-helmet, seemingly oblivious of the murderous heat, and was clawing at the crown of his head with frantic fingers. Convulsions shook his entire body, and the dugout began to rock dangerously as he tossed to and fro in a long paroxysm of manifest agony. His voice mounted to a ceaseless, high, unhuman shrieking.

Thone made a quick decision. There was a break in the lining palisade of somber forest, and he headed the boat for shore immediately. The Indians followed, whispering between themselves and eyeing the sick man with glances of apprehensive awe and terror that puzzled Thone tremendously. He felt that there was some devilish mystery about the whole affair; and he could not imagine what was wrong with Falmer. All the known manifestations of malignant tropical diseases rose before him like a rout of hideous phantasms; but among them, he could not recognize the thing that had assailed his companion.

Having gotten Falmer ashore on a semi-circle of liana-latticed beach without the aid of the reluctant guides, who seemed unwilling to touch or approach the sick man, Thone administered a heavy hypodermic injection of morphine from his medicine chest. This appeared to ease Falmer's suffering, and the convulsions ceased. Thone, taking advantage of their remission, proceeded to examine the crown of Falmer's head.

He was startled to find amid the thick disheveled hair a hard and pointed lump which resembled strangely the tip of a beginning horn, rising under the still unbroken skin. As if endowed with erectile and restless life, it seemed to grow beneath his fingers.

At the same time, abruptly and mysteriously, Falmer opened his eyes and appeared to regain full consciousness, as if he had overcome not only the effects of the hypodermic but the stupor of the unknown malady. For a few minutes, he was more his normal self than at any time since his return from the ruins. He began to talk, as if he were anxious to relieve his mind of some oppressing burden. His voice was peculiarly thick and toneless, but Thone, listening in half-comprehending horror, was able to follow his mutterings and piece them together.

"The pit! The pit!" said Falmer. "The infernal thing that was in the pit, in the deep sepulcher!... I wouldn't go back there for the treasure of a dozen El Dorados... I didn't tell you much about those ruins, Thone. Somehow it was hard—impossibly hard—to talk.

"I guess the Indian knew there was something wrong with those ruins. He led me to the place all right... but he wouldn't tell me anything about it; and he waited by the river-side while I searched for the treasure.

"Great grey walls there were, older than the jungle—old as death and time—not like anything I have ever seen. They must have been quarried and reared by people from some forgotten continent or lost planet. They loomed and leaned at mad, unnatural angles, threatening to crush the trees about them. And there were columns, too: thick, swollen columns of unholy form, whose abominable carvings the jungle had not wholly screened from view.

"My God! that accursed burial-pit! There was no trouble finding it. The pavement above had broken through quite recently, I think. A big tree had pried with its boa-like roots between the yard-deep flagstones that were buried beneath centuries of mould. One of the flags had been tilted back on the pavement, and another had fallen through into the pit. There was a large hole, whose bottom I could see dimly in the forest-strangled light. Something glimmered palely at the bottom; but I could not be sure what it was.

"I had taken along a coil of rope, as you remember. I tied one end to a main root of the tree, dropped the other through the opening, and went down like a monkey. When I got to the bottom I could see little at first in the gloom, except for the whitish glimmering all around me, at my feet. Something broke and crunched beneath me when I began to move—something that was unspeakably brittle and friable. I turned on my flash-light, and saw that the place was fairly littered with bones—human skeletons lay tumbled everywhere. They must have been very old, for they dissolved into powder at a touch.

"The place was a huge sepulchral chamber. After awhile, as I wandered about with the flash-light, I found the steps that led to the blocked-up entrance. But if any treasure had been buried with the bodies, it must have been removed long ago. I groped around amid the bones and dust, feeling pretty much like a ghoul, but couldn't find anything of value, not even a bracelet or a finger-ring on any of the skeletons.

"It wasn't until I thought of climbing out that I noticed the real horror. I didn't mind those skeletons so much: they were lying in attitudes of repose, even if they were a little crowded and it seemed that their owners must have died natural deaths—natural, that is, as we reckon such things.

"Then, in one of the corners—the corner nearest to the opening in the roof—I looked up and saw it in the webby shadows. Ten feet above my head it hung, and I had almost touched it, unknowingly, when I descended the rope.

"It looked like a sort of weird lattice-work at first. Then I saw that the lattice was partly formed of human bones—a complete skeleton, very tall and stalwart, like that of a warrior. I wouldn't have cared if it had been hanging there in any normal fashion—if it had been suspended by metal chains, for instance, or had merely been nailed to the walls. The horror lay in the thing that grew out of the skull—the white, withered thing like a set of fantastic antlers ending in myriads of long and stringy tendrils that had spread themselves on the wall, climbing upward till they reached the roof. They must have lifted the skeleton, or body, along with them as they climbed.

"I examined the thing with my flash-light, and found new horrors. It must have been a plant of some sort, and apparently it had started to grow in the cranium. Some of the branches had issued from the cloven crown, others through the eye-holes and the nose-holes, to flare upward. And the roots of the blasphemous thing had gone downward, trellising themselves on every bone. The very toes and fingers were ringed with them, and they drooped in writhing coils. Worst of all, the ones that had issued from the toe-ends *were rooted in a second skull,* which dangled just below, with fragments of the broken-off root system. There was a litter of fallen bones on the floor in the corner, but I didn't care to inspect it.

"The sight made me feel a little weak, somehow—and more than a little nauseated—that abhorrent, inexplicable mingling of the human and the plant. I started to climb the rope, in a feverish hurry to get out, but the thing fascinated me, in its abominable fashion, and I couldn't help pausing to study it a little more when I had climbed half-way. I leaned toward it too fast, I guess, and the rope began to sway, bringing my face lightly against the leprous, antler-shaped boughs above the skull.

"Something broke—I don't know what—possibly a sort of pod on one of the branches. Anyway, I found my head enveloped in a cloud of pearl-grey powder, very light, fine, and scentless. The stuff settled on my hair, it got into my nose and eyes, nearly choking and blinding me. I tried to shake it off as well as I could. Then I climbed on and pulled myself through the opening…"

As if the effort of coherent narration had been too heavy a strain, Falmer lapsed into disconnected mumblings, some of which were inaudible. The mysterious malady, whatever it was, returned upon him, and his delirious ramblings were mixed with groans of torture. But at moments he regained a flash of coherence.

"My head! My head!" he muttered. "There must be something in my brain, something that grows and spreads; I tell you, I can feel it there. I haven't felt right at any time since I left the burial-pit…. My mind has been queer ever since…. It must have been the spores of the ancient devil-plant…. The spores have taken root… the thing is splitting my skull, going down into my brain—a plant that springs out of a human cranium, as if from a flower-pot!"

The dreadful convulsions began once more, and Falmer writhed uncontrollably in his companion's arms, shrieking with agony. Thone, sick at heart, and horribly shocked by his sufferings, abandoned all effort at restraint and took up the hypodermic. With much difficulty, he managed to inject a triple dose into one of the wildly tossing arms, and Falmer grew quiet by degrees and lay with open glassy eyes, breathing stertorously. Thone, for the first time, perceived an odd protrusion of his eye-balls, which seemed about to start from their sockets, making it impossible for the lids to close, and lending the drawn, contorted features an expression of mad horror and extravagant ghastliness. It was as if something were pushing Falmer's eyes from his head.

Thone, trembling with sudden weakness and terror, felt that he was involved in some unnatural web of nightmare. He could not, dared not, believe the story Falmer had told him, and its implications. The thing was too monstrous, too fantastic; and, assuring himself that his companion had imagined it all, had been ill throughout with the incubation of some strange fever, he stooped over and found that the horn-shaped lump on Falmer's head had now broken through the skin.

Increasingly, with a sense of unreality, he stared at the object that his prying fingers had touched and revealed amid the matted hair. It was unmistakably a plant-bud of some sort, with involuted folds of pale green and bloody pink that seemed about to expand. The thing issued from above the central suture of the skull; and the thought occurred to the horror-sick observer that it had somehow taken root in the very bone; had gone downward, as Falmer had feared, into the brain.

A nausea swept upon Thone, and he recoiled from the lolling head and its baleful outgrowth, averting his gaze. His fever, he felt, was returning; there was a woeful debility in all his limbs; and he heard the muttering voices of incipient delirium through the quinine-induced ringing in his ears. His eyes blurred with a deathly mist, as if the miasma of some equatorial fen had arisen visibly before him.

He fought to subdue his illness and impotence. He must not give way to it wholly; he must go on with Falmer and the Indians, and reach the nearest trading station, many days away on the Orinoco, where Falmer could receive aid.

As if through sheer volition, the clinging vapor cleared from his eyes, and he felt a resurgence of strength. He looked around for the two guides, and saw, with a start of uncomprehending surprise, that they had vanished. Then, peering further, he observed that one of the boats—the dugout used by the Indians—had also disappeared. It was all too evident that he and Falmer had been deserted. Perhaps the Indians had known what was wrong with the sick man, and had been afraid. Their apprehensive glances, their covert whisperings, their patent unwillingness to approach Falmer, all seemed to confirm this. At any rate, they were gone, and they had taken much of the camp equipment and most of the provisions with them.

Thone turned once more to the supine body of Falmer, conquering his fear and repugnance with effort. Something must be done, and they must go on while Falmer still lived. One of the boats remained; and even if Thone became too ill to ply the paddle, the current would still carry them downstream.

Resolutely, he drew out his clasp-knife and, stooping over the stricken man, he excised the protruding bud, cutting as close to the scalp itself as he could with safety. The thing was unnaturally tough and rubbery; it exuded a thin, sanious fluid; and he shuddered when he saw its internal structure, full of nerve-like filaments, with a core that suggested cartilage. He flung it aside quickly on the river sand. Then, lifting Falmer in his arms, he lurched and staggered toward the remaining boat. He fell more than once, and lay half-swooning across the inert body. Alternately carrying and dragging his burden, he reached the boat at last. With the remainder of his failing strength, he contrived to prop Falmer in the stern against the pile of equipment.

His fever was mounting apace. Dimly, with a swimming brain, and legs that bent beneath him like river reeds, he went back for the medicine-kit. After much delay, with tedious, half-delirious exertions, he pushed off from the shore, and got the boat into mid-stream. He paddled with nerveless, mechanical strokes, hardly knowing what he did, till the fever mastered him wholly and the oar slipped from oblivious fingers....

After that, he seemed to be drifting through a hell of strange dreams illumed by an intolerable, glaring sun. He went on in this way for cycles, and then floated into a phantom-peopled darkness, and slumber haunted by innominable voices and faces, all of which became at last the voice and face of Falmer, detailing over and over again a hideous story which Thone still seemed to hear in the utmost abyss of sleep.

He awoke in the yellow glare of dawn, with his brain and his senses comparatively clear. His illness had left a great languor, but his first thought was of Falmer. He twisted about, nearly falling overboard in his debility, and sat facing his companion.

Falmer still reclined, half-sitting, half-lying, against the pile of blankets and other impedimenta. His knees were drawn up, his hands clasping them as if in tetanic rigor. His features had grown as wan and stark and ghastly as those of a dead man, and his whole aspect was one of mortal rigidity. It was this, however, that caused Thone to gasp with unbelieving horror—a horror in which he found himself hoping that Falmer really *was* dead.

During the interim of Thone's delirium and his lapse into slumber, which must have been a whole afternoon and night, the monstrous plant-bud, merely stimulated, it would seem, by the act of excision, had grown again with preternatural and abhorrent rapidity, from Falmer's head. A loathsome pale-green stem was mounting thickly and had started to branch like antlers after attaining a height of six or seven inches.

More dreadful than this, if possible, similar growths had issued from the eyes; and their heavy stems, climbing vertically across the forehead, had entirely displaced the eye-balls. Already they were branching like the thing that mounted from the crown. The antlers were all tipped with pale vermilion. Each of them appeared to quiver with repulsive animation, nodding rhythmically in the warm, windless air.... From the mouth another stem protruded, curling upward like a long and whitish tongue. It had not yet begun to bifurcate.

Thone closed his eyes to shut away the shocking vision. Behind his lids, in a yellow dazzle of light, he still saw the cadaverous, deathly features, the climbing stems that quivered against the dawn like ghastly hydras of tomb-etiolated green. They seemed to be waving toward him, growing and lengthening visibly as they waved. He opened his eyes again, and fancied, with a start of new terror, that the antlers *were* actually taller than they had been a few moments previous.

After that, he sat watching them in a sort of baleful paralysis, with horror curdled at his heart. The illusion of the plant's visible growth and freer movement—if it was illusion—increased upon him by accelerative degrees. Falmer, however, did not stir, and his white, parchment face seemed to shrivel and fall in, as if the roots of the growth were draining him of blood, were devouring his very flesh in their insatiable and ghoulish hunger.

Shuddering, Thone wrenched his eyes away and stared at the river shore. The stream had widened, and the current had grown more sluggish. He sought to recognize their location, looking in vain for some familiar landmark in the monotonous dull-green cliffs of jungle that lined the margin. All was strange to him, and he felt hopelessly lost and alienated. He seemed to be drifting on an unknown tide of nightmare and madness, companioned by something more frightful than corruption itself.

His mind began to wander with an odd inconsequence, coming back always, in a sort of closed circle, to the growth that was devouring Falmer. With a flash of scientific curiosity, he found himself wondering to what genus it belonged. It was neither fungus nor pitcher-plant, nor anything that he had ever encountered or heard of in his explorations. It must have come, as Falmer had suggested, from an alien world; it was nothing that the earth could conceivably have nourished.

He felt, with a comforting assurance, that Falmer was dead, for the roots of the thing must have long since penetrated the brain. That at least, was a mercy. But even as he shaped the thought, he heard a low, guttural moaning, and, peering at Falmer in horrible startlement, saw that his limbs and body were twitching slightly. The twitching increased, and took on a rhythmic regularity, though at no time did it resemble the agonized and violent convulsions of the previous day. It was plainly automatic, like a sort of galvanism; and Thone saw that it was timed with the languorous and loathsome swaying of the plant. The effect on the watcher was insidiously mesmeric and somnolent; and once he caught himself beating the detestable rhythm with his foot.

He tried to pull himself together, groping desperately for something to which his sanity could cling. Ineluctably, he felt the return of his sickness: fever, nausea, and revulsion worse than the loathliness of death. But before he yielded to it utterly, he drew his loaded revolver from the holster and fired six times into Falmer's quivering body. He knew that he had not missed, but, after the final bullet, Falmer still moaned and twitched in unison with the evil swaying of the plant, and Thone, sliding into delirium, heard still the ceaseless, automatic moaning.

There was no time in the world of seething unreality and shoreless oblivion through which he drifted. When he came to himself again, he could not know if hours or weeks had elapsed. But he knew at once that the boat was no longer moving; and lifting himself dizzily, he saw that it had floated into shallow water and mud and was nosing the beach of a tiny, jungle-tufted isle in mid-river. The putrid odor of slime was about him like a stagnant pool, and he heard a strident humming of insects.

It was either late morning or early afternoon, for the sun was high in the still heavens. Lianas were drooping above him from the island trees like uncoiled serpents, and epiphytic orchids, marked with ophidian mottlings, leaned toward him grotesquely from lowering boughs. Immense butterflies went past on sumptuously spotted wings.

He sat up, feeling very giddy and light-headed, and faced again the horror that companioned him. The thing had grown incredibly, enormously: the three-antlered stems, mounting above Falmer's head, had become gigantic and had put out masses of ropy feelers that tossed uneasily in the air, as if searching for support—or new provender. In the topmost antler, issuing from the crown and towering above the others, a prodigious blossom had opened—a sort of fleshy disk, broad as a man's face and pale as leprosy.

Falmer's features had shrunken till the outlines of every bone were visible as if beneath tightened paper. He was a mere death's head in a mask of human skin, and his body seemed to have collapsed and fallen, leaving little more than a skeleton beneath his clothing. He was quite still now, except for the communicated quivering of the stems. The atrocious plant had sucked him dry, had eaten his vitals and his flesh.

Thone wanted to hurl himself forward in a mad impulse to grapple with the loathly growth. But a strange paralysis held him back. The plant was like a living and sentient thing—a thing that watched him, that dominated him with its unclean but superior will. And the huge blossom, as he stared, took on the dim, unnatural semblance of a face. It was somehow like the face of Falmer, but the lineaments were twisted all awry, and were mingled with those of something wholly devilish and non-human. Thone could not move—and he could not take his eyes from the blasphemous, unthinkable abnormality.

By some miracle, his fever had left him; and it did not return. Instead, there came an eternity of frozen fright and madness, in which he sat facing the mesmeric plant. It towered before him from the dry, dead shell that had been Falmer, its swollen, glutted stems and branches swaying in a gentle rhythm, its huge flower leering perpetually upon him with its impious travesty of a human face. He thought that he heard a low singing sound, ineffably, demoniacally sweet, but whether it emanated from the plant or was a mere hallucination of his overwrought senses, he could not know.

The sluggish hours went by, and a gruelling sun poured down upon him like molten lead from some titanic vessel of torture. His head swam with weakness and the fetor-laden heat; but he could not relax the rigor of his posture. There was no change in the nodding monstrosity, which seemed to have attained its full growth above the head of its victim. But after a long interim, Thone's eyes were drawn to the rigid, shrunken hands of Falmer, which still clasped the drawn-up knees in a spasmodic clutch. From the back of each hand, from the ends of the skeleton fingers, tiny white rootlets had broken and were writhing slowly in the air, groping, it seemed, for a new source of nourishment. Then, from the neck and chin, other tips were breaking, and over the whole body the clothing stirred in a curious manner, as if with the crawling and lifting of hidden lizards.

At the same time the singing grew louder, sweeter, more imperious in Thone's ears, and the swaying of the great plant assumed an indescribably seductive tempo. It was like the allurement of voluptuous sirens, the deadly languor of dancing cobras. Thone felt an irresistible compulsion: a summons was being laid upon him, and his drugged mind and body must obey it. The very fingers of Falmer, twisting viperishly, seemed beckoning to him. Then, suddenly he was on his hands and knees in the bottom of the boat.

Inch by inch, with baleful terror and equally baleful fascination contending in his brain, he crept forward, dragging himself over the disregarded bundle of orchid-plants—inch by inch, foot by foot, till his head was against the withered hands of Falmer, from which hung and floated the questing roots.

Some cataleptic spell had made him helpless. He felt the rootlets as they moved like delving fingers through his hair and over his face and neck, and started to strike in with agonizing, needle-sharp tips. He could not stir, he could not even close his lids. In a frozen stare, he saw the gold and carmine flash of a hovering butterfly as the roots began to pierce his pupils.

Deeper and deeper went the greedy roots, while new filaments grew out to enmesh him like a witch's net.... For a while, it seemed that the dead and the living writhed together in leashed convulsions.... At last Thone hung supine amid the lethal, ever-growing web; bloated and colossal, the plant lived on; and in its upper branches, through the still, stifling afternoon, a second flower began to unfold.

THE SECOND INTERMENT

"Well," said Guy Magbane, "I notice that you're still alive." His curtain-shadowed lips, as they shaped the words, took on a thin, ambiguous curve that might have been either smile or sneer. He came forward, peering a little obliquely at the sick man, and held out the glass of garnet-colored medicine.

Sir Uther Magbane, sitting amid the heavy pillows like a death's-head with tawny hair and blue eyes, made no answer and appeared to hesitate before accepting the glass. A dark, formless terror seemed to float upward in his pale gaze, like a drowned object that rises slowly in some autumnal weir. Finally he took the glass and drained its contents with a convulsive gulp, as if the act of swallowing were difficult.

"I'm pretty sick this time, Guy," he said, in a voice that some inner constraint or actual physical constriction had rendered harshly guttural and toneless. "But the worst fear is, that I may not be sick enough... that the thing may happen again as it did before. My God! I can't think of anything else—can't imagine anything else but the black, suffocating agony, the blind, intolerable, stifling horror of it. Promise me—promise me again, Guy, that you'll defer my burial for at least a fortnight, for a month; and swear that when you do put me away you'll make sure that the push-button and electric wiring in my casket are in good order. Merciful God!... supposing I should wake up in the tomb... and find that the alarm didn't work!"

"Don't worry—I'll attend to all that." The tone was soothing, a little contemptuous—and, to the listener, touched with a sinister meaning. Guy Magbane turned to leave the room, and did not see that the floating fear in his brother's gaze had become for the moment a palpable, recognizable thing. He added over his shoulder, negligently and without looking back:

"That idea has grown to be a regular obsession with you. Just because the thing occurred once doesn't mean that it will ever occur again. If you die this time, you'll stay dead, in all likelihood. There won't be any more mistakes about it." With this equivocal and dubious re-assurance, he went out and closed the door behind him.

Sir Uther Magbane leaned back among the pillows and stared at the somber oaken wainscotting. He felt—as he had felt ever since the beginning of his present illness—that the room was too cramped and narrow; that the walls were always threatening to close in upon him, the roof to descend above him, like the sides and lid of a coffin. He could never seem to draw a full breath. All he could do was to lie there, alone with his ghastly fear, his hideous memories and his even more hideous apprehensions. The visits of his younger brother, Guy, for some time past, had served merely to strengthen his feeling of sepulchral oppression... for Guy was now part of the fear.

He had always been afraid of death, even in his boyhood—that time when the specter should normally be dim and far away, if perceived at all. It had begun with the early death of his mother: ever since that black bereavement, a hovering vulturine shadow had seemed to taint and darken the things that were unspoiled for others. His imagination, morbidly acute, sick with suspicion of life itself, had seen everywhere the indwelling skeleton, the flower-shrouded corpse. The kisses of young love were flavored with mortality. The very sap of things was touched with putrefaction.

With heartfelt shudders, as he matured, he had nourished his charnel fancy on all that was macabre in art and literature. Like a seer who gazes into a black crystal, he foresaw with harrowing minuteness the physical and mental agonies of dissolution; he previsioned the activities of decay, the slow toil of the mordant worm, as clearly as if he had descended into the tomb's loathsome oblivion. But he had not imagined or feared the most poignant horror of all—that of premature burial—until he had himself experienced it.

The thing had come without warning, just after his succession to the estate, and his engagement to Alice Margreave, in whose love he had begun to forget a little his boyhood terrors. It was as if the haunting specter had retired, only to strike in a more abhorrent and appalling shape.

Lying there now, the memory seemed to stop his very heart, to throttle his breathing, as it always did. Again, with hallucinatory distinctness, he recalled the first gradual attack of his mysterious malady. He recalled the beginning of his syncope, the lightless gulf into which he had gone down, by timeless degrees, as if through infinite empty space. Somewhere in that gulf, he had found oblivion—the black instant that might have been hours or ages—from which he had awakened in darkness, had tried to sit up, and had bruised his face against an adamantine obstruction that seemed to be only a few inches above him. He had struck out, blindly, in mad, insensate panic, trying to thresh about with hands and feet, and had met on all sides a hard, unyielding surface, more terrifying, because of its inexplicable *nearness*, than the walls of some nighted oubliette.

There was a period of nightmare confusion—and then he knew what had happened. By some ghastly mistake, he had been placed, still alive, in a casket; and the casket was in the old vaults of his family, below the chapel floor. He began to scream then, and his screams, with the dull, muffled repercussion of some underground explosion, were hurled back upon him appallingly in the narrow space. Already the air seemed to stifle him, thick with mortuary odors of wood and cloth.

Hysteria seized him, and he went quite mad, hurling himself against the lid in what seemed an eternity of cramped, hopeless struggle. He did not hear the sound of footsteps that came hurrying to his aid, and the blows of men with chisels and hammers on the heavy lid were mingled indistinguishably with his own cries and clamorings. Even when the lid was wrenched loose, he had become quite delirious with the horror of it all, and had fought against his rescuers, as if they too were part of the suffocating, constrictive nightmare.

Never was he able to believe that his experience had been a matter of a few minutes only—that he had awakened just after the depositing of the coffin in the vault and before the actual lowering of the slab and the departure of the pall-bearers, whose horrified attention he had attracted by the muted sound of his cries and struggles. It seemed to him that he must have fought there for immeasurable cycles.

The shock had left him with shattered nerves that trembled uncontrollably; nerves that found a secret terror, a funereal alarm, in the most innocent, unshadowed things. Three years had gone by since then; but at no time had he been able to master his grisly obsession, to climb from the night-bound pit of his demoralization. His old fear of death was complicated by a new dread: that his illness, recurring, as it was likely to do, would again take the deceptive semblance of death, and again he would awaken in the tomb. With the ceaseless apprehension of a hypochondriac, he watched for the first repetition of the malady's preliminary symptoms; and felt himself irretrievably doomed from their beginning.

His fear had poisoned everything; had even parted him from Alice Margreave. There had been no formal breaking of the engagement: merely a tacit falling apart of the self-preoccupied, self-tortured neurotic and the girl whose love had soon turned, perforce, to a bewildered and horror-mingled pity.

After that, he had abandoned himself more fully, if possible, to his monomania. He had read everything he could find on the subject of premature interment, he had collected clippings that told of known cases: people who had been rescued in time—or whose re-animation had been detected too late, perhaps had been surmised only from some change or contortion of posture noticed after many years in the removal of the body to a new burial-place. Impelled by a shivering fascination, he delved without restraint in the full ghastliness of the abominable theme. And always, in the fate of others, he saw his own fate; and their sufferings, by some vicarious visitation, became his.

Fatally convinced that the insufferable horror would recur, he had made elaborate precautions, equipping the casket in which he was to be buried with an electrical device that would summon help. The least pressure of a button, within easy reach of his right hand, would set an alarm-gong to ringing in the family chapel above, together with a second gong in the nearby manor-house.

Even this, however, did little to assuage his fears. He was haunted by the idea that the push-button might fail to work, or that no one would hear it, or that his rescuers might arrive too late, when he had undergone the full agonies of asphyxiation.

These dismal apprehensions, growing more dolorous and more tyrannous daily, had accompanied the first stages of his second illness. Then, by vacillating degrees, he had begun to doubt his brother, to suspect that Guy, being next in the line of inheritance, might wish for his demise and have an interest in its consummation. Guy had always been a cynical, cold-blooded sort; and his half-concealed contempt and scant sympathy for Uther Magbane's obsession was readily translated into darker terms by a sick fantasy. Gradually, as he grew weaker, the invalid had come to fear that his brother would deliberately hasten the burial—might even disconnect the device for summoning aid, whose care had been confided to him.

Now, after Guy had gone out, the certainty of such treachery, like a black and noxious blossom, leaped full-grown in Sir Uther Magbane's mind. Swept by a cold, devastating panic, he resolved that he would speak, at the first opportunity, to someone else—would confide secretly to another person than Guy the responsibility of seeing that the electrical alarm was kept in good working-order.

Hours went by in a shrouded file as he lay there with his poisonous and sepulchral thoughts. It was afternoon, and the sloping sun should have shone now through the leaded panes, but the yew-fringed sky beyond the window seemed to be overcast, and there was only a sodden glimmering. Twilight began to weave a grey web in the room; and Magbane remembered that it was almost time for the doctor's evening visit.

Could he dare confide in the doctor, he wondered? He did not know the man very well. The family physician had died some time ago, and this new doctor had been called in by Guy. Sir Uther had never cared much for his manner, which was both brisk and saturnine. He might be in league with Guy, might have an understanding as to the way in which the elder brother could be so conveniently disposed of, and his demise made certain. No, he could not speak to the doctor.

Who was there to help him, anyway? He had never made many friends, and even these seemed to have deserted him. The manor-house was in a lonely part of the country; and everything would facilitate the treachery that he apprehended. My God! he was being smothered—buried alive!...

Someone opened the door quietly and came toward him. He felt so hopeless and helpless that he did not even try to turn. Presently the visitor stood before him, and he saw that it was Holton, the aged family butler, who had served three generations of the Magbanes. Probably he could trust Holton; and he would speak about the matter now.

He framed the words with which he would address the butler, and was horrified when his tongue and his lips refused to obey him. He had not noticed anything wrong heretofore: his brain and his senses had been preternaturally clear. But now an icy paralysis appeared to have seized his organs of articulation.

He tried to lift his pale, claw-like hand and beckon to Holton; but the hand lay moveless on the counterpane, in spite of the agonized and herculean effort of will which he exerted. Fully conscious, but powerless to stir by so much as the shifting of a finger or the drooping of an eyelid, he could only lie and watch the dawning concern in the old butler's rheumy eyes.

Holton came nearer, reaching out his tremulous hand. Magbane saw the hand approaching him, saw it hover above his body, descend toward his heart, just below the direct focus of his vision. It seemed never to reach him—at least there was no sensation of contact. The room was dimming rapidly—strange that the darkness should have come so soon—and a faintness was creeping on all his senses, like an insidious mist.

With a start of familiar terror, and a feeling of some intolerable repetition, of doing what he had once done before under circumstances of dire fright, he felt that he was going down into a night-black abyss. Holton's face was fading to a remote star, was receding with awful velocity above unscalable pits at whose bottom nameless, inexorable doom awaited Magbane: a doom to which he had gone at some previous time, and which he had been predestined to meet from the beginning of cycles. Down, forever down he went; the star disappeared; there was no light anywhere; and his syncope was complete.

Magbane's reviving consciousness took the form of a fantastic dream. In this dream, he remembered his descent into the gulf; and he thought that the descent had been prolonged, after a dim interval, by some animate, malignant agency. Great demoniac hands had seemed to grasp him in the nadir-founded gloom, had lifted him, had carried him down immeasurable flights of inframundane stairs and along corridors that lay deeper than hell itself.

There was night everywhere—he could not see the forms of those who bore him, supporting him at feet and head, but he could hear their implacable, unceasing steps, echoing with hollow and sepulchral thunder in the black subterranes; and he could sense the funereal towering of their shapes, oppressing him from about and above in some ultra-tactual fashion, such as is possible only in dreams.

Somewhere in that nether night they laid him down, they left him and went away. In his dream he heard the departing rumble of their footsteps, with leaden reverberations, endless and ominous, through all the stairs and corridors by which they had come with their human burden. At last there was a prolonged clangor as of closing doors, somewhere in the upper profound; a clangor fraught with unutterable despair, like the knell of Titans. After its echoes had died away, the despair seemed to remain, stagnant and soundless, dwelling tyrannically, illimitably, in all the recesses of this sepulchral underworld.

Silence, dank, stifling, aeonian silence prevailed, as if the whole universe had died, had gone down to some infra-spatial burial. Magbane could neither move nor breathe; and he felt, by no physical sense, an infinity of dead things about him, lying hopeless of resurrection, like himself.

Then, within the dream, by no perceptible transition, another dream was intercalated. Magbane forgot the horror and hopelessness of his descent, as a new-born child might forget some former death. He thought that he was standing in a place of soft sunlight and blithe, many-tinted flowers. An April turf was deep and resilient beneath him; the heavens were those of some vernal paradise; and he was not alone in this Eden, for Alice Margreave, his former fiancée, stood lovely and smiling amid the nearer blossoms.

He stepped toward her, filled with ineffable happiness—and in the sward at his feet, a black pit, shaped like the grave, opened and widened and deepened with awful rapidity. Powerless to avert his doom, he went down into the pit, falling, falling interminably; and the darkness closed above him, swooping from all sides on a dim pin-point of light which was all that remained of the April heavens. The light expired, and Magbane was lying once more among dead things, in vaults beneath the universe.

By slow, incalculably doubtful gradations, his dream began to merge into reality. At first, there had been no sense of time; only an ebon stagnation, in which aeons and minutes were equally drowned. Then—through what channel of sense he knew not—there returned to Magbane the awareness of duration. The awareness sharpened, and he thought that he heard, at long, regular intervals, a remote and muffled sound. Insufferable doubt and bewilderment, associated with some horror which he could not recall, awoke and brooded noxiously in his dark mind.

Now he became aware of bodily discomfort. A dank chill, beginning as if in his very brain, crept downward through his body and limbs, till it reached his extremities and left them tingling. He felt, too, that he was intolerably cramped, was lying in some stiff, straitened position. With mounting terror, for which as yet he could find no name, he heard the remote muffled sound draw closer, till it was in his own body, and was no longer a sound, but the palpable hammering of his heart against his side. With this clarifying of his sense-perceptions, he knew, abruptly, as in a flash of black lightning, the thing of which he was afraid.

The terrible knowledge went through him in a lethal shock, leaving him frozen. It was like a tetanic rigor, oppressing all his members, constricting his throat and heart as with iron bands; inhibiting his breath, crushing him like some material incubus. He dared not, *could* not move to verify his fear.

Utterly unmanned by a conviction of atrocious doom, he fought to regain some nominal degree of composure. He must not give way to the horror, or he would go mad. Perhaps it was only a dream after all; perhaps he was lying awake in his own bed, in darkness; and if he reached out his hand, he would encounter free space—not the hideous nearness of a coffin-lid.

In a sick vertigo of irresolution, he tried to summon courage and volition for the test. His sense of smell, awakening now, tended to confirm his despair; for there was a musty closeness, a dismal, sodden reek of wood and cloth... even as once before. It seemed to grow heavier momently with confined impurities.

At first, he thought that he could not move his hand—that the strange paralysis of his malady had not yet left him. With the dread laboriousness of nightmare, he lifted it slowly, tediously, as if overcoming the obstruction of a viscid medium. When, finally, a few inches away, it met the cold, strait surface he had apprehended, he felt the iron tightening of his despair, but was not surprised. There had been no real room for hope: the thing was happening again, just as it had been ordained to happen. Every step he had taken since birth—every motion—every breath—every struggle—had led only to this.

Mad thoughts were milling in his brain—like crowded maggots in a corpse. Old memories and present fears were mingled in strange confusion, steeped with the same charnel blackness. He recalled, in that tumult of disconnected ideas, the push-button he had installed in the casket. At the same moment, his brother's face, callous, ironic, touched with a thin, ambiguous sneer, appeared like a hallucination from the darkness; and the newest of his fears came back upon him with sickening certitude. In a flash, he saw the face presiding above the entire process through which, by the illegal connivance of the doctor, he must have been hurried into the tomb without passing through an embalmer's hands. Fearing that he might revive at any moment, they had taken no chances—and had doomed him to this horror.

The mocking face, the cruel vision, seemed to disappear; and among his disordered, frenzy-driven thoughts there rose an irrational hope. Perhaps he had been wrong in his doubts of Guy. Perhaps the electrical device would work after all; and a light pressure would summon eager hands to loose him from his mortuary confinement. He forgot the ghastly chain of condemning logic.

Quickly, by an automatic impulse, he groped for the button. At first he did not find it, and a sick consternation filled him. Then, at last, his fingers touched it and he pressed the button again and again, listening desperately for the answering clang of the alarm-gong in the chapel above. Surely he would hear it, even through the intervening wood and stone; and he tried insanely to believe that he *had* heard it—that he could even hear the sound of running footsteps somewhere above him. After seeming hours, with a hideous lapse into the most abominable despond, he realized that there was nothing—nothing but the stifled clamor of his own imprisoned heart.

For awhile, he yielded to madness, as on that former occasion—beating obliviously against the sides of the casket, hurling himself blindly at the inexorable lid. He shrieked again and again, and the narrow space seemed to drown him with a volume of thick, demoniacally deep sound, which he did not recognize as his own voice or the voice of anything human. Exhaustion, and the warm, salty taste of blood in his mouth, flowing from his bruised face, brought him back at last to comparative calmness.

He perceived now that he was breathing with great difficulty—that his violent struggles and cries had served only to deplete the scant amount of air in the casket. In a moment of unnatural coolness, he recalled something that he had read, somewhere, about a method of shallow breathing by which men could survive protracted periods of inhumation. He must force himself to inhale lightly, must center all his faculties on the prolongation of life. Perhaps—even yet—if he could hold out—his rescuers would come. Perhaps the alarm *had* rung, and he had not been able to hear it. Men were hurrying to his aid, and he must not perish before they could lift the slab and break open the casket.

He wanted to live, as never before; he longed, with intolerable avidity, to breathe the open air once more, to know the unimaginable bliss of free movement and respiration. Christ! if someone would only come—if he could hear the ring of footsteps, the sullen grating of the slab, the hammers and chisels that would let in the blessed light, the pure air. Was this all that he could ever know, this dumb horror of living interment, this blind, cramped agony of slow suffocation?

He strove to breathe quietly, with no waste or effort; but his throat and chest seemed to constrict as with the inexorable tightening of some atrocious torture instrument. There was no relief, no escape, nothing but a ceaseless, relentless pressure, the strangling clutch of some monstrous garrote that compressed his lungs, his heart, his wind-pipe, his very brain.

The agony increased: there was a weight of piled monuments upon him, which he must lift if he were to breathe freely. He strove against the funereal burden. He seemed to hear, at the same time, the labored sound of some Cyclopean engine that sought to make headway in a subterranean passage beneath fallen masses of earth and stone. He did not know that the sound was his own tortured gasping. The engine seemed to pant, thunderous and stertorous, with earth-shaking vibrations; and upon it, he thought, the foundations of ruined worlds were descending slowly and steadily, to choke it into ultimate silence.

The last agonies of his asphyxiation were translated into a monstrous delirium—a phantasmagoria that seemed to prolong itself for cycles, with one implacable dream passing without transition into another.

He thought that he was lying captive in some Inquisitorial vault whose roof, floor and walls were closing upon him with appalling speed, were crushing him in their adamantine embrace.

For an instant, in a light that was not light, he strove to flee with leaden limbs from a formless, nameless juggernaut, taller than the stars, heavier than the world, that rolled upon him in black, iron silence, grinding him beneath it into the charnel dust of some nethermost limbo.

He was climbing eternal stairs, bearing in his arms the burden of some gigantic corpse, only to have the stairs crumble beneath him at each step, and to fall back with the corpse lying upon him and swelling to macrocosmic proportions.

Eyeless giants had stretched him prone on a granite plain and were building upon his chest, block by colossal block, through aeons of slow toil, the black Babel of a sunless world.

An anaconda of black, living metal, huger than the Python of myth, coiling about him in the pit where he had fallen, constricted his body with its unimaginable folds. In a grey, livid flash, he saw its enormous mouth poised above him, sucking the last breath it had squeezed from his lungs.

With inconceivable swiftness, the head of the anaconda became that of his brother Guy. It mocked him with a vast sneer, it appeared to swell and expand, to lose all human semblance or proportion, to become a blank, dark mass that rushed upon him in cyclonic gloom, driving him down into the space beyond space.

Somewhere in that descent, there came to him the incognizable mercy of nothingness.

UBBO-SATHLA

*... For Ubbo-Sathla is the source and the end. Before the coming of
Zhothaqquah or Yok-Zothoth or Kthulhut from the stars, Ubbo-Sathla
dwelt in the steaming fens of the new-made Earth: a mass without head
or members, spawning the grey, formless efts of the prime and the grisly
prototypes of terrene life.... And all earthly life, it is told, shall go back
at last through the great circle of time to Ubbo-Sathla.*

—The Book of Eibon.

Paul Tregardis found the milky crystal in a litter of oddments from many
lands and eras. He had entered the shop of the curio-dealer through
an aimless impulse, with no particular object in mind, other than the
idle distraction of eyeing and fingering a miscellany of far-gathered things.
Looking desultorily about, his attention had been drawn by a dull glimmering
on one of the tables; and he had extricated the queer orb-like stone from its
shadowy, crowded position between an ugly little Aztec idol, the fossil egg
of a dinornis, and an obscene fetish of black wood from the Niger.

The thing was about the size of a small orange and was slightly flattened at
the ends, like a planet at its poles. It puzzled Tregardis, for it was not like an
ordinary crystal, being cloudy and changeable, with an intermittent glowing in its heart, as if it were alternately illumed and darkened from within.
Holding it to the wintry window, he studied it for awhile without being able
to determine the secret of this singular and regular alternation. His puzzlement was soon complicated by a dawning sense of vague and irrecognizable
familiarity, as if he had seen the thing before under circumstances that were
now wholly forgotten.

He appealed to the curio-dealer, a dwarfish Hebrew with an air of dusty
antiquity, who gave the impression of being lost to commercial considerations
in some web of cabbalistic revery.

"Can you tell me anything about this?"

The dealer gave an indescribable, simultaneous shrug of his shoulders and
his eye-brows.

"It is very old—palaeogean, one might say. I cannot tell you much, for
little is known. A geologist found it in Greenland, beneath glacial ice, in
the Miocene strata. Who knows? It may have belonged to some sorcerer
of primeval Thule. Greenland was a warm, fertile region, beneath the sun

of Miocene times. No doubt it is a magic crystal; and a man might behold strange visions in its heart, if he looked long enough."

Tregardis was quite startled; for the dealer's apparently fantastic suggestion had brought to mind his own delvings in a branch of obscure lore; and, in particular, had recalled *The Book of Eibon*, that strangest and rarest of occult forgotten volumes, which is said to have come down through a series of manifold translations from a prehistoric original written in the lost language of Hyperborea. Tregardis, with much difficulty, had obtained the medieval French version—a copy that had been owned by many generations of sorcerers and Satanists—but had never been able to find the Greek manuscript from which the version was derived.

The remote, fabulous original was supposed to have been the work of a great Hyperborean wizard, from whom it had taken its name. It was a collection of dark and baleful myths, of liturgies, rituals and incantations both evil and esoteric. Not without shudders, in the course of studies that the average person would have considered more than singular, Tregardis had collated the French volume with the frightful *Necronomicon* of the mad Arab, Abdul Alhazred. He had found many correspondences of the blackest and most appalling significance, together with much forbidden data that was either unknown to the Arab or omitted by him... or by his translators.

Was this what he had been trying to recall, Tregardis wondered?—the brief, casual reference, in *The Book of Eibon*, to a cloudy crystal that had been owned by the wizard Zon Mezzamalech, in Mhu Thulan? Of course, it was all too fantastic, too hypothetic, too incredible—but Mhu Thulan, that northern portion of ancient Hyperborea, was supposed to have corresponded roughly with Modern Greenland, which had formerly been joined as a peninsula to the main continent. Could the stone in his hand, by some fabulous fortuity, be the crystal of Zon Mezzamalech?

Tregardis smiled at himself with inward irony for even conceiving the absurd notion. Such things did not occur—at least, not in present-day London; and in all likelihood, *The Book of Eibon* was sheer superstitious fantasy, anyway. Nevertheless, there was something about the crystal that continued to tease and inveigle him. He ended by purchasing it, at a fairly moderate price. The sum was named by the seller and paid by the buyer without bargaining.

With the crystal in his pocket, Paul Tregardis hastened back to his lodgings instead of resuming his leisurely saunter. He installed the milky globe on his writing table, where it stood firmly enough on one of its oblate ends. Then, still smiling at his own absurdity, he took down the yellow parchment manuscript of *The Book of Eibon* from its place in a somewhat inclusive collection of recherché literature. He opened the vermiculated leather cover with hasps of tarnished steel, and read over to himself, translating from the archaic French as he read, the paragraph that referred to Zon Mezzamalech:

"This wizard, who was mighty among sorcerers, had found a cloudy stone, orb-like and somewhat flattened at the ends, in which he could behold many visions of the terrene past, even to the Earth's beginning, when Ubbo-Sathla, the unbegotten source, lay vast and swollen and yeasty amid the vaporing slime.... But of that which he beheld, Zon Mezzamalech left little record; and people say that he vanished presently, in a way that is not known; and after him the cloudy crystal was lost."

Paul Tregardis laid the manuscript aside. Again there was something that tantalized and beguiled him, like a lost dream or a memory forfeit to oblivion. Impelled by a feeling which he did not scrutinize or question, he sat down before the table and began to stare intently into the cold, nebulous orb. He felt an expectation which, somehow, was so familiar, so permeative a part of his consciousness, that he did not even name it to himself.

Minute by minute he sat, and watched the alternate glimmering and fading of the mysterious light in the heart of the crystal. By imperceptible degrees, there stole upon him a sense of dream-like duality, both in respect to his person and his surroundings. He was still Paul Tregardis—and yet he was someone else; the room was his London apartment—and a chamber in some foreign but well-known place. *And in both milieus he peered steadfastly into the same crystal.*

After an interim, without surprise on the part of Tregardis, the process of re-identification became complete. He knew that he was Zon Mezzamalech, a sorcerer of Mhu Thulan, and a student of all lore anterior to his own epoch. Wise with dreadful secrets that were not known to Paul Tregardis, amateur of anthropology and the occult sciences in latter-day London, he sought by means of the milky crystal to attain an even older and more fearful knowledge.

He had acquired the stone in dubitable ways, from a more than sinister source. It was unique and without fellow in any land or time. In its depths, all former years, all things that have ever been, were supposedly mirrored, and would reveal themselves to the patient visionary. And through the crystal, Zon Mezzamalech had dreamt to recover the wisdom of the gods who died before the Earth was born. They had passed to the lightless void, leaving their lore inscribed upon tablets of ultra-stellar stone; and the tablets were guarded in the primal mire by the formless, idiotic demiurge, Ubbo-Sathla. Only by means of the crystal could he hope to find and read the tablets.

For the first time, he was making trial of the globe's reputed virtues. About him an ivory-panelled chamber, filled with his magic books and paraphernalia, was fading slowly from his consciousness. Before him, on a table of some dark Hyperborean wood that had been graven with grotesque ciphers, the crystal appeared to swell and deepen, and in its filmy depth he beheld a swift and broken swirling of dim scenes, fleeting like the bubbles of a mill-race. As if he looked upon an actual world, cities, forests, mountains, seas and meadows flowed beneath him, lightening and darkening as with the passage of days and nights in some weirdly accelerated stream of time.

Zon Mezzamalech had forgotten Paul Tregardis—had lost the remembrance of his own entity and his own surroundings in Mhu Thulan. Moment by moment, the flowing vision in the crystal became more definite and distinct, and the orb itself deepened till he grew giddy, as if he were peering from an insecure height into some never-fathomed abyss. He knew that time was racing backward in the crystal, was unrolling for him the pageant of all past days; but a strange alarm had seized him, and he feared to gaze longer. Like one who has nearly fallen from a precipice, he caught himself with a violent start and drew back from the mystic orb.

Again, to his gaze, the enormous whirling world into which he had peered was a small and cloudy crystal on his rune-wrought table in Mhu Thulan. Then, by degrees, it seemed that the great room with sculptured panels of mammoth ivory was narrowing to another and dingier place; and Zon Mezzamalech, losing his preternatural wisdom and sorcerous power, went back by a weird regression into Paul Tregardis.

And yet not wholly, it seemed, was he able to return. Tregardis, dazed and wondering, found himself before the writing table on which he had set the oblate sphere. He felt the confusion of one who has dreamt and has not yet fully awakened from the dream. The room puzzled him vaguely, as if something were wrong with its size and furnishings; and his remembrance of purchasing the crystal from a curio-dealer was oddly and discrepantly mingled with an impression that he had acquired it in a very different manner.

He felt that something very strange had happened to him when he peered into the crystal; but just what it was he could not seem to recollect. It had left him in the sort of psychic muddlement that follows a debauch of hashish. He assured himself that he was Paul Tregardis, that he lived on a certain street in London, that the year was 1932; but such common-place verities had somehow lost their meaning and their validity; and everything about him was shadow-like and insubstantial. The very walls seemed to waver like smoke; the people in the streets were phantoms of phantoms; and he himself was a lost shadow, a wandering echo of something long forgot.

He resolved that he would not repeat his experiment of crystal-gazing. The effects were too unpleasant and equivocal. But the very next day, by an unreasoning impulse to which he yielded almost mechanically, without reluctation, he found himself seated before the misty orb. Again he became the sorcerer Zon Mezzamalech in Mhu Thulan; again he dreamt to retrieve the wisdom of the antemundane gods; again he drew back from the deepening crystal with the terror of one who fears to fall; and once more—but doubtfully and dimly, like a failing wraith—he was Paul Tregardis.

Three times did Tregardis repeat the experience on successive days; and each time his own person and the world about him became more tenuous and confused than before. His sensations were those of a dreamer who is on the verge of waking; and London itself was unreal as the lands that slip from the dreamer's ken, receding in filmy mist and cloudy light. Beyond it all, he felt the looming and crowding of vast imageries, alien but half-familiar. It was as if the phantasmagoria of time and space were dissolving about him, to reveal some veritable reality—or another dream of space and time.

There came, at last, the day when he sat down before the crystal—and did not return as Paul Tregardis. It was the day when Zon Mezzamalech, boldly disregarding certain evil and portentous warnings, resolved to overcome his curious fear of failing bodily into the visionary world that he beheld—a fear that had hitherto prevented him from following the backward stream of time for any distance. He must, he assured himself, conquer this fear if he were ever to see and read the lost tablets of the gods. He had beheld nothing more than a few fragments of the years of Mhu Thulan immediately posterior to the present—the years of his own life-time; and there were inestimable cycles between these years and the Beginning.

Again, to his gaze, the crystal deepened immeasurably, with scenes and happenings that flowed in a retrograde stream. Again the magic ciphers of the dark table faded from his ken, and the sorcerously carven walls of his chamber melted into less than dream. Once more he grew giddy with an awful vertigo as he bent above the swirling and milling of the terrible gulfs of time in the world-like orb. Fearfully, in spite of his resolution, he would have drawn away; but he had looked and leaned too long. There was a sense of abysmal failing, a suction as of ineluctable winds, of maelstroms that bore him down through fleet unstable visions of his own past life into antenatal years and dimensions. He seemed to endure the pangs of an inverse dissolution; and then he was no longer Zon Mezzamalech, the wise and learned watcher of the crystal, but an actual part of the weirdly racing stream that ran back to re-attain the Beginning.

He seemed to live unnumbered lives, to die myriad deaths, forgetting each time the death and life that had gone before. He fought as a warrior in half-legendary battles; he was a child playing in the ruins of some olden city of Mhu Thulan; he was the king who had reigned when the city was in its prime, the prophet who had foretold its building and its doom. A woman, he wept for the bygone dead in *necropoli* long-crumbled; an antique wizard, he muttered the rude spells of earlier sorcery; a priest of some pre-human god, he wielded the sacrificial knife in cave-temples of pillared basalt. Life by life, era by era, he re-traced the long and groping cycles through which Hyperborea had risen from savagery to a high civilization.

He became a barbarian of some troglodytic tribe, fleeing from the slow, turreted ice of a former glacial age into lands illumed by the ruddy flare of perpetual volcanoes. Then, after incomputable years, he was no longer man, but a man-like beast, roving in forests of giant fern and calamite, or building an uncouth nest in the boughs of mighty cycads.

Through aeons of anterior sensation, of crude lust and hunger, of aboriginal terror and madness, there was someone—or something—that went ever backward in time. Death became birth, and birth was death. In a slow vision of reverse change, the Earth appeared to melt away, and sloughed off the hills and mountains of its latter strata. Always the sun grew larger and hotter above the fuming swamps that teemed with a crasser life, with a more fulsome vegetation. And the thing that had been Paul Tregardis, that had been Zon Mezzamalech, was a part of all the monstrous devolution. It flew with the claw-tipped wings of a pterodactyl, it swam in tepid seas with the vast, winding bulk of an ichthyosaurus, it bellowed uncouthly with the armored throat of some forgotten behemoth to the huge moon that burned through primordial mists.

At length, after aeons of immemorial brutehood, it became one of the lost serpent-men who reared their cities of black gneiss and fought their venomous wars in the world's first continent. It walked undulously in ante-human streets, in strange crooked vaults; it peered at primeval stars from high, Babelian towers; it bowed with hissing litanies to great serpent-idols. Through years and ages of the ophidian era it returned, and was a thing that crawled in the ooze, that had not yet learned to think and dream and build. And the time came when there was no longer a continent, but only a vast, chaotic marsh, a sea of slime, without limit or horizon, without shore or elevation, that seethed with a blind writhing of amorphous vapors.

There, in the grey beginning of Earth, the formless mass that was Ubbo-Sathla reposed amid the slime and the vapors. Headless, without organs or members, it sloughed from its oozy sides, in a slow, ceaseless wave, the amoebic forms that were the archetypes of earthly life. Horrible it was, if there had been aught to apprehend the horror; and loathsome, if there had been any to feel loathing. About it, prone or tilted in the mire, there lay the mighty tablets of star-quarried stone that were writ with the inconceivable wisdom of the pre-mundane gods.

And there, to the goal of a forgotten search, was drawn the thing that had been—or would sometime be—Paul Tregardis and Zon Mezzamalech. Becoming a shapeless eft of the prime, it crawled sluggishly and obliviously across the fallen tablets of the gods, and fought and ravened blindly with the other spawn of Ubbo-Sathla.

Of Zon Mezzamalech and his vanishing, there is no mention anywhere, save the brief passage in *The Book of Eibon*. Concerning Paul Tregardis, who also disappeared, there was a curt notice in several of the London papers. No one seems to have known anything about him: he is gone as if he had never been; and the crystal, presumably, is gone too. At least, no one has found it.

THE DOUBLE SHADOW

My name is Pharpetron, among those who have known me in Poseidonis; but even I, the last and most forward pupil of the wise Avyctes, know not the name of that which I am fated to become ere tomorrow. Therefore, by the ebbing silver lamps, in my master's marble house above the loud, ever-ravening sea, I write this tale with a hasty hand, scrawling an ink of wizard virtue on the grey, priceless, antique parchment of dragons. And having written, I shall enclose the pages in a sealed cylinder of orichalchum, and shall cast the cylinder from a high window into the sea, lest that which I am doomed to become should haply destroy the writing. And it may be that mariners from Lephara, passing to Umb and Pneor in their tall triremes, will find the cylinder; or fishers will draw it from the wave in their seines of byssus; and having read my story, men will learn the truth and take warning; and no man's feet, henceforward, will approach the pale and demon-haunted house of Avyctes.

For six years, I have dwelt apart with the aged master, forgetting youth and its wonted desires in the study of arcanic things. Together, we have delved more deeply than all others before us in an interdicted lore; we have solved the keyless hieroglyphs that guard ante-human formulae; we have talked with the prehistoric dead; we have called up the dwellers in sealed crypts, in fearful abysses beyond space. Few are the sons of mankind who have cared to seek us out among the desolate, wind-worn crags; and many, but nameless, are the visitants who have come to us from further bourns of place and time.

Stern and white as a tomb, older than the memory of the dead, and built by men or devils beyond the recording of myth, is the mansion in which we dwell. Far below, on black, naked reefs, the northern sea climbs and roars indomitably, or ebbs with a ceaseless murmur as of armies of baffled demons; and the house is filled evermore, like a hollow-sounding sepulcher, with the drear echo of its tumultuous voices; and the winds wail in dismal wrath around the high towers, but shake them not. On the seaward side, the mansion rises sheerly from the straight-falling cliff; but on the other sides there are narrow terraces, grown with dwarfish, crooked cedars that bow always beneath the gale. Giant marble monsters guard the landward portals; and huge marble women ward the strait porticoes above the sea; and mighty statues and mummies stand everywhere in the chambers and along the halls. But, saving these, and the spirits we have summoned, there is none to companion us; and liches and shadows have been the servitors of our daily needs.

All men have heard the fame of Avyctes, the sole surviving pupil of that Malygris who tyrannized in his necromancy over Susran from a tower of sable stone; Malygris, who lay dead for years while men believed him living; who, lying thus, still uttered potent spells and dire oracles with decaying lips. But Avyctes lusted not for temporal power in the manner of Malygris; and having learned all that the elder sorcerer could teach him, withdrew from the cities of Poseidonis to seek another and vaster dominion; and I, the youth Pharpetron, in the latter years of Avyctes, was permitted to join him in this solitude; and since then, I have shared his austerities and vigils and evocations… and now, likewise, I must share the weird doom that has come in answer to his summoning.

Not without terror (since man is but mortal) did I, the neophyte, behold at first the abhorrent and tremendous faces of them that obeyed Avyctes: the genii of the sea and earth, of the stars and the heavens, who passed to and fro in his marmorean halls. I shuddered at the black writhing of sub-mundane things from the many-volumed smoke of the braziers; I cried in horror at the grey foulnesses, colossal, without form, that crowded malignly about the drawn circle of seven colors, threatening unspeakable trespass on us that stood at the center. Not without revulsion did I drink wine that was poured by cadavers, and eat bread that was purveyed by phantoms. But use and custom dulled the strangeness, destroyed the fear; and in time I believed implicitly that Avyctes was the lord of all incantations and exorcisms, with infallible power to dismiss the beings he evoked.

Well had it had been for Avyctes—and for me—if the master had contented himself with the lore preserved from Atlantis and Thule, or brought over from Mu and Mayapan. Surely this should have been enough: for in the ivory-sheeted books of Thule there were blood-writ runes that would call the demons of the fifth and seventh planets, if spoken aloud at the hour of their ascent; and the sorcerers of Mu had left record of a process whereby the doors of far-future time could be unlocked; and our fathers, the Atlanteans, had known the road between the atoms and the path into far stars, and had held speech with the spirits of the sun. But Avyctes thirsted for a darker knowledge, a deeper empery; and into his hands, in the third year of my novitiate, there came the mirror-bright tablet of the lost serpent-people.

Strange, and apparently fortuitous, was our finding of the tablet. At certain hours, when the tide had fallen from the steep rocks, we were wont to descend by cavern-hidden stairs to a cliff-walled crescent beach behind the promontory on which stood the house of Avyctes. There, on the dun, wet sands, beyond the foamy tongues of the surf, would lie the worn and curious driftage of alien shores, and trove that hurricanes had cast up from unsounded deeps. And there we had found the purple and sanguine volutes of great shells, and rude lumps of ambergris, and white flowers of perpetually blooming coral; and once, the barbaric idol of green brass that had been the figurehead of a galley from far hyperboreal isles.

There had been a great storm, such as must have riven the sea to its nethermost profound; but the tempest had gone by with morning, and the heavens were cloudless on that fatal day when we found the tablet, and the demon winds were hushed among the high crags and chasms; and the sea lisped with a low whisper, like the rustle of gowns of samite trailed by fleeing maidens on the sand. And just beyond the ebbing wave, in a tangle of russet sea-weed, we beheld a thing that glittered with blinding sun-like brilliance. And running forward, I plucked it from the wrack before the wave's return, and bore it to Avyctes.

The tablet was wrought of some nameless metal, like never-rusting iron, but heavier. It had the form of a triangle and was broader at the widest than a man's heart. On one side it was wholly blank; and Avyctes and I, in turn, beheld our features mirrored strangely, like the drawn, pallid features of the dead, in its burnished surface. On the other side many rows of small crooked ciphers were incised deeply in the metal, as if by the action of some mordant acid; and these ciphers were not the pictorial symbols or alphabetical characters of any language known to the master or to me.

Of the tablet's age and origin, likewise, we could form no conjecture; and our erudition was altogether baffled. For many days thereafter we studied the writing and held argument that came to no issue. And night by night, in a high chamber closed against the perennial winds, we pondered over the dazzling triangle by the tall straight flames of silver lamps. For Avyctes deemed that knowledge of rare value (or haply some secret of an alien or elder magic) was holden by the clueless crooked ciphers. Then, since all our scholarship was in vain, the master sought another divination, and had recourse to wizardy and necromancy. But at first, among the devils and phantoms that answered our interrogation, none could tell us aught concerning the tablet. And any other than Avyctes would have despaired in the end... and well would it have been if he had despaired, and had sought no longer to decipher the writing....

The months and years went by with a slow thundering of seas on the dark rocks, and a headlong clamor of winds around the white towers. Still we continued our delvings and evocations; and further, always further we went into lampless realms of space and spirit; learning, perchance, to unlock the hithermost of the manifold infinities. And at whiles, Avyctes would resume his pondering of the sea-found tablet; or would question some visitant from other spheres of time and place regarding its interpretation.

At last, by the use of a chance formula, in idle experiment, he summoned up the dim, tenuous ghost of a sorcerer from prehistoric years; and the ghost, in a thin whisper of uncouth, forgotten speech, informed us that the letters on the tablet were those of a language of the serpent-men, whose primordial continent had sunk aeons before the lifting of Hyperborea from the ooze. But the ghost could tell us naught of their significance; for, even in his time, the serpent-people had become a dubious legend; and their deep, ante-human lore and sorcery were things irretrievable by man.

Now, in all the books of conjuration owned by Avyctes, there was no spell whereby we could call the lost serpent-men from their fabulous epoch. But there was an old Lemurian formula, recondite and uncertain, by which the shadow of a dead man could be sent into years posterior to those of his own life-time, and could be recalled after an interim by the wizard. And the shade, being wholly insubstantial, would suffer no harm from the temporal transition, and would remember, for the information of the wizard, that which he had been instructed to learn during the journey.

So, having called again the ghost of the prehistoric sorcerer, whose name was Ybith, Avyctes made a singular use of several very ancient gums and combustible fragments of fossil wood; and he and I, reciting the responses to the formula, sent the thin spirit of Ybith into the far ages of the serpent-men. And after a time which the master deemed sufficient, we performed the curious rites of incantation that would recall Ybith from his alienage. And the rites were successful; and Ybith stood before us again, like a blown vapor that is nigh to vanishing. And in words that were faint as the last echo of perishing memories, the specter told us the key to the meaning of the letters, which he had learned in the primeval past; and after this, we questioned Ybith no more, but suffered him to return unto slumber and oblivion.

Then, knowing the import of the tiny, twisted ciphers, we read the writing on the tablet and made thereof a transliteration, though not without labor and difficulty, since the very phonetics of the serpent tongue, and the symbols and ideas expressed in the writing, were somewhat alien to those of mankind. And when we had mastered the inscription, we found that it contained the formula for a certain evocation which, no doubt, had been used by the serpent sorcerers. But the object of the evocation was not named; nor was there any clue to the nature or identity of that which would come in answer to the rites. And moreover there was no corresponding rite of exorcism nor spell of dismissal.

Great was the jubilation of Avyctes, deeming that we had learned a lore beyond the memory or prevision of man. And though I sought to dissuade him, he resolved to employ the evocation, arguing that our discovery was no chance thing but was fatefully predestined from the beginning. And he seemed to think lightly of the menace that might be brought upon us by the conjuration of things whose nativity and attributes were wholly obscure. "For," said Avyctes, "I have called up, in all the years of my sorcery, no god or devil, no demon or lich or shadow, which I could not control and dismiss at will. And I am loath to believe that any power or spirit beyond the subversion of my spells could have been summoned by a race of serpents, whatever their skill in demonism and necromancy."

So, seeing that he was obstinate, and acknowledging him for my master in all ways, I consented to aid Avyctes in the experiment, though not without dire misgivings. And then we gathered together, in the chamber of conjuration, at the specified hour and configuration of the stars, the equivalents of sundry rare materials that the tablet had instructed us to use in the ritual.

Of much that we did, and of certain agents that we employed, it were better not to tell; nor shall I record the shrill, sibilant words, difficult for beings not born of serpents to articulate, whose intonation formed a signal part of the ceremony. Toward the last, we drew a triangle on the marble floor with the fresh blood of birds; and Avyctes stood at one angle, and I at another; and the gaunt umber mummy of an Atlantean warrior, whose name had been Oigos, was stationed at the third angle. And standing thus, Avyctes and I held tapers of corpse-tallow in our hands, till the tapers had burned down between our fingers as into a socket. And in the outstretched palms of the mummy of Oigos, as if in shallow thuribles, talc and asbestos burned, ignited by a strange fire whereof we knew the secret. At one side we had traced on the floor an infrangible ellipse, made by an endless linked repetition of the twelve unspeakable Signs of Oumor, to which we could retire if the visitant should prove inimical or rebellious. We waited while the pole-circling stars went over, as had been prescribed. Then, when the tapers had gone out between our seared fingers, and the talc and asbestos were wholly consumed in the mummy's eaten palms, Avyctes uttered a single word whose sense was obscure to us; and Oigos, being animated by sorcery and subject to our will, repeated the word after a given interval, in tones that were hollow as a tomb-born echo; and I, in my turn, also repeated it.

Now, in the chamber of evocation, before beginning the ritual, we had opened a small window giving upon the sea, and had likewise left open a high door on the hall to landward, lest that which came in answer to us should require a spatial mode of entrance. And during the ceremony, the sea became still and there was no wind, and it seemed that all things were hushed in awful expectation of the nameless visitor. But after all was done, and the last word had been repeated by Oigos and me, we stood and waited vainly for a visible sign or other manifestation. The lamps burned stilly in the midnight room; and no shadows fell, other than were cast by ourselves and Oigos and by the great marble women along the walls. And in the magic mirrors we had placed cunningly, to reflect those that were otherwise unseen, we beheld no breath or trace of any image.

At this, after a reasonable interim, Avyctes was sorely disappointed, deeming that the evocation had failed of its purpose; and I, having the same thought, was secretly relieved. And we questioned the mummy of Oigos, to learn if he had perceived in the room, with such senses as are peculiar to the dead, the sure token or doubtful proof of a presence undescried by us the living. And the mummy gave a necromantic answer, saying that there was nothing.

"Verily," said Avyctes, "it were useless to wait longer. For surely in some way we have misunderstood the purport of the writing, or have failed to duplicate the matters used in the evocation, or the correct intonement of the words. Or it may be that in the lapse of so many aeons, the thing that was formerly wont to respond has long ceased to exist, or has altered in its attributes so that the spell is now void and valueless."

To this I assented readily, hoping that the matter was at an end. So, after erasing the blood-marked triangle and the sacred ellipse of the linked Signs of Oumor, and after dismissing Oigos to his wonted place among the other mummies, we retired to sleep. And in the days that followed, we resumed our habitual studies, but made no mention to each other of the strange triangular tablet or the vain formula.

Even as before, our days went on; and the sea climbed and roared in white fury on the cliffs, and the winds wailed by in their unseen, sullen wrath, bowing the dark cedars as witches are bowed by the breath of Taaran, god of evil. Almost, in the marvel of new tests and cantraips, I forgot the ineffectual conjuration, and I deemed that Avyctes had also forgotten it.

All things were as of yore, to our sorcerous perception; and there was naught to trouble us in our wisdom and power and serenity, which we deemed secure above the sovereignty of kings. Reading the horoscopic stars, we found no future ill in their aspect; nor was any shadow of bale foreshown to us through geomancy, or other modes of divination such as we employed. And our familiars, though grisly and dreadful to mortal gaze, were wholly obedient to us the masters.

Then, on a clear summer afternoon, we walked, as was often our custom, on the marble terrace behind the house. In robes of ocean-purple, we paced among the windy trees with their blown, crooked shadows; and there, following us as we went to and fro, I saw the blue shadow of Avyctes and my own shadow on the marble; and between them, an adumbration that was not wrought by any of the cedars. And I was greatly startled, but spoke not of the matter to Avyctes, and observed the unknown shadow with covert care.

I saw that it followed closely the shadow of Avyctes, keeping ever the same distance. And it fluttered not in the wind, but moved with a flowing as of some heavy, thick, putrescent liquid; and its color was not blue nor purple nor black, nor any other hue to which man's eyes are habituated, but a hue as of some unearthly purulence; and its form was altogether monstrous, having a squat head and a long, undulant body, without similitude to beast or devil.

Avyctes heeded not the shadow; and still I feared to speak, though I thought it an ill thing for the master to be companioned thus. And I moved closer to him, in order to detect by touch or other perception the invisible presence that had cast the adumbration. But the air was void to sunward of the shadow; and I found nothing opposite the sun nor in any oblique direction, though I searched closely, knowing that certain beings cast their shadows thus.

After a while, at the customary hour, we returned by the coiling stairs and monster-flanked portals into the high house. And I saw that the strange adumbration moved ever behind the shadow of Avyctes, falling horrible and unbroken on the steps and passing clearly separate and distinct amid the long umbrages of the towering monsters. And in the dim halls beyond the sun, where shadows should not have been, I beheld with terror the distorted loathly blot, having a pestilent, unnamable hue, that followed Avyctes as if in lieu of his own extinguished shadow. And all that day, everywhere that we went, at the table served by specters, or in the mummy-warded room of volumes and books, the thing pursued Avyctes, clinging to him even as leprosy to the leper. And still the master had perceived it not; and still I forbore to warn him, hoping that the visitant would withdraw in its own time, going obscurely as it had come.

But at midnight, when we sat together by the silver lamps, pondering the blood-writ runes of Hyperborea, I saw that the shadow had drawn closer to the shadow of Avyctes, towering behind his chair on the wall between the huge sculptured women and the mummies. And the thing was a streaming ooze of charnel pollution, a foulness beyond the black leprosies of hell; and I could bear it no more; and I cried out in my fear and loathing, and informed the master of its presence.

Beholding now the shadow, Avyctes considered it closely and in silence; and there was neither fear nor awe nor abhorrence in the deep, graven wrinkles of his visage. And he said to me at last:

"This thing is a mystery beyond my lore; but never, in all the practice of my art, has any shadow come to me unbidden. And since all others of our evocations have found answer ere this, I must deem that the shadow is a veritable entity, or the sign of an entity, that has come in belated response to the formula of the serpent-sorcerers, which we thought powerless and void. And I think it well that we should now repair to the chamber of conjuration, and interrogate the shadow in such manner as we may, to inquire its nativity and purpose."

We went forthwith into the chamber of conjuration, and made such prepa-

rations as were both necessary and possible. And when we were prepared
to question it, the unknown shadow had drawn closer still to the shadow
of Avyctes, so that the clear space between the two was no wider than the
thickness of a necromancer's rod.

Now, in all ways that were feasible, we interrogated the shadow, speaking
through our own lips and the lips of mummies and statues. But there was
no determinable answer; and calling certain of the devils and phantoms
that were our familiars, we made question through the mouths of these, but
without result. And all the while, our magic mirrors were void of any reflection of a presence that might have cast the shadow; and they that had been
our spokesmen could detect nothing in the room. And there was no spell, it
seemed, that had power upon the visitant. So Avyctes became troubled; and
drawing on the floor with blood and ashes the ellipse of Oumor, wherein
no demon nor spirit may intrude, he retired to its center. But still within
the ellipse, like a flowing taint of liquid corruption, the shadow followed his
shadow; and the space between the two was no wider than the thickness of
a wizard's pen.

Now, on the face of Avyctes, horror had graven new wrinkles; and his brow
was beaded with a deathly sweat. For he knew, even as I, that this was a thing
beyond all laws, and foreboding naught but disaster and evil. And he cried
to me in a shaken voice, and said:

"I have no knowledge of this thing nor its intention toward me, and no
power to stay its progress. Go forth and leave me now; for I would not that
any man should witness the defeat of my sorcery and the doom that may
follow thereupon. Also, it were well to depart while there is time, lest you
too should become the quarry of the shadow and be compelled to share its
menace."

Though terror had fastened upon my inmost soul, I was loath to leave
Avyctes. But I had sworn to obey his will at all times and in every respect;
and moreover I knew myself doubly powerless against the adumbration,
since Avyctes himself was impotent.

So, bidding him farewell, I went forth with trembling limbs from the
haunted chamber; and peering back from the threshold, I saw that the alien
umbrage, creeping like a noisome blotch on the floor, had touched the
shadow of Avyctes. And at that moment the master shrieked aloud like one
in nightmare; and his face was no longer the face of Avyctes but was contorted and convulsed like that of some helpless madman who wrestles with
an unseen incubus. And I looked no more, but fled along the dim outer hall
and through the high portals giving upon the terrace.

A red moon, ominous and gibbous, had declined above the terrace and
the crags; and the shadows of the cedars were elongated in the moon; and
they wavered in the gale like the blown cloaks of enchanters. And stooping
against the gale, I fled across the terrace toward the outer stairs that led to

a steep path in the riven waste of rocks and chasms behind Avyctes' house. I neared the terrace edge, running with the speed of fear; but I could not reach the topmost outer stair; for at every step the marble flowed beneath me, fleeing like a pale horizon before the seeker. And though I raced and panted without pause, I could draw no nearer to the terrace edge.

At length I desisted, seeing that an unknown spell had altered the very space about the house of Avyctes, so that none could escape therefrom to landward. So, resigning myself in despair to whatever might befall, I returned toward the house. And climbing the white stairs in the low, level beams of the crag-caught moon, I saw a figure that awaited me in the portals. And I knew by the trailing robe of sea-purple, but by no other token, that the figure was Avyctes. For the face was no longer in its entirety the face of man, but was become a loathly fluid amalgam of human features with a thing not to be identified on earth. The transfiguration was ghastlier than death or the changes of decay; and the face was already hued with the nameless, corrupt and purulent color of the strange shadow, and had taken on, in respect to its outlines, a partial likeness to the squat profile of the shadow. The hands of the figure were not those of any terrene being; and the shape beneath the robe had lengthened with a nauseous undulant pliancy; and the face and fingers seemed to drip in the moonlight with a deliquescent corruption. And the pursuing umbrage, like a thickly flowing blight, had corroded and distorted the very shadow of Avyctes, which was now double in a manner not to be narrated here.

Fain would I have cried or spoken aloud; but horror had dried up the fount of speech. And the thing that had been Avyctes beckoned me in silence, uttering no word from its living and putrescent lips. And with eyes that were no longer eyes, but had become an oozing abomination, it peered steadily upon me. And it clutched my shoulder closely with the soft leprosy of its fingers, and led me half-swooning with revulsion along the hall, and into that room where the mummy of Oigos, who had assisted us in the threefold incantation of the serpent-men, was stationed with several of his fellows.

By the lamps which illumed the chamber, burning with pale, still, perpetual flames, I saw that the mummies stood erect along the wall in their exanimate repose, each in his wonted place with his tall shadow beside him. But the great, gaunt shadow of Oigos on the marble wall was companioned by an adumbration similar in all respects to the evil thing that had followed the master and was now incorporate with him. I remembered that Oigos had performed his share of the ritual, and had repeated an unknown stated word in turn after Avyctes; and so I knew that the horror had come to Oigos in turn, and would wreak itself upon the dead even as on the living. For the foul, anonymous thing that we had called in our presumption could manifest itself to mortal ken in no other way than this. We had drawn it from unfathomable depths of time and space, using ignorantly a dire formula; and the thing had come at its own chosen hour, to stamp itself in abomination uttermost on the evocators.

Since then, the night has ebbed away, and a second day has gone by like a sluggish ooze of horror.... I have seen the complete identification of the shadow with the flesh and the shadow of Avyctes... and also I have seen the slow encroachment of that other umbrage, mingling itself with the lank shadow and the sere, bituminous body of Oigos, and turning them to a similitude of the thing which Avyctes has become. And I have heard the mummy cry out like a living man in great pain and fear, as with the throes of a second dissolution, at the impingement of the shadow. And long since it has grown silent, like the other horror, and I know not its thoughts or its intent.... And verily I know not if the thing that has come to us be one or several; nor if its avatar will rest complete with the three that summoned it forth into time, or be extended to others.

But these things, and much else, I shall soon know; for now, in turn, there is a shadow that follows mine, drawing ever closer. The air congeals and curdles with an unseen fear; and they that were our familiars have fled from the mansion; and the great marble women seem to tremble where they stand along the walls. But the horror that was Avyctes, and the second horror that was Oigos, have left me not, and neither do they tremble. And with eyes that are not eyes, they seem to brood and watch, waiting till I too shall become as they. And their stillness is more terrible than if they had rended me limb from limb. And there are strange voices in the wind, and alien roarings upon the sea; and the walls quiver like a thin veil in the black breath of remote abysses.

So, knowing that the time is brief, I have shut myself in the room of volumes and books and have written this account. And I have taken the bright triangular tablet, whose solution was our undoing, and have cast it from the window into the sea, hoping that none will find it after us. And now I must make an end, and enclose this writing in the sealed cylinder of orichalchum, and fling it forth to drift upon the wave. For the space between my shadow and the shadow of the horror is straitened momently... and the space is no wider than the thickness of a wizard's pen.

THE PLUTONIAN DRUG

"It is remarkable," said Dr. Manners, "how the scope of our pharma-copoeia has been widened by interplanetary exploration. In the past thirty years, hundreds of hitherto unknown substances, employable as drugs or medical agents, have been found in the other worlds of our own system. It will be interesting to see what the Allan Farquar expedition will bring back from the planets of *Alpha Centauri* when—or if—it succeeds in reaching them and returning to Earth. I doubt, though, if anything more valuable than selenine will be discovered. Selenine, derived from a fossil lichen found by the first rocket-expedition to the moon in 1975, has, as you know, practically wiped out the old-time curse of cancer. In solution, it forms the base of an infallible serum, equally useful for cure or prevention."

"I fear I haven't kept up on a lot of the new discoveries," said Rupert Balcoth the sculptor, Manners' guest, a little apologetically. "Of course, everyone has heard of selenine. And I've seen frequent mention, recently, of a mineral water from Ganymede whose effects are like those of the mythical Fountain of Youth."

"You mean *clithni*, as the stuff is called by the Ganymedians. It is a clear, emerald liquid, rising in lofty geysers from the craters of quiescent volca-noes. Scientists believe that the drinking of *clithni* is the secret of the almost fabulous longevity of the Ganymedians; and they think that it may prove to be a similar elixir for humanity."

"Some of the extraplanetary drugs haven't been so beneficial to mankind, have they?" queried Balcoth. "I seem to have heard of a Martian poison that has greatly facilitated the gentle art of murder. And I am told that *mnophka*, the Venerian narcotic, is far worse in its effects on the human system than is any terrestrial alkaloid."

"Naturally, " observed the doctor with philosophic calm, "many of these

239

new chemical agents are capable of dire abuse. They share that liability with any number of our native drugs. Man, as ever, has the choice of good and evil…. I suppose that the Martian poison you speak of is *akpaloli*, the juice of a common russet-yellow weed that grows in the oases of Mars. It is colorless, and without taste or odor. It kills almost instantly, leaving no trace, and imitating closely the symptoms of heart-disease. Undoubtedly many people have been made away with by means of a surreptitious drop of *akpaloli* in their food or medicine. But even *akpaloli*, if used in infinitesimal doses, is a very powerful stimulant, useful in cases of syncope, and serving, not infrequently, to re-animate victims of paralysis in a quite miraculous manner.

"Of course," he went on, "there is an infinite lot still to be learned about many of these ultra-terrene substances. Their virtues have often been discovered quite by accident—and in some cases, the virtue is still to be discovered.

"For example, take *mnophka*, which you mentioned a little while ago. Though allied in a way, to the earth-narcotics, such as opium and hashish, it is of little use for anaesthetic or anodyne purposes. Its chief effects are an extraordinary acceleration of the time-sense, and a heightening and telescoping of all sensations, whether pleasurable or painful. The user seems to be living and moving at a furious whirlwind rate—even though he may in reality be lying quiescent on a couch. He exists in a headlong torrent of sense-impressions, and seems, in a few minutes, to undergo the experiences of years. The physical result is lamentable—a profound exhaustion, and an actual aging of the tissues, such as would ordinarily require the period of real time which the addict has "lived" through merely in his own illusion.

"There are some other drugs, comparatively little known, whose effects, if possible, are even more curious than those of *mnophka*. I don't suppose you have ever heard of plutonium?"

"No, I haven't," admitted Balcoth. "Tell me about it."

"I can do even better than that—I can show you some of the stuff, though it isn't much to look at—merely a fine white powder."

Dr. Manners rose from the pneumatic-cushioned chair in which he sat facing his guest, and went to a large cabinet of synthetic ebony, whose shelves were crowded with flasks, bottles, tubes, and cartons of various sizes and forms. Returning, he handed to Balcoth a squat and tiny vial, two-thirds filled with a starchy substance.

"Plutonium," explained Manners, "as its name would indicate, comes from forlorn, frozen Pluto, which only one terrestrial expedition has so far visited—the expedition led by the Cornell brothers, John and Augustine, which started in 1990 and did not return to Earth till 1996, when nearly everyone had given it up as lost. John, as you may have heard, died during the returning voyage, together with half the personnel of the expedition: and the others reached Earth with only one reserve oxygen-tank remaining.

"This vial contains about a tenth of the existing supply of plutonium. Augustine Cornell, who is an old school-friend of mine, gave it to me three years ago, just before he embarked with the Allan Farquar crowd. I count myself pretty lucky to own anything so rare.

"The geologists of the party found the stuff when they began prying beneath the solidified gases that cover the surface of that dim, starlit planet, in an effort to learn a little about its composition and history. They couldn't do much under the circumstances, with limited time and equipment; but they made some curious discoveries—of which plutonium was far from being the least.

"Like selenine, the stuff is a by-product of vegetable fossilization. Doubtless it is many billion years old, and dates back to the time when Pluto possessed enough internal heat to make possible the development of certain rudimentary plant-forms on its blind surface. It must have had an atmosphere then; though no evidence of former animal-life was found by the Cornells.

"Plutonium, in addition to carbon, hydrogen, nitrogen, and oxygen, contains minute quantities of several unclassified elements. It was discovered in a crystalloid condition, but turned immediately to the fine powder that you see, as soon as it was exposed to air in the rocket-ship. It is readily soluble in water, forming a permanent colloid, without the least sign of deposit, no matter how long it remains in suspension."

"You say it is a drug?" queried Balcoth. "What does it do to you?"

"I'll come to that in a minute—though the effect is pretty hard to describe. The properties of the stuff were discovered only by chance: on the return journey from Pluto, a member of the expedition, half delirious with space-fever, got hold of the unmarked jar containing it and took a small dose, imagining that it was bromide of potassium. It served to complicate his delirium for a while—since it gave him some brand-new ideas about space and time.

"Other people have experimented with it since then. The effects are quite brief (the influence never lasts more than half an hour) and they vary considerably with the individual. There is no bad aftermath, either neural, mental, or physical, as far as anyone has been able to determine. I've taken it myself, once or twice, and can testify to that.

"Just what it does to one, I am not sure. Perhaps it merely produces a derangement or metamorphosis of sensations, like hashish; or perhaps it serves to stimulate some rudimentary organ, some dormant sense of the human brain. At any rate there is, as clearly as I can put it, an altering of the perception of time—of actual duration—into a sort of space-perception. One sees the past, and also the future, in relation to one's own physical self, like a landscape stretching away on either hand. You don't see very far, it is true—merely the events of a few hours in each direction; but it's a very curious experience; and it helps to give you a new slant on the mystery of time and space. It is altogether different from the delusions of *mnophka*."

"It sounds very interesting," admitted Balcoth. "However, I've never tampered much with narcotics myself; though I did experiment once or twice, in my young, romantic days with *cannabis Indica*. I had been reading Gautier and Baudelaire, I suppose. Anyway, the result was rather disappointing."

"You didn't take it long enough for your system to absorb a residuum of the drug, I imagine," said Manners. "Hence the effects were negligible, from a visionary standpoint. But plutonium is altogether different—you get the maximum result from the very first dose. I think it would interest you greatly, Balcoth, since you are a sculptor by profession: you would see some unusual plastic images, not easy to render in terms of Euclidean planes and angles. I'd gladly give you a pinch of it now, if you'd care to experiment."

"You're pretty generous, aren't you, since the stuff is so rare?"

"I'm not being generous at all. For years, I've planned to write a monograph on ultra-terrestrial alkaloids; and you might give me some valuable data. With your type of brain and your highly developed artistic sense, the visions of plutonium should be uncommonly clear and significant. All I ask is, that you describe them to me as fully as you can afterwards."

"Very well," agreed Balcoth. "I'll try anything once." His curiosity was somewhat inveigled, his imagination seduced, by Manners' account of the remarkable drug.

Manners brought out an antique whisky-glass, which he filled nearly to the rim with some golden-red liquid. Uncorking the vial of plutonium, he added to this fluid a small pinch of the fine white powder, which dissolved immediately and without effervescence.

"The liquid is a wine made from a sweet Martian tuber known as *ovvra*," he explained. "It is light and harmless, and will counteract the bitter taste of the plutonium. Drink it quickly and then lean back in your chair."

Balcoth hesitated, eyeing the golden-red fluid.

"Are you quite sure the effects will wear off as promptly as you say?" he questioned. "It's a quarter past nine now, and I'll have to leave about ten to keep an appointment with one of my patrons at the Belvedere Club. It's the billionaire, Claud Wishhaven, who wants me to do a bas-relief in pseudo-jade and neo-jasper for the hall of his country mansion. He wants something really advanced and futuristic. We're to talk it over tonight—decide on the motifs, etc."

"That gives you forty-five minutes," assured the doctor—"and in thirty, at the most, your brain and senses will be perfectly normal again. I've never known it to fail. You'll have fifteen minutes to spare, in which to tell me all about your sensations."

Balcoth emptied the little antique glass at a gulp and leaned back, as Manners had directed, on the deep pneumatic cushions of the chair. He seemed to be falling easily but endlessly into a mist that had gathered in the room with unexplainable rapidity; and through this mist he was dimly aware that Manners had taken the empty glass from his relaxing fingers. He saw the face of Manners far above him, small and blurred, as if in some tremendous perspective of alpine distance; and the doctor's simple action seemed to be occurring in another world.

He continued to fall and float through eternal mist, in which all things were dissolved as in the primordial nebulae of chaos. After a timeless interval, the mist, which had been uniformly grey and hueless at first, took on a flowing iridescence, never the same for two successive moments; and the sense of gentle falling turned to a giddy revolution, as if he were caught in an ever-swiftening vortex.

Coincidentally with his movement in this whirlpool of prismatic splendor, he seemed to undergo an indescribable mutation of the senses. The whirling colors, by subtle, ceaseless gradations, became recognizable as solid forms. Emerging as if by an act of creation from the infinite chaos, they appeared to take their place in an equally infinite vista. The feeling of movement, through decrescent spirals, was resolved into absolute immobility. Balcoth was no longer conscious of himself as a living organic body: he was an abstract eye, a discorporate center of visual awareness, stationed alone in space, and yet having an intimate relationship with the frozen prospect on which he peered from his ineffable vantage.

Without surprise, he found that he was gazing simultaneously in two directions. On either hand, for a vast distance that was wholly void of normal perspective, a weird and peculiar landscape stretched away, traversed by an unbroken frieze or bas-relief of human figures that ran like a straight undeviating wall.

For awhile, the frieze was incomprehensible to Balcoth, he could make nothing of its glacial, flowing outlines with their background of repeated masses and complicated angles and sections of other human friezes that approached or departed, often in a very abrupt manner, from an unseen world beyond. Then the vision seemed to resolve and clarify itself, and he began to understand.

The bas-relief, he saw, was composed entirely of a repetition of his own figure, plainly distinct as the separate waves of a stream, and possessing a stream-like unity. Immediately before him, and for some distance on either hand, the figure was seated in a chair—the chair itself being subject to the same billowy repetition. The background was composed of the reduplicated figure of Dr. Manners, in another chair; and behind this, the manifold images of a medicine cabinet and a section of wall-panelling.

Following the vista on what, for lack of any better name, might be termed the left hand, Balcoth saw himself in the act of draining the antique glass, with Manners standing before him. Then, still further, he saw himself previous to this, with a background in which Manners was presenting him the glass, was preparing the dose of plutonium, was going to the cabinet for the vial, was rising from his pneumatic chair. Every movement, every attitude of the doctor and himself during their past conversation, was visioned in a sort of reverse order, reaching away, unalterable as a wall of stone sculpture, into the weird, eternal landscape. There was no break in the continuity of his own figure; but Manners seemed to disappear at times, as if into a fourth dimension. These times, he remembered later, were the occasions when the doctor had not been in his line of vision. The perception was wholly visual; and though Balcoth saw his own lips and those of Manners parted in the frozen movements of speech, he could hear no word or other sound.

Perhaps the most singular feature of the vision was the utter absence of foreshortening. Though Balcoth seemed to behold it all from a fixed, immovable point, the landscape and the intersecting frieze presented themselves to him without diminution, maintaining a frontal fullness and distinctness to a distance that might have been many miles.

Continuing along the left-hand vista, he saw himself entering Manners' apartments, and then encountered his image standing in the elevator that had borne him to the ninth floor of the hundred story hotel in which Manners lived. Then the frieze appeared to have an open street for background, with a confused, ever-changing multitude of other faces and forms, of vehicles and sections of buildings, all jumbled together as in some old-time futuristic painting. Some of these details were full and clear, and others were cryptically broken and blurred, so as to be scarcely recognizable. Everything, whatever its spatial position and relation, was re-arranged in the flowing frozen stream of this temporal pattern.

Balcoth retraced the three blocks from Manners' hotel to his own studio, seeing all his past movements, whatever their direction in tri-dimensional space, as a straight line in the time-dimension. At last he was in his studio; and there the frieze of his own figure receded into the eerie prospect of space-transmuted time among other friezes formed of actual sculptures. He beheld himself giving the final touches with his chisel to a symbolic statue at the afternoon's end, with a glare of ruddy sunset falling through an unseen window and flushing the pallid marble. Beyond, there was a reverse fading of the glow, a thickening and blurring of the half-chiselled features of the image, a female form to which he had given the tentative name of Oblivion. At length, among half-seen statuary, the left-hand vista became indistinct, and melted slowly in amorphous mist. He had seen his own life as a continuous glaciated stream, stretching for about five hours into the past.

Reaching away on the right hand, he saw the vista of the future. Here there was a continuation of his seated figure under the influence of the drug, opposite the continued bas-relief of Dr. Manners and the repeated cabinet and wall-panels. After a considerable interval, he beheld himself in the act of rising from the chair. Standing erect, he seemed to be talking awhile, as in some silent antique film, to the listening doctor. After that, he was shaking hands with Manners, was leaving the apartment, was descending in the lift and following the open, brightly-litten street toward the Belvedere Club where he was to keep his appointment with Claud Wishhaven.

The Club was only three blocks away, on another street; and the shortest route, after the first block, was along a narrow alley between an office building and a warehouse. Balcoth had meant to take this alley; and in his vision, he saw the bas-relief of his future figure passing along the straight pavement with a background of deserted doorways and dim walls that towered from sight against the extinguished stars.

He seemed to be alone: there were no passers—only the silent, glimmering endlessly repeated angles of arc-lit walls and windows that accompanied his repeated figure. He saw himself following the alley, like a stream in some profound canyon; and there midway, the strange vision came to an abrupt inexplicable end, without the gradual blurring into formless mist, that had marked his retrospective view of the past.

The sculpture-like frieze with its architectural ground appeared to terminate, broken off clean and sharp, in a gulf of immeasurable blackness and nullity. The last wave-like duplication of his own person, the vague doorway beyond it, the glimmering alley-pavement, all were seen as if shorn asunder by a falling sword of darkness, leaving a vertical line of cleavage beyond which there was—nothing.

Balcoth had a feeling of utter detachment from himself, an eloignment from the stream of time, from the shores of space, in some abstract dimension. The experience, in its full realization, might have lasted for an instant only—or for eternity. Without wonder, without curiosity or reflection, like a fourth-dimensional Eye, he viewed simultaneously the unequal cross-sections of his own past and future.

After that timeless interval of complete perception, there began a reverse process of change. He, the all-seeing Eye, aloof in super-space, was aware of movement, as if he were drawn back by some subtle thread of magnetism into the dungeon of time and space from which he had momentarily departed. He seemed to be following the frieze of his own seated body toward the right, with a dimly felt rhythm or pulsation in his movement that corresponded to the merging duplications of the figure. With curious clearness, he realized that the time-unit by which these duplications were determined, was the beating of his own heart.

Now with accelerative swiftness, the vision of petrific form and space was re-dissolving into a spiral swirl of multitudinous colors, through which he was drawn upward. Presently he came to himself, seated in the pneumatic chair, with Dr. Manners opposite. The room seemed to waver a little, as if with some lingering touch of the weird transmutation; and webs of spinning iris hung in the corners of his eyes. Apart from this, the effect of the drug had wholly vanished, leaving, however, a singularly clear and vivid memory of the almost ineffable experience.

Dr. Manners began to question him at once, and Balcoth described his visionary sensations as fully and graphically as he could.

"There is one thing I don't understand," said Manners at the end with a puzzled frown. "According to your account, you must have seen five or six hours of the past, running in a straight spatial line, as a sort of continuous landscape; but the vista of the future ended sharply after you had followed it for three-quarters of an hour; or less. I've never known the drug to act so unequally: the past and future perspectives have always been about the same in their extent for others who have used plutonium."

"Well," observed Balcoth, "the real marvel is that I could see into the future at all. In a way, I can understand the vision of the past. It was clearly composed of physical memories—of all my recent movements; and the background was formed of all the impressions my optic nerves had received during that time. But how could I behold something that hasn't yet happened?"

"There's the mystery, of course," assented Manners. "I can think of only one explanation at all intelligible to our finite minds. This is, that all the events which compose the stream of time have already happened, are happening, and will continue to happen forever. In our ordinary state of consciousness, we perceive with the physical senses merely that moment which we call the present. Under the influence of plutonium, you were able to extend the moment of present cognition in both directions, and to behold simultaneously a portion of that which is normally beyond perception. Thus appeared the vision of yourself as a continuous, immobile body, extending through the time-vista."

Balcoth, who had been standing, now took his leave. "I must be going," he said, "or I'll be late for my appointment."

"I won't detain you any longer," said Manners. He appeared to hesitate, and then added: "I'm still at a loss to comprehend the abrupt cleavage and termination of your prospect of the future. The alley in which it seemed to end was Falman Alley, I suppose—your shortest route to the Belvedere Club. If I were you, Balcoth, I'd take another route, even if it requires a few minutes extra."

"That sounds rather sinister," laughed Balcoth. "Do you think that something may happen to me in Falman Alley?"

"I hope not—but I can't guarantee that it won't." Manners' tone was oddly dry and severe. "You'd best do as I suggest."

Balcoth felt the touch of a momentary shadow as he left the hotel—a premonition brief and light as the passing of some night-bird on noiseless wings. What could it mean—that gulf of infinite blackness into which the weird frieze of his future had appeared to plunge, like a frozen cataract? Was there a menace of some sort that awaited him in a particular place, at a particular moment?

He had a curious feeling of repetition, of doing something that he had done before, as he followed the street. Reaching the entrance of Falman Alley, he took out his watch. By walking briskly and following the alley, he would reach the Belvedere Club punctually. But if he went on around the next block, he would be a little late. Balcoth knew that his prospective patron, Claud Wishhaven, was almost a martinet in demanding punctuality from himself and from others. So he took the alley.

The place appeared to be entirely deserted, as in his vision. Midway, Balcoth approached the half-seen door—a rear entrance of the huge warehouse—which had formed the termination of the time prospect. The door was his last visual impression, for something descended on his head at that moment, and his consciousness was blotted out by the supervening night he had previsioned. He had been sand-bagged, very quietly and efficiently, by a twenty-first century thug. The blow was fatal; and time, as far as Balcoth was concerned, had come to an end.

THE SUPERNUMERARY CORPSE

I t is not remorse that maddens me—that drives me to the penning of this more than indiscreet narrative, in the hope of finding a temporary distraction. I have felt no remorse for a crime to which justice itself impelled me. It is the damnable mystery, beyond all human reason or solution, upon which I have stumbled in the doing of this simple deed, in the mere execution of the justice whereof I speak—it is this that has brought me near to insanity.

My motives in the killing of Jasper Trilt, though imperative, were far from extraordinary. He had wronged me enough, in the course of a twelve years' acquaintance, to warrant his death twice over. He had robbed me of the painfully garnered fruits of a lifetime of labor and research, had stolen, with lying promises, the chemical formulae that would have made me a wealthy man. Foolishly, I had trusted him, believing that he would share with me the profits of my precious knowledge—from which he was to acquire riches and renown. Poor and unknown, I could do nothing for my own redress.

Often I marvel at the long forbearance which I displayed toward Trilt. Something (was it the thought of ultimate revenge?) led me to ignore his betrayals, to dissemble my knowledge of his baseness. I continued to use the laboratory which he had equipped for me, I went on accepting the miserable pittance which he paid me for my toil. I made new discoveries—and I allowed him to cheat me of their usufruct.

Moreover, there was Norma Gresham, whom I had always loved in my halting, inarticulate fashion, and who had seemed to like me well enough before Trilt began to pay her his dashing and gallant addresses. She had speedily forgotten the timid, poverty-stricken chemist, and had married Trilt. This, too, I pretended to ignore, but I could not forget…. As you see, my grievances were such as have actuated many others in the seeking of vengeance: they were in no sense unusual; and like everything else about the affair, they served by their very commonplaceness to throw into monstrous relief the abnormal and inexplicable outcome.

I cannot remember when it was that I first conceived the idea of killing my betrayer. It has been so long an integral part of my mental equipment, that I seem to have nurtured it from all pre-eternity. But the full maturing, the perfection of my murderous plans, is a thing of quite recent date.

For years, apart from my usual work, I have been experimenting with poisons. I delved in the remote arcana and by-ways of toxicology, I learned all that chemistry could tell me on the subject—and more. This branch of my research was wholly unknown to Trilt; and I did not intend that he should profit by anything that I had discovered or devised in the course of my investigations. In fact, my aims were quite different, in regard to him.

From the beginning, I had in mind certain peculiar requisites, which no poison familiar to science could fulfil. It was after endless groping and many failures that I succeeded in formulating a compound of rare toxic agents which would have the desired effect on the human system.

It was necessary, for my own security, that the poison should leave no trace, and should imitate closely the effects of some well-known malady, thus precluding even the chance of medical suspicion. Also, the victim must not die too quickly and mercifully. I devised a compound which, if taken internally, would be completely absorbed by the nervous system within an hour and would thereafter be indetectable through analysis. It would cause an immediate paralysis, and would present all the outward effects of a sudden and lethal stroke of apoplexy. However, the afflicted person—though seemingly insensible—would retain consciousness and would not die till the final absorption of the poison. Though utterly powerless to speak or move, he would still be able to hear and see, to understand—and suffer.

Even after I had perfected this agent, and had satisfied myself of its efficacy, I delayed the crowning trial. It was not through fear or compunction that I waited; rather, it was because I desired to prolong the delicious joys of anticipation, the feeling of power it gave me to know that I could sentence my betrayer to his doom and could execute the sentence at will.

It was after many months—it was less than a fortnight ago—that I decided to withhold my vengeance no longer. I planned it all very carefully, with complete forethought; and I left no loophole for mischance or accident. There would be nothing, not even the most tenuous thread, that could ever lead any one to suspect me.

To arouse the cupidity of Trilt, and to insure his profound interest, I went to him and hinted that I was on the brink of a great discovery. I did not specify its nature, saying that I should reveal it all at the proper time, when success had been achieved. I did not invite him to visit the laboratory. Cunningly, by oblique hints, I stimulated his curiosity; and I knew that he would come. Perhaps my caution was excessive; but it must not even seem that I had prearranged the visit that would terminate in his seizure and death. I could, perhaps, have found opportunity to administer the poison in his own home, where I was still a fairly frequent caller. But I wished him to die in my presence and in the laboratory that had been the scene of my long, defrauded toils.

I knew, by a sort of prescience, the very evening when he would come, greedy to unearth my new secret. I prepared the draft that contained the poison—a chemist's glass of water colored with a little grenadine—and set it aside in readiness among my tubes and bottles. Then I waited.

The laboratory—an old and shabby mansion converted by Trilt to this purpose—lay in a well-wooded outskirt of the town, at no great distance from my employer's luxurious home. Trilt was a gourmand; and I knew that he would not arrive till well after the dinner hour. Therefore, I looked for him about nine o'clock. He must indeed have been eager to filch my supposed new formula; for, half an hour before the expected time, I heard his heavy, insolent knock on the door of the rear room in which I was waiting amid my chemical apparatus.

He came in, gross and odious, with the purple of overfeeding upon his puffy jowls. He wore an azure blue tie and a suit of pepper-and-salt—a close-fitting suit that merely emphasized the repulsive bulkiness of his figure.

"Well, Margrave, what is it now?" he asked. "Have you finished the experiments you were hinting about so mysteriously? I hope you've really done something to earn your pay, this time."

"I have made a tremendous discovery," I told him—"nothing less than the Elixir of the alchemists—the draft of eternal life and energy."

He was palpably startled, and gave me a sharp, incredulous stare.

"You are lying," he said—"or fooling yourself. Everyone knows, and has known since the Dark Ages, that the thing is a scientific impossibility."

"Others may lie," I said sardonically. "But it remains to be seen whether or not I have lied. That graduated glass which you see on the table is filled with the Elixir."

He stared at the vessel which I had indicated.

"It looks like grenadine," he remarked, with a certain perspicacity.

"There is a superficial likeness—the color is the same.... But the stuff means immortality for any one who dares to drink it—also it means inexhaustible capacity for pleasure, a freedom from all satiety or weariness. It is everlasting life and joy."

He listened greedily. "Have you tried it yourself?"

"Yes, I have experimented with it," I countered.

He gave me a somewhat contemptuous and doubtful glance. "Well, you do look rather animated tonight—at least, more so than usual—and not so much like a mackerel that's gotten soured on life. The stuff hasn't killed you, at any rate. So I think I'll try it myself. It ought to be a pretty good commercial proposition, if it only does a tenth of what you say it will. We'll call it Trilt's Elixir."

"Yes," said I, slowly, echoing him: "Trilt's Elixir."

He reached for the glass and raised it to his lips.

"You guarantee the result?" he asked.

"The result will be all that one could desire," I promised, looking him full in the eyes, and smiling with an irony which he could not perceive.

He drained the glass at a gulp. Instantly, as I had calculated, the poison took effect. He staggered as if he had received a sudden, crushing blow, the empty vessel fell from his fingers with a crash, his heavy legs seemed to collapse beneath him, he fell on the laboratory floor between the laden benches and tables, and lay without stirring again. His face was flushed and congested, his breathing stertorous, as in the malady whose effects I had chosen to simulate. His eyes were open—horribly open and glaring; but there was not even the least flicker of their lids.

Coolly, but with a wild exultation in my heart, I gathered up the fragments of the broken glass and dropped them into the small heating-stove that stood at the room's end. Then, returning to the fallen and helpless man, I allowed myself the luxury of gloating over the dark, unutterable terror which I read in his paralytic gaze. Knowing that he could still hear and comprehend, I told him what I had done and listed the unforgotten wrongs which he thought I had accepted so supinely.

Then, as an added torture, I emphasized the indetectable nature of the poison, and I taunted him for his own folly in drinking the supposed elixir. All too quickly did the hour pass—the hour which I had allowed for the full absorption of the poison and the victim's death. The breathing of Trilt grew slower and fainter, his pulse faltered and became inaudible; and at last he lay dead. But the terror still appeared to dwell, dark and stagnant and nameless, in his ever-open eyes.

Now, as was part of my carefully laid plan, I went to the laboratory telephone. I intended to make two calls—one, to tell Norma, Trilt's wife, of his sudden and fatal seizure while visiting me—and the other, to summon a doctor.

For some indefinable reason, I called Norma first—and the outcome of our conversation was so bewildering, so utterly staggering, that I did not put in the second call.

Norma answered the telephone herself, as I had expected. Before I could frame the few short words that would inform her of Trilt's death, she cried out in a shaken, tremulous voice:

"I was just going to call you, Felton. Jasper died a few minutes ago, from an apoplectic stroke. It's all so terrible, and I am stunned by the shock. He came into the house about an hour ago, and dropped at my feet without saying a word.... I thought he had gone to see you—but he could hardly have done that and gotten back so quickly. Come at once, Felton."

The dumbfoundment which I felt was inexpressible. I think I must have stammered a little as I answered her:

"Are you sure—quite sure that it's Jasper?"

"Of course, it's incredible. But he is lying here now on the library sofa—dead. I called a doctor when he was stricken; and the doctor is still here. But there is nothing more to be done."

It was impossible then for me to tell her, as I had intended—that Trilt had come to the laboratory—that his dead body was lying near me in the rear room at that moment. Indeed, I doubted my own senses, doubted my very brain, as I hung up the telephone. Either I—or Norma—was the victim of some strange and unaccountable delusion.

Half expecting that the gross cadaver would have vanished like an apparition, I turned from the telephone—and saw it, supine and heavy, with stiffening limbs and features. I went over, I stooped above it and dug my fingers roughly into the flabby flesh to make sure that it was real—that Trilt's visit and the administering of the poison had not been a mere hallucination. It was Trilt himself who lay before me: no one could mistake the obese body, the sybaritic face and lips, even with the chill of death descending upon them. The corpse I had touched was all too solid and substantial.

It must be Norma then, who was demented or dreaming, or who had made some incredible mistake. I should go to the house at once and learn the true explanation. There would be time enough afterward to do my own explaining.

There was no likelihood that any one would enter the laboratory in my absence. Indeed, there were few visitors at any time. With one backward look at the body, to assure myself anew of its materiality, I went out into the moonless evening and started toward my employer's residence.

I have no clear recollection of the short walk among shadowy trees and bushes and along the poorly litten streets with their scattered houses. My thoughts, as well as the external world, were a night-bound maze of baffling unreality and dubiety.

Into this maze I was plunged to an irremeable depth on my arrival. Norma, pale and stunned rather than grief-stricken (for I think she had long ceased to love Trilt), was at the door to meet me.

"I can't get over the suddenness of it," she said at once. "He seemed all right at dinner-time, and ate heartily, as usual. Afterwards he went out, saying that he would walk as far as the laboratory and look in on you.

"He must have felt ill, and started back after he had gone half-way. I didn't even hear him come in. I can't understand how he entered the house so quietly. I was sitting in the library, reading, when I happened to look up, just in time to see him cross the room and fall senseless at my feet. He never spoke or moved after that."

I could say nothing as she led me to the library. I do not know what I had expected to find; but certainly no sane man, no modern scientist and chemist, could have dreamed of what I saw—the body of Jasper Trilt, reposing still and stiff and cadaverous, on the sofa: the same corpse, to all outward seeming, which I had left behind me in the laboratory!

The doctor, Trilt's family physician, whom Norma had summoned, was about to leave. He greeted me with a slight nod and a cursory, incurious glance.

"There's nothing whatever to be done," he said—"it's all over."

"But—it doesn't seem possible," I stammered. "Is it really Jasper Trilt—isn't there some mistake?"

The doctor did not seem to hear my question. With reeling senses, doubting my own existence, I went over to the sofa and examined the body, touching it several times to make sure—if assurance were possible—of its substantiality. The puffy, purplish features, the open, glaring eyes with the glacial terror, the suit of pepper-and-salt, the azure blue tie—all were identical with those I had seen and touched a few minutes previous, in another place. I could no longer doubt the materiality of the second corpse—I could not deny that the thing before me, to all intents and purposes, was Jasper Trilt. But in the very confirmation of its incredible identity, there lay the inception of a doubt that was infinitely hideous....

A week has gone by since then—a week of unslumbering nightmare, of all-prevailing, ineluctable horror.

Going back to the laboratory, I found the corpse of Jasper Trilt on the floor, where he had fallen. Feverishly, I applied to it all possible tests: it was solid, clammy, gross, material, like the other. I dragged it into a dusty, little-used storeroom, among cobwebby cartons and boxes and bottles, and covered it with sacking.

For reasons that must be more than obvious, I dared not tell any one of its existence. No one, save myself, has ever seen it. No one—not even Norma—suspects the unimaginable truth....

Later, I attended the funeral of Trilt, I saw him in his coffin, and as one of the pall-bearers I helped to carry the coffin and lower it into the grave. I can swear that it was tenanted by an actual body. And on the faces of the morticians and my fellow pall-bearers there was no shadow of doubt or misgiving as to the identity and reality of the corpse. But afterwards, returning home, I lifted the sacking in the store-room, and found that the thing beneath—cadaver or ka, doppelgänger or phantom, whatever it was—had not disappeared or undergone the least change.

Madness took me then for awhile, and I knew not what I did. Recovering my senses in a measure, I poured gallon after gallon of corrosive acids into a great tub; and in the tub I placed the thing that had been Jasper Trilt, or which bore the semblance of Trilt. But neither the clothing nor the body was affected in any degree by the mordant acid. And since then, the thing has shown no sign of normal decay, but remains eternally and inexplicably the same. Some night, before long, I shall bury it in the woods behind the laboratory; and the earth will receive Trilt for the second time. After that, my crime will be doubly indetectable—if I have really committed a crime, and have not dreamed it all or become the victim of some hallucinative brain-disease.

I have no explanation for what has happened, nor do I believe that any such can be afforded by the laws of a sane universe. But—is there any proof that the universe itself is sane, or subject to rational laws?

Perhaps there are inconceivable lunacies in chemistry itself, and drugs whose action is a breach of all physical logic. The poison that I administered to Trilt was an unknown quantity, apart from its deadliness, and I cannot be wholly sure of its properties, of its possible effect on the atoms of the human body—and the atoms of the soul. Indeed, I can be sure of nothing, except that I too, like the laws of matter, must go altogether mad in a little while.

THE COLOSSUS OF YLOURGNE

1. THE FLIGHT OF THE NECROMANCER

The thrice-infamous Nathaire, alchemist, astrologer and necromancer, with his ten devil-given pupils, had departed very suddenly and under circumstances of strict secrecy from the town of Vyônes. It was widely thought, among the people of that vicinage, that his departure had been prompted by a salutary fear of ecclesiastical thumbscrews and fagots. Other wizards, less notorious than he, had already gone to the stake during a year of unusual inquisitory zeal; and it was well-known that Nathaire had incurred the reprobation of the Church. Few, therefore, considered the reason of his going a mystery; but the means of transit which he had employed, as well as the destination of the sorcerer and his pupils, were regarded as more than problematic.

A thousand dark and superstitious rumors were abroad; and passers made the sign of the Cross when they neared the tall, gloomy house which Nathaire had built in blasphemous proximity to the great cathedral and had filled with a furniture of Satanic luxury and strangeness. Two daring thieves, who had entered the mansion when the fact of its desertion became well established, reported that much of this furniture, as well as the books and other paraphernalia of Nathaire, had seemingly departed with its owner, doubtless to the same fiery bourn. This served to augment the unholy mystery: for it was patently impossible that Nathaire and his ten apprentices, with several cart-loads of household belongings, could have passed the ever-guarded city gates in any legitimate manner without the knowledge of the custodians.

It was said by the more devout and religious moiety that the Archfiend, with a legion of bat-winged assistants, had borne them away bodily at moonless midnight. There were clerics, and also reputable burghers, who professed to have seen the flight of dark, man-like shapes upon the blotted stars together with others that were not men, and to have heard the wailing cries of the hell-

257

bound crew as they passed in an evil cloud over the roofs and city walls.

Others believed that the sorcerers had transported themselves from Vyônes through their own diabolic arts, and had withdrawn to some unfrequented fastness where Nathaire, who had long been in feeble health, could hope to die in such peace and serenity as might be enjoyed by one who stood between the flames of the *auto-da-fé* and those of Abaddon. It was thought that he had lately cast his own horoscope, for the first time in his fifty-odd years, and had read therein an impending conjunction of disastrous planets, signifying early death.

Others still, among whom were certain rival astrologers and enchanters, said that Nathaire had retired from the public view merely that he might commune without interruption with various coadjutive demons; and thus might weave, unmolested, the black spells of a supreme and lycanthropic malice. These spells, they hinted, would in due time be visited upon Vyônes and perhaps upon the entire region of Averoigne; and would no doubt take the form of a fearsome pestilence or a wholesale invultuation or a realm-wide incursion of succubi and incubi.

Amid the seething of strange rumors, many half-forgotten tales were recalled, and new legends were created overnight. Much was made of the obscure nativity of Nathaire and his dubitable wanderings before he had settled, six years previous, in Vyônes. People said that he was fiend-begotten, like the fabled Merlin: his father being no less a personage than Alastor, de-mon of revenge; and his mother a deformed and dwarfish sorceress. From the former, he had taken his spitefulness and malignity; from the latter, his squat, puny physique.

He had travelled in Orient lands, and had learned from Egyptian or Sara-cenic masters the unhallowed art of necromancy, in whose practice he was unrivalled. There were black whispers anent the use he had made of long dead bodies, of fleshless bones, and the service he had wrung from buried men that the angel of doom alone could lawfully raise up. He had never been popular, though many had sought his advice and assistance in the further-ing of their own more or less dubious affairs. Once, in the third year after his coming to Vyônes, he had been stoned in public because of his bruited necromancies, and had been permanently lamed by a well directed cobble. This injury, it was thought, he had never forgiven; and he was said to return the antagonism of the clergy with the hellish hatred of an Antichrist.

Apart from the sorcerous evils and abuses of which he was commonly suspected, he had long been looked upon as a corrupter of youth. Despite his minikin stature, his deformity and ugliness, he possessed a remarkable power, a mesmeric persuasion; and his pupils, whom he was said to have plunged into bottomless and ghoulish iniquities, were young men of the most brilliant promise. On the whole, his vanishment was regarded as a quite providential riddance.

Among the people of the city, there was one man who took no part in the somber gossip and lurid speculation. This man was Gaspard du Nord, himself a student of the proscribed sciences, who had been numbered for a year among the pupils of Nathaire but had chosen to withdraw quietly from the master's household after learning the enormities that would attend his further initiation. He had, however, taken with him much rare and peculiar knowledge, together with a certain insight into the baleful powers and night-dark motives of the necromancer.

Because of this knowledge and insight, Gaspard preferred to remain silent when he heard of Nathaire's departure. Also, he did not think it well to revive the memory of his own past pupilage. Alone with his books, in a sparsely furnished attic, he frowned above a small, oblong mirror, framed with an arabesque of golden vipers, that had once been the property of Nathaire.

It was not the reflection of his own comely and youthful though subtly lined face that caused him to frown. Indeed, the mirror was of another kind than that which reflects the features of the gazer. In its depths, for a few instants, he had beheld a strange and ominous-looking scene, whose participants were known to him but whose location he could not recognize or orientate. Before he could study it closely, the mirror had clouded as if with the rising of alchemic fumes, and he had seen no more.

This clouding, he reflected, could mean only one thing: Nathaire had known himself watched and had put forth a counterspell that rendered the clairvoyant mirror useless. It was the realization of this fact, together with the brief, sinister glimpse of Nathaire's present activities, that troubled Gaspard and caused a chill horror to mount slowly in his mind: a horror that had not yet found a palpable form or a name.

2. THE GATHERING OF THE DEAD

The departure of Nathaire and his pupils occurred in the late spring of 1281, during the interlunar dark. Afterwards, a new moon waxed above the flowery fields and bright-leafed woods, and waned in ghostly silver. With its waning, people began to talk of other magicians and fresher mysteries.

Then, in the moon-deserted nights of early summer, there came a series of disappearances far more unnatural and inexplicable than that of the dwarf-ish, malignant necromancer.

It was found one day, by grave-diggers who had gone early to their toil in a cemetery outside the walls of Vyônes, that no less than six newly occupied graves had been opened, and the bodies, which were those of reputable citizens, removed. On closer examination, it became all too evident that this removal had not been effected by robbers. The coffins, which lay aslant or stood protruding upright from the mould, offered all the appearance of having been shattered from within as if by the use of extrahuman strength; and the fresh earth itself was upheaved, as if the dead men, in some awful, untimely resurrection, had actually *dug* their way to the surface.

The corpses had vanished utterly, as if hell had swallowed them; and, as far as could be learned, there were no eyewitnesses of their fate. In those devil-ridden times, only one explanation of the happening seemed credible: demons had entered the graves and taken bodily possession of the dead, compelling them to arise and go forth.

To the dismay and horror of all Averoigne, the strange vanishment was followed with appalling promptness by many others of a like sort. It seemed as if an occult, resistless summons had been laid upon the dead. Nightly, for a period of two weeks, the cemeteries of Vyônes, and also those of other towns, of villages and hamlets, gave up a ghastly quota of their tenants. From brazen-bolted tombs, from common charnels, from shallow, unconsecrated trenches, from the marble-lidded vaults of churches and cathedrals, the weird exodus went on without cessation.

Worse than this, if possible, there were newly ceremented corpses that leapt from their biers or catafalques, and disregarding the horrified watchers, ran with great bounds of automatic frenzy into the night, never to be seen again by those who lamented them.

In every case, the missing bodies were those of young stalwart men who had died but recently and had met their death through violence or accident rather than wasting illness. Some were criminals who had paid the penalty of their misdeeds; others were men-at-arms or constables, slain in the execution of their duty. Knights who had died in tourney or personal combat were numbered among them; and many were the victims of the robber-bands who infested Averoigne at that time. There were monks, merchants, nobles, yeomen, pages, priests; but none, in any case, who had passed the prime of life. The old and infirm, it seemed, were safe from the animating demons.

The situation was looked upon by the more superstitious as a veritable omening of the world's end. Satan was making war with his cohorts and was carrying the bodies of the holy dead into hellish captivity. The consternation increased a hundred-fold when it became plain that even the most liberal sprinkling of holy water, the performance of the most awful and cogent exorcisms, failed utterly to give protection against this diabolic ravishment. The Church owned itself powerless to cope with the strange evil; and the forces of secular law could do nothing to arraign or punish the intangible agency.

Because of the universal fear that prevailed, no effort was made to follow the missing cadavers. Ghastly tales, however, were told by late wayfarers who had met certain of these liches, striding alone or in companies along the roads of Averoigne. They gave the appearance of being deaf, dumb, totally insensate, and of hurrying with horrible speed and sureness toward a remote, predestined goal. The general direction of their flight, it seemed, was eastward; but only with the cessation of the exodus, which had numbered several hundred people, did anyone begin to suspect the actual destination of the dead.

This destination, it somehow became rumored, was the ruinous castle of Ylourgne, beyond the werewolf-haunted forest, in the outlying, semi-mountainous hills of Averoigne.

Ylourgne, a great, craggy pile that had been built by a line of evil and marauding barons now extinct, was a place that even the goatherds preferred to shun. The wrathful specters of its bloody lords were said to move turbulently in its crumbling halls; and its châtelaines were the Undead. No one cared to dwell in the shadow of its cliff-founded walls; and the nearest abode of living men was a small Cistercian monastery, more than a mile away on the opposite slope of the valley.

The monks of this austere brotherhood held little commerce with the world beyond the hills; and few were the visitors who sought admission at their high-perched portals. But, during that dreadful summer, following the disappearances of the dead, a weird and disquieting tale went forth from the monastery throughout Averoigne.

Beginning with late spring, the Cistercian monks were compelled to take cognizance of sundry odd phenomena in the old, long-deserted ruins of Ylourgne, which were visible from their windows. They had beheld flaring lights, where lights should not have been: flames of uncanny blue and crimson that shuddered behind the broken, weed-grown embrasures or rose starward above the jagged crenellations. Hideous noises had issued from the ruin by night together with the flames; and the monks had heard a clangor as of hellish anvils and hammers, a ringing of gigantic armor and maces, and had deemed that Ylourgne was become a mustering-ground of devils. Mephitic odors as of brimstone and burning flesh had floated across the valley; and even by day, when the noises were silent and the lights no longer flared, a thin haze of hell-blue vapor hung upon the battlements.

It was plain, the monks thought, that the place had been occupied from beneath by subterrestrial beings; for no one had been seen to approach it by way of the bare, open slopes and crags. Observing these signs of the Archfoe's activity in their neighborhood, they crossed themselves with new fervor and frequency, and said their Paters and Aves more interminably than before. Their toils and austerities, also, they redoubled. Otherwise, since the old castle was a place abandoned by men, they took no heed of the supposed occupation, deeming it well to mind their own affairs unless in case of overt Satanic hostility.

They kept a careful watch; but for several weeks they saw no one who actually entered Ylourgne or emerged therefrom. Except for the nocturnal lights and noises, and the hovering vapor by day, there was no proof of tenantry either human or diabolic.

Then, one morning, in the valley below the terraced gardens of the monastery, two brothers, hoeing weeds in a carrot-patch, beheld the passing of a singular train of people who came from the direction of the great forest of Averoigne and went upward, climbing the steep, chasmy slope toward Ylourgne.

These people, the monks averred, were striding along in great haste, with stiff but flying steps; and all were strangely pale of feature and were habited in the garments of the grave. The shrouds of some were torn and ragged; and all were dusty with travel or grimed with the mould of interment. The people numbered a dozen or more; and after them, at intervals, there came several stragglers, attired like the rest. With marvellous agility and speed, they mounted the hill and disappeared at length amid the lowering walls of Ylourgne.

At this time, no rumor of the ravished graves and biers had reached the Cistercians. The tale was brought to them later, after they had beheld, on many successive mornings, the passing of small or great companies of the dead toward the devil-taken castle. Hundreds of these liches, they swore, had filed by beneath the monastery; and doubtless many others had gone past unnoted in the dark. None, however, were seen to come forth from Ylourgne, which had swallowed them up like the undisgorging Pit.

Though direly frightened and sorely scandalized, the brothers still thought it well to refrain from action. Some, the hardiest, irked by all these flagrant signs of evil, had desired to visit the ruins with holy water and lifted crucifixes. But their abbot, in his wisdom, enjoined them to wait. In the meanwhile, the nocturnal flames grew brighter, the noises louder.

Also, in the course of this waiting, while incessant prayers went up from the little monastery, a frightful thing occurred. One of the brothers, a stout fellow named Théophile, in violation of the rigorous discipline, had made overfrequent visits to the wine-casks. No doubt he had tried to drown his pious horror at these untoward happenings. At any rate, after his potations, he had the ill-luck to wander out among the precipices and break his neck.

Sorrowing for his death and dereliction, the brothers laid Théophile in the chapel and chanted their masses for his soul. These masses, in the dark hours before morning, were interrupted by the untimely resurrection of the dead monk, who, with his head lolling horribly on his broken neck, rushed as if fiend-ridden from the chapel and ran down the hill toward the demon flames and clamors of Ylourgne.

3. THE TESTIMONY OF THE MONKS

Following the above-related occurrence, two of the brothers who had previously desired to visit the haunted castle, again applied to the abbot for this permission, saying that God would surely aid them in avenging the abduction of Théophile's body, as well as the taking of many others from consecrated ground. Marvelling at the hardihood of these lusty monks, who proposed to beard the Archenemy in his lair, the abbot permitted them to go forth, furnished with aspergillums and flasks of holy water, and bearing great crosses of hornbeam, such as would have served for maces with which to brain an armored knight.

The monks, whose names were Bernard and Stéphane, went boldly up at middle forenoon to assail the evil stronghold. It was an arduous climb, among overhanging boulders and along slippery scarps; but both were stout and agile, and, moreover, well accustomed to such climbing. Since the day was sultry and airless, their white robes were soon stained with sweat; but pausing only for brief prayer, they pressed on; and in good season they neared the castle, upon whose grey, time-eroded ramparts they could still descry no evidence of occupation or activity.

The deep moat that had once surrounded the place was now dry, and had been partly filled by crumbling earth and detritus from the walls. The drawbridge had rotted away; but the blocks of the barbican, collapsing into the moat, had made a sort of rough causey on which it was possible to cross. Not without trepidation, and lifting their crucifixes as warriors lift their weapons in the escalade of an armed fortress, the brothers climbed over the ruin of the barbican into the courtyard.

This too, like the battlements, was seemingly deserted. Overgrown nettles, rank grasses and sapling trees were rooted between its paving-stones. The high, massive donjon, the chapel, and that portion of the castellated structure containing the great hall, had preserved their main outlines after centuries of dilapidation. To the left of the broad bailey, a doorway yawned like the mouth of a dark cavern in the cliffy mass of the hall-building; and from this doorway there issued a thin, bluish vapor, writhing in phantom coils toward the unclouded heavens.

Approaching the doorway, the brothers beheld a gleaming of red fires within, like the eyes of dragons blinking through infernal murk. They felt sure that the place was an outpost of Erebus, an antechamber of the Pit; but nevertheless, they entered bravely, chanting loud exorcisms and brandishing their mighty crosses of hornbeam.

Passing through the cavernous doorway, they could see but indistinctly in the gloom, being somewhat blinded by the summer sunlight they had left. Then, with the gradual clearing of their vision, a monstrous scene was limned before them, with ever-growing details of crowding horror and grotesquery. Some of these details were obscure and mysteriously terrifying; others, all too plain, were branded as if with sudden, ineffaceable hell-fire on the minds of the monks.

They stood on the threshold of a colossal chamber, which seemed to have been made by the tearing down of upper floors and inner partitions adjacent to the castle hall, itself a room of huge extent. The chamber seemed to recede through interminable shadow, shafted with sunlight falling through the rents of ruin: sunlight that was powerless to dissipate the infernal gloom and mystery.

The monks averred, later, that they saw many people moving about the place, together with sundry demons, some of whom were shadowy and gigantic, and others barely to be distinguished from the men. These people, as well as their familiars, were occupied with the tending of reverberatory furnaces and immense pear-shaped and gourd-shaped vessels such as were used in alchemy. Some, also, were stooping above great fuming cauldrons, like sorcerers busy with the brewing of terrible drugs. Against the opposite wall, there were two enormous vats, built of stone and mortar, whose circular sides rose higher than a man's head, so that Bernard and Stéphane were unable to determine their contents. One of the vats gave forth a whitish glimmering; the other, a ruddy luminosity.

Near the vats, and somewhat between them, there stood a sort of low couch or litter, made of luxurious, weirdly figured fabrics such as the Saracens weave. On this the monks discerned a dwarfish being, pale and wizened, with eyes of chill flame that shone like evil beryls through the dusk. The dwarf, who had all the air of a feeble moribund, was supervising the toils of the men and their familiars.

The dazed eyes of the brothers began to comprehend other details. They saw that several corpses, among which they recognized that of Théophile, were lying on the middle floor, together with a heap of human bones that had been wrenched asunder at the joints, and great lumps of flesh piled like the carvings of butchers. One of the men was lifting the bones and dropping them into a cauldron beneath which there glowed a ruby-colored fire; and another was flinging the lumps of flesh into a tub filled with some hueless liquid that gave forth an evil hissing as of a thousand serpents.

Others had stripped the grave-clothes from one of the cadavers, and were starting to assail it with long knives. Others still were mounting rude flights of stone stairs along the walls of the immense vats, carrying vessels filled with semi-liquescent matters which they emptied over the high rims.

Appalled at this vision of human and Satanic turpitude, and feeling a more than righteous indignation, the monks resumed their chanting of sonorous exorcisms and rushed forward. Their entrance, it appeared, was not perceived by the heinously occupied crew of sorcerers and devils.

Bernard and Stéphane, filled with an ardor of godly wrath, were about to fling themselves upon the butchers who had started to assail the dead body. This corpse they recognized as being that of a notorious outlaw, named Jacques Le Loupgarou, who had been slain a few days previous in combat with the officers of the state. Le Loupgarou, noted for his brawn, his cunning and his ferocity, had long terrorized the woods and highways of Averoigne. His great body had been half-eviscerated by the swords of the constabulary; and his beard was stiff and purple with the dried blood of a ghastly wound that had cloven his face from mouth to temple. He had died unshriven, but nevertheless, the monks were unwilling to see his helpless cadaver put to some unhallowed use beyond the surmise of Christians.

The pale, malignant-looking dwarf had now perceived the brothers. They heard him cry out in a shrill, imperatory tone that rose above the ominous hiss of the cauldrons and the hoarse mutter of men and demons.

They knew not his words, which were those of some outlandish tongue and sounded like an incantation. Instantly, as if in response to an order, two of the men turned from their unholy chemistry, and lifting copper basins filled with an unknown, fetid liquor, hurled the contents of these vessels in the faces of Bernard and Stéphane.

The brothers were blinded by the stinging fluid, which bit their flesh as with many serpents' teeth; and they were overcome by the noxious fumes, so that their great crosses dropped from their hands and they both fell unconscious on the castle floor.

Recovering anon their sight and their other senses, they found that their hands had been tied with heavy thongs of gut, so that they were now helpless and could no longer wield their crucifixes or the sprinklers of holy water which they carried.

In this ignominious condition, they heard the voice of the evil dwarf, commanding them to arise. They obeyed, though clumsily and with difficulty, being denied the assistance of their hands. Bernard, who was still sick with the poisonous vapor he had inhaled, fell twice before he succeeded in standing erect; and his discomfiture was greeted with a cachinnation of foul, obscene laughter from the assembled sorcerers.

Now, standing, the monks were taunted by the dwarf, who mocked and reviled them, with appalling blasphemies such as could be uttered only by a bond servant of Satan. At last, according to their sworn testimony, he said to them:

"Return to your kennel, ye whelps of Ialdabaoth, and take with you this message: *They that came here as many shall go forth as one.*"

Then, in obedience to a dreadful formula spoken by the dwarf, two of the familiars, who had the shape of enormous and shadowy beasts, approached the body of Le Loupgarou and that of Brother Théophile. One of the foul demons, like a vapor that sinks into a marsh, entered the bloody nostrils of Le Loupgarou, disappearing inch by inch, till its horned and bestial head was withdrawn from sight. The other, in like manner, went in through the nostrils of Brother Théophile, whose head lay wried athwart his shoulder on the broken neck.

Then, when the demons had completed their possession, the bodies, in a fashion horrible to behold, were raised up from the castle floor, the one with ravelled entrails hanging from its wide wounds, the other with a head that drooped forward loosely on its bosom. Then, animated by their devils, the cadavers took up the crosses of hornbeam that had been dropped by Stéphane and Bernard; and using the crosses for bludgeons, they drove the monks in ignominious flight from the castle, amid a loud, tempestuous howling of infernal laughter from the dwarf and his necromantic crew. And the nude corpse of Le Loupgarou and the robed cadaver of Théophile followed them far on the chasm-riven slopes below Ylourgne, striking great blows with the crosses, so that the backs of the two Cistercians were become a mass of bloody bruises.

After a defeat so signal and crushing, no more of the monks were emboldened to go up against Ylourgne. The whole monastery, thereafter, devoted itself to triple austerities, to quadrupled prayers; and awaiting the unknown will of God, and the equally obscure machinations of the Devil, maintained a pious faith that was somewhat tempered with trepidation.

In time, through goatherds who visited the monks, the tale of Stéphane and Bernard went forth throughout Averoigne, adding to the grievous alarm that had been caused by the wholesale disappearance of the dead. No one knew what was really going on in the haunted castle or what disposition had been made of the hundreds of migratory corpses; for the light thrown on their fate by the monks' story, though lurid and frightful, was all too inconclusive; and the message sent by the dwarf was somewhat cabbalistic.

Everyone felt, however, that some gigantic menace, some black, infernal enchantment, was being brewed within the ruinous walls. The malignant, moribund dwarf was all too readily identified with the missing sorcerer, Nathaire; and his underlings, it was plain, were Nathaire's pupils.

4. THE GOING-FORTH OF GASPARD DU NORD

Alone in his attic chamber, Gaspard du Nord, student of alchemy and sorcery, and quondam pupil of Nathaire, sought repeatedly, but always in vain, to consult the viper-circled mirror. The glass remained obscure and cloudy, as with the risen fumes of Satanical alembics or baleful necromantic braziers. Haggard and weary with long nights of watching, Gaspard knew that Nathaire was even more vigilant than he.

Reading with anxious care the general configuration of the stars, he found the foretokening of a great evil that was to come upon Averoigne. But the nature of the evil was not clearly shown.

In the meanwhile, the hideous resurrection and migration of the dead were taking place. All Averoigne shuddered at the manifold enormity. Like the timeless night of a Memphian plague, terror settled everywhere; and people spoke of each new atrocity in bated whispers, without daring to voice the execrable tale aloud. To Gaspard, as to everyone, the whispers came; and likewise, after the horror had apparently ceased in early mid-summer, there came the appalling story of the Cistercian monks.

Now, at last, the long-baffled watcher found an inkling of that which he sought. The hiding-place of the fugitive necromancer and his apprentices, at least, had been uncovered; and the disappearing dead were clearly traced to their bourn. But still, even for the percipient Gaspard, there remained an undeclared enigma: the exact nature of the abominable brew, the hell-dark sorcery, that Nathaire was concocting in his remote den. Gaspard felt sure of one thing only: the dying, splenetic dwarf, knowing that his allotted time was short, and hating the people of Averoigne with a bottomless rancor, would prepare an enormous and maleficent magic without parallel.

Even with his knowledge of Nathaire's proclivities, and his awareness of the well-nigh inexhaustible arcanic science, the reserves of pit-deep wizardry possessed by the dwarf, he could form only vague, terrifical conjectures anent the incubated evil. But, as time went on, he felt an ever-deepening oppression, the adumbration of a monstrous menace crawling from the dark rim of the world. He could not shake off his disquietude; and finally he resolved, despite the obvious perils of such an excursion, to pay a secret visit to the neighborhood of Ylourgne.

Gaspard, though he came of a well-to-do family, was at that time in straitened circumstances; for his devotion to a somewhat doubtful science had been disapproved by his father. His sole income was a small pittance, purveyed secretly to the youth by his mother and sister. This sufficed for his meager food, the rent of his room, and a few books and instruments and chemicals; but it would not permit the purchase of a horse or even a humble mule for the proposed journey of more than forty miles.

Undaunted, he set forth on foot, carrying only a dagger and a wallet of food. He timed his wanderings so that he would reach Ylourgne at nightfall in the rising of a full moon. Much of his journey lay through the great, lowering forest, which approached the very walls of Vyônes on the eastern side and ran in a somber arc through Averoigne to the mouth of the rocky valley below Ylourgne. After a few miles, he emerged from the mighty wood of pines and oaks and larches; and thenceforward, for the first day, followed the river Isoile through an open, well-peopled plain. He spent the warm summer night beneath a beech-tree, in the vicinity of a small village, not caring to sleep in the lonely woods where robbers and wolves—and creatures of a more baleful repute—were commonly supposed to dwell.

At evening of the second day, after passing through the wildest and oldest portion of the immemorial wood, he came to the steep, stony valley that led to his destination. This valley was the fountain-head of the Isoile, which had dwindled to a mere rivulet. In the brown twilight, between sunset and moonrise, he saw the lights of the Cistercian monastery; and opposite, on the piled, forbidding scarps, the grim and rugged mass of the ruinous stronghold of Ylourgne, with wan and wizard fires flickering behind its high embrasures. Apart from these fires, there was no sign of occupation; and he did not hear at any time the dismal noises reported by the monks.

Gaspard waited till the round moon, yellow as the eye of some immense nocturnal bird, had begun to peer above the darkling valley. Then, very cautiously, since the neighborhood was strange to him, he started to make his way toward the somber, brooding castle.

Even for one well-used to such climbing, the escalade would have offered enough difficulty and danger by moonlight. Several times, finding himself at the bottom of a sheer cliff, he was compelled to retrace his hard-won progress; and often he was saved from falling only by stunted shrubs and briars that had taken root in the niggard soil. Breathless, with torn raiment, and scored and bleeding hands, he gained at length the shoulder of the craggy height, below the walls.

Here he paused to recover breath and recuperate his flagging strength. He could see from his vantage the pale reflection as of hidden flames, that beat upward on the inner wall of the high-built donjon. He heard a low hum of confused noises, whose distance and direction were alike baffling. Sometimes they seemed to float downward from the black battlements, sometimes to issue from subterranean depths far in the hill.

Apart from this remote, ambiguous hum, the night was locked in a mortal stillness. The very winds appeared to shun the vicinity of the dread castle. An unseen, clammy cloud of paralyzing evil hung removeless upon all things; and the pale, swollen moon, the patroness of witches and sorcerers, distilled her green poison above the crumbling towers in a silence older than time.

Gaspard felt the obscenely clinging weight of a more burdenous thing than his own fatigue when he resumed his progress toward the barbican. Invisible webs of the waiting, ever-gathering evil seemed to impede him. The slow, noisome flapping of intangible wings was heavy in his face. He seemed to breathe a surging wind from unfathomable vaults and caverns of corruption. Inaudible howlings, derisive or minatory, thronged in his ears, and foul hands appeared to thrust him back. But, bowing his head as if against a blowing gale, he went on and climbed the mounded ruin of the barbican, into the weedy courtyard.

The place was deserted, to all seeming; and much of it was still deep in the shadows of the walls and turrets. Nearby in the black, silver-crenelated pile, Gaspard saw the open, cavernous doorway described by the monks. It was lit from within by a lurid glare, wannish and eerie as marsh-fires. The humming noise, now audible as a muttering of voices, issued from the doorway; and Gaspard thought that he could see dark, sooty figures moving rapidly in the lit interior.

Keeping in the further shadows, he stole along the courtyard, making a sort of circuit amid the ruins. He did not dare to approach the open entrance for fear of being seen; though, as far as he could tell, the place was unguarded.

He came to the donjon, on whose upper wall the wan light flickered obliquely through a sort of rift in the long building adjacent. This opening was at some distance from the ground; and Gaspard saw that it had been formerly the door to a stone balcony. A flight of broken steps led upward along the wall to the half-crumbled remnant of this balcony; and it occurred to the youth that he might climb the steps and peer unobserved into the interior of Ylourgne.

Some of the stairs were missing; and all were in heavy shadow. Gaspard found his way precariously to the balcony, pausing once in considerable alarm when a fragment of the worn stone, loosened by his footfall, dropped with a loud clattering on the courtyard flags below. Apparently it was unheard by the occupants of the castle; and after a little he resumed his climbing.

Cautiously he neared the large, ragged opening through which the light poured upward. Crouching on a narrow ledge, which was all that remained of the balcony, he peered in on a most astounding and terrific spectacle, whose details were so bewildering that he could barely comprehend their import till after many minutes.

It was plain that the story told by the monks—allowing for their religious bias—had been far from extravagant. Almost the whole interior of the half-ruined pile had been torn down and dismantled to afford room for the activities of Nathaire: in itself a superhuman task for whose execution the sorcerer must have employed a legion of familiars as well as his ten pupils.

The vast chamber was fitfully illumed by the glare of athanors and braziers; and, above all, by the weird glimmering from the huge stone vats. Even from his high vantage, the watcher could not see the contents of these vats; but a white luminosity poured upward from the rim of one of them, and a flesh-tinted phosphorescence from the other.

Gaspard had seen certain of the experiments and evocations of Nathaire, and was all too familiar with the appurtenances of the dark arts. Within certain limits, he was not squeamish; nor was it likely that he would have been terrified overmuch by the shadowy, uncouth shapes of demons who toiled in the pit below him side by side with the black-clad pupils of the sorcerer. But a cold horror clutched his heart when he saw the incredible, enormous thing that occupied the central floor: the colossal human skeleton a hundred feet in length, stretching for more than the extent of the old castle hall; the skeleton whose bony right foot the group of men and devils, to all appearance, were busily clothing with human flesh!

The prodigious and macabre framework, complete in every part, with ribs like arches of some Satanic nave, shone as if it were still heated by the fires of an infernal welding. It seemed to shimmer and burn with unnatural life, to quiver with malign disquietude in the flickering glare and gloom. The great finger-bones, curving claw-like on the floor, appeared as if they were about to close upon some helpless prey. The tremendous teeth were set in an everlasting grin of sardonic cruelty and malice. The hollow eye-sockets, deep as Tartarean wells, appeared to seethe with myriad, mocking lights, like the eyes of elementals swimming upward in obscene shadow.

Gaspard was stunned by the shocking and stupendous phantasmagoria that yawned before him like a peopled hell. Afterwards, he was never wholly sure of certain things, and could remember very little of the actual manner in which the work of the men and their assistants was being carried on. Dim, dubious, bat-like creatures seemed to be flitting to and fro between one of the stone vats and the group that toiled like sculptors, clothing the bony foot with a reddish plasm which they applied and moulded like so much clay. Gaspard thought, but was not certain later, that this plasm, which gleamed as if with mingled blood and fire, was being brought from the rosy-litten vat in vessels borne by the claws of the shadowy flying creatures. None of them, however, approached the other vat, whose wannish light was momently enfeebled, as if it were dying down.

He looked for the minikin figure of Nathaire, whom he could not distinguish in the crowded scene. The sick necromancer—if he had not already succumbed to the little-known disease that had long wasted him like an inward flame—was no doubt hidden from view by the colossal skeleton and was perhaps directing the labors of the men and demons from his couch.

Spell-bound on that precarious ledge, the watcher failed to hear the furtive, cat-like feet that were climbing behind him on the ruinous stairs. Too late, he heard the clink of a loose fragment close upon his heels; and turning in startlement, he toppled into sheer oblivion beneath the impact of a cudgel-like blow, and did not even know that the beginning fall of his body toward the courtyard had been arrested by his assailant's arms.

5. The Horror of Ylourgne

Gaspard, returning from his dark plunge into Lethean emptiness, found himself gazing into the eyes of Nathaire: those eyes of liquid night and ebony, in which swam the chill, malignant fires of stars that had gone down to irremeable perdition. For some time, in the confusion of his senses, he could see nothing but the eyes, which seemed to have drawn him forth like baleful magnets from his swoon. Apparently disembodied, or set in a face too vast for human cognizance, they burned before him in chaotic murk. Then, by degrees, he saw the other features of the sorcerer, and the details of a lurid scene; and became aware of his own situation.

Trying to lift his hands to his aching head, he found that they were bound tightly together at the wrists. He was half-lying, half-leaning against an object with hard planes and edges that irked his back. This object he discovered to be a sort of alchemic furnace, or athanor, part of a litter of disused apparatus that stood or lay on the castle floor. Cupels, aludels, cucurbits, like enormous gourds and globes, were mingled in strange confusion with the piled, iron-clasped books and the sooty cauldrons and braziers of a darker science.

Nathaire, propped among Saracenic cushions with arabesques of sullen gold and fulgurant scarlet, was peering upon him from a kind of improvised couch, made with bales of Orient rugs and arrases, to whose luxury the rude walls of the castle, stained with mould and mottled with dead fungi, offered a grotesque foil. Dim lights and evilly swooping shadows flickered across the scene; and Gaspard could hear a guttural hum of voices behind him. Twisting his head a little, he saw one of the stone vats, whose rosy luminosity was blurred and blotted by vampire wings that went to and fro.

Gaspard and Nathaire, it seemed, were alone. The assailants of the youth, whoever or whatever they had been, had presumably returned to another task after bringing their bound, unconscious captive before the sorcerer.

"Welcome," said Nathaire, after an interval in which the student began to perceive the fatal progress of illness in the pain-pinched features before him. "So Gaspard du Nord has come to see his former master!" The harsh, imperatory voice, with demoniac volume, issued appallingly from the wizened frame.

"I have come," said Gaspard, in laconic echo. "Tell me, what devil's work is this in which I find you engaged? And what have you done with the dead bodies that were stolen by your accursed familiars?"

The frail, dying body of Nathaire, as if possessed by some sardonic fiend, rocked to and fro on the luxurious couch in a long, violent gust of laughter, without other reply.

"If your looks bear creditable witness," said Gaspard, when the baleful laughter had ceased, "you are mortally ill, and the time is short in which you can hope to atone for your deeds of malefice and make your peace with God—if indeed it still be possible for you to make peace. What foul and monstrous brew are you preparing, to insure the ultimate perdition of your soul?"

The dwarf was again seized by a spasm of diabolic mirth.

"Nay, nay, my good Gaspard," he said finally. "I have made another bond than the one with which puling cowards try to purchase the good will and forgiveness of the heavenly Tyrant. Hell may take me in the end, if it will; but Hell has paid, and will still pay, an ample and goodly price. I must die soon, it is true, for my doom is written in the stars: but in death, by the grace of Satan, I shall live again, and shall go forth endowed with the mighty thews of the Anakim, to visit vengeance on the people of Averoigne, who have long hated me for my necromantic wisdom and have held me in derision for my dwarf stature."

"What madness is this whereof you dream?" asked the youth, appalled by the more than human frenzy and malignity that seemed to dilate the shrunken frame of Nathaire and stream in Tartarean luster from his eyes.

"It is no madness, but a veritable thing: a miracle, mayhap, as life itself is a miracle.... From the fresh bodies of the dead, which otherwise would have rotted away in charnel foulness, my pupils and familiars are making for me, beneath my instruction, the giant form whose skeleton you have beheld. My soul, at the death of its present body, will pass into this colossal tenement through the working of certain spells of transmigration in which my faithful assistants have also been carefully instructed.

"If you had remained with me, Gaspard, and had not drawn back in your petty, pious squeamishness from the marvels and profundities that I should have unveiled for you, it would now be your privilege to share in the creation of this prodigy.... And if you had come to Ylourgne a little sooner in your presumptuous prying, I might have made a certain use of your stout bones and muscle... the same use I have made of other young men, who died through accident or violence. But it is too late even for this, since the building of the bones has been completed, and it remains only to invest them with human flesh. My good Gaspard, there is nothing whatever to be done with you—except to put you safely out of the way. Providentially, for this purpose, there is an oubliette beneath the castle: a somewhat dismal lodging-place, no doubt, but one that was made strong and deep by the grim lords of Ylourgne."

Gaspard was unable to frame any reply to this sinister and extraordinary speech. Searching his horror-frozen brain for words, he felt himself seized from behind by the hands of unseen beings who had come, no doubt, in answer to some gesture of Nathaire: a gesture which the captive had not perceived. He was blindfolded with some heavy fabric, mouldy and musty as a grave-cloth, and was led stumbling through the litter of strange apparatus, and down a winding flight of ruinous, narrow stairs from which the noisome breath of stagnating water, mingled with the oily muskiness of serpents, arose to meet him.

He appeared to descend for a distance that would admit of no return. Slowly the stench grew stronger, more insupportable; the stairs ended; a door clanged sullenly on rusty hinges; and Gaspard was thrust forward on a damp, uneven floor that seemed to have been worn away by myriad feet.

He heard the grating of a ponderous slab of stone. His wrists were untied, the bandage was removed from his eyes, and he saw by the light of flickering torches a round hole that yawned in the oozing floor at his feet. Beside it was the lifted slab that had formed its lid. Before he could turn to see the faces of his captors, to learn if they were men or devils, he was seized rudely and thrust into the gaping hole. He fell through Erebus-like darkness, for what seemed an immense distance, before he struck bottom. Lying half-stunned in a shallow, fetid pool, he heard the funereal thud of the heavy slab as it slid back into place far above him.

6. THE VAULTS OF YLOURGNE

Gaspard was revived, after a while, by the chillness of the water in which he lay. His garments were half-soaked; and the slimy, mephitic pool, as he discovered by his first movement, was within an inch of his mouth. He could hear a steady, monotonous dripping somewhere in the rayless night of his dungeon. He staggered to his feet, finding that his bones were still intact, and began a cautious exploration. Foul drops fell upon his hair and lifted face as he moved; his feet slipped and splashed in the rotten water; there were angry, vehement hissings, and serpentine coils slithered coldly across his ankles.

He soon came to a rough wall of stone, and following the wall with his finger-tips, he tried to determine the extent of the oubliette. The place was more or less circular, without corners, and he failed to form any just idea of its circuit. Somewhere in his wanderings, he found a shelving pile of rubble that rose above the water against the wall; and here, for the sake of comparative dryness and comfort, he ensconced himself, after dispossessing a number of outraged reptiles. These creatures, it seemed, were inoffensive, and probably belonged to some species of water-snake; but he shivered involuntarily at the touch of their clammy scales.

Sitting on the rubble-heap, Gaspard reviewed in his mind the various horrors of a situation that was infinitely dismal and desperate. He had learned the incredible, soul-shaking secret of Ylourgne, the unimaginably monstrous and blasphemous project of Nathaire; but now, immured in this noisome hole as in a subterranean tomb, in depths beneath the devil-haunted pile, he could not even warn the world of the imminent menace.

The wallet of food, now more than half-empty, with which he started from Vyônes, was still hanging at his back; and he assured himself by investigation that his captors had not troubled to deprive him of his dagger. Gnawing a crust of stale bread in the darkness, and caressing with his hand the hilt of the precious weapon, he sought for some rift in the all-environing despair.

He had no means of measuring the black hours that went over him with the slowness of a slime-clogged river, crawling in blind silence to a subterrene sea. The ceaseless drip of water, probably from sunken hill-springs that had supplied the castle in former years, alone broke the stillness; but the sound became in time an equivocal monotone that suggested to his half-delirious mind the mirthless and perpetual chuckling of unseen imps. At last, from sheer bodily exhaustion, he fell into troubled nightmare-ridden slumber.

He could not tell if it were night or noon in the world without when he awakened; for the same stagnant darkness, unrelieved by ray or glimmer, brimmed the oubliette. Shivering, he became aware of a steady draft that blew upon him: a dank, unwholesome air, like the breath of unsunned vaults that had wakened into cryptic life and activity during his sleep. He had not noticed the draft heretofore; and his numb brain was startled into sudden hope by the intimation which it conveyed. Obviously there was some underground rift or channel through which the air entered; and this rift might somehow prove to be a place of egress from the oubliette.

Getting to his feet, he groped uncertainly forward in the direction of the draft. He stumbled over something that cracked and broke beneath his heels, and narrowly checked himself from falling on his face in the slimy, serpent-haunted pool. Before he could investigate the obstruction or resume his blind groping, he heard a harsh, grating noise above, and a wavering shaft of yellow light came down through the oubliette's opened mouth. Dazzled, he looked up and saw the round hole ten or twelve feet overhead, through which a dark hand had reached down with a flaring torch. A small basket, containing a loaf of coarse bread and a bottle of wine, was being lowered at the end of a cord.

Gaspard took the bread and wine, and the basket was drawn up. Before the withdrawal of the torch and the redepositing of the slab, he contrived to make a somewhat hasty but thorough survey of his dungeon.

The place was roughly circular, as he had surmised, and was perhaps fifteen feet in diameter. The thing over which he had stumbled was a human skeleton, lying half on the rubble-heap, half in the filthy water. It was brown and rotten with age, and its garments had long melted away in patches of liquid, running mould.

The walls were guttered and runneled by centuries of ooze, and their very stone, it seemed, was rotting slowly to decay. In the opposite side, at the bottom, he saw the opening he had suspected: a low mouth, not much bigger than a fox's hole, into which the sluggish water flowed. His heart sank at the sight; for, even if the water were deeper than it seemed, the hole was far too strait for the passage of a man's body. In a state of hopelessness that was like a veritable suffocation, he found his way back to the rubble-pile when the light had been withdrawn.

The loaf of bread and the bottle of wine were still in his hands. Mechanically, with dull, sodden hunger, he munched and drank. Afterwards, he felt stronger; and the sour, common wine served to warm him and perhaps helped to inspire him with the idea which he presently conceived.

Finishing the bottle, he found his way across the dungeon to the low, burrow-like hole. The entering air-current had strengthened, and this he took for a good omen. Drawing his dagger, he started to pick with the point at the half-rotten, decomposing wall, in an effort to enlarge the opening. He was forced to kneel in noisome silt; and the writhing coils of water-snakes, hissing frightfully, crawled across his legs as he worked. Evidently the hole was their means of ingress and egress, to and from the oubliette.

The stone crumbled readily beneath his dagger, and Gaspard forgot the horror and ghastliness of his situation in the hope of escape. He had no means of knowing the thickness of the wall, or the nature and extent of the subterranes that lay beyond; but he felt sure that there was some channel of connection with the outer air.

For hours or days, it seemed, he toiled with his dagger, digging blindly at the soft wall and removing the debris that splashed in the water beside him. After a while, prone on his belly, he crept into the hole he had enlarged; and burrowing like some laborious mole, he made his way onward inch by inch.

At last, to his prodigious relief, the dagger-point went through into empty space. He broke away with his hands the thin shell of obstructing stone that remained; then, crawling on in the darkness, he found that he could stand upright on a sort of shelving floor.

Straightening his cramped limbs, he moved on very cautiously. He was in a narrow vault or tunnel, whose sides he could touch simultaneously with his outstretched finger-tips. The floor was a downward incline; and the water deepened, rising to his knees and then to his waist. Probably the place had once been used as an underground exit from the castle; and the roof, falling in, had dammed the water.

More than a little dismayed, Gaspard began to wonder if he had exchanged the foul, skeleton-haunted oubliette for something even worse. The night around and before him was still untouched by any ray, and the air-current, though strong, was laden with a dankness and mouldiness as of interminable vaults.

Touching the tunnel-sides at intervals as he plunged hesitantly into the deepening water, he found a sharp angle, giving upon free space at his right. The space proved to be the mouth of an intersecting passage, whose flooded bottom was at least level and went no deeper into the stagnant foulness. Exploring it, he stumbled over the beginning of a flight of upward steps. Mounting these through the shoaling water, he soon found himself on dry stone.

The stairs, narrow, broken, irregular, without landings, appeared to wind in some eternal spiral that was coiled lightlessly about the bowels of Ylourgne. They were close and stifling as a tomb, and plainly they were not the source of the air-current which Gaspard had started to follow. Whither they would lead he knew not; nor could he tell if they were the same stairs by which he had been conducted to his dungeon. But he climbed steadily, pausing only at long intervals to regain his breath as best he could in the dead, mephitis-burdened air.

At length, in the solid darkness, far above, he began to hear a mysterious, muffled sound: a dull but recurrent crash as of mighty blocks and masses of falling stone. The sound was unspeakably ominous and dismal, and it seemed to shake the unfathomable walls around Gaspard, and to thrill with a sinister vibration in the steps on which he trod.

He climbed now with redoubled caution and alertness, stopping ever and anon to listen. The recurrent crashing noise grew louder, more ominous, as if it were immediately above; and the listener crouched on the dark stairs for a time that might have been many minutes, without daring to go further. At last, with disconcerting suddenness, the sound came to an end, leaving a strained and fearful stillness.

With many baleful conjectures, not knowing what fresh enormity he should find, Gaspard ventured to resume his climbing. Again, in the blank and solid stillness, he was met by a sound: the dim, reverberant chanting of voices, as in some Satanic mass or liturgy with dirge-like cadences that turned to intolerably soaring paeans of evil triumph. Long before he could recognize the words, he shivered at the strong malefic throbbing of the measured rhythm, whose fall and rise appeared somehow to correspond to the heartbeats of some colossal demon.

The stairs turned, for the hundredth time in their tortuous spiral; and coming forth from that long midnight, Gaspard blinked in the wan glimmering that streamed toward him from above. The choral voices met him in a more sonorous burst of infernal sound, and he knew the words for those of a rare and potent incantation, used by sorcerers for a supremely foul, supremely maleficent purpose. Affrightedly, as he climbed the last steps, he knew the thing that was taking place amid the ruins of Ylourgne.

Lifting his head warily above the castle floor, he saw that the stairs ended in a far corner of the vast room in which he had beheld Nathaire's unthinkable creation. The whole extent of the internally dismantled building lay before him, filled with a weird glare in which the beams of the slightly gibbous moon were mingled with the ruddy flames of dying athanors and the coiling, multi-colored tongues that rose from necromantic braziers.

Gaspard, for an instant, was puzzled by the flood of full moonlight amid the ruins. Then he saw that almost the whole inner wall of the castle, giving on the courtyard, had been removed. It was the tearing-down of the prodigious blocks, no doubt through an extrahuman labor levied by sorcery, that he had heard during his ascent from the subterrene vaults. His blood curdled, he felt an actual horripilation, as he realized the purpose for which the wall had been demolished.

It was evident that a whole day and part of another night had gone by since his immurement; for the moon rode high in the pale sapphire welkin. Bathed in its chilly glare, the huge vats no longer emitted their eerie and electric phosphorescence. The couch of Saracen fabrics, on which Gaspard had beheld the dying dwarf, was now half-hidden from view by the mounting fumes of braziers and thuribles, amid which the sorcerer's ten pupils, clad in sable and scarlet, were performing their hideous and repugnant rite, with its malefically measured litany.

Fearfully, as one who confronts an apparition reared up from nether hell, Gaspard beheld the colossus that lay inert as if in Cyclopean sleep on the castle flags. The thing was no longer a skeleton: the limbs were rounded into bossed, enormous thews, like the limbs of Biblical giants; the flanks were like an insuperable wall; the deltoids of the mighty chest were broad as platforms; the hands could have crushed the bodies of men like millstones.... *But the face of the stupendous monster, seen in profile athwart the pouring moon, was the face of the Satanic dwarf, Nathaire—remagnified a hundred times, but the same in its implacable madness and malevolence!*

The vast bosom seemed to rise and fall; and during a pause of the necromantic ritual, Gaspard heard the unmistakable sound of a mighty respiration. The eye in the profile was closed; but its lid appeared to tremble like a great curtain, as if the monster were about to awake; and the outflung hand, with fingers pale and bluish as a row of corpses, twitched unquietly on the cold flags.

An insupportable terror seized the watcher; but even this terror could not induce him to return to the noisome vaults he had left. With infinite hesitation and trepidation, he stole forth from the corner, keeping in a zone of ebon shadow that flanked the castle wall.

As he went, he saw for a moment, through bellying folds of vapor, the couch on which the shrunken form of Nathaire was lying pallid and motionless. It seemed that the dwarf was dead, or had fallen into a stupor preceding death. Then the choral voices, crying their dreadful incantation, rose higher in Satanic triumph; the vapors eddied like a hell-born cloud, coiling about the sorcerers in python-shaped volumes, and hiding again the Orient couch and its corpse-like occupant.

A thralldom of measureless evil oppressed the air. Gaspard felt that the awful transmigration, evoked and implored with ever-swelling, liturgic blasphemies, was about to take place—had perhaps already occurred. He thought that the breathing giant stirred, like one who tosses in light slumber.

Soon the towering, massively recumbent bulk was interposed between Gaspard and the chanting necromancers. They had not seen him; and he now dared to run swiftly, and gained the courtyard unpursued and unchallenged. Thence, without looking back, he fled like a devil-hunted thing upon the steep and chasm-riven slopes below Ylourgne.

7. THE COMING OF THE COLOSSUS

After the cessation of the exodus of liches, a universal terror still prevailed; a wide-flung shadow of apprehension, infernal and funereal, lay stagnantly on Averiogne. There were strange and disastrous portents in the aspect of the skies: flame-bearded meteors had been seen to fall beyond the eastern hills; a comet, far in the south, had swept the stars with its luminous besom for a few nights, and had then faded, leaving among men the prophecy of bale and pestilence to come. By day the air was oppressed and sultry, and the blue heavens were heated as if by whitish fires. Clouds of thunder, darkling and withdrawn, shook their fulgurant lances on the far horizons, like some beleaguering Titan army. A murrain, such as would come from the working of wizard spells, was abroad among the cattle. All these signs and prodigies were an added heaviness on the burdened spirits of men, who went to and fro in daily fear of the hidden preparations and machinations of hell.

But, until the actual breaking-forth of the incubated menace, there was no one, save Gaspard du Nord, who had knowledge of its veritable form. And Gaspard, fleeing headlong beneath the gibbous moon toward Vyônes, and fearing to hear the tread of a colossal pursuer at any moment, had thought it more than useless to give warning in such towns and villages as lay upon his line of flight. Where, indeed—even if warned—could men hope to hide themselves from the awful thing, begotten by Hell on the ravished charnel, that would walk forth like the Anakim to visit its roaring wrath on a trampled world?

So, all that night, and throughout the day that followed, Gaspard du Nord, with the dried slime of the oubliette on his briar-shredded raiment, plunged like a madman through the towering woods that were haunted by robbers and werewolves. The westward-falling moon flickered in his eyes betwixt the gnarled, somber boles as he ran; and the dawn overtook him with the pale shafts of its searching arrows. The moon poured over him its white sultriness, like furnace-heated metal sublimed into light; and the clotted filth that clung to his tatters was again turned into slime by his own sweat. But still he pursued his nightmare-harried way, while a vague, seemingly hopeless plan took form in his mind.

In the interim, several monks of the Cistercian brotherhood, watching the grey walls of Ylourgne at early dawn with their habitual vigilance, were the first, after Gaspard, to behold the monstrous horror created by the necromancers. Their account of its epiphany may have been somewhat tinged by a pious exaggeration; but they swore that the giant rose abruptly, standing more than waist-high above the ruins of the barbican, amid a sudden leaping of long-tongued fires and a swirling of pitchy fumes erupted from Malebolge. The giant's head was level with the high top of the donjon, and his right arm, outthrust, lay like a bar of stormy cloud athwart the new-risen sun.

The monks fell grovelling to their knees, thinking that the Archfoe himself had come forth, using Ylourgne for his gateway from the Pit. Then, across the mile-wide valley, they heard a thunderous peal of demoniac laughter; and the giant, climbing over the mounded barbican at a single step, began to descend the scarped and craggy hill.

When he drew nearer, bounding from slope to slope, his features were manifestly those of some great devil animated with ire and malice toward the sons of Adam. His hair, in matted locks, streamed behind him like a mass of black pythons; his naked skin was livid and pale and cadaverous, like the skin of the dead; but beneath it, the stupendous thews of a Titan swelled and rippled. The eyes, wide and glaring, flamed like lidless cauldrons heated by the fires of the unplumbed Pit.

The rumor of his coming passed like a gale of terror through the monastery. Many of the brothers, deeming discretion the better part of religious fervor, hid themselves in the stone-hewn cellars and vaults. Others crouched in their cells, mumbling and shrieking incoherent pleas to all the Saints. Still others, the most courageous, repaired in a body to the chapel and knelt in solemn prayer before the wooden Christ on the great crucifix.

Bernard and Stéphane, now somewhat recovered from their grievous beating, alone dared to watch the advance of the giant. Their horror was inexpressibly increased when they began to recognize in the colossal features a magnified likeness to the lineaments of that evil dwarf who had presided over the dark, unhallowed activities of Ylourgne; and the laughter of the colossus, as he came down the valley, was like a tempest-borne echo of the damnable cachinnation that had followed their ignominious flight from the haunted stronghold. To Bernard and Stéphane, however, it seemed merely that the dwarf, who was no doubt an actual demon, had chosen to appear in his natural form.

Pausing in the valley-bottom, the giant stood opposite the monastery with his flame-filled eyes on a level with the window from which Bernard and Sté-phane were peering. He laughed again—an awful laugh, like a subterranean rumbling—and then, stooping, he picked up a handful of boulders as if they had been mere pebbles, and proceeded to pelt the monastery. The boulders crashed against the walls, as if hurled from great catapults or mangonels of war; but the stout building held, though shaken grievously.

Then, with both hands, the colossus tore loose an immense rock that was deeply embedded in the hill-side; and lifting this rock, he flung it at the stubborn walls. The tremendous mass broke in an entire side of the chapel; and those who had gathered therein were found later, crushed into bloody pulp amid the splinters of their carven Christ.

After that, as if disdaining to palter any further with a prey so insignificant, the colossus turned his back on the little monastery, and like some fiend-born Goliath, went roaring down the valley into Averoigne.

As he departed, Bernard and Stéphane, still watching from their window, saw a thing they had not perceived heretofore: a huge basket made of planking, that hung suspended by ropes between the giant's shoulders. In the basket, ten men—the pupils and assistants of Nathaire—were being carried like so many dolls or puppets in a peddler's pack.

Of the subsequent wanderings and depredations of the colossus, a hundred legends were long current throughout Averoigne: tales of an unexampled ghastliness, a wanton diabolism without parallel in all the histories of that demon-pestered land.

The goatherds of the hills below Ylourgne saw him coming, and fled with their nimble-footed flocks to the highest ridges. To these he paid little heed, merely trampling them down like beetles when they could not escape from his path. Following the hill-stream that was the source of the river Isoile, he came to the verge of the great forest; and here, it is related, he tore up a towering ancient pine by the roots, and snapping off the mighty boughs with his hands, shaped it into a cudgel which he carried henceforward.

With this cudgel, heavier than a battering-ram, he pounded into shapeless ruin a wayside shrine in the outer woods. A hamlet fell in his way, and he strode through it, beating in the roofs, toppling the walls, and crushing the inhabitants beneath his feet.

To and fro in a mad frenzy of destruction, like a death-drunken Cyclops, he wandered all that day. Even the fierce beasts of the woodland ran from him in fear. The wolves, in mid-hunt, abandoned their quarry and retired, howling dismally with terror, to their rocky dens. The black, savage hunting-dogs of the forest barons would not face him, and hid whimpering in their kennels.

Men heard his mighty laughter, his stormy bellowing; they saw his approach from a distance of many leagues, and fled or concealed themselves as best they could. The lords of moated castles called in their men-at-arms, drew up their drawbridges and prepared as if for the siege of an army. The peasants hid themselves in caverns, in cellars, in old wells, and even beneath hay-mounds, hoping that he would pass them by unnoticed. The churches were crammed with refugees who sought protection of the Cross, deeming that Satan himself, or one of his chief lieutenants, had risen to harry and lay waste the land.

In a voice like summer thunder, mad maledictions, unthinkable obscenities and blasphemies were uttered ceaselessly by the giant as he went to and fro. Men heard him address the litter of black-clad figures that he carried on his back, in tones of admonishment or demonstration such as a master would use to his pupils. People who had known Nathaire recognized the incredible likeness of the huge features, the similarity of the swollen voice, to his. A rumor went abroad that the dwarf sorcerer, through his loathly bond with the Adversary, had been permitted to transfer his hateful soul into this Titanic form; and, bearing his pupils with him, had returned to vent an insatiable ire, a bottomless rancor, on the world that had mocked him for his puny physique and reviled him for his sorcery. The charnel genesis of the monstrous avatar was also rumored; and, indeed, it was said that the colossus had openly proclaimed his identity.

It would be tedious to make explicit mention of all the enormities, all the atrocities, that were ascribed to the marauding giant…. There were people—mostly priests and women, it is told—whom he picked up as they fled, and pulled limb from limb as a child might quarter an insect…. And there were worse things, not to be named in this record….

Many eye-witnesses told how he hunted Pierre, the Lord of La Frênaie, who had gone forth with his dogs and men to chase a noble stag in the nearby forest. Overtaking horse and rider, he caught them with one hand, and bearing them aloft as he strode over the tree-tops, he hurled them later against the granite walls of the Château of La Frênaie in passing. Then, catching the red stag that Pierre had hunted, he flung it after them; and the huge bloody blotches made by the impact of the pashed bodies remained long on the castle stone, and were never wholly washed away by the autumn rains and the winter snows.

Countless tales were told, also, of the deeds of obscene sacrilege and profanation committed by the colossus: of the wooden Virgin that he flung into the Isoile above Ximes, lashed with human gut to the rotting, mail-clad body of an infamous outlaw; of the wormy corpses that he dug with his hands from unconsecrated graves and hurled into the courtyard of the Benedictine abbey of Périgon; of the Church of Ste. Zénobie, which he buried with its priests and congregation beneath a mountain of ordure made by the gathering of all the dungheaps from neighboring farms.

8. THE LAYING OF THE COLOSSUS

Back and forth, in an irregular, drunken, zig-zag course, from end to end and side to side of the harried realm, the giant strode without pause, like an energumen possessed by some implacable fiend of mischief and murder, leaving behind him, as a reaper leaves his swath, an ever-lengthening zone of havoc, of rapine and carnage. And when the sun, blackened by the smoke of burning villages, had set luridly beyond the forest, men still saw him moving in the dusk, and heard still the portentous rumbling of his mad, stormy cachinnation.

Nearing the gates of Vyônes at sunset, Gaspard du Nord saw behind him, through gaps in the ancient wood, the far-off head and shoulders of the terrible colossus, who moved along the Isoile, stooping from sight at intervals in some horrid deed.

Though numb with weariness and exhaustion, Gaspard quickened his flight. He did not believe, however, that the monster would try to invade Vyônes, the especial object of Nathaire's hatred and malice, before the following day. The evil soul of the sorcerous dwarf, exulting in its almost infinite capacity for harm and destruction, would defer the crowning act of vengeance, and would continue to terrorize, during the night, the outlying villages and rural districts.

In spite of his rags and filth, which rendered him practically unrecognizable and gave him a most disreputable air, Gaspard was admitted without question by the guards at the city gate. Vyônes was already thronged with people who had fled to the sanctuary of its stout walls from the adjacent country-side; and no one, not even of the most dubious character, was denied admittance. The walls were lined with archers and pike-bearers, gathered in readiness to dispute the entrance of the giant. Cross-bowmen were stationed above the gates, and mangonels were mounted at short intervals along the entire circuit of the ramparts. The city seethed and hummed like an agitated hive.

Hysteria and pandemonium prevailed in the streets. Pale, panic-stricken faces milled everywhere in an aimless stream. Hurrying torches flared dolorously in the twilight that deepened as if with the shadow of impending wings arisen from Erebus. The gloom was clogged with intangible fear, with webs of stifling oppression. Through all this rout of wild disorder and frenzy, Gaspard, like a spent but indomitable swimmer breasting some tide of eternal, viscid nightmare, made his way slowly to his attic lodgings.

Afterwards, he could scarcely remember eating and drinking. Overworn beyond the limit of bodily and spiritual endurance, he threw himself down on his pallet without removing his ooze-stiffened tatters, and slept soddenly till an hour halfway between midnight and dawn.

He awoke with the death-pale beams of the gibbous moon shining upon him through his window; and rising, spent the balance of the night in making certain occult preparations which, he felt, offered the only possibility of coping with the fiendish monster that had been created and animated by Nathaire.

Working feverishly by the light of the westering moon and a single dim taper, Gaspard assembled various ingredients of familiar alchemic use which he possessed, and compounded from these, through a long and somewhat cabbalistic process, a dark-grey powder which he had seen employed by Nathaire on numerous occasions. He had reasoned that the colossus, being formed from the bones and flesh of dead men unlawfully raised up, and energized only by the soul of a dead sorcerer, would be subject to the influence of this powder, which Nathaire had used for the laying of resurrected liches. The powder, if cast in the nostrils of such cadavers, would cause them to return peacefully to their tombs and lie down in a renewed slumber of death.

Gaspard made a considerable quantity of the mixture, arguing that no mere finger-pinch would suffice for the lulling of the gigantic charnel monstrosity. His guttering yellow candle was dimmed by the white dawn as he ended the Latin formula of fearsome verbal invocation from which the compound would derive much of its efficacy. The formula, which called for the cooperation of Alastor and other evil spirits, he used with unwillingness. But he knew that there was no alternative: sorcery could be fought only with sorcery.

Morning came with new terrors to Vyônes. Gaspard had felt, through a sort of intuition, that the vengeful colossus, who was said to have wandered with unhuman tirelessness and diabolic energy all night through Averoigne, would approach the hated city early in the day. His intuition was confirmed; for, scarcely had he finished his occult labors, when he heard a mounting hubbub in the streets, and above the shrill, dismal clamor of frightened voices, the far-off roaring of the giant.

Gaspard knew that he must lose no time, if he were to post himself in a place of vantage from which he could throw his powder into the nostrils of the hundred-foot colossus. The city walls, and even most of the church spires, were not lofty enough for this purpose; and a brief reflection told him that the great cathedral, standing at the core of Vyônes, was the one place from whose roof he could front the invader with success. He felt sure that the men-at-arms on the walls could do little to prevent the monster from entering and wreaking his malevolent will. No earthly weapon could injure a being of such bulk and nature; for even a cadaver of normal size, reared up in this fashion, could be shot full of arrows or transfixed by a dozen pikes without retarding its progress.

Hastily he filled a huge leathern pouch with the powder; and carrying the pouch at his belt, he joined the agitated press of people in the street. Many were fleeing toward the cathedral, to seek the shelter of its august sanctity; and he had only to let himself be borne along by the frenzy-driven stream.

The cathedral nave was packed with worshippers, and solemn masses were being said by priests whose voices faltered at times with inward panic. Unheeded by the wan, despairing throng, Gaspard found a flight of coiling stairs that led tortuously to the gargoyle-warded roof of the high tower.

Here he posted himself, crouching behind the stone figure of a cat-headed griffin. From his vantage he could see, beyond the crowded spires and gables, the approaching giant, whose head and torso loomed above the city walls. A cloud of arrows, visible even at that distance, rose to meet the monster, who apparently did not even pause to pluck them from his hide. Great boulders hurled from mangonels were no more to him than a pelting of gravel; the heavy bolts of arbalists, embedded in his flesh, were mere slivers.

Nothing could stay his advance. The tiny figures of a company of pikemen, who opposed him with outthrust weapons, were swept from the wall above the eastern gate by a single sidelong blow of the seventy-foot pine that he bore for a cudgel. Then, having cleared the wall, the colossus climbed over it into Vyônes.

Roaring, chuckling, laughing like a maniacal Cyclops, he strode along the narrow streets between houses that rose only to his waist, trampling without mercy everyone who could not escape in time, and smashing in the roofs with stupendous blows of his bludgeon. With a push of his left hand, he broke off the protruding gables, and overturned the church steeples with their bells clanging in dolorous alarm as they went down. A woeful shrieking and wailing of hysteria-laden voices accompanied his passing.

Straight toward the cathedral he came, as Gaspard had calculated, feeling that the high edifice would be made the special butt of his malevolence.

The streets were now emptied of people; but, as if to hunt them out and crush them in their hiding places, the giant thrust his cudgel like a battering-ram through walls and windows and doors as he went by. The ruin and havoc that he left were indescribable.

Soon he loomed opposite the cathedral tower on which Gaspard waited behind the gargoyle. His head was level with the tower, and his eyes flamed like unfathomable wells of burning brimstone as he drew near. His lips were parted over stalactitic fangs in a hateful snarl; and he cried out in a voice like the rumbling of articulate thunder:

"Ho! ye puling priests and devotees of a powerless God! *Come forth and bow to Nathaire the master, before he sweeps you into limbo!"*

It was then that Gaspard, with a hardihood beyond comparison, rose from his hiding place and stood in full view of the raging colossus.

"Draw nearer, Nathaire, if indeed it be you, foul robber of tombs and charnels," he taunted. "Come close, for I would hold speech with you."

A monstrous look of astonishment dimmed the diabolic rage on the colossal features. Peering at Gaspard as if in doubt or incredulity, the giant lowered his lifted cudgel and stepped close to the tower, till his face was only a few feet from the intrepid student. Then, when he had apparently convinced himself of Gaspard's identity, the look of maniacal wrath returned, flooding his eyes with Tartarean fire and twisting his lineaments into a mask of Apollyon-like malignity. His left arm came up in a prodigious arc, with twitching fingers that poised horribly above the head of the youth, casting upon him a vulture-black shadow in the full-risen sun. Gaspard saw the white, startled faces of the necromancer's pupils, peering over his shoulder from their plank-built basket.

"Is it you, Gaspard, my recreant pupil?" the colossus roared stormily. "I thought you were rotting in the oubliette beneath Ylourgne—and now I find you perched atop of this accursed cathedral which I am about to demolish!... You had been far wiser to remain where I left you, my good Gaspard."

His breath, as he spoke, blew like a charnel-polluted gale on the student. His vast fingers, with blackened nails like shovel-blades, hovered in ogreish menace. Gaspard had furtively loosened his leathern pouch that hung at his belt, and untied its mouth. Now, as the twitching fingers descended toward him, he emptied the contents of the pouch in the giant's face, and the fine powder, mounting in a dark-grey cloud, obscured the snarling lips and palpitating nostrils from his view.

Anxiously, he watched the effect, fearing that the powder might be useless after all, against the superior arts and Satanical resources of Nathaire. But miraculously, as it seemed, the evil lambence died in the pit-deep eyes, as the monster inhaled the flying cloud. His lifted hand, narrowly missing the crouching youth in its sweep, fell lifelessly at his side. The anger was erased from the mighty, contorted mask, as if from the face of a dead man; the great cudgel fell with a crash to the empty street; and then, with drowsy, lurching steps and listless, hanging arms, the giant turned his back to the cathedral and retraced his way through the devastated city.

He muttered dreamily to himself as he went; and people who heard him swore that the voice was no longer the awful, thunder-swollen voice of Nathaire, but the tones and accents of a multitude of men, amid which the voices of certain of the ravished dead were recognizable. And the voice of Nathaire himself, no louder now than in life, was heard at intervals through the manifold mutterings, as if protesting angrily.

Climbing the eastern wall as it had come, the colossus went to and fro for many hours, no longer wreaking a hellish wrath and rancor, but searching, as people thought, for the various tombs and graves from which the hundreds of bodies that composed it had been so foully reft. From charnel to charnel, from cemetery to cemetery it went, through all the land; but there was no grave anywhere in which the dead colossus could lie down.

Then, toward evening, men saw it from afar on the red rim of the sky, digging with its hands in the soft, loamy plain beside the river Isoile. There, in a monstrous and self-made grave, the colossus laid itself down, and did not rise again. The ten pupils of Nathaire, it was believed, unable to descend from their basket, were crushed beneath the mighty body; for none of them was ever seen thereafter.

For many days no one dared to approach the place where the corpse lay uncovered in its self-dug grave. And so the thing rotted prodigiously beneath the summer sun, breeding an almighty stench that wrought pestilence in that portion of Averoigne. And they who ventured to go near in the following autumn, when the stench had lessened greatly, swore that the voice of Nathaire, still protesting angrily, was heard by them to issue from the enormous, rook-haunted bulk.

Of Gaspard du Nord, who had been the savior of the province, it was related that he lived in much honor to a ripe age, being the one sorcerer of that region who at no time incurred the disapprobation of the Church.

THE GOD OF THE ASTEROID

Man's conquest of the interplanetary gulfs has been fraught with many tragedies. Vessel after vessel, like a venturous mote, has disappeared in the infinite—and has not returned. Inevitably, for the most part, the lost explorers have left no record of their fate. Their ships have flared as unknown meteors through the atmosphere of the further planets, to fall like shapeless metal cinders on a never-visited terrain; or have become the dead, frozen satellites of other worlds or moons. A few, perhaps, among the unreturning fliers, have succeeded in landing somewhere, and their crews have perished immediately, or survived for a little while amid the inconceivably hostile environment of a cosmos not designed for men.

In later years, with the progress of exploration, more than one of the early derelicts has been descried, following its solitary orbit; and the wrecks of others have been found on ultra-terrene shores. Occasionally—not often—it has been possible to reconstruct the details of the lone, remote disaster. Sometimes, in a fused and twisted hull, a log or record has been preserved intact. Among others, there is the case of the *Selenite*, the first known rocket-ship to dare the zone of the asteroids.

At the time of its disappearance, fifty years ago, in 1980, a dozen voyages had been made to Mars, and a rocket-base had been established in Syrtis Major, with a small permanent colony of terrestrials, all of whom were trained scientists as well as men of uncommon hardihood and physical stamina.

The effects of the Martian climate, and the utter alienation from familiar conditions, as might have been expected, were extremely trying and even disastrous. There was an unremitting struggle with deadly or pestiferous bacteria new to science, a perpetual assailment by dangerous radiations of soil and air and sun. The lessened gravity played its part also, in contributing to curious and profound disturbances of metabolism. The worst effects were nervous and mental. Queer, irrational animosities, manias or phobias never classified by alienists, began to develop among the personnel at the rocket-base.

Violent quarrels broke out between men who were normally controlled and urbane. The party, numbering fifteen in all, soon divided into several cliques, one against the others; and this morbid antagonism led at times to actual fighting and even bloodshed.

One of the cliques consisted of three men, Roger Colt, Phil Gershom and Edmond Beverly. These three, through banding together in a curious fashion, became intolerably antisocial toward all the others. It would seem that they must have gone close to the borderline of insanity, and were subject to actual delusions. At any rate, they conceived the idea that Mars, with its fifteen earth-men, was entirely too crowded. Voicing this idea in a most offensive and belligerent manner, they also began to hint their intention of faring even further afield in space.

Their hints were not taken seriously by the others, since a crew of three was insufficient for the proper manning of even the lightest rocket-vessel used at that time. Colt, Gershom, and Beverly had no difficulty at all in stealing the *Selenite*, the smaller of the two ships then reposing at the Syrtis Major base. Their fellow-colonists were aroused one night by the cannon-like roar of the discharging tubes, and emerged from their huts of sheet-iron in time to see the vessel departing in a fiery streak toward Jupiter.

No attempt was made to follow it; but the incident helped to sober the remaining twelve and to calm their unnatural animosities. It was believed, from certain remarks that the malcontents had let drop, that their particular objective was Ganymede or Europa, both of which were thought to possess an atmosphere suitable for human respiration. It seemed very doubtful, however, that they could pass the perilous belt of the asteroids. Apart from the difficulty of steering a course amid these innumerable, far-strewn bodies, the *Selenite* was not fuelled or provisioned for a voyage of such length. Gershom, Colt and Beverly, in their mad haste to quit the company of the others, had forgotten to calculate the actual necessities of their proposed voyage, and had wholly overlooked its dangers.

After that departing flash on the Martian skies, the *Selenite* was not seen again; and its fate remained a mystery for thirty years. Then, on tiny, remote Phocea, its dented wreck was found by the Holdane expedition to the asteroids.

Phocea, at the time of the expedition's visit, was in aphelion. Like others of the planetoids, it was discovered to possess a rare atmosphere, too thin for human breathing. Both hemispheres were covered with thin snow; and lying amid this snow, the *Selenite* was sighted by the explorers as they circled about the little world.

Much interest prevailed, for the shape of the partially bare mound was plainly recognizable and not to be confused with the surrounding rocks.

Holdane ordered a landing, and several men in space-suits proceeded to examine the wreck. They soon identified it as the long-missing *Selenite*.

Peering in through one of the thick, unbreakable neo-crystal ports, they met the eyeless gaze of a human skeleton, which had fallen forward against the slanting, overhanging wall. It seemed to grin a sardonic welcome. The vessel's hull was partly buried in the stony soil, and had been crumpled and even slightly fused, though not broken, by its plunge. The manhole lid was so thoroughly jammed and soldered that it was impossible to effect an entrance without the use of a cutting-torch.

Enormous, withered, cryptogamous plants with the habit of vines, that crumbled at a touch, were clinging to the hull and the adjacent rocks. In the light snow beneath the skeleton-guarded port, a number of sharded bodies were lying, which proved to be those of tall insect forms, like giant *phasmidae*. From the posture and arrangement of their lank, pipy members, longer than those of a man, it seemed that they had walked erect. They were unimaginably grotesque, and their composition, due to the almost non-existent gravity, was fantastically porous and insubstantial. Many more bodies, of a similar type, were afterwards found on other portions of the planetoid; but no living thing was discovered. All life, it was plain, had perished in the trans-arctic winter of Phocea's aphelion.

When the *Selenite* had been entered, the party learned, from a sort of log or notebook found on the floor, that the skeleton was all that remained of Edmond Beverly. There was no trace of his two companions; but the log, on examination, proved to contain a record of their fate as well as the subsequent adventures of Beverly almost to the very moment of his own death from a doubtful, unexplained cause.

The tale was a strange and tragic one. Beverly, it would seem, had written it day by day, after the departure from Syrtis Major, in an effort to retain a semblance of morale and mental coherence amid the black alienation and disorientation of infinitude. I transcribe it herewith, omitting only the earlier passages, which were full of unimportant details and personal animadversions. The first entries were all dated, and Beverly had made an heroic attempt to measure and mark off the seasonless night of the void in terms of earthly time. But after the disastrous landing on Phocea, he had abandoned this; and the actual length of time covered by his entries can only be conjectured.

THE LOG

S ept. 10th. Mars is only a pale-red star through our rear ports; and according to my calculations we will soon approach the orbit of the nearer asteroids. Jupiter and its system of moons are seemingly as far off as ever, like beacons on the unattainable shore of immensity. More even than at first, I feel that dreadful, suffocating illusion, which accompanies ether-travel, of being perfectly stationary in a static void.

Gershom, however, complains of a disturbance of equilibrium, with much vertigo and a frequent sense of falling, as if the vessel were sinking beneath him through bottomless space at a headlong speed. The causation of such symptoms is rather obscure, since the artificial gravity regulators are in good working-order. Colt and I have not suffered from any similar disturbance. It seems to me that the sense of falling would be almost a relief from this illusion of nightmare immobility; but Gershom appears to be greatly distressed by it, and says that his hallucination is growing stronger, with fewer and briefer intervals of normality. He fears that it will become continuous.

Sept. 11th. Colt has made an estimate of our fuel and provisions and thinks that with careful husbandry we will be able to reach Europa. I have been checking up on his calculations, and find that he is altogether too sanguine. According to my estimate, the fuel will give out while we are still midway in the belt of asteroids; though the food, water and compressed air would possibly take us most of the way to Europa. This discovery I must conceal from the others. It is too late to turn back. I wonder if we have all been mad, to start out on this errant voyage into cosmical immensity with no real preparation or thought of consequences. Colt, it would seem, has lost even the power of mathematical calculation: his figurings are full of the most egregious errors.

Gershom has been unable to sleep, and is not even fit to take his turn at the watch. The hallucination of falling obsesses him perpetually, and he cries out in terror, thinking that the vessel is about to crash on some dark, unknown planet to which it is being drawn by an irresistible gravitation. Eating, drinking and locomotion are very difficult for him, and he complains that he cannot even draw a full breath—that the air is snatched away from him in his precipitate descent. His condition is indeed painful and pitiable.

Sept. 12th. Gershom is worse—bromide of potassium and even a heavy dose of morphine from the *Selenite*'s medicine lockers, have not relieved him or enabled him to sleep. He has the look of a drowning man and seems to be on the point of strangulation. It is hard for him to speak.

Colt has become very morose and sullen, and snarls at me when I address him. I think that Gershom's plight has preyed sorely upon his nerves—as it has on mine. But my burden is heavier than Colt's: for I know the inevitable doom of our insane and ill-starred expedition. Sometimes I wish it were all over…. The hells of the human mind are vaster than space, darker than the night between the worlds… and all three of us have spent several eternities in hell. Our attempt to flee has only plunged us into a black and shoreless limbo, through which we are fated to carry still our own private perdition.

I, too, like Gershom, have been unable to sleep. But, unlike him, I am tormented by the illusion of eternal immobility. In spite of the daily calculations that assure me of our progress through the gulf, I cannot convince myself that we have moved at all. It seems to me that we hang suspended like Mohammed's coffin, remote from earth and equally remote from the stars, in an incommensurable vastness without bourn or direction. I cannot describe the awfulness of the feeling.

Sept. 13th. During my watch, Colt opened the medicine locker and managed to shoot himself full of morphine. When his turn came, he was in a stupor and I could do nothing to rouse him. Gershom had gotten steadily worse and seemed to be enduring a thousand deaths... so there was nothing for me to do but keep on with the watch as long as I could. I locked the controls, anyway, so that the vessel would continue its course without human guidance if I should fall asleep.

I don't know how long I kept awake—nor how long I slept. I was aroused by a queer hissing whose nature and cause I could not identify at first. I looked around and saw that Colt was in his hammock, still lying in a drug-induced sopor. Then I saw that Gershom was gone, and began to realize that the hissing came from the air-lock. The inner door of the lock was closed securely—but evidently someone had opened the outer manhole, and the sound was being made by the escaping air. It grew fainter and ceased as I listened.

I knew then what had happened—Gershom, unable to endure his strange hallucination any longer, had actually flung himself into space from the *Selenite!* Going to the rear ports, I saw his body, with a pale, slightly bloated face and open, bulging eyes. It was following us like a satellite, keeping an even distance of ten or twelve feet from the lee of the vessel's stern. I could have gone out in a space suit to retrieve the body; but I felt sure that Gershom was already dead, and the effort seemed more than useless. Since there was no leakage of air from the interior, I did not even try to close the manhole.

I hope and pray that Gershom is at peace. He will float forever in cosmic space—and in that further void where the torment of human consciousness can never follow.

Sept. 15th. We have kept our course somehow, though Colt is too demoralized and drug-sodden to be of much assistance. I pity him when the limited supply of morphine gives out.

Gershom's body is still following us, held by the slight power of the vessel's gravitational attraction. It seems to terrify Colt in his more lucid moments; and he complains that we are being haunted by the dead man. It's bad enough for me, too, and I wonder how much my nerves and mind will stand. Sometimes I think that I am beginning to develop the delusion that tortured Gershom and drove him to his death. An awful dizziness assails me, and I fear that I shall start to fall. But somehow I regain my equilibrium.

S ept. 16th. Colt used up all the morphine, and began to show signs of intense depression and uncontrollable nervousness. His fear of the satellite corpse appeared to grow upon him like an obsession; and I could do nothing to reassure him. His terror was deepened by an eerie, superstitious belief.

"I tell you, I hear Gershom calling us," he cried. "He wants company, out there in the black, frozen emptiness; and he won't leave the vessel till one of us goes out to join him. You've got to go, Beverly—it's either you or me—otherwise he'll follow the *Selenite* forever."

I tried to reason with him, but in vain. He turned upon me in a sudden shift of maniacal rage.

"Damn you, I'll throw you out, if you won't go any other way!" he shrieked.

Clawing and mouthing like a mad beast, he leapt toward me where I sat before the *Selenite*'s control-board. I was almost overborne by his onset, for he fought with a wild and frantic strength.... I don't like to write down all that happened, for the mere recollection makes me sick.... Finally he got me by the throat, with a sharp-nailed clutch that I could not loosen, and began to choke me to death. In self-defense, I had to shoot him with an automatic which I carried in my pocket. Reeling dizzily, gasping for breath, I found myself staring down at his prostrate body, from which a crimson puddle was widening on the floor.

Somehow, I managed to put on a space-suit. Dragging Colt by the ankles, I got him to the inner door of the air-lock. When I opened the door, the escaping air hurled me toward the open manhole together with the corpse; and it was hard to regain my footing and avoid being carried through into space. Colt's body, turning transversely in its movement, was jammed across the manhole; and I had to thrust it out with my hands. Then I closed the lid after it. When I returned to the ship's interior, I saw it floating, pale and bloated, beside the corpse of Gershom.

S ept. 17th. I am alone—and yet most horribly I am pursued and companioned by the dead men. I have sought to concentrate my faculties on the hopeless problem of survival, on the exigencies of space navigation; but it is all useless. Ever I am aware of those stiff and swollen bodies, swimming in the awful silence of the void, with the white, airless sun like a leprosy of light on their upturned faces. I try to keep my eyes on the control-board— on the astronomic charts—on the log I am writing—on the stars toward which I am travelling. But a frightful and irresistible magnetism makes me turn at intervals, mechanically, helplessly, to the rearward ports. There are no words for what I feel and think—and words are as lost things along with the worlds I have left so far behind. I sink in a chaos of vertiginous horror, beyond all possibility of return.

S ept. 18th. I am entering the zone of the asteroids—those desert rocks, fragmentary and amorphous, that whirl in far-scattered array between Mars and Jupiter. Today the *Selenite* passed very close to one of them—a small body like a broken-off mountain, which heaved suddenly from the gulf with knife-sharp pinnacles and black gullies that seemed to cleave its very heart. The *Selenite* would have crashed full upon it in a few instants, if I had not reversed the power and steered in an abrupt diagonal to the right. As it was, I passed near enough for the bodies of Colt and Gershom to be caught by the gravitational pull of the planetoid; and when I looked back at the receding rock, after the vessel was out of danger, they had disappeared from sight. Finally I located them with the telescopic reflector, and saw that they were revolving in space, like infinitesimal moons, about that awful, naked asteroid. Perhaps they will float thus forever, or will drift gradually down in lessening circles, to find a tomb in one of those bleak, bottomless ravines.

S ept. 19th. I have passed several more of the asteroids—irregular fragments, little larger than meteoric stones; and all my skill of spacemanship has been taxed severely to avert collision. Because of the need for unrelaxing vigilance, I have been compelled to keep awake at all times. But sooner or later, sleep will overpower me, and the *Selenite* will crash to destruction.

After all, it matters little: the end is inevitable, and must come soon enough in any case. The store of concentrated food, the tanks of compressed oxygen, might keep me alive for many months, since there is no one but myself to consume them. But the fuel is almost gone, as I know from my former calculations. At any moment, the propulsion may cease. Then the vessel will drift idly and helplessly in this cosmic limbo, and be drawn to its doom on some asteroidal reef.

S ep. 21st (?). Everything I have expected has happened, and yet by some miracle of chance—or mischance—I am still alive.

The fuel gave out yesterday (at least I think it was yesterday). But I was too close to the nadir of physical and mental exhaustion to realize clearly that the rocket-explosions had ceased. I was dead for want of sleep, and had gotten into a state beyond hope or despair. Dimly I remember setting the vessel's controls through automatic force of habit; and then I lashed myself in my hammock and fell asleep instantly.

I have no means of guessing how long I slept. Vaguely, in the gulf beyond dreams, I heard a crash as of far-off thunder, and felt a violent vibration that jarred me into dull wakefulness. A sensation of unnatural, sweltering heat began to oppress me as I struggled toward consciousness; but when I had opened my heavy eyes, I was unable to determine for some little time what had really happened.

Twisting my head so that I could peer out through one of the ports, I was startled to see, on a purple-black sky, an icy, glittering horizon of saw-edged rocks.

For an instant, I thought that the vessel was about to strike on some looming planetoid. Then, overwhelmingly, I realized *that the crash had already occurred*—that I had been awakened from my coma-like slumber by the falling of the *Selenite* upon one of those barren cosmic islets.

I was wide-awake now, and I hastened to unlash myself from the hammock. I found that the floor was pitched sharply, as if the *Selenite* had landed on a slope or had buried its nose in the alien terrain. Feeling a queer, disconcerting lightness, and barely able to re-establish my feet on the floor at each step, I made my way to the nearest port. It was plain that the artificial gravity-system of the flier had been thrown out of commission by the crash, and that I was now subject only to the feeble gravitation of the asteroid. It seemed to me that I was light and incorporeal as a cloud—that I was no more than the airy specter of my former self.

The floor and walls were strangely hot; and it came to me that the heating must have been caused by the passage of the vessel through some sort of atmosphere. The asteroid, then, was not wholly airless, as such bodies are commonly supposed to be; and probably it was one of the larger fragments, with a diameter of many miles—perhaps hundreds. But even this realization failed to prepare me for the weird and surprising scene upon which I gazed through the port.

The horizon of serrate peaks, like a miniature mountain-range, lay at a distance of several hundred yards. Above it, the small, intensely brilliant sun, like a fiery moon in its magnitude, was sinking with visible rapidity in the dark sky that revealed the major stars and planets.

The *Selenite* had plunged into a shallow valley, and had half-buried its prow and bottom in a soil that was formed by decomposing rock, mainly basaltic. All about were fretted ridges, guttering pillars and pinnacles; and over these, amazingly, there clambered frail, pipy, leafless vines with broad, yellow-green tendrils flat and thin as paper. Insubstantial-looking lichens, taller than a man, and having the form of flat antlers, grew in single rows and thickets along the valley beside rills of water like molten moonstone.

Between the thickets, I saw the approach of certain living creatures who rose from behind the middle rocks with the suddenness and lightness of leaping insects. They seemed to skim the ground with long, flying steps that were both easy and abrupt.

There were five of these beings, who, no doubt, had been attracted by the fall of the *Selenite* from space and were coming to inspect it. In a few moments, they neared the vessel and paused before it with the same effortless ease that had marked all their movements.

What they really were, I do not know; but for want of other analogies, I must liken them to insects. Standing perfectly erect, they towered seven feet in air. Their eyes, like faceted opals, at the end of curving protractile stalks, rose level with the port. Their unbelievably thin limbs, their stem-like bodies, comparable to those of the *phasmidae,* or "walking-sticks", were covered with grey-green shards. Their heads, triangular in shape, were flanked with immense, perforated membranes, and were fitted with mandibular mouths that seemed to grin eternally.

I think that they saw me with those weird, inexpressive eyes; for they drew nearer, pressing against the very port, till I could have touched them with my hand if the port had been open. Perhaps they too were surprised: for the thin eye-stalks seemed to lengthen as they stared; and there was a queer waving of their sharded arms, a quivering of their horny mouths, as if they were holding converse with each other. After a while they went away, vanishing swiftly beyond the near horizon.

Since then, I have examined the *Selenite* as fully as possible, to ascertain the extent of the damage. I think that the outer hull has been crumpled or even fused in places: for when I approached the manhole, clad in a spacesuit, with the idea of emerging, I found that I could not open the lid. My exit from the flier has been rendered impossible, since I have no tools with which to cut the heavy metal or shatter the tough, neo-crystal ports. I am sealed in the *Selenite* as in a prison; and the prison, in due time, must also become my tomb.

Later. I shall no longer try to date this record. It is impossible, under the circumstances, to retain even an approximate sense of earthly time. The chronometers have ceased running, and their machinery has been hopelessly jarred by the vessel's fall. The diurnal periods of this planetoid are, it would seem, no more than an hour or two in duration; and the nights are equally short. Darkness swept upon the landscape like a black wing after I had finished writing my last entry; and since then, so many of these ephemeral days and nights have shuttled by, that I have now ceased to count them. My very sense of duration is becoming oddly confused. Now that I have grown somewhat used to my situation, the brief days drag with immeasurable tedium.

The beings whom I call the walking-sticks have returned to the *Selenite,* coming daily, and bringing scores and hundreds of others. It would seem that they correspond in some measure to humanity, being the dominant lifeform of this little world. In most ways, they are incomprehensibly alien; but certain of their actions bear a remote kinship to those of men, and suggest similar impulses and instincts.

Evidently they are curious. They crowd around the *Selenite* in great numbers, inspecting it with their stalk-borne eyes, touching the hull and ports with their attenuated members. I believe they are trying to establish some sort of communication with me. I cannot be sure that they emit vocal sounds, since the hull of the flier is sound-proof; but I am sure that the stiff, semaphoric gestures which they repeat in a certain order before the port as soon as they catch sight of me, are fraught with conscious and definite meaning.

Also, I surmise an actual veneration in their attitude, such as would be accorded by savages to some mysterious visitant from the heavens. Each day, when they gather before the ship, they bring curious spongy fruits and porous vegetable forms which they leave like a sacrificial offering on the ground. By their gestures, they seem to implore me to accept these offerings.

Oddly enough, the fruits and vegetables always disappear during the night. They are eaten by large, luminous, flying creatures with filmy wings, that seem to be wholly nocturnal in their habits. Doubtless, however, the walking-sticks believe that I, the strange ultra-stellar god, have accepted the sacrifice.

It is all strange, unreal, immaterial. The loss of normal gravity makes me feel like a phantom; and I seem to live in a phantom world. My thoughts, my memories, my despair—all are no more than mists that waver on the verge of oblivion. And yet, by some fantastic irony, I am worshipped as a god!

Innumerable days have gone by since I made the last entry in this log. The seasons of the asteroid have changed: the days have grown briefer, the nights longer; and a bleak wintriness pervades the valley. The frail, flat vines are withering on the rocks, and the tall lichen-thickets have assumed funereal autumn hues of madder and mauve. The sun revolves in a low arc above the saw-toothed horizon, and its orb is small and pale as if it were receding into the black gulf among the stars.

The people of the asteroid appear less often, they seem fewer in number, and their sacrificial gifts are rare and scant. No longer do they bring sponge-like fruits, but only pale and porous fungi that seem to have been gathered in caverns.

They move slowly, as if the winter cold were beginning to numb them. Yesterday, three of them fell, after depositing their gifts, and lay still before the flier. They have not moved, and I feel sure that they are dead. The luminous night-flying creatures have ceased to come, and the sacrifices remain undisturbed beside their bearers.

The awfulness of my fate has closed upon me today. No more of the walking-sticks have appeared. I think that they have all died—the ephemerae of this tiny world that is bearing me with it into some Arctic limbo of the solar system. Doubtless their life-time corresponds only to its summer—to its perihelion.

Thin clouds have gathered in the dark air, and snow is falling like fine powder. I feel an unspeakable desolation—a dreariness that I cannot write. The heating-apparatus of the *Selenite* is still in good working-order; so the cold cannot reach me. But the black frost of space has fallen upon my spirit. Strange—I did not feel so utterly bereft and alone while the insect people came daily. Now that they come no more, I seem to have been overtaken by the ultimate horror of solitude, by the chill terror of an alienation beyond life. I can write no longer, for my brain and my heart fail me.

Still, it would seem, I live, after an eternity of darkness and madness in the flier, of death and winter in the world outside. During that time, I have not written in the log; and I know not what obscure impulse prompts me to resume a practice so irrational and futile.

I think it is the sun, passing in a higher and longer arc above the dead landscape, that has called me back from the utterness of despair. The snow has melted from the rocks, forming little rills and pools of water; and strange plant-buds are protruding from the sandy soil. They lift and swell visibly as I watch them. I am beyond hope, beyond life, in a weird vacuum; but I see these things as a condemned captive sees the stirring of spring from his cell. They rouse in me an emotion whose very name I had forgotten.

My food-supply is getting low, and the reserve of compressed air is even lower. I am afraid to calculate how much longer it will last. I have tried to break the neo-crystal ports with a large monkey-wrench for hammer; but the blows, owing partly to my own weightlessness, are futile as the tapping of a feather. Anyway, in all likelihood, the outside air would be too thin for human respiration.

The walking-stick people have re-appeared before the flier. I feel sure, from their lesser height, their brighter coloring, and the immature development of certain members, that they all represent a new generation. None of my former visitors have survived the winter; but somehow, the new ones seem to regard the *Selenite* and me with the same curiosity and reverence that were shown by their elders. They, too, have begun to bring gifts of insubstantial-looking fruit; and they strew filmy blossoms below the port... I wonder how they propagate themselves, and how knowledge is transmitted from one generation to another....

The flat, lichenous vines are mounting on the rocks, are clambering over the hull of the *Selenite*. The young walking-sticks gather daily to worship me—they make those enigmatic signs which I have never understood, and they move in swift gyrations about the vessel, as in the measures of a hieratic dance.... I, the lost and doomed, have been the god of two generations. No doubt they will still worship me when I am dead. I think the air is almost gone—I am more light-headed than usual today, and there is a queer constriction in my throat and chest....

Perhaps I am a little delirious, and have begun to imagine things; but I have just perceived an odd phenomenon, hitherto unnoted. I don't know what it is. A thin, columnar mist, moving and writhing like a serpent, with opal colors that change momently, has appeared among the rocks and is approaching the vessel. It seems like a live thing—like a vaporous entity; and somehow, it is poisonous and inimical. It glides forward, rearing above the throng of *phasmidae*, who have all prostrated themselves as if in fear. I see it more clearly now: it is half-transparent, with a web of grey threads among its changing colors; and it is putting forth a long, wavering tentacle.

It is some rare life-form, unknown to earthly science; and I cannot even surmise its nature and attributes. Perhaps it is the only one of its kind on the asteroid. No doubt it has just discovered the presence of the *Selenite*, and has been drawn by curiosity, like the walking-stick people.

The tentacle has touched the hull—it has reached the port behind which I stand, pencilling these words. The grey threads in the tentacle glow as if with sudden fire. My God—*it is coming through the neo-crystal lens—*

APPENDIX ONE:
STORY NOTES

Abbreviations Used:

AHT   Arkham House Transcripts: a set of transcriptions and excerpts from the letters of H. P. Lovecraft prepared by Donald Wandrei and August Derleth after Lovecraft's death in preparation for what would be five volumes of *Selected Letters* (Sauk City, WI: Arkham House, 1965-1976).

AWD   August W. Derleth (1909-1971), Wisconsin novelist, *Weird Tales* author, and co-founder of Arkham House.

AY   *The Abominations of Yondo* (Sauk City, WI: Arkham House, 1960).

BB   *The Black Book of Clark Ashton Smith* (Sauk City, WI: Arkham House, 1979).

BL   Bancroft Library, University of California at Berkeley.

CAS   Clark Ashton Smith (1893-1961).

DAW   Donald A. Wandrei (1908-1987), poet, *Weird Tales* writer and co-founder of Arkham House.

DS   *The Door to Saturn: The Collected Fantasies of Clark Ashton Smith, Volume Two.* Ed. Scott Connors and Ron Hilger (San Francisco: Night Shade Books, 2007).

EOD   *Emperor of Dreams: A Clark Ashton Smith Bio-Bibliography* by Donald Sidney-Fryer et al. (West Kingston, RI: Donald M. Grant, 1978).

ES   *The End of the Story: The Collected Fantasies of Clark Ashton Smith, Volume One.* Ed. Scott Connors and Ron Hilger (San Francisco: Night Shade Books, 2006).

FFT   *The Freedom of Fantastic Things.* Ed. Scott Connors (New York: Hippocampus Press, 2006).

FW   Farnsworth Wright (1888-1940), editor of *Weird Tales* from 1924 to 1939.

GL   *Genius Loci and Other Tales* (Sauk City, WI: Arkham House, 1948).

HPL   Howard Phillips Lovecraft (1890-1937), informal leader of a circle of writers for *Weird Tales* and related magazines, and probably the leading exponent of weird fiction in the twentieth century.

JHL   Clark Ashton Smith Papers and H. P. Lovecraft Collection, John Hay Library, Brown University.

LL   *Letters to H. P. Lovecraft.* Ed. Steve Behrends (West Warwick, RI: Necronomicon Press, 1987).

LW   *Lost Worlds* (Sauk City, WI: Arkham House, 1944).

MHS   Donald Wandrei Papers, Minnesota Historical Society.

OD   *Other Dimensions* (Sauk City, WI: Arkham House, 1970).

OST   *Out of Space and Time* (Sauk City, WI: Arkham House, 1942).

PD   *Planets and Dimensions: Collected Essays.* Ed. Charles K. Wolfe (Baltimore: Mirage Press, 1973).

PP   *Poems in Prose* (Sauk City, WI: Arkham House, 1965).

RA   *A Rendezvous in Averoigne* (Sauk City, WI: Arkham House, 1988).

RHB   Robert H. Barlow (1918-1951), correspondent and collector of manuscripts of CAS, HPL, and other *WT* writers.

RW   *Red World of Polaris.* Ed. Ronald S. Hilger and Scott Connors (San Francisco: Night Shade Books, 2003).

SHSW   August Derleth Papers, State Historical Society of Wisconsin Library.

SL   *Selected Letters of Clark Ashton Smith.* Ed. David E. Schultz and Scott Connors (Sauk City, WI: Arkham House, 2003).

SS   *Strange Shadows: The Uncollected Fiction and Essays of Clark Ashton Smith.* Ed. Steve Behrends with Donald Sidney-Fryer and Rah Hoffman (Westport, CT: Greenwood Press, 1989).

ST   *Strange Tales of Mystery and Terror*, a pulp edited by Harry Bates in competition with *WT.*

TI   *Tales of India and Irony.* Ed. Scott Connors and Ron Hilger (San Francisco: Night Shade Books, 2007).

TSS   *Tales of Science and Sorcery* (Sauk City, WI: Arkham House, 1964).

WS   *Wonder Stories*, a pulp published by Hugo Gernsback and edited first by David Lasser and then Charles D. Hornig.

WT   *Weird Tales*, Smith's primary market for fiction, edited by FW (1924-1940) and later Dorothy McIlwraith (1940-1954).

The Holiness of Azédarac

Smith began the composition of "The Holiness of Azédarac" (originally called "The Satanic Prelate") in late April 1931, but put it aside in order to write "The Hunters from Beyond."[1] He completed the story on May 21, and it was readily accepted by Farnsworth Wright, appearing in the November 1933 issue of *Weird Tales*. Smith received eighty dollars for this tale.[2] August Derleth apparently did not find it sufficiently outré, since CAS wrote to him "I agree with you about 'Azédarac', which is more piquant than weird. But I like to do something in lighter vein occasionally."[3] This text is based upon a carbon of the original typescript at JHL. It was collected in both *LW* and *RA*.

At one point CAS contemplated writing a sequel to the story, which he would have called "The Doom of Azédarac":

> Azédarac, sorcerer-bishop of Ximes, supposedly dying in the odour of sanctity, in reality transports himself to an other-dimensional world which represents an alternative development of the Earth-sphere from the same primal causes and origins. In this world, many peculiar laws and conditions prevail, together with certain distorted resemblances to the Earth. Azédarac finds himself in a curiously topsy-turvy Averoigne whose people are only vaguely human. He meets a being who is the otherworld alternative of himself, and a weird duel ensues between the two, each using all his resources of wizardry and necromancy. In the end Azédarac, being out of his normal element, loses, and is absorbed like a shadow by the other.[4]

1. CAS, letter to AWD, May 1, 1931 (SHSW).
2. Popular Fiction Publishing Company, letters to CAS, March 30, 1934 and April 28, 1934 (ms, JHL).
3. CAS, letter to AWD, June 15, 1931 (*SL* 154).
4. *BB* item 49.

The Maker of Gargoyles

During the summer of 1931 Smith had an idea for a story about "a gargoyle on the new-built cathedral of Vyônes which comes to life at night and terrorizes the town with eerie and prankish depredations." The plot took a more sinister turn as he expanded this germ into what he called "The Carver of Gargoyles," later changed to "The Maker of Gargoyles:"

> Two gargoyles, wrought by the same carver, on the new-built ca-thedral of Vyônes, one of which is expressive of malignant hatred, and the other of unclean lust. These gargoyles come to life at night, and terrorize the town, appearing in different places, as if they were seeking someone. At last they find the house of the carver, who has recently married a girl of Vyônes. The next day, the carver is found dead, with a torn throat, and his wife raving mad, with her clothing in shreds. On the teeth of the malignant gargoyle, in its usual position in the cathedral cornice, is human blood; and there are fragments of a woman's dress on the claws of the other.[1]

The story was completed on June 16, 1931, and promptly submitted to Harry Bates at *Strange Tales*.

Smith circulated the carbon copy among the Lovecraft Circle for their comments and suggestions. By coincidence, the plot of "The Maker of Gargoyles" is similar to a story-idea recorded by Lovecraft in his "Commonplace Book."[2] Smith expressed the "hope [that] you won't let any coincidence of idea in the gargoyle yarn prevent you from developing your own tale. Your treatment, I imagine, would be quite different from mine; and certainly there is plenty of room. I've never seen a story at all similar to the 'Maker of Gargoyles'; but the notion is one that might readily occur to imaginative minds".[3]

Derleth liked the story, but "found one thing about which I might make a suggestion—the end":

> I think it's pretty evident what's causing all the trouble, since you play up the gargoyles so, so that the climax being the maker's realization seems weak to the reader. Why not have him go up and destroy the gargoyles, and in their destruction, himself be killed? Say he goes up to roof, there is a moment of cataclysmic realization; then in sudden repentant horror he seizes something and begins to demolish them, tumbling them from the roof. Suddenly he feels something pulling at him, he loses his hold and plunges downward. In the morning he is found crushed on the cathedral steps, his clothes still caught firmly on a claw of one of the gargoyle s—a claw on a limb distended in a fashion which the bishop or whoever sees *knows* was not wrought in the original stone.[4]

Smith wrote back to Derleth that he thought "[y]our suggestion anent 'The Maker of Gargoyles' is damn good, and I shall adopt it if the tale comes back from [Harry] Bates, who is evidently holding it for the publisher's reaction ...", adding "Funny—I seem to have more trouble with the endings of stories than anything else. God knows how many I have had to re-write".[5] Bates returned the story, so CAS rewrote the ending on August 27, 1932, and submitted the revised version to Farnsworth Wright at *Weird Tales.*[6]

Unfortunately, "[s]omewhat to my disgust, Wright] returned 'Gargoyles' as melodramatic and unconvincing',"[7] leading to a resubmission of the revised version to Bates. He rejected it once more, but admitted "that the new ending was better and that the story was now 'right on the line' and *could* possibly be bought".[8] After this Smith put the story aside for several months before rewriting two paragraphs "so as to make the fight between Reynard and the gargoyles a little more plausible". In his letter to Derleth announcing the sale, Smith added that "I certainly admire your perseverance in sending in stuff as much as ten or twelve times—so far, I haven't had the nerve to go beyond a third submission".[9] *Weird Tales* paid Smith fifty-six dollars and published it in the August 1932 issue.[10] It was collected posthumously in *TSS*. This text is based upon a carbon copy of the final revised typescript at

JHL. (A copy of the original version presented to HPL forms part of their Lovecraft Collection.)

1. *SS* 167.
2. Item 76 of HPL's "Commonplace Book," written in 1919, reads: "Ancient cathedral—hideous gargoyle—man seeks to rob—found dead—gargoyle's jaw bloody." (*Miscellaneous Writings*, Ed. S. T. Joshi [Sauk City, WI: 1995], p. 91.)
3. CAS, letter to HPL, [c. late August 1931] (*LL* 30).
4. AWD, letter to CAS, 14 August [1931] (ms, SHSW).
5. CAS, letter to AWD, August 18, 1931 (*SL* 160).
6. CAS, letter to AWD, August 28, 1931 (*SL* 161).
7. CAS, letter to AWD, October 23, 1931 (ms, SHSW).
8. CAS, letter to AWD, November 21, 1931 (ms, SHSW).
9. CAS to AWD, March 15, 1932 (*SL* 173).
10. Popular Fiction Publishing Company, letter to CAS, July 27, 1932 (ms, JHL).

Beyond the Singing Flame

As a result of the success of "The City of the Singing Flame," Smith undertook the writing of a sequel, completing it on June 30, 1931. In his cover letter to David Lasser of *Wonder Stories*, which published "Beyond the Singing Flame" in the November 1931 issue, Smith wrote that

> I have found it advisable to maintain the same suggestive vagueness that characterized the other story; though I have explained many things that were left obscure in the other. The description of the Inner Dimension is a daring flight; and I seem almost to have set myself the impossible task which Dante attempted in his account of Paradise. Granting that human beings could survive the process of revibration in the Flame, I think that the new-sense-faculties and powers developed by Hastane, Angarth and Ebbonly are quite logical and possible. Most writers of trans-dimensional tales do not seem to postulate any change of this nature; but it is really quite obvious that there might be something of the kind, since the laws and conditions of existence would be totally different in the new realm.[1]

Smith wrote to Donald Wandrei that "This is, by all odds, my best recent story".[2] He eventually received sixty-eight dollars from the notoriously delinquent Hugo Gernsback, after engaging the services of New York attorney Ione Weber.[3]

In 1940 Walter Gillings, editor of the British science fiction magazine *Tales of Wonder*, reprinted both "The City of the Singing Flame" and "Beyond the Singing Flame" together for the first time. Rather than reprinting them separately, Gillings edited them together, rewriting portions of Smith's prose and adding a bridging paragraph. Mr. Gillings admitted this to Donald Sidney-Fryer some years later.[4] When CAS was putting together *OST*, he could not locate either his carbon of "The City of the Singing Flame" or the original *WS* appearance, so he sent along tear sheets from the Spring 1940 issue of *Tales of Wonder* containing the conjoined stories. This text was duly included in both *OST* and in August Derleth's 1949 anthology *The Other Side of the Moon* (Pellegrini & Cudahy), but not, contrary to what we stated in *DS* 298, in *From Off This World*, a collection of "Hall of Fame" stories reprinted in the pulp magazine *Startling Stories*, edited by Oscar Friend and Leo Margulies (Merlin Press, 1949), which published each tale separately. The present text is based upon a carbon of the original typescript at JHL.

1. *PD* 11.
2. CAS, letter to DAW, August 18, 1931 (ms, MHS).
3. See Mike Ashley, "The Perils of Wonder: Clark Ashton Smith's Experiences with *Wonder Stories.*" *Dark Eidolon* no. 2 (July 1989): 2-8.
4. *EOD* 175.

Seedling of Mars

Hugo Gernsback had some unique ideas regarding how his writers should be compensated, preferring to hold contests rather than offering authors a fixed scale of payment. Since the purpose of his magazines was to increase popular interest in scientific progress in general, and space travel in particular, he and editor David Lasser announced a contest for the best interplanetary plot in the Spring 1931 issue of *Wonder Stories Quarterly*. The readers who submitted the best seven plots would win a cash prize, and the plot would be assigned to a professional writer for further development. E. M. Johnston (1873-1946), of Collingwood, Ontario, won Second Prize for an idea called "The Martian."[1] Lasser offered Smith the assignment of turning Johnston's raw conception into a story, adding "We have no objections of your revising the plots for the purpose of the story as long as the fundamental idea is retained. We are perfectly willing to pay you our usual rate for your completed story".[2] Smith wrote the 16,000 word story in less than a week, completing it on July 20. He wrote to Lovecraft that "the plot … was pretty good, so the job wasn't so disagreeable as it sounds." Smith was to have received one hundred and eighteen dollars for "The Martian," which was published under the title "The Planet Entity" in the Fall 1931 issue of *Wonder Stories Quarterly*. Smith later changed the title to "Seedling of Mars" when he assembled the contents of his fifth Arkham House collection, *TSS*, which was published posthumously.

1. See Mike Ashley and Robert A. W. Lowndes, *The Gernsback Days: A Study of the Evolution of Modern Science Fiction from 1911 to 1936* (Holicong, PA: Wildside Press, 2004), p. 187.
2. David Lasser, letter to CAS, July 10, 1931 (ms, JHL).
3. CAS, letter to HPL, [c. early August 1931] (*SL* 159).

The Vaults of Yoh-Vombis

The following plot synopsis was found among Smith's papers (which he originally titled "The Vaults of Abomi"):

> Some human explorers on a dying world who are driven to take shelter in subterranean vaults by a strange, crawling, mat-like monstrosity called the *vortlup*. The vaults are evidently of mausolean nature, and contain the mummies of an unknown race, some of which lack the upper portion of the head. The explorers become separated in the dark, winding passages, and one is lost from the others. They hear a muffled cry at some distance, followed by silence; and going in the direction of the cry with their flashlights, meet a terrible sight—the body of their comrade which still walks erect, with a great black, slug-like creature attached to the half-eaten head. The thing is controlling the corpses which passes its friends, enters another catacomb, and removes a heavy boulder from the mouth of a deeper vault, beneath the direction of the slug. Following, the others shoot the creature, which dissolves in a sort of liquid putrescence, and, at the same time, the animated corpse drops dead. Then, from the uncovered pit, there emerges a hoard of the black monsters, and the men flee. They are not followed into the sunlight; and fortunately the *vortlup* has disappeared.[1]

At some point Smith changed "Abomi" to "Yoh-Vombis" and the references to a "dying world" and "unknown race" to "a deserted ancient city on Mars" and "ancient Martian;" perhaps the composition of "Seedling of Mars" had stimulated his interest in the Red Planet. Steve Behrends also suggests that the setting might have been influenced by a series of wildfires that Smith battled during the summer of 1931, pointing out that in a letter to August Derleth he described the sky after one such blaze as being "as dark and dingy as the burnt-out sky of the planet Mars".[2] The story, which he described to Derleth as a "rather ambitious hunk of extra-planetary weirdness",[3] was completed on September 12, 1931.

We have not seen Lovecraft's original remarks to Smith regarding the story, but he wrote to Donald Wandrei at the time that he thought it was "great—replete with the musty, tenebrous, & menacing atmosphere of alien & unholy arcana."[4] Derleth's response was more qualified, taking issue with the choice of some words and adding that he "would have liked it much much better had it been set on earth, minus the interplanetary Martian angle."[5] Smith defended the extraterrestrial setting of "Yoh-Vombis" against objections that it might well be set among the ruins of an earthly antiquity: "I suppose the interplanetary angle is a matter of taste. As far as I am concerned, it adds considerably to the interest, particularly since the tale has little or nothing in common with the usual science fiction stuff".[6]

Wright rejected "The Vaults of Yoh-Vombis" on its first submission, telling Smith "to speed up the first half… on the plea that many of his readers would never get to the interesting portion as it stands." This did not please Smith: "Oh hell… I suppose I can leave out a lot of descriptive matter; but it's a crime all the same.[7] Lovecraft encouraged him to stand his ground, writing "if I were in your place I'd tell Wright to go to Hades & take my chances on rejection. He would probably take the tale in the end, even if not now; & any change in so well-balanced a narrative would be the sheerest vandalism".[8] But as Smith poignantly pointed out, his situation was different from that of Lovecraft:

> I *would* have told Wright to go chase himself in regard to "The Vaults of Yoh-Vombis", if I didn't have the support of my parents, and debts to pay off. For this reason it's important for me to place as many stories as possible and have them coming out at a tolerably early date. However, I did not reduce the tale by as much as Wright suggested, and I refused to sacrifice the essential details and incidents of the preliminary section. What I did do, mainly, was to condense the descriptive matter, some of which had a slight suspicion of prolixity anyhow. But I shall restore most of it, if the tale is ever brought out in book form. W. accepted the revised version by return mail.[9]

Smith completed the desired revisions on October 24, 1931, and he then resubmitted "Yoh-Vombis" to *Weird Tales*. Wright was enthusiastic about the story, writing in his letter of acceptance that it was "a tremendous tale, a powerful story".[10] Smith received sixty-three dollars for the story, wryly noting to Derleth that "I mulcted myself out of 17 dollars on the price by the surgical excisions which I performed".[11] It appeared in the May 1932 issue, where it tied with David H. Keller's "The Last Magician" as the most popular story in that issue. The tale is included in *OST* and *RA*. Smith also included it among the contents of *Far from Time*, a collection of his stories that he submitted to Ballantine Books in the 1950s; Ray Bradbury wrote a foreword for this anthology that was included in Jack L. Chalker's tribute collection *In Memoriam: Clark Ashton Smith* (Baltimore: Anthem, 1963), and later in *RA*. The present text was established by a comparison of the typescript of the original version, originally presented by Smith to Robert H. Barlow and now in a private collection (a photocopy of which was provided by Rah Hoffman), with the typescript of the published version, with consultation of the published versions in *WT* and *OST.*

In describing the origins of "The Vault of Yoh-Vombis," as well as in determining its present text, the current editors must acknowledge the pioneering work of Steve Behrends. It is impossible to walk this path without following his footsteps.

1. *SS* 162-63.

2. CAS, letter to AWD, September 6, 1931; quoted in Steve Behrends, "Introduction" to *The Unexpurgated Clark Ashton Smith: The Vaults of Yoh-Vombis* (West Warwick, RI: Necronomicon Press, March 1988), p. 5.

3. CAS, letter to AWD, September 6, 1931 (*SL* 162).

4. HPL to DAW, September 25, 1931, (*Mysteries of Time and Spirit: The Letters of H. P. Lovecraft and Donald Wandrei*, Ed. S. T. Joshi and David E. Schultz [San Francisco: Night Shade Books, 2002], p. 286).

5. AWD, letter to CAS, 18 September 1931 (ms, JHL). Behrends (*supra*) notes that Smith incorporated the suggested changes. In his response to Derleth on September 19, 1931 (ms, SHSW), CAS explained his earlier choices: "'Foreprescience' was both punk and needless, and probably it *isn't* in any dictionary. I must have wanted a trisyllable for the rhythm, or something, and didn't stop to consider its exact meaning. 'Presentiment' would fill the bill; and 'anything of the sort' could be put 'anything of peril'."

6. CAS, letter to AWD, September 19, 1931 (ms, SHSW). Part of Derleth's objection to the setting of the story on Mars may be due to his attitude towards contemporary science fiction: "As a rule I don't read scientifiction stuff at all. I regard it as a sort of bastard growth on the true weird tale, though I suppose that would be a sort of blasphemy to H. P. and his stressing of the 'cosmic beyond'. ..." AWD, letter to CAS, October 26 [1931] (ms, JHL).

7. CAS, letter to HPL, [c. 20 October 1931] (*LL* 31).

8. HPL, letter to CAS [Postmarked October 30, 1931] (ms, private collection).

9. CAS, letter to HPL, [c. early November 1931] (*SL* 165). Smith took a different slant on the subject in correspondence with Derleth. On November 12, 1931, he wrote that "'Yoh-Vombis' was injured little if at all by the excisions which I made, since I refused to sacrifice the essential details and incidents, and merely condensed the preliminary descriptive matter. There were certain paragraphs that had a suspicion of prolixity anyhow" (ms, SHSW).

10. FW, letter to CAS, October 29, 1931 (ms, JHL).

11. CAS, letter to AWD, November 3, 1931 (*SL* 164).

The Eternal World

Smith called "The Eternal World" the "best and most original of my super-scientific tales".[1] He described the story to August Derleth on September 22, 1931 as having a "speculative basis [that] would give Einstein a headache".[2] On that same day he jotted down the basic plot for a story that he then called "Across the Time-Stream:"

> A man invents a mechanism, utilizing a force which can project him *laterally* in universal time, thus achieving instantaneous space-transit. The force projects him *beyond* time and space, as we know them, into a universe with different properties, into a sort of eternity, peopled with strange, frozen figures, where he and his machine are unable to function, as if they were caught in a block of ice, though he maintains a sort of consciousness, such as might characterize the unmoving things about him. Into this timelessness, there come invading entities, who, by means of some sort of super-magnetic force, are able to move and live, albeit sluggishly. They take the explorer in his mechanism, and certain of the timeless ones, back to their own world, intending to enslave them and release the dynamic power of the eternal beings in a war against rival peoples. Evidently they have taken the explorer for one of the timeless things.
> In this world, subject to ordinary time-space conditions, the statue-like entities become instantly alive and tremendously active and defy all control of their captors. They burst like genii the time-traversing mechanism in which they are confined, catch up the human explorer, and proceed to devastate the planet by means of cataclysmic and varied force-manifestations, before going back to eternity. On their way to the timelessness, they drop the human back into his own world.[3]

Although CAS wrote to Derleth that the writing of this story was "the toughest job I have ever attempted",[4] he completed the story the next day. The story was then submitted to *Wonder Stories*. David Lasser's reaction is recorded in his letter of October 21, 1931: the story possessed "an excellent idea", but Smith's descriptions relied too heavily on "strange and bizarre words" and that they were "so long that the story hardly moves and although it is true that you are describing a timeless world in which nothing happens, you cannot afford to have your story be a 'timeless one'".[5] Smith undertook the required revisions, eliminating what he considered to be some genuine redundancies, but characterized the admonition to "put 'more realism' into my future stories [because] the late ones were 'verging dangerously on the weird'" as "really quite a josh—as well as a compliment".[6] The story appeared in the March 1932 issue, and Smith was eventually paid the sum of sixty dollars. "The Eternal World" was collected in *GL*, and was slated for inclusion in *Far from Time*.

The current text is based upon a carbon of a typescript at JHL dated September 27, 1931. Despite telling both Derleth and Lovecraft that he had pruned the story (he noted that "The tale really needed it in places, since there were genuine redundancies of thought and image"[7]), this manuscript, which would appear to predate any revisions, does not differ markedly from the published versions, outside of the simplification of a few words. Perhaps Smith was able to replace just the affected pages and did not bother retyping the entire story.

1. CAS, letter to AWD, January 31, 1932 (ms, SHSW). See also Smith's remarks in "An Autobiography of Clark Ashton Smith," *Science Fiction Fan*, August 1936 (*PD* 43): "Of all the tales published in science fiction magazines, 'The Eternal World' and 'The City of the Singing Flame,' are in my opinion, the most outstanding".

2. CAS, letter to AWD, September 22, 1931 (ms, SHSW).

3. *SS* 172.

4. CAS, letter to AWD, September 26, 1931 (*SL* 163).

5. David Lasser, letter to CAS, October 21, 1931 (ms, JHL).

6. CAS, letter to AWD, November 21, 1931 (ms, SHSW).

7. CAS to HPL, [c. early November 1931] (*SL* 166).

The Demon of the Flower

"The Demon of the Flower" is an expansion of an earlier prose poem, "The Flower-Devil," that appeared in his self-published collection *Ebony and Crystal: Poems in Prose and Verse* (*Auburn Journal*, 1922). CAS completed the tale on October 17, 1931, and sent it along to Harry Bates. Derleth wrote to Smith that he "found it very colourful, got a strong impression of colour-movement due to your vivid descriptive phrases and sentences. I don't think Bates will take this, however, good as it is. Not enough action. Still, he took 'The Door to Saturn;' but this latter was more whimsical, not so?"[1] But Bates surprised both Smith and Derleth by tentatively accepting the tale for *Strange Tales*; unfortunately, the magazine's publisher, William Clayton, ended up vetoing it.[2] Farnsworth Wright rejected it "with some quibbling comments about the diction, which he seems to think might prove a trifle too recherché, for the semi-illiterates among his readers".[3] Smith resubmitted it with some minor changes, but to no avail.

Smith at one point considered including "The Demon of the Flower" in a pamphlet of stories he had the *Auburn Journal* print for him (*The Double Shadow and Other Fantasies*, 1933), but when F. Orlin Tremaine took over the editorship of *Astounding Stories* he submitted several stories there, and Tremaine accepted the story for the December 1933 issue. Smith included it in *LW*. The current text is based upon a copy of the October 17, 1931 version forming part of the papers of Genevieve K. Sully.

1. AWD, letter to CAS, 26 October [1931] (ms, JHL).
2. Harry Bates, letter to CAS, December 15, 1931 (ms, JHL).
3. CAS, letter to AWD, January 9, 1932 (ms, SHSW).

The Nameless Offspring

Although completed on November 12, 1931, the origins of this story date to January 1931. Smith had been re-reading Arthur Machen's collection *The House of Souls*, lent to him by Bernard Austin Dwyer (a mutual correspondent from upstate New York). As he described to Lovecraft:

> "Pan"…has suggested to me an idea so hellish that I am almost afraid to work it out in story-form. It involves a cataleptic woman who was placed alive in the family vaults. Days later, a scream was heard within the family vaults, the door was unlocked, and the woman was found sitting up in her *open* coffin, babbling deliriously of some terrible demoniac face whose vision had awakened her from her death-like sleep. Eight or nine months afterwards, she gives birth to a child and dies. The child is so monstrous that no one is permitted to see it. It is kept in a locked room; but many years later, *after* the death of the woman's husband, it escapes; and co-incidentally the corpse of the deceased is found in a condition not to be described. Also, there are monstrous footprints leading *toward* the vaults, but not away from them. If I do this tale, I shall head it with a text from the *Necronomicon,* which certainly did great service in "Carnby." The "atmosphere" wouldn't have been half so good without it…[1]

Lovecraft's response was typically encouraging and enthusiastic:

> That daemoniac-spawn plot of yours is tremendously powerful—a genuine improvement, I think, on the idea of which Machen is so fond—"Great God Pan," "Black Seal," &c. I once had the idea of having a daemon begotten through some hellish evocation, & having the birth attended by the death, from shock, of both mother & physician—followed by the swift growth of the nameless thing which escapes unseen from the fateful birth-chamber. The thing was to be a terror of the night in the rural region concerned—a looker into windows & devourer of lone travellers. But I gave up the notion when I saw how Machen had used it before me. Your tomb idea, though, is new—implying that the begetting entity was one of Those whom

Harley Warren glimpsed far down beneath the archaic necropolis before he perished from fright—in the darkness. The way you subsequently dispose of the ghoul-spawn—including Its final exit—is truly powerful & terrifying. In describing the way the Thing is kept locked in secret, you might get an idea or two from the similar (though not supernatural) situation in that Austrian play which made such a furore a few years ago—"Goat Song," by Franz Werfel. If you can't get the text of that, H. Warner Munn could lend it to you. I am sure that the *Necronomicon*, at least in the original Arabic version, must have some nighted text balefully appropriate as a motto for such a narrative. Of course, you would have to use great care & subtlety in suiting the tale to Wright's idea of its reception by the Indiana Parent-Teacher Association—& even so, his timidity might bring about rejection in the end. Poor chap—he'll never forget the row that Eddy's "Loved Dead" stirred up some seven years ago! But the thing is abundantly worth trying, & I certainly hope you'll go to it. It will certainly have a highly appreciative MS. reading amongst the gang, whatever its professional fortunes may be.[2]

Smith then composed the tremendous passage from the *Necronomicon* that prefaces the tale, but the remainder of the story was not completed until November 12, 1931. Lovecraft wrote after reading it "Nggrrhh... I can still hear that *clawing!* I think you managed the terrestrial setting very well—indeed, I think your results in that line are always excellent, even though the process of achievement may not be congenial. For my part, I like to delineate a prosaic earthly setting—& *then* let the cosmic abnormality intrude."[3]

CAS submitted it directly to Harry Bates, who accepted it immediately, but offered the following suggestion, which he told Smith he was free to use or reject:

It occurs to me that two little things would improve this last story somewhat. I wonder if you will agree. If somewhere in the body of the story you inserted the idea that the ghoul would eat human flesh, you would not have to be so specific on page 22 where you say in so many words that Sir John had been partly devoured. In this place you could just hint at something too horrible and gruesome to be put into the words: the reader will know that the man has been partly devoured. Then, I think it would improve the end of the story to have the ghoul followed into the vault and a search made—a search which would reveal no trace of it. This would be more reasonable than to cut short the pursuit at the gate of the vault, which would enable the monster to get out for dirty work on other occasions; also I think it would give a slightly better "feeling" to the end.[4]

Smith readily accepted Bates' suggestion, "since it lifts the whole business more into the realm of the supernatural to have the monster vanish utterly."[5] It appeared in the June 1932 issue of *Strange Tales*. It was not collected until the last Arkham House collection to be published in Smith's lifetime, *AY*. The current text is based on a carbon typescript at JHL.

It is probable that "The Nameless Offspring" would not have been written, let alone published, had *Strange Tales* not existed, since Smith recognized that "its commercial chances are pretty nil."[6] As Lovecraft mentioned, Wright would probably have been too squeamish to take the story, both because of the necrophagia and the sexual element; Smith felt that the latter was no worse than in Machen's story or even Lovecraft's own "The Dunwich Horror", but fumed that "by some curious twist of convention, editors will probably think that it is."[7] Bates, on the other hand, was more open to purely gruesome material, such as "The Return of the Sorcerer," also rejected by Wright, while also being personally receptive to Smith's more outré stories such as "The Door to Saturn" and "The Demon of the Flower." At the time CAS wrote "The Nameless Offspring" he was writing regularly for three main markets, *WT, WS*, and *ST*, and was still trying to crack magazines such as *Ghost Stories*. The worsening depression would soon lead to the collapse of the Clayton and McFadden magazines, would also adversely affect the ability of those that survived to pay in a timely manner, and would do nothing to encourage Smith to continue the writing of fiction.

Having Henry Chaldane running a bee ranch in Canada was a tip of the hat to Smith's correspondent Frank Lillie Pollock (1876-1957), who operated just such a facility in Shedden, Ontario.[8]

1. CAS, letter to HPL, [c. January 27, 1931] (*SL* 145-46).
2. HPL, letter to CAS, February 8, 1931 (ms, MHS; included in part in *Selected Letters III*, Ed. August Derleth and Donald Wandrei [Sauk City, WI: Arkham House, 1972], p. 286).
3. HPL, letter to CAS [early December 1931] (ms, JHL).
4. Harry Bates, letter to CAS, December 15, 1931 (ms, JHL).
5. CAS, letter to AWD, December 31, 1931 (*SL* 168).
6. CAS, letter to HPL, [c. early November 1931] (*SL* 166).
7. CAS, letter to AWD, November 12, 1931 (ms, SHSW).
8. See notes to "The Planet of the Dead," *ES* 273.

A Vintage from Atlantis

Farnsworth Wright used short stories of three thousand words or less as "filler" to occupy the holes left in each issue by the larger stories, and many of Smith's stories ("The Gorgon," "The Supernumerary Corpse," etc.) fall into this category. By late 1931 Wright had published all such stories of Smith's, leading CAS to write to Derleth in late November 1931 that he was composing a filler of this title that dealt "with the unique brand of d.t. induced in a crew of pirates by drinking the contents of an antique wine-jar, crusted with barnacles and corals, which they had found cast up on the beach of a West Indian isle."[1] A plot synopsis found among his papers describes his conception thus:

> A crew of pirates have landed on a desert West Indian isle to bury their loot, and find a strange antique jar that has been washed up out of the sea. The thing is made of a strong, heavy, almost infrangible earthenware; but they manage to break off the neck with hammers, and discover that the jar is filled with a dark, aromatic wine. All of them drink the wine, excepting one Puritan abstainer, who tells the story. After drinking it, they go mad and begin to babble in an unknown tongue, and to perform strange rites on the beach, including the sacrifice, in a very peculiar manner, of the pirate captain on an improvised altar. Some of them seize the Puritan, and make him swallow a little of the wine; and though he does not become so demented as the others, he has a shadowy vision of some monstrous being that comes up out of the sea, and of shimmering, mirage-like domes and walls that rise from the waters. He is overcome with terror, and flees in one of the boats to the ship, leaving the others to continue their mad revel, which ends in death.[2]

Wright was ambivalent about the story, writing "I think it best to follow my usual practice of rejecting when in doubt."[3] The rejection puzzled Smith, but he accepted it philosophically, observing "I dare say he goes by precedent; and this tale, in style and substance, was a little off the beaten track."[4] Lovecraft encouraged him to submit the story to *Strange Tales*, adding that the tale "surely grips the reader by the throat by the time it is ended! It has a touch of Dunsanian phantasy about it, & ought to be acceptable to Bates if he liked 'The Door to Saturn' or Whitehead's 'Moon Dial'. Those *visions* are really tremendous, & the climax is satisfyingly adequate."[5] Bates rejected it on December 15. Wright finally ended up taking the story after Smith's third revision, publishing it in the September 1933 issue.[6] It was collected in *AY*. The current text is based upon an undated carbon copy of the typescript at JHL.

1. CAS, letter to AWD, November 21, 1931 (ms, SHSW).
2. *SS* 168.
3. FW, letter to CAS, December 1, 1931 (ms, JHL).
4. CAS, letter to AWD, December 12, 1931 (ms, SHSW).
5. HPL, letter to CAS, [c. early December 1931] (ms, JHL).
6. CAS, letter to AWD, October 8, 1932 (*SL* 193).

The Weird of Avoosl Wuthoqquan

One of Smith's most frequently reprinted stories, this tale was completed on November 25, 1931. A plot synopsis found among his papers describes the story thus:

> ^Ootal^ [Zoon] Wuthoqquan, rich usurer of Uzuldaroum, denies an alms to aged beggar on the street. Thereupon the beggar proceeds to utter a cryptically disagreeable prophecy concerning Ootal Wuthoqquan's future fate. This prophecy is fulfilled. A strange man appears and asks the usurer for a loan of money, offering three huge emeralds as security. The loan is accorded; but that night, as Ootal Wuthoqquan is looking at the emeralds, they start to roll away from him, as if bewitched. He follows them; but keeping just beyond his reach, they lead him through the nocturnal streets of the moonlit city and into the country. Here they vanish into a hole or cave. Wild with avarice, the usurer still follows, and finds himself in a phosphorescent cavern heaped with jewels, where a terrible, formless, multiform entity broods on a pile of gems. This creature proceeds to devour the unfortunate usurer.[1]

Smith submitted the story to Harry Bates, telling Derleth that he felt "Wright would perhaps consider it too fantastic,"[2] but it failed to get past publisher William Clayton.[3] Wright accepted the story apparently without hesitation and offered Smith thirty-three dollars for it.[4] It appeared in the June 1932 issue of *Weird Tales*, and was collected in *OST* and *RA*. Smith also planned to include it in *Far from Time*, which indicates that he possibly regarded it as more than a mere filler.

1. *SS* 166.
2. CAS, letter to AWD, December 2, 1931 (ms, SHSW).
3. Harry Bates, letter to CAS, December 15, 1931 (ms, JHL).
4. Popular Fiction Publishing Company, letter to CAS May 28, 1932 (ms, JHL).

The Invisible City

Harry Bates, editor of *Strange Tales of Mystery and Terror*, edited a sister genre magazine for publisher William Clayton, *Astounding Stories of Super-Science*. Smith had not submitted any stories to it despite his success with *Strange Tales* because its basic formula could be summed up as cowboys and Indians in space. It comes as no surprise that CAS did not have a high opinion of the magazine, telling Lovecraft "*Astounding* absolutely gags me—in one of the stories, for example, there is a Man from Mars who talks American slang! I shall not buy the magazine again".[1] On the other hand,

Bates had already bought two stories from Smith for *Strange Tales*, and was about to buy three more, one of which he had specially commissioned. It is not surprising, then, that Bates wrote to Smith on October 16, 1931 to solicit submission for his science fiction magazine: "I wonder why you can't write an acceptable short story for our *Astounding Stories*. I see you do it for our competitors".[2]

"The Invisible City" was the first "scientifiction" story Smith wrote after receiving this invitation. Two plot synopses exist for this story among Smith's papers. The first dates approximately to 1930, and reads simply "An invisible barrier, like a city wall, is encountered by explorers in the Gobi desert. Groping, they find a gate in this wall—and are trapped in an unseen labyrinth of buildings. They spend a night in this labyrinth before escaping."[3] He would later develop this idea further:

> Two explorers, wandering in the Gobi desert, lost, and searching for water, come to a series of strange, regular-shapen pits in the desert floor. Examining these, they find to their amazement that the pits are covered with an invisible, solid substance, that they are walking among unseen walls, on unseen pavements, in what appears to be a maze of buildings wrought of an ice-cold substance absolutely permeable to light. In some of the pits they see the apparently floating bodies of strange creatures, which they take to be mummies. One of the two men falls down a flight of steps, drops his rifle, and is attacked by an unseen monster, the minotaur of this strange labyrinth. The other man, following more carefully, manages to shoot the monster in a vital spot, and kills it. The thing becomes visible in death, and putrefies with amazing rapidity. The men escape from the city; and crossing a low ridge, find themselves on the bank of a river which will take them to the huts of desert tribesmen.[4]

Smith found the actual composition of the story less than satisfying, and expressed concern that it would prove unsaleable. The problem was that it had "not enough atmosphere to make it really good—and too many unexplained mysteries for the scientifiction readers, who simply must have their little formulae. A story in which the 'heroes' don't solve anything would hardly go. To hell with heroes anyway."[5] His fears were realized when, after completing the story on December 15, 1931, Bates rejected it as "too vague and pointless."[6] After finishing some revisions on February 2, 1932, Smith resubmitted the story, but to no avail. Bates' letters do not survive, but according to Smith it was felt that his stories lacked "human interest" and his heroes "didn't show enough excitement over their prodigious adventures."[7] (To this last criticism Smith wryly observed "But if anything could be more insouciant than some of the birds who figure in the A.S. yarns—"[8]) Having already invested more effort in the story than he probably felt it deserved, Smith sent it along to *Wonder Stories*, where it was accepted by David Lasser on March 5, 1932.[9] It appeared on the cover of the June 1932 issue, and Ione Weber was eventually able to extract sixty-five dollars for it from Gernsback's purse.

Smith probably didn't know it, but it appears that Gernsback sold the foreign language rights to his story. "The Invisible City" was translated as "Die unsichtbare Stadt" in the ninth issue for 1933 of the German magazine *Bibliothek der Unterhaltung und des Wissens*, published in Stuttgart by Union Deutsche Verlagsgesellschaft. Smith would later sell the rights to the story to the British magazine *Tales of Wonder*, edited by Walter Gillings, and would also take the cover spot.

Smith called the story "a hunk of tripe,"[10] although Lovecraft praised it as "vivid & ingenious in the extreme—& with enough 'eckshun' to please the most exacting clientele".[11] Lovecraft would later write a story with a similar theme ("In the Walls of Eryx," *Weird Tales*, October 1939), but the idea for this story came from his teenage collaborator, Kenneth Sterling (1920-1995), who identified his inspiration as Edmond Hamilton's "The Monster-God of Mamurth" (*Weird Tales*, August 1926).[12]

1. CAS, letter to HPL, [c. late October 1930 (*SL* 123)].
2. Harry Bates, letter to CAS, October 16, 1931 (ms, JHL).
3. *SS* 158-59.
4. *SS* 172-73.
5. CAS, letter to AWD, December 12, 1931 (ms, SHSW).
6. CAS, letter to AWD, January 31, 1932 (ms, SHSW).
7. CAS, letter to AWD, February 10, 1932 (ms, SHSW).
8. CAS, letter to AWD, February 24, 1932 (ms, SHSW).
9. David Lasser, letter to CAS, March 5, 1932 (private collection).
10. CAS, letter to AWD, March 15, 1932 (*SL* 173).
11. HPL, note to CAS [Postmarked May 13, 1932] (courtesy of S. T. Joshi and David E. Schultz).
12. S. T. Joshi, *H. P. Lovecraft: A Life* (West Warwick, RI: Necronomicon Press, 1996), p. 604.

The Immortals of Mercury

Despite his unpleasant experience with "The Invisible City," Smith found the two cents a word paid by the Clayton magazines as alluring as any pilgrim to Ydmos found the call of the Singing Flame. His next attempt to storm the barricades at *Astounding Stories* was "The Immortals of Mercury." The planet closest to the sun apparently excited his imagination, as story ideas such as "The Ghoul from Mercury" and "The Conquest of Mercury" were found among his papers. One such idea, "A Sojourn in Mercury," follows:

"The terrestrial explorer, landing in the twilight zone of the dark frozen side of Mercury, who is driven forth by the inhabitants toward the burning desert of the side toward the sun."[1] A later version of this idea follows immediately after the second outline of "The Invisible City," the title now reading "The Immortals of Mercury":

> An explorer caught by the aboriginals of Mercury, who is tied to the back of a salamander-like monster that carries him away into the sun-ward deserts of the planet. Almost swooning with the insupportable heat, he sees the lifting of an artificial lid in the desert floor, and is rescued and carried into subterranean regions by strange beings who have achieved immortality by wearing clothes of a material that excludes the destructive cosmic rays.[2]

Smith began the composition of the story around the middle of December 1931, but its completion was delayed until mid-January because his mother became ill with an infected heel, which required him both to care for her and to accomplish the chores she usually performed. He was not overly pleased with the completed product, describing it as "a lot of tripe, I'm afraid; but if it brings me a 200.00 dollar check, [it] will have served its purpose".[3] Lovecraft, as usual, offered his support, telling Smith encouragingly "What you suggest about 'The Immortals of Mercury' sounds alluring, even though concessions to Claytonism may have been made".[4] Unfortunately, Bates rejected the story for the same reasons discussed above (see "The Invisible City").

In order to increase the chances of its acceptance by Farnsworth Wright, Smith rewrote the tale to give it "a grim and terrific ending,"[5] which led HPL to observe ironically "for once commercial pressure may have an effect other than deleterious—leading you into some potent realism which you would not otherwise have introduced."[6] (This remark was related to a running exchange between Smith and Lovecraft concerning the relative merits of romanticism versus realism in the weird tale.) Wright declined to use "The Immortals of Mercury," preferring instead to serialize such immortal classics as Victor Rousseau's "The Phantom Hand" (*Weird Tales*, July through November 1932) and public domain novels like *Frankenstein*.

David Lasser accepted "The Immortals of Mercury," mentioning that they might print it as a separate pamphlet rather than use it in either *Wonder Stories* or its sister quarterly.[7] The booklet appeared early that summer, with Lovecraft writing Smith that he found it waiting for him upon his return from a trip to New Orleans:

> It would have been much better, I fancy, if not deprived of the parts you mention—but even as it is it furnishes more than one authentic shudder. It ought to have "eckshun" enough to suit even the canny

Gernsback, & in addition, the later parts give a very real thrill of subterrene horror. Glad that Hugo & Co. didn't demand a happy ending—the present abrupt punch comes as a magnificently ironic touch.[8]

According to the accounts obtained by his attorney, Ione Weber, Smith was due eighty dollars from Gernsback's Stellar Publication Corporation for the story's publication as *Science Fiction Series* no. 16, a rather unprepossessing pamphlet issued with no cover illustration. The story was included in *TSS*. No complete manuscript exists, although we were able to examine several pages of a first draft for "Immortals." We also compared the text from *TSS* with that of a copy of the 1932 pamphlet corrected by Smith, and between them were able to correct most of the numerous typographical errors that crept into both editions.

1. *SS* 160.
2. *SS* 173.
3. CAS, letter to Derleth, January 19, 1932 (ms, SHSW). Two hundred dollars is what *Astounding Stories* would have paid for the ten thousand word novelette.
4. HPL, letter to CAS [postmarked January 28, 1932] (ms, JHL).
5. CAS, letter to AWD, February 21, 1932 (ms, SHSW).
6. HPL, letter to CAS, February 26, 1932 (AHT).
7. David Lasser, letter to CAS, March 16, 1932 (ms, JHL).
8. HPL, letter to CAS, July 10, 1932 (AHT).

The Empire of the Necromancers

In this story Smith introduced what Brian Stableford has called "the most dramatically appropriate"[1] of his secondary worlds, Zothique. Will Murray,[2] Steve Behrends[3] and Jim Rockhill[4] have all discussed the origins of this series in some depth, tracing its origins as far back as Smith's 1911 poem "The Last Night"[5] and a brief sketch "Account of an Actual Dream—1912."[6] CAS described it to L. Sprague de Camp as "the last inhabited continent of earth" where the "science and machinery of our present civilization have long been forgotten, together with our present religions. But many gods are worshipped; and sorcery and demonism prevail again as in ancient days."[7] The first use of the name occurs in a synopsis for "Vizaphmal in Ophiuchus," a never-completed sequel to "The Monster of the Prophecy," where it referred to a world in another solar system, that he plotted in April 1930.[8] In February 1931 he came up with the idea of "Gnydron, a continent of the far future, in the South Atlantic, which is more subject to incursions of 'outsideness' than any former terrene realm; and more liable to the visitation of beings from galaxies not yet visible; also, to shifting admixtures and interchanges with other dimensions or planes of entity."[9]

Also in 1930 CAS scribbled an idea about the exploitation of the dead by the living, which he called "The Empire of the Necromancers": "Two sorcerers, who raise up an entire people from the dead, in order that they may reign over them. The dead, however, revolt against being brought back to life."[10] The idea laid dormant, much like the people of Cincor, until he developed the plot further in August or September 1931:

> A story told by a man centuries dead—the prince of a perished people. He and all his subjects are raised up from death to be the slaves of two necromancers greedy of dominion and power. These people, living a ghostly, hollow, shadow-like existence, are driven to toil for the necromancers, are tortured for their sadistic plea- sure, made to serve their necrophilic lusts. The prince, learning the secret of their power, and throwing off their spell in a measure, resolves to rescue his people from this terrible doom. He contrives that the necromancers shall themselves die, to awaken at a stated time and find themselves among the living dead. Then he and his people, freed from their slavery, seek the oblivion of a second death by flinging themselves into the subterranean fires beneath the kingdom.[11]

Smith worked on it at the same time as, and possibly as an antidote to, "The Invisible City" and "The Immortals of Mercury," completing it on January 7, 1932. "There is a queer mood in this little tale; and, like my forth- coming, 'The Planet of the Dead,' it is muchly overgreened with what H. P. once referred to as the 'verdigris of decadence'."[12] HPL called it "great—one of the best things I've seen lately—& I'm immensely glad to learn that it has landed with Wright."[13] "The Empire of the Necromancers" was the most popular story in the September 1932 issue of *Weird Tales*. It was collected in *LW* and *RA*. This text is based upon two carbon copies of the typescript, one at JHL forming part of Smith's papers, and another presented by CAS to Lester Anderson, a Bay Area science fiction fan, that incorporates some holograph changes that do not appear on either the JHL copy or the pub- lished text . This presentation copy was purchased by the Bancroft Library a few years ago as part of a large lot of Smith's letters, manuscripts and other ephemera.

1. Brian Stableford, "Outside the Human Aquarium: The Fantastic Imagination of Clark Ashton Smith." In *FFT* 161.
2. Will Murray, "Introduction" to *Tales of Zothique* by Clark Ashton Smith (West Warwick, RI: Necronomicon Press, 1995), p. 7-12.
3. Steve Behrends, chapter 2, "Zothique," *Clark Ashton Smith*, Starmont Reader's Guide 49 (Mercer Island, WA: Starmont House, 1990), pp. 24-37.

4. Jim Rockhill, "As Shadows Wait Upon the Sun: Clark Ashton Smith's Zothique." In *FFT* 277-92.

5. *The Star-Treader and Other Poems* (San Francisco: A. M. Robertson, 1912), p. 31.

6. *SS* 245.

7. CAS, letter to L. Sprague de Camp, November 3, 1953 (*SL* 374).

8. *ES* 266.

9. *SS* 165.

10. *SS* 158.

11. *SS* 170.

12. CAS, letter to AWD, January 9, 1932 (ms, SHSW).

13. HPL, letter to CAS [postmarked January 28, 1932] (ms, JHL).

The Seed from the Sepulcher

If we use the number of times a story has been anthologized as an indication of its popularity, then "The Seed from the Sepulcher," at eight times (not counting different editions of the same anthology), is Smith's most popular story, beating "The Return of the Sorcerer" (five times), "The City of the Singing Flame" (four times), "A Rendezvous in Averoigne" (four times), and "The Weird of Avoosl Wuthoqquan" (three times)—and it wasn't even included in one of his collections until after his death!

Timeus Ashton-Smith (1855-1937), the father of Clark Ashton Smith, was the son of a wealthy British industrialist who used his patrimony for travel and gambling. Based upon accounts received from his friend, H. P. Lovecraft described Timeus as "something of a soldier of fortune [who had] travelled in many odd corners of the earth, including the Amazon jungles of South America. Clark probably derives much of his exotic taste from the tales told him by his father when he was very small—he was especially impressed by accounts of the gorgeously plumed birds and bizarre tropical flowers of equatorial Brazil."[1] These stories undoubtedly were on Smith's mind when he conceived of this story.

Steve Behrends, in his notes to Smith's story-ideas published in *Strange Shadows*, identifies this plot germ, originally called "A Bottle on the Amazon" (later changed to "Orinoco") as the genesis of "The Seed from the Sepulcher":

> A whisky-bottle floating in the ^Orinoco^ [Amazon] is picked up near the river's mouth, and is found to contain a ms. which details the adventures of two explorers in an untrodden country of Venezuela. Here one of the two men is bitten by a monstrous fanged vegetable growth ^having a vague, distorted likeness to a human figure^, and shortly after, begins to show signs of an appalling transformation.

Little by little he is turned into a replica of the thing that had bitten him. Finally, he takes root in the jungle—and stings the narrator of the story, just as the other is about to abandon him in horror and despair.[2]

According to Behrends, this synopsis probably dates to the summer of 1931. He began working on the tale toward the end of January 1932, mentioning in a letter that he was "doing another story, 'The Seed from the Sepulcher,' for submission to *Strange Tales*... 'The Seed from the Sepulcher' will be the best of the lot, from my standpoint. It describes a monstrous plant growing out of a man's skull, eyes, etc., and trellising the roots on all his bones, *while he was still alive.*"[3] It was completed by February 10, since in a discussion of his recent stories Smith told Derleth "I like 'The Seed from the Sepulcher' best, for its imaginative touches, but am going to chuck the malignant plant idea after this. I don't want to run it into the ground!"[4] When he submitted it to Harry Bates,

> he wanted me to make some slight alterations before showing it to Clayton. He seemed to think there was an inconsistency in the development of the devil-plant; but, as I pointed out to him, the plant merely propagated itself through spores, *after death,* but had the power of extending its *individual life-term* through an extension of the root-system from one victim to another. However, I made several minor changes, adding some horrific details, and mentioning a *second skull* in the lattice-work of bones, roots, etc, in the burial-pit. Derleth's suggestions were very good, but I rather like the thing as it stands. It might have been worked out more gradually, at greater length, as Wandrei suggests; but the present development, as far as I am concerned, has, through its very acceleration, a strong connotation of the unnatural, the diabolic, the supernatural.[5]

Bates accepted the revised story for *Strange Tales*, but now informed Smith that payment would have to wait until publication. This was a precursor to even worse news: facing the threat of bankruptcy, publisher William Clayton gave Bates orders to shut down the magazine with the January 1933 issue.[6] Bates had been holding three of Smith's stories, including "Seed," which he had already copy-edited and marked with instructions for the printer, and returned them to Smith. A new copy was promptly typed and submitted to Farnsworth Wright at *Weird Tales*; CAS took the opportunity to add a few details and "verbal emendations" that added "from my standpoint... to the literary value of the tale, which was a little hasty and hacky in spots before."[7] Wright rejected it, telling Smith that it had "many excellent features; but as a whole, it seems too long drawn out—at least, that is my reaction to it."[8]

The next month Smith revised the story, eliminating "all repetitional detail [and] cutting the yarn to 4500 [words]"; Wright accepted this trimmed version.[9] Smith received forty-five dollars for the story after it appeared in the October 1933 issue of *Weird Tales*.[10] It was collected in *TSS*.

The current text is based upon the typescript edited by Harry Bates, which Smith had given to R. H. Barlow and who in turn donated it to the Bancroft Library, and the later typescripts at JHL. Some descriptive material from the first version that was cut for *Weird Tales* has been restored, but the repetitive material that Smith had cut—and there was a lot of repetition in the Bates-edited version—has not been restored.

1. HPL, letter to F. Lee Baldwin, March 27, 1934 (in *FFT* 66).
2. *SS* 167.
3. CAS, letter to AWD, January 31, 1932 (ms, SHSW).
4. CAS, letter to AWD, February 10, 1932 (ms, SHSW).
5. CAS, letter to HPL, [c. March 1932] (*SL* 171-72).
6. Mike Ashley and Robert A. W. Lowndes, *The Gernsback Days: A Study of the Evolution of Modern Science Fiction from 1911 to 1936* (Holicong, PA: Wildside Press, 2004), p. 203.
7. CAS, letter to AWD, October 16, 1932 (ms, SHSW).
8. FW, letter to CAS, October 21, 1932 (ms, JHL).
9. CAS, letter to AWD, December 3, 1932 (ms, SHSW).
10. Popular Fiction Publishing Company to CAS, February 24, 1934 (ms, JHL).

The Second Interment

As in the case of "An Adventure in Futurity" and "Seedling of Mars," "The Second Interment" originated with a suggestion from one of Smith's editors. Harry Bates forwarded to Smith the following suggestion from William Clayton:

> Mr. Clayton recently suggested to me that he would like to see a story recounting the horror a man might feel at being buried alive. His sensations, all the awful things—the states of mind—he would go through. He might prolong his agony by shallow breathing a la Houdini. It would add to the horror of things if he had for years been afraid of being buried alive, and had an obsession that he would. Perhaps he had a push button or some other device in the casket of summoning aid just in case, and perhaps it does not work. Perhaps he has had one unfortunate experience from which he was rescued in time, which would give far more point and tension to a repetition of it for a climax.... The thing would, of course, be a naturalistic horror story.[1]

Smith apparently felt the suggestion a congenial one, for he had completed the story by January 29, 1932, less than a week after receiving the suggestion. He added to Clayton's basic idea "the suggestion of foul play that was apprehended by Uther; and it seems to me that the thing could hardly have happened in any other way than through dirty work. The younger brother, with the dr.'s connivance, must have hustled him away in a terrible hurry, fearing that he might wake up at any moment, if they took the chance of committing him to an embalmer's care. But maybe I should have inserted a more direct hint of this somewhere in this tale."[2]

Although Smith called "The Second Interment" a "detailed and remorseless study in naturalistic horror," the technique he used was vividly impressionistic in its depiction of the psychological and physiological agonies experienced by the unfortunate Uther Magbane. In doing so he perhaps unconsciously made reference to some of the nightmare visions found in "The Hashish-Eater." The images of eyeless giants, the black Babel of a sunless world, and the huge Python of myth with unimaginable folds, are all reminiscent of this poem. The fevered rush from horror to horror also duplicates much of the tone used throughout Smith's most famous poem, but the most striking similarity occurs in the final sentences of the story:

> With inconceivable swiftness, the head of the anaconda became that of his brother Guy. It mocked him with a vast sneer, it appeared to swell and expand, to lose all human semblance or proportion, to become a blank, dark mass that rushed upon him in cyclonic gloom, driving him down into the space beyond space.

Compare the above paragraph with the final lines from "The Hashish-Eater":

> It grows and grows, a huge white eyeless Face,
> That fills the void and fills the universe,
> And bloats against the limits of the world
> With lips of flame that open.[3]

"The Second Interment" appeared in the last issue of *Strange Tales*, January 1933. Donald Wandrei called the story "a fine piece of craftsmanship, one of the best tales you have yet spun. Derleth raised a question about insoluble problems of technique involved in such a presentation, but I answered with the simple assertion that certain types of potential or actual experience can not be handled at all except by such methods as were employed in your story; and of course, where the question is one of to have or not to have, the affirmative wins".[4] CAS agreed that "the method employed was the only feasible one. The tale was written to order, as I may have told you, and it is almost the only instance where I have done anything good under such conditions."[5] Smith confirmed his good opinion of the story by allowing August Derleth to include it in *OST*.[6]

1. Bates, letter to CAS, January 22, 1932 (ms, JHL).
2. CAS, letter to AWD, February 24, 1932 (ms, SHSW).
3. CAS, "The Hashish-Eater; or, the Apocalypse of Evil." In *The Last Oblivion: Best Fantastic Poems of Clark Ashton Smith*, Ed. S. T. Joshi and David E. Schultz (NY: Hippocampus Press, 2002), p. 29.
4. DAW, letter to CAS, October 31, 1932 (ms, JHL).
5. CAS, letter to DAW, November 10, 1932 (*SL* 195).
6. See CAS, letter to AWD, September 5, 1941 (*SL* 333).

Ubbo-Sathla

Completed on February 15, 1932, "Ubbo-Sathla" originated in the following note:

> A man, who, in trance, goes back in earthly time to the very beginning, when Ubbo-Sathla, the primal one, out of whom all terrestrial life has sprung, lay wallowing in the mist and slime, playing idiotically with the tablets on which are writ the wisdom of vanished pre-mundane gods. In his trance, the man believes that he has been sent to retrieve these tablets; but, approaching Ubbo-Sathla, he seems to revert to some primordial life-form; and forgetting his mission, wallows and ravens in the ooze with the spawn of Ubbo-Sathla. He does not re-emerge from the trance. Ubbo-Sathla is a vast, yeasty mass, sloughing off continuously various rudimentary life-forms.[1]

Douglas A. Anderson suggests that "Ubbo-Sathla" may have been influenced by Leonard Cline's visionary novel *The Dark Chamber* (1927),[2] but as of December 1933 Smith had not read it.[3] Cline's novel may have exerted some influence at second hand, though, since Donald Wandrei is known to have read *The Dark Chamber*, and CAS wrote him that the story's "ideation may remind you a little of your own tale, '[The Lives of] Alfred Kramer'" [*WT*, December 1932]. In the same letter CAS stated that "The main object of Ubbo-Sathla was to achieve a profound and manifold dissolution of what is known as reality—which, come to think of it, is the animus of nearly all my tales, more or less."[4]

"Ubbo-Sathla" was submitted to *Weird Tales*, but was rejected. Wright's rejection letter does not survive, but CAS remarked to HPL that he seemed "to think that it would be over the heads of his clientele."[5] He continued in the same vein in his next letter to Lovecraft:

Wright must have rejected "Ubbo-Sathla" because it didn't remind him of anything that had ever made a hit with his readers. I can't see myself that it's especially difficult or "high-brow." Where Wright errs is in playing safe when he can't find a precedent for some particular tale—a method of selection that is none too favourable to originality. It will be interesting to see what he says to "The Double Shadow"—a tale that I am inclined (though I may be wrong) to rate above "Ubbo-Sathla."[6]

Wright did accept the story upon re-submission, apparently after Lovecraft "had raked him over about the rejection,"[7] publishing it in the July 1933 issue. This issue also contained Lovecraft's "The Dreams in the Witch House" as well as Hazel Heald's "The Horror in the Museum" (which was actually ghost-written by Lovecraft). All three stories contained references to the mythical *Book of Eibon,* which excited a lot of questions among credulous fans. Smith responded to one such query from Charles D. Hornig, David Lasser's successor at *Wonder Stories* and editor of the fanzine *Fantasy Fan:*

"Necronomicon," "Book of Eibon" etc I am sorry to say, are all fictitious. Lovecraft invented the first, I the second.... It is really too bad that they don't exist as objective, bonafide compilations of the elder and darker Lore! I have been trying to remedy this, in some small measure, by cooking up a whole chapter of Eibon. It is still unfinished, and I am now entitling it "The Coming of the White Worm."....[8]

After Hornig inadvertently published Smith's letter in the November 1933 issue, CAS remarked in a postcard to Lovecraft: " I was a little vexed by Brother Hornig's 'scoop' in utilizing my letter about Eibon, etc. He asked me where and how the books could be obtained; and I didn't think to stipulate that the answer was for his private information! Dumb of me, I'll admit. However, as you say, the hoax might easily go too far."[9] CAS included "Ubbo-Sathla" among the "Hyperborean Grotesques" of *OST.* This text is derived from a carbon typescript at JHL.

1. *SS* 174.
2. Douglas A. Anderson, "Introduction." In *The Dark Chamber* by Leonard Cline (Cold Spring Harbor, NY: Cold Spring Press, 2005), p. 9.
3. CAS, letter to HPL, [c. December 4, 1933] (*SL* 240).
4. CAS, letter to DAW, February 17, 1932 (*SL* 170).
5. CAS, letter to HPL, [c. March 1932] (*SL* 172).
6. CAS, letter to HPL, [c. mid-March 1932] (*LL* 35-36).

7. CAS, letter to DAW, May 4, 1932 (ms, MHS).

8. *PD* 29.

9. CAS, postcard to HPL, postmarked November 24, 1933 (private collection).

The Double Shadow

When H. P. Lovecraft first read "The Double Shadow," he called it "magnificent… full of vivid colour & creeping menace, & with an atmosphere worthy of E. A. P."[1] Smith thought that it was the "most demoniac of my recent tales"[2] and called it a personal favorite.[3] Yet Farnsworth Wright's continued refusal to buy the story until Smith had almost ceased the composition of fiction was probably a contributing factor in that cessation, and led Smith to the drastic and ultimately unprofitable step of self-publication.

The germ of the story may be found in the following note: "A man sees a monstrous shadow following his own and merging with it gradually, day by day; while coincidentally with this merging, he loses his own entity and becomes possessed by an evil thing from unknown worlds. In his personality, the hideous invading spirit takes form and becomes manifest till his shadow is that which had followed him."[4] Smith completed it on March 14, 1932, and immediately submitted it to *Weird Tales*, perhaps feeling that its exotic setting in Atlantis might not be to the liking of the Babbitesque William Clayton. Wright's original rejection letter apparently does not survive, but according to Smith he wrote "that it was 'interesting, in a way,' but he feared that his readers wouldn't care for it. I fear that Wright, in his anxiety to publish nothing that would be disliked by any of his readers, will get to the point where he won't publish anything that any one will like very much."[5] He then submitted it to *Strange Tales*, where much to his surprise it was accepted. However, there was a catch:

> Both Mr. Clayton and I have tentatively approved both of them: but because of their type I can only buy one. I am hoping that one will be the longer, but at this time, with *Strange Tales* appearing so infrequently, I cannot make the decision. I hope you do not mind if I hold your two stories, "The Double Shadow" and "The Colossus of Ylourgne" for a while longer.[6]

Smith was therefore elated when Bates later wrote to him later "that in some mysterious manner, both 'The Double Shadow' and 'The Colossus of Ylourgne' have passed successfully through Mr. Clayton's critical craw. I expect to buy both!"[7] Unfortunately, in October 1932 Clayton ordered Bates to shut down both *Strange Tales* and *Astounding Stories*, which had the dual effect of drastically cutting down Smith's sources of income (for all his philistine thickheadedness, Clayton paid better rates than any other genre publication) and leaving Wright in command of the field. "My own prospective income is sadly nicked by the failure of S. T.," CAS wrote to Derleth. "I am out five hundred bucks, unless I can re-sell part or all of the unused tales to Wright. I don't believe he will buy 'The Double Shadow;' but the chances seem fair for the other two."[8] Sadly, Smith's prediction proved correct, as Wright once again rejected "The Double Shadow" in November.[9] Smith finally ended up publishing the story himself as the title story of his first collection, which he published himself in 1933 utilizing the services of the local newspaper. In an advertising flyer that he printed to promote *The Double Shadow and Other Fantasies*, he described the tale as "a strange tale of two Atlantean sorcerers, who made use of a dreadful antehuman spell, without knowing what would come in answer to their evocation."

Smith's fiction output fell off for several reasons starting in late 1933. However, Wright had a sufficient backlog of stories that this didn't begin to become apparent until after 1936. Coupled with the deaths of Robert E. Howard in 1936 and H. P. Lovecraft in 1937, this was a blow which lead to Wright frantically trying to get stories from one of his few remaining stars. Smith insisted that Wright first purchase stories that he had previously rejected, which brought about the appearance in *Weird Tales* of several stories from *The Double Shadow and Other Fantasies*, including the title story. Ironically, when it appeared in the February 1939 in a slightly pruned version, "The Double Shadow" was voted the most popular story in that issue by the readers. Smith used tear sheets from that issue for *OST*, and he planned to include the story in *Far from Time*. We are using the text from a copy of *The Double Shadow and Other Fantasies* that features Smith's handwritten corrections of typographical errors.

1. HPL, letter to DAW, March 26, 1932 (*Mysteries of Time and Spirit: The Letters of H. P. Lovecraft and Donald Wandrei*, Ed. S. T. Joshi and David E. Schultz [San Francisco: Night Shade Books, 2002], p. 304).

2. CAS, letter to DAW, April 6, 1932 (ms, MHS).

3. CAS, letter to DAW, April 14, 1932 (ms, MHS).

4. *SS* 174.

5. CAS, letter to AWD, April 5, 1932 (ms, SHSW).

6. Harry Bates, letter to CAS, June 11, 1932 (ms, JHL).

7. Quoted in CAS, letter to AWD, September 28, 1932 (ms, SHSW).

8. CAS, letter to AWD, October 16, 1932 (ms, SHSW).

9. CAS, letter to AWD, November 15, 1932 (ms, SHSW).

The Plutonian Drug

Smith wrote August Derleth in February 1932 that "I've begun a short pseudo-scientific tale, dealing with a drug that changed a man's perception of time into a sort of space-perception. He saw himself as a continuous body—a sort of infinite frieze—stretching both into the past and future." He added that he found the writing of the story "hellishly hard to do."[1] He put the story aside for a month, completing it on April 5, 1932.

Although he had submitted stories to a wide variety of publications, CAS had so far managed to sell his stories to just three magazines with any degree of regularity. One pulp that he had yet to "crack" was the oldest of the "scientifiction" magazines, *Amazing Stories*. By late 1931 he had just about given up, telling Derleth that "The same editorial crew is still in force, and I understand there will be no change in policy. They seem to have a fixed prejudice against my stuff as not being sufficiently scientific."[2] With "The Plutonian Drug" CAS thought that he had managed to inject enough science that it might meet with success, so he submitted "The Plutonian Drug" to its editor, T. O'Conor Sloane (1851-1940).[3] As was his practice, Sloane held on to the manuscript for several months before publishing it in the September 1934 issue of *Amazing Stories*. Smith received only ½ cent a word for the story,[4] less than either *Weird Tales* (one cent) or *Wonder Stories* (¾ cent), and far less than the two cents paid by the Clayton *Strange Tales*. CAS collected it in *LW*. It also formed part of the proposed contents for *Far from Time*.

In 1951 August Derleth asked Smith to select a favorite story for an anthology. He chose this story:

> "The Plutonian Drug" is, in my opinion, among my best in the genre of science-fiction. For one thing, it is the sort of tale that can hardly become "dated" in spite of changing vogues and varying themes. And it has the advantages of conciseness and brevity.
> The field of speculation that it opens is a fascinating one, and hardly to be exhausted. Benjamin Paul Blood (and, no doubt, others) has hinted that our deepest perceptions of reality may come to us beneath the influence of drugs: a proposition equally impossible to prove or disprove. *Quien Sabe?*[5]

1. CAS, letter to AWD, February 24, 1932 (ms, SHSW).
2. CAS, letter to AWD, October 15, 1931 (ms, SHSW).
3. CAS, letter to HPL, [c. early April 1932] (*SL* 175).
4. CAS, letter to AWD, October 27, 1932 (ms, SHSW).
5. *PD* 74.

The Supernumerary Corpse

The concept of "The Supernumerary Corpse" occurred to Smith early in his career as a fiction writer; the title appears in a list of possible titles that dates to late 1929. His notes for the story describe it succinctly: "A man dies, and leaves two corpses, in two different places."[1] CAS first discusses the story in a letter to Lovecraft in mid-November 1930.[2] It apparently failed to fire his imagination sufficiently as it was not completed until April 10, 1932. CAS submitted it to Wright, wryly noting that it "may be punk enough for him to buy," and adding that he could not decide if "the carbon is worth circulating."[3] It was published in the November 1932 issue, and remained uncollected until after Smith's death, in *OD*. The current text is based upon a carbon of the typescript at JHL.

1. *SS* 159.
2. CAS, letter to HPL, [c. November 16, 1930] (*SL* 136).
3. CAS, letter to HPL, [c. early April 1932] (ms, JHL).

The Colossus of Ylourgne

The story germ of this story may be found in Smith's "Black Book," which he described in the fanzine the *Acolyte* as "a notebook containing used and unused plot-germs, notes on occultism and magic, synopses of stories, fragments of verse, fantastic names for people and places, etc., etc.,"[1] under the title "The Colossal Incarnation":

> An immense giant, moulded from innumerable dead bodies by a sorcerer. The tale to be told by one of his assistants, who has helped to collect the bodies, stealing them from graves and charnels. Having read his own horoscope, and knowing that his death is imminent, the sorcerer plans to have his spirit pass into the vast body through which, among other things, he will take revenge on a city that had flouted him. But the body, being composed of the dead, is not sufficiently subject to his control. Its elements long only for sleep and oblivion; and instead of destroying the city, it proceeds to dig itself a colossal grave.[2]

Completed on May 1, 1932, Smith described the story as "about the most horrific of my tales dealing with the mythical province of Averoigne."[3] It was accepted by Harry Bates for *Strange Tales*, but as in the case of "The Double Shadow" and "The Seed from the Sepulcher," it was returned to Smith after the magazine folded. It was the most popular story in the June 1934 issue of *Weird Tales* and was included in both GL and RA.

The next year Smith was approached by Universal Pictures regarding whether he had any stories that might be suitable for adaptation as screenplays.[4] Smith offered "The Colossus of Ylourgne" and "The Dark Eidolon." Apparently the studio expressed interest in these properties, since Smith asked Wright to release the motion-picture rights, which he did on October

11, 1935,[5] but the Laemmele family lost control the next year, and the new management may not have cared for such unconventionally imaginative material.

1. "Excerpts from the *Black Book*," *The Acolyte* (Spring 1944), reprinted in *BB* 77.
2. *BB* item 57.
3. CAS, letter to DAW, May 4, 1932 (ms, MHS).
4. Universal Pictures (Edward Churchill), letter to CAS, August 21, 1935 (ms, JHL).
5. FW, letter to CAS, October 11, 1935 (ms, JHL).

The God of the Asteroid

This story is yet another testament to Gernsback's proclivity for changing the titles of stories without first consulting the authors. First published in the October 1932 issue of *Wonder Stories* under the title of "Master of the Asteroid," and receiving a fine cover illustration by Frank R. Paul, all contemporary references to the story by Smith use the present title, which dates back to a listing of possible story titles he recorded in late 1929 or early 1930.[1] For instance, he refers in a letter to the Lovecraft-revised story "The Man of Stone" by Hazel Heald as "a story in the Oct. Wonder Stories (which featured my 'God of the Asteroid') ...."—after he had learned of the title-change to "Master of the Asteroid."[2]

A synopsis titled "The God of the Asteroid" was found among Smith's papers: "A space-ship manned by three terrestrial explorers is wrecked on an asteroid. One of the three survives, and is worshipped as a god by the grotesque inhabitants. He goes stark mad, but lives for years, still revered and tended as a deity".[3] The present story was completed on June 9, 1932. Smith received forty dollars for the story.

Smith refers in the story to Mohammed's coffin, which was supposed to have been suspended between Heaven and Earth. He had written another story, "Like Mohammed's Tomb," that unfortunately has not been located and may not survive.

The first indication that Smith had resigned himself to the name-change was when he allowed the story to be reprinted as "Master of the Asteroid" in August Derleth's anthology *Strange Ports of Call* (Pellegrini & Cudahy, 1948). This might have been due to purely commercial considerations, since under the published title it was a well-known and popular story. Sometime in the late 1950s Smith's wife Carol prepared a new typescript using the title given to the story by *WS*, and it is under this title that it was collected posthumously in *TSS*, and later in *RA*. Surprisingly, in light of the praise lent the tale by Ray Bradbury in his foreword to the unpublished paperback collection *Far from Time*, Smith did *not* include this story in that book.

1. *SS* 182.
2. CAS, letter to AWD, December 24, 1932 (*SL* 198).
3. *SS* 155.

Appendix Two: The Flower-Devil

(The Prose Poem that "The Demon of the Flower" Was Based Upon)

In a basin of porphyry, at the summit of a pillar of serpentine, the thing has existed from primeval time, in the garden of the kings that rule an equatorial realm of the planet Saturn. With black foliage, fine and intricate as the web of some enormous spider; with petals of livid rose, and purple like the purple of putrefying flesh; and a stem rising like a swart and hairy wrist from a bulb so old, so encrusted with the growth of centuries that it resembles an urn of stone, the monstrous flower holds dominion over all the garden. In this flower, from the years of oldest legend, an evil demon has dwelt—a demon whose name and whose nativity are known to the superior magicians and mysteriarchs of the kingdom, but to none other. Over the half-animate flowers, the ophidian orchids that coil and sting, the bat-like lilies that open their ribbēd petals by night, and fasten with tiny yellow teeth on the bodies of sleeping dragon-flies; the carnivorous cacti that yawn with green lips beneath their beards of poisonous yellow prickles; the plants that palpitate like hearts, the blossoms that pant with a breath of poisonous perfume—over all these, the Flower-Devil is supreme, in its malign immortality, and evil, perverse intelligence—inciting them to strange maleficence, fantastic mischief, even to acts of rebellion against the gardeners, who proceed about their duties with wariness and trepidation, since more than one of them has been bitten, even unto death, by some vicious and venefic flower. In places, the garden has run wild from lack of care on the part of the fearful gardeners, and has become a monstrous tangle of serpentine creepers, and hydra-headed plants, convolved and inter-writhing in lethal hate or venomous love, and horrible as a rout of wrangling vipers and pythons.

And, like his innumerable ancestors before him, the king dares not destroy the Flower, for fear that the devil, driven from its habitation, might seek a new home, and enter into the brain or body of one of the king's subjects—or even the heart of his fairest and gentlest, and most beloved queen!

Appendix Three:
Bibliography

"The Holiness of Azédarac." *WT* 22, 3 (November 1933): 594-607. In *LW*, *RA*.

"The Maker of Gargoyles." *WT* 20, 2 (August 1932): 198-207. In *TSS*.

"Beyond the Singing Flame." *WS* 3, 6 (November 1931): 752-761. *Tales of Wonder* no. 10 (Spring 1940): 6-31 (combined with "The City of the Singing Flame"). *Startling Stories* 11, 1 (Summer 1944): 90-99. In *OST* (combined with "The City of the Singing Flame"). Reprinted (combined with "The City of the Singing Flame") in *The Other Side of the Moon*. Edited by August Derleth (NY: Pellegrini and Cudahy, 1949). Reprinted in *From Off This World*. Edited by Leo Margulies and Oscar J. Friend (NY: Merlin Press, 1949).

"Seedling of Mars." *WS Quarterly* 3, 1 (Fall 1931): 110-125, 136 (as "The Planet Entity"). In *TSS*.

"The Vaults of Yoh-Vombis." *WT* 19, 5 (May 1932): 599-610. In *OST, RA*. Reprinted in *Avon Fantasy Reader* no. 1. Edited by Donald A. Wollheim (NY: Avon, 1947).

"The Eternal World ." *WS* 3, 10 (March 1932): 1130-1137. In *GL*.

"The Demon of the Flower." *Astounding Stories* 12, 4 (December 1933): 131-138. In *LW*.

"The Nameless Offspring." *ST* 2, 2 (June 1932): 264-276. *Strange Tales of the Mysterious and Supernatural* Second Selection [Edited by Walter H. Gillings] (London: Utopian Publications [1946]): 16-27. In *AY*.

"A Vintage from Atlantis." *Weird Tales* 22, 3 (September 1933): 394-399. In *AY*.

"The Weird of Avoosl Wuthoqquan." *WT* 19, 6 (June 1932): 835-840. In *OST, RA*. Reprinted in *And the Darkness Falls*. Edited by Boris Karloff (Cleveland: World, 1946).

"The Invisible City." *WS* 4, 1 (June 1932): 6-13, 86. *Tales of Wonder* no. 9 (Winter 1939): 50-63. *Bibliothek der Unterhaltung und des Wissens,* Band IX (Stuttgart: Union Deutsche Verlagsgesellschaft, 1933): 5-16 (as "Die unsichtbare Stadt"). In *OD.*

"The Immortals of Mercury." *Science Fiction Series* no. 16 (NY: Stellar Publishing Corp., 1932). In *TSS.*

"The Empire of the Necromancers." *WT* 20, 3 (September 1932): 338-344. In *LW, RA.* Reprinted in *Avon Fantasy Reader* no. 7. Edited by Donald A. Wollheim (NY: Avon, 1947).

"The Seed from the Sepulcher." *WT* 22, 4 (October 1933): 497-505. In *TSS.* Reprinted in *Tales of the Undead.* Edited by Elinore Blaisdell (NY: Thomas Y. Crowell, 1947).

"The Second Interment." *ST* 3, 1 (January 1933): 8-16. In *OST.*

"Ubbo-Sathla." *WT* 22, 1 (July 1933): 112-116. In *OST.* Reprinted in *Avon Fantasy Reader* no. 15. Edited by Donald A. Wollheim (NY: Avon, 1951).

"The Double Shadow." Original version: in *The Double Shadow and Other Fantasies* (Auburn Journal Press, 1933). Revised version: in *WT* 33, 2 (February 1039): 47-55. In *OST.* Reprinted in *The Sleeping and the Dead: Thirty Uncanny Tales.* Edited by August Derleth (NY: Pellegrini & Cudahy, 1947; Toronto: George J. McLeod Ltd., 1947).

"The Plutonian Drug." *Amazing Stories* 9, 5 (September 1934): 41-48. In *LW.* Reprinted in *The Outer Reaches. Favorite Science Fiction Tales Chosen By Their Authors.* Edited by August Derleth (NY: Pellegrini & Cudahy, 1951; NY: Berkley, 1951).

"The Supernumerary Corpse." *WT* 20, 5 (November 1932): 693-698. In *OD.*

"The God of the Asteroid" (as "The Master of the Asteroid"). *WS* 4, 5 (October 1932): 435-439, 469. *Tales of Wonder* no. 11 (Summer 1940): 46-55. *Bibliothek der Unterhaltung und des Wissens,* Band V (Stuttgart: Union Deutsche Verlagsgesellschaft, 1933): 5-22 (as "Die Geheimnis des Asteroiden"). In *AY, RA.* Reprinted in *Strange Ports of Call.* Edited by August Derleth (NY: Pellegrini & Cudahy, 1948; Toronto: George J. McLeod, 1948; NY: Berkley, 1948, 1958)

"The Colossus of Ylourgne." *WT* 23, 6 (June 1934): 696-720. In *GL, RA.*

"The Flower-Devil." In *Ebony and Crystal: Poems in Verse and Prose* (Auburn Journal Press, 1922). In *PP.*